Submissive Lies

SHANE STARRETT

Editor: Nerine Dorman

Cover Design by: Eris Adderly

"But to sacrifice what you are...is a fate more terrible than dying."

- Joan of Arc

ONE

I could see the beginning of the end the night Thomas tried to 'fuck me hard.'

Not all problems couples face start with sex. There's money, careers, who's responsible for cleaning out the cat litter box... a ton of reasons that can be the catalyst for relationship troubles. The issues Thomas and I were facing... they started with sex. It was as simple as that. The complication in our case was that only *one* of us knew it. I knew there was a problem. I knew *I* had a problem. Thomas? All Thomas knew was that something was bothering me. He just didn't know *what* it was.

Yet.

'Hard' wasn't the way we normally had sex. Not the way we'd *ever* had sex. And the morning prior to Thomas trying to fuck me hard the sex had been anything but that. That morning we'd made love.

Sweet, gentle lovemaking no different from what we'd had in the six months we'd been together.

Normal sex. 'Vanilla' sex. Boring sex.

Ugh.

That morning, as I laid there nestled into him, the thoughts running through my head were at complete odds with where I was. I could have—should have—been doing so many things right then.

Things that in previous weeks would have come naturally to me. Now, as I stretched out watching him in silence, my eyes taking in the angles of his chest, the whorls of hair, I couldn't focus on any of them. Instead I was bathing in self-doubt. That was the problem. In my current state of mind, my thoughts weren't centered in the same place they'd been in the past. Where they should be. Focused on the good, sweet, *'oh this feels so nice'* kind you'd expect. No, instead, my thoughts were fixated yet again on the one thing that had been worrying at me for weeks now. Another repetition of an internal dialogue that had begun as whispers but had grown to shouts. One that had started the moment I realized the enormity of the mistake I had made.

This morning though, something inside me clicked. As I lay there, his fingers stroking my hair, I decided there would never be a *perfect* moment for the conversation I needed to have with him. So I did what seemed reasonable. Blurted out the perfect opening line.

"Thomas, can we talk?"

His hand stopped mid-stroke. The room froze, and when he eventually responded, it was with the tone of voice I expected— cautious, edged with tension.

"Of course." Thomas pushed himself up onto an elbow, looking down at me.

I adjusted myself, gazing up into his face. His brow furrowed slightly, the warm smile fading into a tightening around the corners of his eyes that signaled 'Serious Thomas' mode. I was well aware he knew something was going on with me. He'd asked about it often enough in the last couple of weeks. The look he was giving me now telegraphed he was steeling himself for whatever bomb I was about to drop.

"It's nothing bad, I swear. It's probably not what you're think-ing!" Even though I saw a bit of tension release from around his eyes,

Thomas—ever the lawyer—remained wary. "Good to know... So, what *do* you want to talk about?"

I sighed. "I haven't really told you much about my past relationships, have I?"

"No." He drew the word out, his voice cautious. "Is there something you need to tell me that I should be concerned about?"

His response puzzled me, and I wasn't sure why. I repeated what I'd just said in my head. And realized with horror how he may have perceived it.

"Fuck!" I made a frantic waving motion with my hand. "Okay, okay, okay, I need to make one thing clear. This isn't a conversation about STDs or anything like that, okay?"

"Okay. Jen." His shoulders relaxed in another small increment as he gave me a wry chuckle. "Just for future reference, though, you might want to think of another way of starting a conversation right after we've had sex other than 'Can we talk?' followed by 'Have I ever told you about my past lovers?'"

"Ugh." I slumped back, groaning. "This is getting all twisted around..."

He laughed and then bent down, kissing the top of my head. "It's fine. Just tell me what this is about."

"In my past relationships, I..." I paused, letting out a small sigh. "Well, there have been certain things about them that were... well, aspects of them that have included... umm..." I wasn't sure exactly how to approach this. This was not a conversation I'd thought I'd ever have with him, and coupled with the fact that the discussion had already gotten off to an awkward start, I was losing my resolve.

However, Thomas was patient, waiting for me to continue.

"Certain"—I picked up where I had stopped— "... certain, uh, what people might call... kinky things." I looked up at him, hopeful, expectant. His expression change from mild uncertainty to one of bemusement.

"Kinky things?"

"Yeah, you know, kinky... sexual things."

"Okay." Thomas frowned, his brows knitting together. He was deep in lawyer mode, and I could see his brain attacking this. "Are we talking about things like the toys in your drawer?" He made a slight motion towards the nightstand on my side of the bed.

"Well..." I pursed my lips together, taking a deep breath, trying not to let my frustration show. "Those could be considered part of it, I suppose. But what I'm referring to are things that would be a little more... pronounced than that."

"Okay. Help me out, Jen." Thomas' voice was sober in a way he got at times. "How *pronounced* are we talking about here? Spanking? Dirty talk? Stuff like that?"

It was at that very moment it became perfectly clear just how 'vanilla' Thomas was. And how this conversation was very likely not going to end the way I had hoped it might. I understood my kink—BDSM, and specifically Dominant/submissive dynamics—quite well. I had what I considered an insider's point of view of it. What I'd not done is give much thought to how the ignorance of someone who had little knowledge of D/s dynamics would present itself. And now I was finding out.

Thomas was an intelligent man. I'm sure if I had gone into the details of what I was trying to describe, he would have recognized some of what I meant when trying to relate my version of 'kinky.' Those things that had been part and parcel of my previous sexual relationships. And while he might have understood the terms and known the dictionary descriptions for them, I was quickly getting the gut-level impression that he wouldn't quite comprehend the reason someone would want these things. Desire them. Crave engaging in them with their partner. 'Spanking? Dirty talk? Stuff like that?' No, I was talking about things much more explicit, and it was becoming clear that Thomas wouldn't understand why someone would *want* to engage in the kinds of things I had. And wanted to again.

That's when the light bulb went off in my head. This was not going to happen right now. This wouldn't be the moment when things would be resolved. Much as I had hoped differently, this wouldn't be the conversation where I could break out of my lie.

"Well, yes, again, things along those lines." My voice was stumbling, and I sensed Thomas was picking up every tell I was handing him like a defendant being cross-examined.

"What I'm saying is that... well, I experimented with certain things like that, and I found there were things that I liked, and..." I flailed, desperately looking for a way to ripcord out of this conversation as quickly as I could.

His eyes narrowed in increments to my every word. It only intensified the feeling that I was on the witness stand, and I hated that I was responding to it as if I was.

"And?"

"Well..." I gulped, gesturing towards him. "Are there any..."

Jesus Christ, Jen! Just ask him the goddamn question!

"Is there anything like that... that you, you know, ever did? Or wanted to do?" I blurted it out, the last few words tumbling over themselves.

Thomas looked down at me with lingering traces of confusion in his eyes, the corners of his mouth turned down. I had seen this look before, most often when he was listening to an argument. It was as if he was not only absorbing the words but also looking for the subtext behind them. But this wasn't another lawyer he was listening to. It was me. I felt like I was the one on trial even if he acted as if *he* was the one waiting for whatever I would spring on him. After a few seconds of thought, a gentle, knowing smile began to crease his face.

"Are you asking me if I like... rough sex, Jen?"

I almost couldn't stop myself. I wanted to burst out laughing. I wanted to roll on my back and squeal until my sides hurt.

Rough sex? Seriously?

But I did stop myself. I had seen this before. As a submissive—back when I'd actually been engaging in my kink—I'd read all sorts of online posts where people described this very thing. New people who came into the scene fresh, still clinging to an outsider's preconceived notion of what BDSM and D/s dynamics were all about. Sometimes it was the supposition that whips and chains were involved, and at others, it was all about spankings—*thank you very much Anne Rice*. And with still others, it was nearly word for word what Thomas had just said.

Kink, BDSM, whatever label was applied, it all equaled one thing.

Rough sex.

To be fair, I had never talked to Thomas about BDSM, whether in this conversation or any other prior. It was certainly not something he'd ever brought up during the six months of our relationship. I could only assume he had no inkling that was where my mind was. I had said 'kinky,' and while the two were intertwined in my mind, any assumption I had that Thomas would equate them the same way was a poor expectation on my part. As I stared up at him I caught myself thinking this, and in that moment I became uneasy. Nervous of where Thomas' vanilla lawyer brain might take this and head off to.

"Yeah, that's it. You know... rough," I said with a weak smile, my voice faltering. I hated myself so much as the words came out. It was a lie. Yet another lie in a string that had become par for the course for me lately. I had been living a lie to deal with the painful implosion of my previous relationship. And like most of us are taught when we're children, lies have a way of coming back around on us. I was being forced to confront this, and in doing so, I was struggling with whether I could keep telling this lie until it became our truth—my truth. Or if I would have to handle this differently. At this point, the only person I'd admitted my deception to was myself. I was continuing to perpetuate the lie on Thomas because the solutions to ending it were not proving to be as simple and easy as I'd thought. For a woman as strong and intelligent as I believed I was, this whole situation was turning out to be a lot more difficult to maintain control over than I'd anticipated. I couldn't bring myself to make the hard choice to tell him the truth.

That, in turn, became the starting point of a vicious loop of self-destructive thoughts racing around inside my head.

Why? Why, for fuck's sake, am I doing this to the both of us right now?

I didn't have the answer to that. However, I did know that one way or another, something had to be done. I was struggling to come to terms with my circumstances. I had no one but myself to blame for this. This was a situation I had created, and for some time I had made it work. But now it felt as if it was slowly coming apart. Thomas thought he'd met a woman who was one thing, and at that time I *had* been that person. I had *made* myself into that person.

Now, not so much.

I had lied. First to myself, and then by living that lie, to Thomas.

Now the foundation to my lie was showing signs of strain. I was starting to feel unsure. On increasingly shaky ground. The reemergence of my submissive desires had so many thoughts from my past worming back into my head, eating away at the conviction I'd used to help prop up my deception. The choices I'd made back then now seemed so very wrong, and yet the idea of approaching Thomas about my dishonesty, even the baby step I'd just tried, left me feeling uncertain. Edgy of all the potential risks in what I was doing. Anxious that any false move would send it all spiraling out of control.

I had to extract myself from this situation, and it wasn't as simple as just ending this conversation. As I lay there staring into Thomas' smiling face, I understood I had a choice: bear down and get my head back in the game, continue to maintain the lie as I had done so for the past six months.

Or...

That *or* was not just the obvious solution of telling him the truth. While that might be the simplest option, it was also the one that held the most risk. Risk that was all bound up in Thomas' perception of kink. Of 'rough sex'. Because in the solution where I told Thomas the truth about who I was, told him what *I* was thinking about when I used terms like 'kinky things' and 'rough sex', the danger wasn't in the telling. The danger lay in how he would respond. That was the part which bothered me more than I wanted to admit. It bothered me because buried within it lay something dark, menacing. A single destructive word that sat at its core.

Over.

That word sat there waiting silently, ready to be the end of it all.

No.

No, I wasn't ready to confront that. Not yet.

Thomas, no doubt having convinced himself he'd broken the Da Vinci Code of our relationship, beamed with self-satisfaction. All the concerns he'd expressed over the past couple of weeks about what was bothering me were a thing of the past. The smug set of his grin seemed ample validation of just how proud of himself he was. Leaning down, he kissed me on the forehead.

"I understand, Jen. You shouldn't feel uncomfortable with those thoughts, okay? They're perfectly natural. Don't feel ashamed."

I smiled back weakly.

Oh, God. Oh my fucking God. What have I done?

I spent most of the day in an existential crisis of my own making. While I went through the motions of doing the mundane things that make up the fabric of a day, what was really going on inside my head was a stream of bitter, depressing thoughts. Bleak reflections that plagued every hour. Thomas did not pick up on my mood. Whether that was a function of how well I hid it, or how smug he was feeling, I didn't know. It was most likely the latter, given the smirk that seemed perpetually plastered across his face. The way he grinned at me every time he stopped to give me a kiss. The wink he gave me as he walked by on his way to the living room. All of those things simply confirmed my worst anxieties and did nothing to slow my train of thought. And for the first time in our relationship, I was dreading going to bed that night.

Fuck, fuck, fuck, fuck, fuck! What did I do?

— ⟐ —

Thomas cooked dinner and afterwards we watched a movie. Never had I wanted a film to go on forever as much as I did then. Of course it didn't. The credits were barely rolling when Thomas had me in his arms, pulling me tight and kissing me with a fierceness more than he ever had before. As he gripped me, fingers digging into my skin, I felt a momentary sense of buoyancy. Maybe I had been over thinking this. Maybe this wouldn't go as badly as I had built up in my mind.

Maybe, maybe, maybe.

He gathered me up in his arms and I snaked my legs around him, drawing my body tight to his. My arms pulled against his back, my fingers biting into muscles I could feel working as he held me. He carried me to the bedroom while our mouths crashed together in urgent, hungry bites, an intertwining of tongues that had heat flaring inside me. Thomas had been passionate with me before, but nothing to the degree I felt from him now. It was a taste of the kind of spontaneous, aggressive play I'd experienced with other lovers, and I'd be lying if I said I didn't like it. We were suddenly in the bedroom, still kissing, and then we were yanking clothes off. Thomas didn't rip my clothes away, but he came as close to it as his controlled, precise nature would allow. I was starting to get into it. I pulled at his pants, fumbling with the buttons, his hands taking over mine as he shoved them down.

His shirt came up and disappeared as he flung it away. His cock tented his underwear, then was free as he shed the last of his clothing. He moved up to me, our eyes locked together. He gripped my shoulder and spun me around. I felt him pull the catches of my bra apart with a fierce tug, and then his hands were up under the cups, fondling me. Hands pressing into my flesh, my body responded in turn, my nipples drawing tight. He continued to hold me firmly as I pushed at my jeans, shoving them down, wriggling against him as I slipped free. My panties followed suit, and soon both were piled around my feet in a tangle. Thomas' hands released my breasts as he slipped around my side, his body never leaving contact with mine. When he came into view, the look on his face was different from when we normally made love. It was darker, more aggressive than I'd ever seen him. My breath hitched, and my earlier thoughts and fears seemed stupid. He was definitely stepping up his game. Working me up in a way I craved. It was a step in a direction I couldn't have envisioned from our earlier conversation.

"On the bed. Now." His voice was a low growl I'd never heard him use before. It was nothing of the disciplined, almost formal way he normally spoke, and it sent a shiver shooting through me.

"Yes, sir." My voice was a whisper as I moved to the bed, climbing on top of it. Kneeling, I positioned myself as a long-forgotten familiarity washed over me.

I remember this.

Looking up at him from beneath lowered lashes, I watched as he moved up with me. He slid over, one hand gripping my shoulder, the other snaking around my waist. Suddenly he flipped me roughly onto my stomach, and then he was straddling me, one knee spreading me wide. He moved to position himself, his erection gliding against my thigh before pushing into the cleft between my cheeks. He rode up against me at the same time his voice rumbled in my ear.

"I am going to fuck you hard, Jen."

I thrilled at his words. This was so much more than I had expected. It wasn't Ben, but it was as close as I'd felt in six months to what he'd been, and that had me incredibly wet for Thomas right now. Every nerve in my body was tense. Not just for what was happening this moment, but with anticipation for what would follow next.

I waited for that next. It never came.

I felt him slide inside of me, his cock stretching me open. I knew what I expected, what I wanted. Hard, savage thrusts that would drive his cock deep inside. Fingers digging into my thighs, rough words breathed into my ear, maybe a hand gripping my hair in a knot of fingers and strands that would strain my neck in that way I loved. I waited for that, any of it, and as the moments went by, I felt tendrils of disappointment begin their insidious creep through me.

Thomas didn't 'fuck' me. He made love to me.

From the moment he entered me, it was little different from what we had done that morning. Or any other time during the months we'd been together. We did it doggie style. That was his version of rough sex—rear entry. The realization that this was what I would get, the entirety of it, made a slow, hollow feeling build inside of me. Sure, he wasn't as gentle as he normally was. I'd little doubt his impression was he was truly fucking me hard. But the things I had anticipated, that my body had desired?

Nothing. Not a single thing.

He grunted as he stroked in and out of me at the same intensity and pace he did when we were doing it missionary style. He reverted to the gentle, considerate lover he had always been, and my body shook with the urge to scream in exasperation.

No! No, no, no, no, no! Please! This isn't fair!

He vocalized what he obviously thought I was feeling.

"You like that, don't you?" His voice was less the deep rumble than it had been. Now it was the more attentive Thomas I was so familiar with. "You like the way I'm fucking you. I know you do."

I buried my face into the covers. The appreciative noises I made were ones I knew he wanted to hear. Noises that were as much a lie as anything else I'd done before. Every bit of hope that had sprung up in me blew away in a whirlwind. I could feel the smooth, even timing of his thrusts that were every bit the controlled, practiced lover he was. A lover any woman would be—should be—happy with, as long as that woman wasn't me. I closed my eyes, gritting my teeth. In the end I did what was easiest. I simply gave in and followed his lead.

Thomas was trying, and he truly believed he was giving me *exactly* what I had been dancing around during our conversation. The thought that this was his idea of rough sex made it even worse. I lay there, and all I felt was a ramping sense of frustration. And—*goddammit!*—I had enjoyed sex with him in the past. There had been a time when I loved everything about the way he made love to me. The gentle attentiveness, the way he cradled, caressed, and cherished me as if I was some sort of goddess to be worshipped. Now I was struggling to show my appreciation for the effort he was putting into this and failing. That was wrong because, dammit, I owed him that! None of this was his fault. He was a good man trying to do the right thing for the woman he loved, but who wasn't giving that back in return. I was just all manner of shit right now, because keeping this lie propped up was becoming harder than hell.

-How can you claim to love a man you can't even be truthful with?-

That was a knife to the gut.

I don't want to hurt him. He doesn't deserve to be hurt.

-Oh, how noble *of you. Your trust in him to love and accept you for who you are is extraordinary. Truly stunning in the shallowness of its depth and scope. Bravo.-*

I don't want to hurt him! I can do this. I can control these thoughts and feelings. He doesn't need to know. At least for right now. When the time is right, I'll know. And I'll do it then.

-I swear, sometimes I think you can't say anything stupider, and then you turn around and prove me wrong.-

Lying there while Thomas fucked me required every effort to keep the thoughts going through my head under control. So he wouldn't suspect. For God's sake, I was in the middle of having what in any other circumstances would be fantastic sex. And what was I doing?

Realizing the futility of believing I could keep the burgeoning return of my submissiveness from intruding back into my life. I'd flipped off my submissive switch when I'd told myself that it would be the solution to all of my problems. But now that light was blinking back on, and it was becoming apparent I did not have the mental fortitude to stop it. Even worse, the thought of trying to throttle back those desires made me cringe. I had made my choice back then, but now I was questioning it. Second-guessing not only my decision, but myself too.

And the conclusion I was coming to was not reassuring. I had made the wrong choice. Not only that, I'd involved someone else in my choice, even though they knew nothing about it. I'd drawn them into my lie without their knowledge. Made it so they believed it. And now I needed to make a new choice. Come to a decision.

Except I couldn't make myself do it.

I couldn't bring myself to follow through on the obvious solution that faced me. The one that would require me to sit Thomas down and be open and honest with him. To tell him in clear, concise, truthful terms who I was, what I wanted, and what I desired sexually. I couldn't force myself to take the risk, because I feared what the result might be.

No. It was so much easier to keep propping up the lie.

Thomas continued thrusting inside me. He was building to his peak, and I was as far away from mine as I could be. The in-out-in-out pacing of cock to pussy was a fucking metronome, and in my current mood it was maddening. It did, however, interrupt the angst I was feeling, drawing me back to the reality of the moment. I took stock of my body. At least I was wet, thank God. That made the cock-beat cadence he had set up at least manageable. The worst part of this situation was what was missing. Where earlier I had hoped for fingers digging into my skin, crescent marks to be left on my flesh that I would cherish for hours, if not days, there was only Thomas' firm yet gentle caress as he held me in place. There was no slamming of his hips into my ass, balls slapping against me. *Shit.* If it wasn't for the fact that the bed was rocking I might have questioned whether he was back there at all. The thrusts themselves, which were building in speed, had lost any semblance of being rough. A week ago, everything Thomas was doing would have had me at the brink of my own orgasm. Now, as frustration pushed tears against the back of my eyes, I knew just one thing: I wasn't making love with Thomas. Right now, I was nothing more than a blow-up doll. And all I wanted was for this to be over.

"Yes! Fuck. Fuck, yes!" His voice was in perfect timing with his hips connecting with my rear, a growl full of the passion that *he* was feeling for me. As he jerked, coming inside me, I did something I'd never done with him before.

I faked it.

I faked my orgasm, because I needed every ounce of strength I possessed to avoid breaking down in tears. Because there was no way in hell I wanted to try to explain *that* reaction to Thomas—especially after this morning and what he'd just done.

After he finished, he pulled out, rolling to his side. I remained where I was for a moment, unmoving. He reached for me, wrapping an arm around my chest to pull me close.

"So?" he asked with a voice filled with pride. His expression told me he didn't need to hear my answer. It was obvious in the way he looked at me, the satisfied smile, the crinkle at the corners of his eyes. *Mission accomplished!*

I buried my face into his chest, not looking at him. I couldn't. "Mmm. Yes, nice." The words were as fake as my release.

"See? I told you not to worry. I told you I understood what you were looking for." He pulled me tighter, his fingers running gently through my mussed hair. Where now I would have arched and hissed with pleasure had he twisted those fingers tight to my scalp and wrenched my head back, Thomas caressed me with post-orgasmic sweetness.

Fuck.

I could do nothing more than nod. The words would not form. Sleep didn't come easily for me that night. For Thomas, however, it did. We lay there together, and soon the motion of his hand slowed.

Before long, while I lay trapped in thought, his gentle breathing made clear he'd drifted off.

I did cry at that point. It was soft, and I slowly, deliberately turned away from him so he wouldn't be able to feel my chest heaving. I choked back as much of it as I could. I must have done well, because he never woke. Railing at myself, I cried, mentally beating myself bloody not only for what I was doing to Thomas but also for what I had done to myself.

It was a horrible feeling, and it was tearing me up. This whole thing was turning out so different, so *wrong,* from where I'd imagined Thomas and I being the first day we'd met. The reasons for how and why it had ended up this way landed squarely in my lap. There was no way I could find to excuse myself, even though there was a part of me that wanted nothing more than that.

I scrubbed at my face, pushing the tears away as they slipped from my eyes. Feeling them against my skin frustrated me as much as anything else. What I wanted was an easy way to shift all the blame for this situation off me and onto someone else. My former lover Ben. Thomas. Someone. *Anyone.* But so many past conversations I'd had were like Marley's ghosts coming back to haunt me. They rattled their chains, reminding me I knew exactly who was at fault here, who needed to own this place I found myself in. I gulped in air as quietly as I could and considered how I'd let myself get to this point. And why.

I wasn't tracking on time, unsure exactly how long I'd laid there until Thomas' breathing smoothed into a deep sleep. All that 'rough sex' had worn him out. It should have been funny, but it wasn't. Once I was certain he was out, I gently slipped from under his arm and padded to the bathroom. Closing the door, I turned the light on.

I didn't like the person I saw staring back at me.

I didn't start with half-measures when I did something, and right now I was all in with the self-loathing. In the zone. Using a hand towel, I wiped at the tears that streaked my face. Standing there, it was easy to convince myself I was truly the most horrible, despicable, loathsome person that one could ever hope to meet. One step above Ben, but not a very big one, that was for sure. If only I could pull on my big girl pants, wake Thomas up, sit him down and really, truly, honestly tell him what I'd been talking about that morning.

'Thomas, I'm a submissive. I don't like gentle sex, or 'rough' sex the way you think of it. I like sex where I'm tied up, spanked, even whipped. I want you to grab me by my hair, by my neck, force me to my knees, tell me that I belong to you, and that you are going to fuck the shit out of me.'

Yeah. Yeah, that's what I should have done. Cleared the air completely. But I didn't. Because I was weak and even trying to convince myself I could do it would be nothing more than another fucking lie compounding those I'd already told myself. Instead of marching myself back to the bedroom and coming clean with Thomas, I evaded the issue one more time. Turning off the bathroom light, I slipped silently out to the living room couch and curled up. I pulled the throw off the back and wrapped myself in it. Thin bands of pale-yellow light coming through the curtain openings cast patterns of shadow and light across the room. I shrank down into the cover, letting my thoughts take over.

How? How had I gotten here?

My self-loathing was a voice of spite, contempt.

-You know the answer to that.- Why? Why did he do it?

-Does it fucking matter? He did it. But the lie... oh, the lie wasn't him. That was you.-

He hurt me!

-Big fucking deal. People get hurt all the time. You made the choice to lie to yourself. And then later to Thomas. He wasn't the one who made that *decision.-*

I thought it would help with the pain...

-Grow up. That's not the way adults deal with pain. What are you, twelve?-

IT HURT!

20

-Some fucking submissive you are. Aren't you supposed to like pain?-

Fuck you. That's different. Liking pain in the bedroom is completely *fucking different. I may be a submissive, but my desire for pain does not extend to that.*

Not to the pain Ben inflicted on me the moment I walked through that door.

TWO

I'd been so pleased with myself that day.

Burrowing into the throw I'd wrapped myself up in, feet curled up underneath me, I played out a movie in my head I'd seen a thousand times, and would see a thousand times more. I wasn't sitting on a couch in Thomas' apartment. In my mind, I was trapped in a memory I couldn't put behind me no matter how much I'd tried. In there, I was miles away, heading up the walk to the house where I'd once lived with Ben.

Ben Devers. My Dom. My *former* Dom.

I was returning home from a company trade show two days early. As part of my job as a marketing and communications manager for a biomed corporation, these shows were a regular occurrence. Ben, my boyfriend of three years, the man with whom I lived with—the one I was walking up the path towards—had grown used to me being away at these events whenever they came up.

For me to be coming home early was unusual. It was my boss's idea. She'd thought it would be a nice treat for Ben and I to have a few extra days to spend together since I'd been gone for over a week. It was her way of giving us a mini-vacation of sorts.

I wanted to surprise him, to make my coming home early extra special, so I did nothing to let on I'd be arriving ahead of schedule. I kept it secret. Made no hint of it in my e-mails, texts, or calls that I wasn't still going to be at the show for another two days. On my way to the airport I texted Ben to find out what his plans were for the day. If he expected to be home.

He'd texted me back: *lol! yeah, cleaning up*

Me: *Really? Trying to hide the evidence? :-)*

Ben: *lol it's all the crazy parties I've been having!*

The exchange made me smile. The image of him working like a busy little beaver around the house, getting it straightened out, made me grin. My mind swirled with delightful, devilish thoughts of the reward I'd give him once I arrived home and surprised him.

I caught a cab from the airport and gave a sigh of relief when I got to the house and saw his car in the driveway. I paid the cabbie then started that unforgettable walk up the path to the door. Fishing out my key, I undid the lock, moving quiet as I could letting myself in. If I was lucky, he'd have his headphones on listening to music while he worked. I'd snuck up on him like that on more than one occasion. I set my bag down inside the door, looking around. The house was silent, and there was no sign of him. I slipped into the kitchen, cracking open the door to the garage. Empty. Hmm. That only left a few other options. The most obvious was him being back in our bedroom, or...

It was the second choice that made me grin even wider. Our playroom.

The playroom was a private space in the house that Ben and I had created to play our kinky games. People sometimes referred to spaces like ours as a dungeon, but I hated that name. It sounded so... weird. Medieval. And there was nothing about our room that justi-fied it being called that. It was not dark. There weren't chains on the walls. And while we had a St. Andrews cross, and there was a bondage bench, and a horse—no Sybian yet; *that was on the to-buy list*—there wasn't anything else that warranted the term. The walls were a pleasant sage green, the flooring bland oak hardwood, and it was as far from anything dungeon-like as could be imagined. We had built the room for ourselves, kitted it out with things we liked, and for us the term playroom was much more appropriate.

I smiled as I crept down the hallway. Tiptoeing, I heard a thump come from the direction of the playroom, followed by quiet. I chuckled. Ben was a busy little boy, getting things squared away so he could properly greet me when I arrived home. At the time I was scheduled to. Well, I had a different plan. I would turn the tables on him. The thought of surprising him tugged a wicked grin across my face. Oh, I was being a very naughty girl, and that, I hoped, would result in me receiving some appropriately delightful punishments.

As I drew closer, another thudding noise came from behind the closed door. My smile faltered.

Wait.

I knew that sound. It was a sound I recognized all too well. The sound of a flogger hitting flesh. And... and that was a muted cry.

I stopped cold.

I suddenly felt lightheaded, as if the hallway was growing smaller, narrower, the door into the playroom receding into the distance. The noise repeated itself. My feet moved, bringing me up to the doorway.

Again. Another strike. A muffled whimpering cry.

That should be my voice.

In that room, I was the one who was supposed to make that noise. I heard Ben's voice, a low chuckle, followed by a rumble of words that were unclear. I reached for the doorknob, even as a flood of adrenalin pumped into my system.

It's a video. He's watching porn.

-No, it's not.-

He wouldn't do this to me...

-You're about to find out just how fucking wrong you are.-

I pushed the door open, stepping through. Ben was in mid-swing as I came into the room. He twisted to face me as the leather falls landed heavily against her skin.

25

"Holy fuck." His voice cracked on the words. The arm holding the flogger fell to his side, and he just stood there, staring at me as if I was an apparition rather than the lover of three years whom he had just destroyed.

It was eerie how calm I felt. Composed and yet filled with a rage unlike anything I'd ever experienced before. I took in the room, slowly turning my head. Ben, standing there in his black pants, black tee, the flogger hanging limply from his hand. A young woman —*call her Submissive Number Two*—hung naked, suspended from the rigging Ben had done her up in. Her head was turned back over her shoulder, staring at us with deer-like wide eyes. I swung back to face Ben, the sound of blood pounding in my ears.

"You're home," he croaked in a voice filled with both panic and disbelief.

"That's it?" I hissed as my body began to quiver, my fury banking to blast furnace temperature. "That's it? *That's* what you have to say?" My voice grew in volume to every syllable.

"I—"

"Can explain!" My voice rose to a crescendo. "Is that what you're going to say? Because there is *nothing for you to explain, you fucking sonofabitch!*"

"Jen, you need to calm down..." He took a step toward me.

"Are you fucking insane? Did you really just say that?" I was screaming now. I stood there, fists clenched at my sides, as Ben stopped mid-step. My breathing was labored from the strain of suddenly having my life destroyed. He stared at me, his face twitching, each tic giving life to a random emotion or thought that flew across it like dust before a storm.

"You need to stop yelling. Now!" He scrambled to put on his Dom voice, trying for that sharp hard tone as if it would somehow cause me to back down.

You idiot. I couldn't hold back the maniacal laughter which poured out of me.

"Oh my God! Really? Nice try, asshole! Fuck! You!"

Now he looked panicked. His head swiveled back and forth between me and the girl still hanging there silently.

"Okay, Jen. We can work this out like adults." He held his hands palms up towards me.

"We can? We can?" The sound of my laughter had reached pyscho-killer stage. I stepped towards him, rolling my eyes. "Get. Out."

"Jen..." He took a tentative step backwards.

"*Get! Out!*" I took another step forward, and this time he did not yield. Stopping just shy of him, I stood there, my body shaking. He held his ground, observing me. I hadn't started crying. My face felt hot, livid with rage that poured through me, but there were no tears.

He nodded.

Letting the flogger drop to the floor, he turned away. Moving out of the room, he marched down the hallway. I followed to just outside the door, watching as he strode to the living room. My eyes never left him as he grabbed up his wallet and keys from the end table. He went to the front door and stopped. My gaze must have seared his flesh because he turned his head towards me.

The look he gave me was filled with concern. Sympathy.

Pity.

"*Out!*" I screamed, flying down the hall in a surge of violence. It was the pity. That he would have the gall to stare at me with that look in his eyes was all my rage needed to ignite into an all-consuming fury.

I would not be pitied. Not by this bastard. Not after what he had done.

He fled through the door, slamming it behind him. I tore down the hallway until I came up to the door, stopping to lean with my forehead against it. His car started, tires screeching as he pulled out of the driveway and roared down the street. I rested there, closing my eyes.

And then I cried.

Adrenalin was still pulsing through my body, and I was doing everything I could not to fall apart. I was in pain, serious pain, and not the good kind of pain that I expected Ben to provide. I was definitely on the opposite end of the desired, craved, get-down-on-my-knees-and- beg-him-to-provide spectrum. What I was experiencing was the pain you get when you discover that someone you trusted, who you loved and you thought loved you in return, decided instead that they'd rather rip your heart out by the root, tear your soul from your body, and then casually take a shit on them.

I sobbed, my eyes blurred with tears, and for a moment all I could think of was my missed opportunity. My missed chance to call Ben all the things I should have. Cheater. Liar. Piece of shit. Not just those, but other things too—things that were bad, really bad, but not nearly bad enough. I gasped, ran my wrist across my eyes to wipe away the wetness, doing my best to get myself back under control. My sobs shifted from choking to heaving, finally to just sucking deep breaths. I didn't remember moving, but I found I was standing in the living room, staring at a picture on the wall. It an abstract print, black flowing lines on stark white simulating in minimalist fashion a woman in repose. Her head was turned, looking back over her shoulder at something, someone, out of sight. The only color on the print was the red slash that indicated her lips. I'd bought that for Ben. Purchased it because I thought it symbolic of who we were. An abstract representation of our dynamic.

Now. Now it was blood—blood from my heart—splashed against canvas. I wanted to rip it down, tear it into a million pieces. Burn it in the fireplace below. Once again, anger stoked itself to replace the grief of only moments before. I was moving, crossing the space that separated me from the image when I heard it.

"Hello?"

It was a soft voice.

It was coming from the playroom.

Oh. Fuck.

I stopped cold, closing my eyes as I realized to whom the voice belonged.

Submissive Number Two.

What a perfect fucking metaphor for Ben. He screwed me over until he got caught, then fled without taking care of the one thing he absolutely should have. I'd thought him such a perfect Dom. The sound of her voice shattered that illusion in an instant, leaving me to feel even more humiliated at how gullible I'd been. Asshole. Fucking asshole. He'd bailed, and now I would have to clean up his mess. I turned and tiptoed back down the hallway. Coming up to the playroom door, I stopped and looked inside.

There she was, still suspended.

As I stepped into the room, her head snapped up. She twisted ever so slightly in the rigging. Her eyes were wide, looking at me with a just-was-in-subspace-but-now-possibly-facing-my-own-death stupor. For a moment, neither of us spoke, but we studied each other silently.

Her lips quivered. She took a gulp of air, then asked, "I... could you, umm... let me down? Please?"

I wanted to hate her. I really did. But even in that moment I understood it wasn't her fault. I knew, at some instinctual level, that she didn't have a fucking clue what was going on. What exactly had just happened here. No, this was all on Ben.

I said nothing as I crossed to the wall where the suspension ropes came together. I looked up at the lines, down to the cleat they were lashed to, and then to her.

"Okay."

I pulled, taking up some of the tension. Gathering the lines together, I unwound them from the cleat and started lowering. I warned her, "Listen, I'm going to try to lower you slowly, but no guarantees..."

I could have been an ass. I could have let go. Let her fall. I didn't. Being careful and going slow I got her down without issue. She came to rest on the floor of the playroom in a lump, still trussed up. Ben had prided himself on his ropework, and this Shibari was no different, so it took me some time to get her completely unbound. That gave us both time to talk.

"You know who I am?"

She nodded her head, eyes tracking my every movement. "Ben's other sub."

I grunted. "His *other* sub..."

She gave a suppressed yelp as I yanked on a knot. Maybe a little harder than was necessary.

"I'm guessing you didn't know Ben lived with me?"

"Umm... he said that he had another play partner, but that you were both poly, and that you were out of town for a while and you wanted him to have fun...."

"Yeah, I'll bet he did."

There was silence for a while as I worked at the rope and got her arms free. Then I started working on the bindings crisscrossing her legs.

"That... that was a lie, wasn't it?" Her voice was deflated recognition.

"Yeah, that was a lie."

"Oh."

As I finished untying the last of the rope, I gave her a condensed version of the relationship Ben and I had shared. At the end, she sat there, rubbing the marks on her legs, looking dazed and sad.

"I... I'm sorry. I didn't know. That's not what Ben told me when we first met."

I nodded. "Yeah, I'll bet it wasn't."

I found her clothes, scooping them up and handing them to her. As she dressed, she filled me in on the dynamic she had had with Ben. It seemed this wasn't their first play session. Ben had met her at a munch, no doubt one he'd attended while I was away for work. He'd sold her a bill of goods on how we were a couple who had our own play partners, and that while we were committed to each other, when we were separated we could play with other people. *'He said that was why he couldn't be in another exclusive relationship.'*

"This wasn't my first time playing, so I really didn't think anything of it." Her eyes pleaded for understanding. "I'm really sorry. If I'd known..."

I made a dismissive motion with my hand. I understood what had happened here. It was a part of the lifestyle I knew a lot of people engaged in. Multiple partners. Ben had convinced her that our dynamic included that. I had nothing against nor judged others who engaged in it. But it was not—and never would be—a part of any dynamic I would be involved in. I had made that clear to Ben from day one.

"I understand," I said gruffly. "Not your fault."

Everything that Submissive Number Two—*I didn't remember her name, even if she told it to me at some point*—had just told me should have enraged me even further. However, by that point I was feeling a sense of dislocation. Numbness. Ben had fucked me, and not in the fun way. He'd broken that most core concept of a D/s relationship: each partner must trust the other implicitly. What was clear the longer I'd listened to Ms. Number Two was that he'd broken that trust early on in our relationship. Violated that trust without much thought given to the consequences. I had made it clear to Ben from the get-go that I was monogamous. No one desiring multiple partners need apply. He had assured me he was of a like mind. That he would never think to be with anyone else while we were together. He was smooth, he was sincere, and the fucker played a well-run game. I never once felt the need to question him, never felt my trust misplaced, or suspected him capable of doing what he'd done.

Right up to the moment I opened that playroom door.

Fucking bastard.

"I... I should go."

I looked over to her, coming out of my reverie.

"Yeah, that would probably be a good idea." I left the playroom, heading down the hallway to the front door. She followed me silently, and I shooed her out of the house. I should have been mad, should have been furious, but I just didn't have the mental or emotional energy in me for it. I was exhausted. Drained. Once she was out, I closed the door, turned, and leaned my back against it. My mind was already slipping into damage control mode, working overtime to triage my emotional state and psyche, especially those that related to the parts of my life that in the last thirty minutes had been completely torn apart.

That was what began to consume me—trying to come to terms with what Ben had done. Trying to wrap my head around the what and the why. Why had he done it? What had I done wrong? What had I not given him that he needed, aside from the obvious?

I spent much of that day and night trying to figure it out. I didn't. It took time. A lot of time. And many tears flowed before I formed my ultimate conclusions.

Ben was a narcissistic, cheating, lying, piece-of-shit asshole who had screwed me over royally.

I was done with BDSM.

The first was easy to come to terms with. Ben had taken me for a ride from day one. He'd had no intention of being true to me. He had used me, gotten what he wanted for three years, and had his little dessert side dishes to boot. I had trusted him. I had believed him because he had spouted off all the right things to me. Ben was my first true Dominant, and he knew the language of our kink so well. Knew all the right words, could spell out all the right RACK —*Risk Aware Consensual Kink*—and SSC—*Safe, Sane, Consensual* —phrases rote.

And I accepted without question everything he said. Believed him when he told me 'Jennifer Boyd, you are the submissive I have been looking for my entire life. There will never be another for me, because you are perfection.'

Oh, God, I bought into that. I had wanted those words with every molecule of my being, and when he said them, I drew them in like smack to a junkie. And now I'd paid the price. A butcher's bill settled with a shattered heart. For believing and accepting without question.

The latter conclusion was not as easy to process. It took time for me to come to a resolution with that one. My reasoning was neither rational nor cohesive, but while wallowing in the sea of pain I was in, it all made perfectly logical sense somehow. All of what had happened wasn't just Ben's fault. No. BDSM was equally to blame. Everything about our dynamic had been a sham. The entire life-style, and all the people involved in it, were bullshit. All of it filled with false ideals, unrealistic expectations, and people who were as deceitful and disingenuous as the day was long. If you looked at it that way, there was obviously only one logical course of action—I had to get out. I had to cast off anything and everything having to do with BDSM and the lifestyle surrounding it. And that meant I would no longer be a submissive. Submission wasn't going to be a part of my sexuality, or any part of my life for that matter. I would be strictly 'vanilla' from here on out. The benefits were clear. Every-thing would be so much easier, so much less complicated. No worries about cheating, multiple partners, etcetera.

Yep. That was it. That was what I would do. That quick. That easy.

THREE

I blinked.

I was in the living room of the apartment, sitting in the dark.

Shaking myself out of my reverie, I took a deep breath then let it out slowly.

"Goddammit," I whispered. My frustration here was the implied question behind the expletive: to whom did it apply? Ben, or myself? Because the real issue—the one that had sent me out here to the couch to cocoon myself in the throw and remember that life-defining day from my past—wasn't something that Ben had created alone. He may have set it in motion, but I was the one who had conceived the lie that had me sitting here thinking about myself with pity and disgust.

I heard a small creaking noise from back in the house. For a panicked moment I thought it might be Thomas, awake and coming to find out where I was. I did not want to explain why I was out here. That was not a conversation I wanted to have yet. I sat motionless for a moment, but silence returned and there was no further sound. I got up, shrugged off the throw, folded it carefully and placed it over the back of the couch. Moving down the hall, I quietly slipped back to bed. Thomas was still asleep, back facing me as I sat at the edge of my side.

He was a good man.

Thomas Kiernan was a good man. I'd known that from the very first day I'd met him.

He didn't deserve this. He didn't deserve to be on the receiving end of whatever shit would eventually come down because of the lie I had dragged him into.

I slid under the covers next to him and he shifted back, pressing against me. I could smell him, that distinctive scent that was him—traces of the body wash he used, the slight tang of the sweat from the sex we'd had. Tears began to well up in my eyes, but I squeezed tight to force them back. I would not cry again tonight. I was determined. Adjusting my pillows, I spooned tight to him.

I lay there trying, but failing, to fall asleep. He deserved better, I kept thinking. I remembered how I'd first met Thomas. The first day I'd gone back to work after the playroom incident.

Somehow, I'd pulled myself together to the point where I believed I might make it through the workday without coming apart. Patched myself up, slapped on clothes that would pass as reasonable work wear, and hauled my ass in. As soon as I stepped out onto the Marketing Department floor, my boss Loren approached me.

"So? Did Ben enjoy your little surprise?" She winked at me with a knowing smile.

I almost lost it then, and I hadn't even made it to my office. I bore down and smiled weakly, but it was obvious my response lacked the appropriate enthusiasm. It didn't take long before she was watching me with concern, gently probing if there was anything I wanted to talk about. I avoided it that day, and then the next, but eventually I broke down and accepted her offer. We went out for drinks, and sufficiently lubricated, I filled her in on what had taken place. I kept my story lean, providing only the minimum amount of details. Loren didn't know of my kink and none of the intricacies of my relationship with Ben. She knew that we were a couple who'd been living together for three years, and from all the limited information I'd shared with her during that time the impression was that I'd been happy. Which, truthfully, had been the case. Leaving out most of the gory details, I told her I'd left Ben because I'd found out he'd cheated on me. She was both filled with indignation and touchingly supportive.

"You are going to get through this and be stronger and better for it in the end."

"That's what they say."

"Jen, I swear it. You have to be one of the strongest people I know.

I know you. You will not let this define you nor weaken you. If ever there was a woman I could say has the 'warrior' spirit, it's you."

Wonder how much of a 'warrior' you'd think I am, Loren, if you knew how much I miss Ben? Miss feeling him tying me spread eagle to the cross and then flogging me. That thought went through my head, but only briefly. She meant well, and there was no way in hell I would spring something like my former submissive lifestyle on her.

Loren may have been the first to notice that something had happened to me, but it didn't take long for others to do so too. Soon, through that wonderful communication medium known as office gossip, everyone knew that my boyfriend had cheated on me and that I was suddenly single. Between Loren and a few other co-workers and friends, eventually the inevitable happened; they started trying to hook me up. I had known it was likely to come to this at some point, and so when it did I was neither upset nor surprised. For each attempt sent my way I begged off, saying that I had no desire to jump back into the dating (cess)pool just yet. And that was the truth. It didn't matter how great this guy was going to be or how they were sure we'd hit it off. I just wasn't interested.

"Listen, at the very least, from everything I've heard, you'll get some great sex out of it."

That had come from one of my marketing co-workers, and while it had been candid and refreshing—and the only one I'd paused to consider—I still politely declined. What I really needed was time. Some time, some space, and a lot of healing. And, God bless them, there was no real pressure. They did what they did because they cared about me and wanted to see me happy. It was sweet, touching, and frustrating all at the same time. Eventually everyone seemed to get the subtle message, and the offers dwindled. At that point all of those things I wanted—the time, the space, the room to heal—I got.

And it was good... until it wasn't.

I had forgotten one key thing about being in a D/s relationship; the intensity. The absolute passion with which you become connected to the person you're engaging with. At its core there was one central tenet to most BDSM relationships. Trust. When you had created your own dynamic one of the most powerful aspects of it was how much you grew to trust that person. How much you came to trust your partner to take care of you even as they were doing these things that had the potential to be very harmful, whether emotionally, physically, or both. You trusted your partner to engage in these things and still cherish you, protect you, and look at you as the beautiful, incredible, desirable person you were. Outsiders' often viewed BDSM as being all about pain—whips and chains, trussed up in ropes, clad in leather or latex.

And in any given dynamic those things could be important. But the one thing that held it all together, the glue that allowed people to do these crazy, kinky things to each other, was trust. It was a hard thing to describe, but once you'd had that kind of relationship, it could be hard to give it up for something that seemed less in comparison. Difficult not to despair at the void its absence created and be desperate to have it back again.

That's where I eventually ended up.

It was nine months after my separation from Ben when the itch grew to a point where I couldn't ignore it any longer. It came on slowly at first. An ache I felt when I was alone, realizing the silence that surrounded me was no longer comforting. It wasn't that I'd become a hermit. I'd kept up a social life of sorts both in and outside of work. It wasn't strictly sexual either, since I had more than enough toys and a vivid imagination to help overcome those needs when they arose.

Still, all that aside, I knew what those pangs were, and I fought to keep them at bay. Loneliness is an insidious thing though. It creeps up on you, taking root in those safe spaces you've created. Then it breaks apart the foundation until, before you know it, they are cracking and falling down around you. That's when loneliness can really do its job. Create the real damage it's capable of. When it can wrap its tendrils around your thoughts, remind you of what you once had and whisper seductively how horrible your current life is.

-So, this spinsterhood thing really suits you! Could have saved yourself a lot of time and pain if you'd known how wonderful this was going to be before Ben.-

Stop. I don't need this shit right now.

-Then fucking do something about it!-

My self-loathing loved what I was going through. It was having a field day, and I became ever more frustrated that it showed no signs of letting up. No sign that it would allow me to go back to the peace I'd had immediately after Ben was out of my life.

While my personal life was reaching a crisis point, my work life continued blithely along. I had an upcoming show for which I needed to prepare, but there was one slight twist. Our corporation had recently purchased a smaller company and folded them in under our corporate umbrella. I hadn't worked with anyone who'd come over yet, but that would change for this upcoming show. We would highlight both lines of products in the booth simultaneously, and I would be getting my first taste of working with some of the team from the other company.

Part of my job in handling our trade show presence was FDA

compliance. Ultimately, what that boiled down to was making sure the FDA didn't think we were trying to sell snake oil to an unsuspecting public. I didn't write the copy for our marketing materials, but I was the lucky soul who had to run each submission past our lawyers and get them to approve it before we sent it along.

Thomas Kiernan was a new lawyer at our corporation, one who had come over from the purchased company after the merger. His specialty was compliance, and within our corporate structure he was now low man on the totem pole. Not quite at the bottom, but close enough that for FDA marketing compliance—as opposed to the sexier drug compliance—he drew the short straw. When told to forward all the materials requiring review to a lawyer whom I had never worked with before, I prepared myself for a long, ugly slog.

But that didn't happen.

I sent him a review request along with all the associated materials.

In response, I received a single two-word reply:

Thank you.

Then he went radio silent. I did not hear a peep out of him for several days. What I had prepared for was pushback of the kind I was familiar with from our lawyers. Requests demanding further details, clarification of the procedures required for these types of submissions, and the dreaded meetings. Multiple unnecessary, repetitious, frustrating meetings. As the days passed, the silence from Thomas started to make me nervous. By day three, I was sufficiently rattled enough that I decided I had to know if he was outright ignoring the matter or being passive aggressive and waiting for me to make the first move.

So I did.

At least that was the plan. Before I could finish typing my e-mail, I received one from him. In it, he provided an index of all the files he had reviewed, a link to copies where he had made amendments and revisions, and a concise outline of where he expected there to be rejections. Along with this he provided suggestions on how we could handle those should they occur. In short, it was as complete and thorough a review as I could have hoped for.

I was stunned. And intrigued.

I wrote him back, thanking him for the exemplary job, saying I was both grateful and impressed; some of our own corporate lawyers could take lessons from him. I ended it by asking if he would have some time to go over everything in detail, given that I wasn't as familiar with their product line as he was. I wanted to make sure I had at least a basic idea of what they might ask me to explain.

Thomas: *Lunch? Thur. good?*

Me: *Sure! Sounds great!*

I went to Loren immediately.

"What do you know about Thomas Kiernan?"

She gave me a blank stare, voice tinged with confusion. "Who?"

"Thomas Kiernan. In Legal. He's one of the lawyers who came over during the merger."

"Hmm. I *think* I might have met him once? I dunno, honestly. There've been so many new people coming in that I've had a tough time keeping track of all of them. Why?"

"Well... he did the entire compliance package for the AACN show in three days, no questions, no pushback, nothing. I submitted the files, he reviewed them, then he sent back a packet that is so thorough it makes our guys look like kindergartners. I think I'm in love."

"Oh, really?" Loren grinned, an eyebrow arching upwards.

"And he just asked me to lunch to go over all of it."

"Oh. *Really?*" Loren's eyebrow shot up another degree. This time she said it in a suggestive tone that I did not want or need.

"Oh, God. Don't even." I rolled my eyes, letting a sigh emphasize my annoyance.

"Hey, just saying. Lawyer, smart, competent at his job..." She wiggled her eyebrows salaciously, eyes twinkling.

"Umm... probably married, or in a relationship, or not my type."

"You don't know that."

"Okay, Loren, thanks for all your help." I waved at her over my shoulder as I slipped away. "Buh-bye!"

Her laughter followed me all the way back to my office. This Thomas Kiernan was intriguing, but not in the way that

Loren was suggesting. Well, okay, maybe he was a tiny bit, but that was it. Even with the pangs of loneliness increasing daily, I still wasn't ready to cast my line and start fishing. I'd be lying, however, if I said that there weren't a few occasions when the thought of *'Wouldn't it be interesting if...'* crossed my mind. The mind can be tricksy like that when you're lonely.

Thursday afternoon rolled around. I'd been trying to catch a glimpse of Mystery Lawyer when he showed up, but as luck would have it, I was on a phone call when he eventually arrived. Engrossed in the paperwork I was discussing with a vendor, I didn't notice him as he stood in the hallway outside my door. He was the one who got the drop on me, standing there watching me for a good five minutes while I argued over the phone. It was only towards the end of the call that I glanced up and saw him there.

Oh! Oh, okay. Not bad. A little taller than me. Blond, curly hair. Hmm... kinda an upscale SoCal surfer vibe. Obviously takes care of himself. Pleasant, if somewhat bland face.

No, not bad. Not bad at all.

I smiled at him, making an *'I'm sorry!'* motion at the phone and my desk. He returned the smile and made a *'don't worry about it'* wave. I finished the call as quickly as I could, glancing between the paperwork and him. Once the handset was back in its cradle, I came around my desk, hand extended.

"I'm sorry about that! I'm Jennifer."

"I totally understand." He gave me a firm handshake as we came together. "I'm Thomas."

His smile was warm and damned if I didn't feel a slight tingle go up my spine.

"Ready for lunch?"

"Yes, definitely. Let me just grab a few things." I turned back to my desk to dump the folder I'd already put together into my bag, and then we were off.

Lunch went much better than I could have imagined. It was pleasant, enlightening, and at moments downright fun. Thomas—he was Thomas, never Tom—was intelligent, amiable, personable, funny, and confident. All attributes that in my current state were Tomahawk missiles straight to my relationship triggers. Even if I had still been embracing my submissive nature, he would have been intriguing. Since I had put that part of my personality aside, there was no denying the attraction and the chemistry I sensed taking place between us. At this point in my life, coming off of Ben, my confidence in my ability to read people wasn't at its highest. By the same token I didn't think I was a total failure at it either. My Spidey-senses were tingling during our lunch, and I felt there was a decent chance Thomas was catching the same vibes.

"Hey, this has been fun. I can honestly say this has been the most relaxing power lunch I've had since coming over." Thomas grinned across the table at me like a boy caught doing something he shouldn't have.

"I've enjoyed it, too. We should do it again." I smiled. It shouldn't have sounded like a request for a date, and yet it did.

"Yes," he looked at me with eyes that narrowed at the same time his smile shifted subtly. "Yes, we should."

We weren't flirting with each other. At least that's what I tried to convince myself. We were heading in that direction, though. Taking those first tentative steps off the trail of simply co-workers and into the forest of I-like-you-you-like-me-what-do-you-say and all things beyond.

Smiling softly at that memory, I closed my eyes as sleep began to overtake me. In that dreamy half-state, I put my hand to Thomas' back, feeling his breathing. It was peaceful, relaxing, and something I'd grown to love. It was something that I'd found comforting from the first night we'd spent together. A night that hadn't been long in coming after our lunch date. After that day things had progressed quickly. We did the relationship dance for two months and by the third we'd become the perfect couple.

And then, in the span of the next three short months, it all started to go to hell.

FOUR

I woke the next morning to Thomas shifting in bed.

I'd nestled to his back, and he rolled to me, eyes blinking owlishly as he came awake. His face wrinkled into a soft smile as he gazed at me. "Hey beautiful."

I smiled back, cupping my hand to his cheek, feeling the coarse stubble. "Hey you."

He leaned forward and kissed me gently. After a moment, he pulled away, brushing my hair out of my eyes.

"Mmm..." I sighed at the intimacy of the gesture, letting myself drift into the cocoon of affection he'd created.

"How are you feeling this morning? Little sore?"

My eyes almost snapped open.

Oh no.

I forced myself to lie motionless. I couldn't let Thomas see my reaction. See the dismay those two little words had spawned within me. I kept my eyes closed so he couldn't read the disappointment that might show if I dared to open them. Remaining silent, I let his words hang between us, keeping my face as neutral as I could. *Dear God.* He seriously thought his rough sex from last night had made me sore. I centered myself, straining to keep my breathing relaxed and then slowly let the air trickle out.

"No, I'm fine. Thanks." I kept my eyes closed for a bit longer. I knew I couldn't trust myself not to react if I opened them and saw the air of self-satisfied, peacocking pride I suspected from his tone. No. I was certain I would unravel at the seams if I peeked and found him staring back at me like that. Fortunately, Thomas solved the problem. Chuckling softly, he slid to the edge of the mattress and then slipped off the bed. Cracking one eye open, I watched as he padded to the bathroom, closing the door behind him.

I leaned back against my pillow and groaned.

God dammit. What am I going to do?

-Okay, here's a thought: his belt is right there at the end of the bed. Why don't you pick it up, go into the bathroom, lean your hands on the counter, then when he comes out, tell him you want him to whip your ass red?-

Oh, God, yes. But... fuck no! He thinks what he did last night made me sore!

-Well, now's your chance to show him what would really *make you feel sore.-*

In the end, I just lay there burrowing into the covers, attempting to hide from what was waiting out there. Him. Smiling *that* smile.

Eventually he came out and—*goddammit*—there it was. That expression of smug satisfaction plastered across his face, exactly as I'd been afraid of.

"I'm gonna head downstairs and make coffee, start on some breakfast, okay?"

"Sure," I nodded, slapping on a smile. "I'll be down in a few."

He came over to the bed and kissed me. The whole time that superior look never left his face, and I knew exactly what was going on in that head of his.

-Oh, look at that! Isn't it cute! He thinks he knows your dirty little secret!-

Shut it. Shut. The. Fuck. Up.

-You made this bed. Enjoy lying in it.-

Gritting my teeth, I waited until Thomas left the room. Once he was gone I scrambled up, wrenching the covers aside until they were wadded in a heap at the foot of the bed. I sat for a moment, legs dangling over the edge as I tried to calm myself. Maybe my reaction was irrational, but right now I wasn't sure of anything except that this was wrong. Everything about this was just wrong. I had to do something. I had to speak to him. Now. Today. Soon. He was just going to go on thinking he had this entire situation sewed up. That he had me pegged. That he knew exactly what my *needs* were.

My needs. My desires.

-And... what? Hmm? You do that, tell him everything, and exactly

how *do you think he's going to react?-* I don't know.

-Oh, bullshit. You do *know. You know exactly how he'll react if you suddenly open up about your submissive desires.-* Well, what then? Just...

-Yes?-

Just go on doing what I've been doing?

-Hey, don't ask me, friend. You created this. I thought you had a plan.-

I did.

-Seems to be working out great to me. Well done. Keep up the good work!-

I rubbed my eyes, grabbed my robe and slipped it on. I sat there, hands clenched in my lap. Fuck my self-loathing. I had to do it. Sit Thomas down, talk to him, clear this up. He needed to know the truth. That no, no I wasn't sore, because he *hadn't* fucked me rough. He'd just fucked me in a different position, and that was *not* what I had been talking about yesterday morning.

No, he needed to know who I was. What I was. Because it was the fair and right thing to do.

As I walked towards the kitchen, I could hear him moving

around, smell the coffee brewing. Each step I took made me more determined. I was strong. What was it Loren had said? I had the warrior spirit. Hell yeah! I was a *warrior*! I was a badass warrior who would march in there and get this shit sorted out right now!

Right up to the moment I rounded the corner.

He was so cute. It wasn't the first time I'd thought that, seeing him puttering around the kitchen in his sleep pants, the tight black tee shirt he wore stretched nicely along the vee his muscles made down the length of his back. I bit down on my lower lip as a flood of blissful warmth poured through me while I watched him make breakfast. For me. His lover.

-*Yep. Some warrior...*-

Fuck you. Soon. Tomorrow. Just... not now. Not... right now.

-*Sure.*-

Thomas grinned at me as he went about finishing breakfast while I sat down at the counter. He put my coffee mug in front of me and I took a sip. Perfect. Just the way I liked it. I cupped my hands around the mug, sipping slowly and thinking.

For the six months Thomas and I had been a couple, it had been good. No, that wasn't fair. In the beginning, it was more than just good. It had been incredible. Life affirming, rejuvenating, inspiring.

And the sex had been great too!

Thomas was an incredible guy. In those first months I was not only happy, I thought things were finally turning around for me. I was starting to put Ben behind me, I'd stopped thinking so much about the damage he'd done because I realized it wouldn't define me forever. Therein lay the problem though. The day eventually came when I realized that since my decision, what I had in fact been doing was trying to redefine who I was. What Ben had done to me got parsed out in simple terms: the path to recovery was for me to step away from the submissive part of myself entirely.

It seemed so rational then.

Thomas came to the counter and set a plate in front of me. I wasn't a breakfast person during the week, but this cooking for us on the weekends had become a little ritual that Thomas had created in our time together. It was sweet, romantic, and I loved him for it. It was things like this that I didn't want to give up. Why couldn't these moments be enough? Why did all those other things need to come into play?

Why can't you be something that you aren't?

For a time, the idea of submission, of *being* a submissive, was so distinctly associated with a period in my life of such terrible pain that I determined I would no longer allow it to define my sexuality. Instead, I pushed it away. Denied it. Buried it. The thought of being in a relationship, of trusting and being intimate with someone that way triggered so many emotions, all of them negative, that I couldn't even consider it. Then Thomas had come along. He'd showed up at my office, taken me to lunch, and then taken me to his bed. Those wounds had started healing, and that had been a good thing. But it came with consequences. The most significant of which was that, gradually, as time went on, those submissive tendencies that had been such a large part of how I identified before began to creep back in. I had thought pushing them away, shoving them into neat little boxes and slamming the door closed would be simple. A way to drive out a pain center that Ben's cheating and dishonesty had created.

-But then you discovered a little flaw in your grand plan, didn't you, Jen?-

Yes.

Ben had lied to me. And of all the things he'd done, his lies hurt the most. My solution to the pain those lies had inflicted on me was to create a lie of my own. A lie which I then imposed upon myself. *I am no longer a submissive.* Once Thomas came along and the hurt began to fade, the pain healed, those parts of my sexuality so integral to who I once was began to creep back in. Slowly, insidiously. The solution was no longer working. The lie was coming undone.

-You thought you could just walk away from it all. Easy-peasy...-

It was supposed to be simple.

It wasn't.

"You haven't finished eating."

I started at the sound of his voice, my head coming up from where I'd been staring down at my plate, lost in this miasma of self-loathing and doubt. "Oh, God... sorry."

Thomas leaned on an elbow, staring at me with mild apprehension in his frown. "Everything okay?"

"Just thinking..."

"About?"

I panicked. I'd prepared for battle earlier, ready to have that come- to-Jesus meeting with him I needed to have. Now it was the last thing I wanted to do. I thought fast.

"Just thinking about the upcoming show."

"Ah..." Thomas paused for a second, mouth open as if he were about to say more. A second later he closed it, giving a quick nod before he leaned over and kissed my forehead.

This. This was becoming a problem. Thomas was not stupid. Over the past two months he'd started asking questions when he found me lost in thought like this. *Penny for your thoughts? What's going on up inside there, Jen? Is everything okay?* Each time he caught me I piled another lie on top of the ones before them. To dodge answering the questions, to avoid telling him the truth.

The fucking irony was not lost on me. I hated lying to him. Lies to myself I could deal with. The consequences of those were mine to own and suffer through. The lies I told Thomas would be his to deal with at some point, and through no fault of his own.

I wasn't ready to tell him the truth, however. At least not now. Not today. I wasn't strong enough to do that yet.

I looked down at my plate. When my desires began to reassert themselves, they'd started as brief flashes of memory that would appear at random moments, and not always when we were having sex. Simple touches prompted explicit memories that they shouldn't have. Memories that triggered feelings that ran up my spine like little jolts of electricity, calling for me to react in ways that would have definitely raised Thomas' eyebrow. Hell, couples who aren't into any sort of kink do shit like that all the time! Except when they did, they didn't suddenly want to fall to their knees, head bent, waiting with quivering anticipation for a fist to wrap in their hair. For me, however, that was what was happening with far too much frequency. Triggered reactions that were not conducive to maintaining the persona I had taken on. I was struggling to keep them in check and losing the battle. Those thoughts that urged me to kneel before Thomas, offering myself to him, begging him to dominate me were winning.

-Oh, yeah, you should do that. Definitely do every one of those things. That *will go over well.-*

I sighed. Right. *Sure.* As if I could. I couldn't tell him those thoughts, unless I was willing to admit to something much larger. If I were to just come clean with him about my sexuality now, he wouldn't understand. That wasn't the person who Thomas thought I was, nor the one he loved. I hadn't sold him on *that* person.

I'd sold him on a lie.

Our recent conversation and his discovery of my dirty little secret notwithstanding, none of the things I wanted to tell Thomas about what I desired sexually would be things he'd be willing to—or want to— engage in. That wasn't who Thomas was. No, he was a good boy, as clean-cut as his blond, all-American, boyish looks portrayed. Rough sex. Yep, that right there, what he had done last night, was as far as Thomas Kiernan would ever go. I had little doubt that even *that* had made him feel giddy with the absolute filthy wickedness of it.

Dear God.

For a moment, I'd thought his finding out about my kinky desires might have bought me some time. Thrown him off the scent that there was something bothering me. Now, I wasn't so sure. That look he'd given me when he'd caught me wool-gathering, the unspoken question that he'd withheld... *Shit.* Maybe I had gained nothing. Maybe he still knew that there was something more bothering me. *Fuck.* What if nothing I was doing to hide my apprehension was working?

Thomas was moving about the kitchen, cleaning up. I pulled out of my musing and watched him, feeling both sadness and frustration in equal parts. The problem here was I was talking myself to fucking death about this, rather than meeting it head on. I debated with myself in circles around the issue, but not once did I bear down and do what I needed to do — just talk to Thomas. I had gotten myself to this point, but I couldn't seem to get the traction to go further.

All I did know was one thing: this situation wasn't going to get any better. In fact, unless something happened, it would only get worse.

Next week I had to go out of town for one of our corporate trade shows. This upcoming event wasn't a big one, so I would be the only person from my department in attendance. Loren wouldn't be there, and aside from a few regional and corporate salespeople who would show up on the actual show days, this was my gig to run solo. I would handle things the way I saw fit with a minimal amount of input from others, which was a blessing unto itself. Shows like this where I'd be holding down the fort on my own were the ones I enjoyed the most.

There was a secondary benefit this time. It would give me a chance to get my head screwed on straight. Come up with a real game plan on how to deal with my relationship with Thomas. I watched as he finished the last of the dishes. He glanced up at me, looking at me with a smile.

The one that said 'Oh, I know what you like, and I'm gonna take *real* good care of you.'

Fuck.

This was a monster of my own creation. No one to blame but myself.

I had to take care of it and take care of it soon.

FIVE

We had argued.

Again.

The day I flew out for the show, Thomas had driven me to the airport. All that morning I had been irritable, fighting with myself to do what I knew I needed to. Thomas had picked up on it, and as we rode in the car, he called me out.

"Jen, come on. Seriously, talk to me. Something's been bugging you. What's wrong?"

"Nothing! I told you before, it's just... work. This trip. I'm fine. Fine."

Arguments like this had been happening off and on since that night. The Night of the Rough Sex, as I'd begun referring to it. At first Thomas had thought he'd discovered my secret, and in doing so the explanation behind why I had been so reticence and distracted lately. But when nothing had changed, my attitude the same if not worse than it had been before, Thomas began to show signs of frustration of his own.

After I checked my bag, Thomas stood with me as I waited to join the line for security. There was still the barrier of tension that separated us after this morning's argument, although to give Thomas credit he was doing his best not to let it show.

"Have a good show. Come back soon." He held me in his arms and kissed me, but I could feel the stiffness in both acts. Tears welled up in my eyes. I felt so bad for what I was doing to him, and though a part of me still wished there was some easy way out of this, I knew there wasn't.

Do it, Jen.

"Thomas..." I faltered, unable to force out another word. Talk or continue with the lie. Those were my choices. Neither was ideal, neither was easy, and both had built up a death grip level of frustration inside me. Still, I knew I had to do something.

Thomas wiped away the tears that spilled down my cheeks. He pulled me tight to his chest again, and then gently leaned back, letting go.

"What, Jen? What is it? Please. Just tell me what's going on."

"I..." I choked. *We need to talk about our relationship, Thomas. I have something I need to tell you. About me. About who I am. About us.* I needed to say one of these things, the right one, but in the end, I said nothing at all.

"Jen." I watched as his jaw went tight. "Dammit. Come on. Talk to me."

I kicked the can down the road. "It's...nothing. I'll see you when I get home. Love you." I gave him a hurried peck on the cheek, sniffling.

"Okay." For a second his voice sounded different. An undercurrent I couldn't pinpoint that disappeared as fast as it had come. "Okay."

The smile he gave me at first I took for tenderness, but as I stared back at him silently, it suddenly looked like something else. Something that was less sympathy and more like disappointment.

Thomas gently pushed me away. "Love you too. Now, go. Before you get me started."

I did. Snapping my mouth shut, I let the words I should have said wither and die inside me. I walked into the line, looked up once to see him still standing there, and did not look again until I was at the other end of the conveyor. Looking back, he was still there, distant now, waving at me. I gave a quick wave then headed for the departure gate.

Sitting in the waiting area, looking out of the large glass windows, I stared at the white plane that idled at the gate waiting to take me away. The show ahead of me was in Chicago, at McCormick Place. I'd done shows there several times before and I knew the things I needed to look out for. An easy show is what I wanted, and my reasons were simple. I needed time to think. I didn't want to focus on the show. What I wanted was the space to concentrate on what I'd been avoiding addressing with Thomas. Looking in the show packet, I'd seen only one minor change that indicated anything different from the last time I'd been there, and that was nothing I couldn't handle.

I was still mulling these things over when they began boarding us. The flight was almost empty, a blessing I rarely experienced. I held my breath as the rest of the passengers settled in. I didn't want a companion this trip. A grandmother who'd want to chat and ask me why I wasn't married yet, popping out babies. Or—even worse— another business person, a guy who'd want to know all the details of what I did to either try and sell me whatever it was he peddled, figure out if he had a chance of getting me into his hotel room, or maybe both.

Right now, either would have had me at the brink.

I had thoughts to think, and I just wanted to be left alone in blissful peace. I sighed with palpable relief when the last passenger was aboard and the remaining seat in my row was still vacant. Settling in as we taxied out to the runway, I listened to that weird drone aircraft engines make as they build up for take off. I took the free drink offered, opened my computer bag and pulled out my folder of paperwork to spread out in front of me.

I intended to read it one more time, but the effort was in vain.

Soon my mind was drifting as I'd often found it doing in the past week.

My submissive desires had awoken from their slumber. And in any other situation that should have been a wonderful thing. But I had poisoned the well big time in that regard. Rather than embracing it, I started to resent it. The frustration the reemergence of those thoughts and desires brought on became traitorous tendrils that twined themselves to choke out everything I had worked hard to do to turn 'normal.' *Vanilla.* I tried slashing them away whenever they appeared but for each I destroyed a new one replaced it. And as much as I railed against it, I knew my aggravation was only growing more pronounced. I'd thought Thomas had taken his discovery of my rough sex fetish as sign he'd solved whatever was bugging me. In the week after The Night of the Rough Sex that assumption had proven wrong. My exasperation with myself had turned into resentment and try as hard as I might it trickled over into my relationship with Thomas. And he picked up on it. Prior to that night he'd simply questioned me, asking me what was going on.

'Jen, what's wrong? Is something bothering you?'

'No. I'm fine. I've just got a lot going on at work right now.'

It was another lie, and each lie I told piled on top of the last, notching my irritation level up even further.

'Hey. Is everything okay? You seem kind of tense.' 'It's fine, Thomas. Nothing's wrong.'

After that night, though, despite my best efforts otherwise, my reticence and distraction made things increasingly difficult between us. He caught it in pensive looks I had while sitting at the kitchen counter, thinking. Or when he came around the corner and into my office as I sat lost in some thought of 'what I needed to do.' It was in car rides where he'd be talking and I was staring out the window, not tracking on what he was saying until it was too late.

"Jen."

"Huh?" *Crap.*

"Oh, yeah, umm... we should do that."

"Do...what?"

Panic. "Uh... what you just said."

"I said have you noticed your car's got a weird shimmy in the front end."

"Uh..." *Think, goddammit! Think!* "Yeah, yeah, right. We should... do that. Thing. To get it fixed."

Shit!

We'd rarely fought. At worst animated discussions where he might call me out on my behavior. But Thomas was no fool. He was a goddamn lawyer. His job was to see when people were hiding something, lying. And now our conversations were devolving. Becoming less questioning and more demanding. More heated. *Tell me what's going on, Jen. I want to know what you're thinking about? Don't give me that. Talk to me.* He *knew* something was bothering me, and the discovery that my fetish for rough sex—*God please kill me—* wasn't it had him as exasperated as I was.

'Just tell me.'

'There's nothing to tell!'

'Jen...'

'I. Am. Fine, dammit! Just leave it alone, Thomas.'

I deflected every time Thomas brought the subject up, or just outright lied because I had no intention of telling him anything about the thoughts and images flowing through my head with increasing frequency. I shouldn't need to because that wasn't a part of who I was any longer! It wasn't a part of *us*. I'd put that part of my life behind me, and that's where it would goddamn well stay because I willed it to be so. I kept telling myself that even as we sat in bed discussing work, and yet in my head all my thoughts were of him shoving me onto my back, grabbing my wrists and binding them together. Wrenching them up and lashing them to the headboard above my head.

'Jen? Jen? Earth to Jen...' He'd looked across at me, waving a hand in front of my face.

'Sorry. Just trying to think through that... what we were talking about... thing.'

Fuck.

I was mentally slapping myself on a regular basis as a reminder I was no longer that person. Yet it would be moments, an hour, or a day later and I would catch myself at it again, pulling out from a daydream of him fisting my hair, pulling my head back so I was staring up into his eyes, his cock touching my...

God. Dammit! What the fuck is wrong with you?

As my imagination continued to refuse to give up its single-minded grip on me, the realization that I needed to address this in some fashion continued being pounded home. Frustration became exasperation became infuriation, and none of it helped by my forced acknowledgement that I wasn't nearly as strong as I'd always believed I was. That hurt. It was a blade to the gut that carved out a little part of me every time I confronted it.

Some warrior you've turned out to be...

To say that this revelation upset me would be an understatement. I was a strong, independent woman, and yet I didn't have the fortitude to get what I was sometimes thinking of as *my kink issues* under control. That didn't fit the model of the person I thought of myself as. So now I was dealing with self-respect issues on top of everything else. My inner critic was eating it up.

-You are the worst. No, seriously. The absolute worst. I'm trying to think of a way that you could screw this whole thing up more, and... nope. I got nothing.-

I fought back against that, told myself I wasn't the worst; this was simply a phase that I could work through. When it became clear that wouldn't happen, part of me still pushed back like a petulant child.

Come on, Jen! You can do this! You're strong! You're not some sort of weird sex addict! You can stop this from getting the best of you!

I looked down at the paperwork laid out in front of me, thumbing through it idly. My focus wasn't really on it, though.

Instead, my attention was on the choices in front of me. I could keep propping up the lie until it became reality. Somebody had once said that a lie told often enough will eventually become the truth. I'd considered that option at first, but as time went on, I rejected it. It was a non-starter. My thoughts and desires had come back, and there was no putting that genie back in the bottle. That left me with option number two. I could come clean with Thomas. Every time those submissive thoughts and desires got their hooks deep into me this seemed the most viable solution. But there was a catch. Each time I tried to force myself to have The Conversation, I either screwed it up, or backed out entirely.

-Or...-

I pursed my lips. I hated the way my inner voice drew the word out. Taunting me.

Or... what? Option three? The nuclear option. The one where I tell Thomas that we need to...

-Yes. That. Say it, Jen. Say it.-

No. No, it doesn't need to come to that. Not yet.

-If you say so.-

The plane droned on and I shuffled the paperwork back together in a neat stack. I sipped my soda, thinking about the 'come clean' option. It was the one that made the most sense. Of course, that was because it was the one that was proving to be the most difficult to do. There was one other drawback to it, too.

Thomas.

Maybe he'll understand. Maybe he's actually into it, too. Maybe he's been hiding it from me as much as I've been hiding it from him.

-Sure. You go with that.- *He's a good man.*

-And you're a terrible woman. Good luck thinking you can drag him down to your level.-

I closed my eyes, gritting my teeth as I leaned back in the chair. I couldn't believe I'd just thought that. *Down to my level.* That was utter bullshit. There was nothing wrong with my sexuality, and I *wasn't* a bad person, my internal dialogue notwithstanding. But, yeah, it was a delusion to think Thomas had any of my inclinations in the bedroom. We'd been together long enough to see the likelihood of that.

He was a good man. He was also as vanilla as they came, and nothing would ever change that. Rough sex or no.

I drifted off thinking of that. My sleep was uneven, troubled. I woke twice, shifting in my seat to get comfortable before dozing off again. The final time I awoke it was to the sound of the engines shifting tone as we made our approach to O'Hare.

A simple, easy show was exactly what I needed. So I could refocus and decide what the next step in my relationship should be. Make a choice, and then follow through on it. A week to gather my thoughts, prepare myself, then do what was required, no matter how painful. For both of us.

— · 🙢 · —

"Yes, ma'am, I have your reservation right here." The desk clerk tapped at her keyboard. "You'll be staying for five days, four nights, yes?"

"Yes."

"One key or will there be another guest staying with you?" I smiled, shaking my head. "No. One key is fine."

I found my room, dumped my things, then settled in for the evening. Sipping at my glass of exorbitantly overpriced red wine from the mini-bar, I went over all the files one more time.

I just wanted any easy show, so I could have time to think. No muss, no fuss.

No complications.

Famous last words.

SIX

"This is your 5am wake-up call, Ms. Boyd."

I thanked the desk clerk, and hung up the phone. Rolling out of bed, I scrubbed my hands across my face. The Hyatt was close by the McCormick, which meant I could somewhat maintain my normal morning schedule. I threw my exercise clothes on, managing to fit in a quick workout at the hotel gym before heading back to the room for a shower. Dressed in my work clothes, I went downstairs to grab breakfast, with enough time left afterwards to walk to the convention center so I'd arrive before 7am.

The McCormick Center could be an intimidating place to work. However, I'd done this enough times by now I knew a few tricks to getting around, and I could avoid the pitfalls others fell victim to. I swung by the Installation & Dismantle—I&D—service desk, and checked in with Tony, the local City Manager. Tony and I had worked together on previous shows, and I smiled as I saw him sitting behind the service desk, poring over paperwork. As I approached, he glanced up, a smile creasing his worn face.

"Hey! Miss Jen! How you doing?" He got up and came around to give me a big hug. He was a large man, gregarious, with a deep rich baritone voice that was distinctly Chicagoan. I loved Tony, and over the years I'd worked with him, he'd always done right by me. I gave him a hug in return.

"Doing good, Tony, doing good! It's great to see you!"

We made small talk for a few minutes, catching up with each other before I broached the subject I'd been mulling over since the night before.

"Tony, I noticed I have a new leadman this show. Where's Mitch? You know I love Mitch! If you've yanked him off my booth and given him to some other client, I may just have to pull this account from you." I said it in jest, but the look that came over his face was unexpected.

"Oh, wow. I forgot you ain't been here in over a year." Tony's brows furrowed, distress showing in hound-dog eyes and a voice that went soft. "Mitch had a heart-attack about nine months back. He had to take an early pension."

My hand flew to my mouth, breath catching in my throat. The breezy attitude I'd come in with this morning disappeared. "Oh, God, I am so sorry! I didn't know!"

"It's all right." Tony moved beside me. His beefy arm came around my shoulder, giving me a gentle squeeze. "You couldn't have known."

I smiled weakly, doing everything I could to put on my best face. Everything going on in my life right now was clearly coloring my reaction, but it was more than just that. Mitch had been an amazing person to work with. He'd always treated me as an equal, never looking or talking down to me. It hurt to think of him gone. I looked at Tony and mumbled, "Well, I'm sure this new guy will be just fine."

"We're going to make sure you're taken care of, Miss Jen. You gotta trust me." Tony's fingers dug into my shoulder before letting go. His head bobbed in time to his words of reassurance as he added, "You're going to be in good hands with Stevie."

I nodded as he said this, but the thought of what had happened to Mitch rattled me. While I appreciated Tony's reassurance, I still felt unsure about how this might end up. I was off my stride already, and I hadn't even entered the booth. I wanted a nice, uncomplicated show, and it wasn't off to the best start. All I could hope for now was that Tony was telling the truth. That they'd take care of me and this "Stevie" wouldn't be some hack artist I ended up having to chase out of the booth.

Tony excused himself as one of the service people pulled him away to deal with another client. I took that opportunity to head over to the booth space. The hall was already alive with movement as I walked through the main doors. The sound of voices yelling across the floor, of forklifts shuttling about the hall, the occasional beep of a warning horn, the smell of propane exhaust that built on the thickness of the humid air that was Chicago in spring. One thing I'd learned over the years was once you were inside a convention center at the start of an install it could feel as if you were in any city in the U.S., no different from another a thousand miles away. It felt that way now as I walked across the floor towards the exhibit.

Our booth space was just off the center of the hall, trending towards the front entrance. While we weren't one of the biggest players on the show floor, we at least avoided being buried in the back corner near the bathrooms. As I came up to our space, I saw that someone from the I&D company had got there first and set up a card table to use as a desk during the set. It was also clear some work had started ahead of my arrival. Looking around, I saw two men talking to each other. One I vaguely remembered from the last time I'd been here. The other I didn't recognize at all.

Both men looked up from their discussion as I walked in, and I'll admit, the one I didn't know caught my attention. He was taller, at least six feet, stocky build, arms corded with muscle. He had dark hair cropped short. Looking at him, my guess was he couldn't be over five years older than I. Both men stared at me with polite looks, and then the new guy moved, approaching me with a warm smile.

"Morning! I'm going to guess you're Ms. Boyd." He offered his hand in greeting. "I'm Steve Friess."

I took his hand. It was a warm, welcoming handshake. Gray eyes with faint traces of blue stared back at me as we assessed each other. I recognized what we were doing. Each of us looking for anything that would give a clue about the other, good or bad. He gave me a small nod, giving my hand a final firm shake before he let go.

"Morning! Yes, I'm Jennifer Boyd. Nice to meet you." I could still feel the warmth of his palm. I didn't break away, but scrutinized him, uncertain why I was doing so. He was an attractive man, there was no escaping that, but beyond that there was something else. It was in the way he stared at me, assessing me. There was a quality to it that seemed… familiar. Familiar in a way I couldn't quite place. I knew it was more than just him being the new guy in my booth and me trying to predict by looking at him how the next few days would go. Whatever it was, I didn't feel uncomfortable. Just… intrigued.

He was the first to break the gaze we'd been holding, glancing over his shoulder. "I think you probably know Keith." He motioned towards the other worker.

I looked at the man I had recognized from previous shows. Once I heard his name it clicked into place. He'd been one of Mitch's assistants the last time I had been here, and though I'd only worked with him a little, I now connected the name and face.

"Yes, we've worked together before."

Keith approached me, holding out his hand. He had a solemn, serious expression. "Good to see you again, Ms. Boyd."

"Good to see you again too, Keith." I shook hands with him politely before turning my gaze back to Steve. He was staring at me once more.

"We've got a table all set up here if you'd like to get settled in." He pointed over towards the one I'd noticed earlier. "Can I get you coffee, something to drink?"

I nodded, eyes flicking from him to the table and then back. "Coffee would be great, thank you."

He smiled at me again before moving off. I walked to the table, opened my bag, and began spreading out my files and drawings. Keith went back to work while I set up my things. I had just finished when Steve returned. The cup he handed me bore a familiar green logo on a white background. I raised an eyebrow. This was not what I'd expected when he left. I'd assumed coffee from the pot they had at the service desk.

"Well, to what do I owe this special treatment?"

He gave me an amused look, and a low chuckle. "Beg pardon?"

"Starbucks?" I raised the cup up slightly. "I've never rated anything more than Tony's coffee before."

Steve gave a short laugh, the sound reflected in eyes that went from a slate gray to burnished steel with eagerness. "I thought it best to make as good an impression as I could right from the start. I know Mr. Kourdris took good care of you, and I don't want to be *that* guy that ruins his legacy."

At the mention of Mitch's last name, I hesitated as a pang of pain pricked at me. I forced a smile across my face, nodding. Taking a sip of the coffee, a familiar flavor hit my tongue, and I pulled the cup back in surprise. It was prepared exactly the way I liked it. I glanced at him, and then took another taste. I was intrigued. How he could have known how I liked my coffee I had no idea. Maybe it'd been a lucky guess, but I knew the chances of that were unlikely. Few people drank coffee with the amount of extra syrup pumps I did. Just the mention of the number would send most people into a diabetic shock.

I looked from the cup to Steve again, my eyes narrowing. He noticed my gaze, and his smile grew perceptibly wider. He didn't say a word but continued to watch, waiting.

"How did you know?"

"Now what kind of leadman would I be if I didn't do my home-work, Ms. Boyd?" His smile brightened by a few more degrees as he looked at me with quiet satisfaction.

I saw no arrogance in his expression, and I couldn't begrudge him for looking pleased. It was a neat trick he'd pulled off, and I let out an appreciative chuckle.

Well, well. This was growing more interesting by the moment.

"Okay, fair enough. You've gotten my attention. Now let's see how well you do getting my booth set up."

Steve grinned at me and gave a slight nod. "All right! Let's go."

Pulling his own set of drawings out, he spread them across the table. I looked at them as he pushed the first page down flat. It only took a quick glance to see that Steve had done his homework. He'd marked up his copies of the drawings up with notes, and it was obvious he'd looked the prints over in sufficient detail to know what was in store for us.

"So, we'll get the A/V cords down, the electrical laid, the base plates in position, and if all that looks good to you, then I'll have the guys start laying the carpet and pad. That should go fast, and the way I see it, there shouldn't be any issue getting the tower panels started, if not complete before we break tonight."

I listened as he described how he saw the set going. If he was trying to impress me in a manner similar to what he'd done with the coffee, he was doing a damned good job.

"So, what do you think, Ms. Boyd? Sound like a reasonable plan?" He shot me an inquiring look. "If you saw anything I missed, or that doesn't sound right, let me know, okay? This is my first time with your booth, so I'll defer to you on most things. If you have any suggestions or know of any tricks you want to let me in on, please do."

Okay, now I was *definitely* impressed. The way Steve was handling things was different. I had been on more installs than I cared to count where the leadman assumed I knew nothing about erecting my exhibit. He would go off on his own, not even giving me the opportunity to give my input. When I was new to this part of my job, I had accepted dismissal of that sort as just part of the way things were. After time and experience... not so much. Leadmen I came across who tried to take that approach with me ended up in one of two situations. Either they learned to listen and heed my say, or they found themselves kicked off the call. I paid the bills. I'd be damned if I would let someone bust my budget to line their own pockets thinking they could roll over me. Or because their precious ego wouldn't allow them to take direction from a woman.

Steve was in a rare category. I hadn't needed to prompt him. He'd straight up requested my feedback rather than assume I had none to give. That was unique. It showed a sign of confidence and respect I couldn't help but take notice of. If I'd had concerns about having a new leadman this morning after learning about Mitch, the last thirty minutes had done wonders in wiping them away.

But there was another unexpected effect from all of this. I felt a tingle run up my spine.

It was one I hadn't felt since that first day at lunch with Thomas.

Wait, what?

-Oh my God, are you... are you checking this guy out? Are you sniffing around him? You are, aren't you?-

It's not like that! I'm just... looking.

-Uh, huh. You are a piece of work... -

But it *wasn't* like that. Sure, he was attractive, without a doubt. Damn attractive. As he and the crew went about their jobs, I kept glancing at him. Watching his arms, looking at his chest. There was no doubt he was built. Fit. In addition, he carried himself with a level of confidence that was hard not to notice. He gathered the crew, spoke with them, and they listened. None of them wandered off, no one rolled their eyes or ignored what he had to say. I'd seen that in the past with other leadmen, and it was never a good sign. But the thing that really struck me was that Steve listened. When one of the crew asked a question, he never cut the person off but paused, listened, and then responded calmly, sometimes joking, but never condescending. When the crew worked, he worked with them, only stopping to answer a question or to point something out when needed. There was something about the way he moved, the way he led the crew that sparked a memory in me. Something I recognized in the back of my head, but couldn't quite place.

-He's ex-military, Jen. Come on. Look at him. You recognize it.-

Shit! He is. He's just like some of the guys that worked under Dad.

The more I watched him, the more I could see it. My father was a retired Army officer, and I grew up around people that carried themselves the way Steve was doing. I recognized the leadership methods he was using. Steve didn't speak down to the crew or force his authority on them. He let his demeanor and actions speak for him. As the installation continued, one thing became clear. There wasn't anyone on the crew that did not follow his lead. Watching him, I remembered what my dad had once said: 'Respect the man, not the rank.'

The crew respected Steve. That was clear. And it was obvious he'd earned their trust and respect because he knew what he was doing.

And that was the thing. As I'd been doing from the moment we'd met, I was assessing Steve. Tallying up all those little positives and not finding the negatives. I realized how preposterous that sounded. No one was perfect... but there I was still marking the tallies. And they were all coming up in the 'good' column. The research he'd done on the booth, the investigation he'd carried out on me, and the way he'd asked for my input rather than assuming I was ignorant... These were all points in his favor. The assurance and confidence with which he carried himself were things I found personally attractive, and the rapport he had with the crew was something more uncommon than common in my experience. I kept trying to find something negative about him, something to offset all those other things, and it was almost grating that I couldn't. For me, if I was listing out my triggers, Steve was hitting every one of them dead on.

-Ooo, yeah. He's a fucking hottie, isn't he? I wonder what he's like in bed. Assertive, aggressive...-

Shut the fuck up. It is not like that.

-Yeah, it better not be. Need I remind you that you and Thomas are still in a relationship. No matter what you may be thinking lately. Or are you going to pull a Ben here?-

Fuck. Off. It is not like that. Give it a rest!

It was a distraction throughout the morning. I tried not to stare, but I caught myself watching him, tracking his movements. At one point he came up, a smile on his face, and I felt that tingle run up my spine again. It had barely run its course when I pushed back and pushed back hard.

"Everything looking good so far, Ms. Boyd?"

"Yes, absolutely. And, please, call me Jen."

"If you're sure..."

"Of course!"

"Well, my dad raised me to always address someone by their last name until given permission to do otherwise. Sir and ma'am, that sort of thing."

"I know exactly what you mean. My dad was the same way." I gave him a warm smile, enjoying the idea we shared something in common.

He gave me a boyish grin in return, and then headed back to resume working with the crew.

Since Steve had left me feeling at ease with how he was handling the install, that put me in a somewhat interesting position. I had less to do now than I normally did during the exhibit set up. I wasn't having to check to make sure no mistakes were being made or double-check to make sure my directions were being followed. This allowed me the luxury to continue doing what I'd been doing earlier.

Watch him.

-Seriously, this is messed up.-

I'm just looking. There's no harm in it. What's the old saying? He's easy on the eyes.

-I swear I can't believe I'm you sometimes...-

69

I felt more than a little guilty for ogling Steve. No question. But that wasn't stopping me from doing it. I was having no problem justifying it either. It wasn't as if I were going to pursue anything with him. Under different circumstances, maybe. But not right now. I was in a relationship. And even if I was having doubts about Thomas and I, that did *not* mean I planned to go chasing after this guy. What I was doing was nothing more than some harmless guy-watching. That was it. Just me covertly watching a good-looking man who just happened to be working in my booth. It wasn't as if I was wolf-whistling him or slapping him on his sculpted ass. I was just observing him. Making sure he was doing his job.

Yeah, that was it. I was being a conscientious manager. Hell, I deserved a gold star!

My justifications may have sounded like bullshit even to me, but the level of self-confidence and poise he carried himself with provoked a response. He was assertive and charming, self-assured without being bullish. I was determined, however, that I would not let his attributes, no matter how positive, affect my judgement any further than simply watching him. Outwardly I was keeping every-thing professional between us. So why shouldn't I enjoy the view as much as propriety and common sense allowed? Men did it all the time. Why not me?

As the morning went on, there were two additional details about Mr. Friess I discovered, both in the form of tattoos. The first peeked out from under the bottom edge of his shirtsleeve. It was the Marine Corps emblem with the words SEMPER FI inked in below that. Given my military upbringing, the symbol was easy to recognize. Seeing it confirmed my earlier suspicion. He *had* served in the military and now I was certain which branch it had been.

The other was more subtle. It was a smaller tattoo on his wrist. At first glance it looked like it might be a Celtic rune of some sort, or perhaps a type of Taoist symbol. Since he was constantly moving around within the exhibit, it was hard to see. However, at one point

I caught a good glimpse of it. When I did, my stomach did a little flip.

It looked like a triskelion.

Shit.

For someone outside the BDSM community that probably meant nothing in particular. Just another tattoo design that looked impressive. For someone experienced in the lifestyle, the emblem—three yin-yang shapes chasing each other within a circle—held much greater symbolism. In general it showed to others that the person wearing it was a fellow traveler. Someone practicing their own BDSM dynamic. I had seen it before. Many times.

Almost immediately I began second-guessing myself. It was hard to see it with complete clarity. Maybe it wasn't what I thought it was. Maybe he didn't know what the symbol meant and had just had it inked on himself because he thought it looked cool.

Yeah. That's what it has to be...

It wasn't as if I could—or would—call Steve over and say, 'Hey! Let me look at the tattoo you have on your wrist!' As the morning went on, I kept trying to steal a glimpse of it every chance I got, looking to convince myself one way or the other of what I thought I'd seen. It remained elusive, however, and I was no more certain of what it was as the lunch break approached than I had been when I'd first noticed it. As we came up on the noon hour I saw Steve walking across the booth towards me. I tried not to stare at his wrist as he approached the table, a perturbed look on his face.

"Ms. Boy—Jen, we have a small problem."

I took a deep breath. Let it out. *Here we go.* "And that is?"

"Here, let me show you." Steve came around the edge of the table, and bent over, flipping through my drawing package. He pulled out the ground plan and electrical layout drawings. Laying down the ground plan first, he circled a spot on the paper.

"Right here is where we need to put down the baseplate for your main tower." He flipped to the electrical layout. "And here is where your electrical drawing says we're supposed to pull power into the tower for all the A/V and lighting." He pointed to a spot on that drawing.

I scanned both drawings, focusing on the section he emphasized, and saw nothing wrong. Lips pursed, I turned from the drawings to him. "Yes?"

"Well, someone got it wrong somewhere. The floor pocket for the power isn't here." He pointed once again to the spot on the electrical drawing. He flipped back to the ground plan and pointed to where the baseplate lay. "It's here."

My brows scrunched together as the information sank in. Just what I had hoped to avoid. An issue. There were two possibilities for what had happened here: either he had the baseplate in the wrong location, or someone had given our engineer the wrong information. As if reading my mind, Steve cleared his throat.

"I've run a tape on it twice, and I swear I'm reading the dims correctly. Maybe you should come check it to make sure I'm not missing something."

I looked at him, head cocked at a slight angle. Was he seriously asking me to double check him? That was unique.

"No, no, I don't doubt you." I looked down where his hand held the drawing in place and sighed. This was exactly what I didn't need right now. A problem. At that moment, however, something else attracted my attention, and it had nothing to do with an electrical floor pocket that wasn't where it should to be. As he held the drawing in place, I got a closer look at the small tattoo on his wrist.

It *was* a triskelion.

Sonofabitch...

I must have been staring at it for longer than I thought, my mind racing, because I heard him clear his throat. When I looked up, he was staring at me.

"Umm...Jen? You there? You kinda zoned out for a minute."

"Yes, sorry. Just thinking..."

Yeah, I was thinking all right. Just not what I should be thinking about. There were about a thousand questions and thoughts suddenly careening through my mind, and not even one of them was pertinent to what we were discussing. Or had any right occupying my time right now.

Come on, Jen! What the hell is wrong with you? Get your head out of your ass!

"Okay, where is the closest available floor pocket?" I reengaged my brain, forcing it back to the task at hand.

"Well, there's one here." Steve pointed to another spot on the drawing. "And one here."

"Hmm." I mulled over the two locations he'd pointed to. Both had potential issues. Running cords underneath the tower panels was never ideal. I'd dealt with similar circumstances before, so I knew it wasn't insurmountable. However, it was one of those pain in the ass situations I'd hoped to avoid.

"This one is the closest, so I suppose that'd be our best bet." I pointed to the floor pocket nearest to where the tower structure would stand. I looked up at Steve, and while he was nodding in agreement, there was a frown pulling at his mouth.

"You're right, that one is the closest. I was thinking, though, that coming from that floor pocket might cause us a couple of issues. We'll have a big bundle of cords passing right through where a lot of your clients will be walking, even if we channel out the padding. The other thing I'm guessing is when this tower is up it is fairly heavy, and when it settles, I'm a little worried the cords might actually rack it."

And then he did something for which I was completely unprepared.

He gripped my hand with his and moved it to where the other floor pocket was on the drawing.

He gripped my hand.

Uh oh.

Umm... uh-fucking-oh.

He laid his finger atop mine, and with firm pressure, he moved both our hands together as he continued talking. The problem was that whatever he was saying, I heard none of it.

Nope. I was gone.

Oh God. Oh my God. What the hell? He's holding my hand. No, wait, wait, he's not just holding my hand. He's gripping it. With his. Firmly. Tightly.

Holy shit.

After a moment, my head cleared. I caught up with what Steve was proposing, but I was not truly processing it. What I was registering was his presence next to me, our shoulders touching, his hand guiding mine over the drawing. He traced a path with my finger, emphasizing his solution to the problem. In response, a surge of submissive reactions I'd buried deep within me whipped back with a vengeance. They boiled up inside me, a sensory overload I was unprepared for. I felt flustered. Lightheaded. Giddy.

Like I was some 16-year-old pubescent girl with her first crush.

Jesus. Christ.

I heard the sharp intake of my breath when he stopped and tapped my finger at the spot on the drawing where the tower was. *Shit.* I wondered if he heard that. I couldn't be sure, but if I'd heard it, then I assumed he must have. There was no way he could not have. On top of that, he had to feel the ever so slight trembling in my hand.

"So, if we run it that way, it'll avoid most foot traffic. No one comes into the booth from that side anyway, right?"

My voice was a little breathy when I answered him. "Uh... yes, um... yeah, that... that makes a lot of sense." *Shit.* Even I could hear it.

Oh God, please, no hormones, not right now. Please, goddammit. Not. Now.

He stopped speaking, and for a moment we both stood there. His hand was still holding mine, the gentle pressure of his finger pushing mine into the paper. Grip tightening, his shoulder pressed against mine. His calm, measured breathing filled my ears.

I almost leaned into him.

Jesus Christ, Jen! What the hell are you doing!

He must have noticed. He had to. The man was no fool. After what could only have been a few seconds but seemed far longer, he let go of me, leaning back from the table. I stayed where I was for a moment longer before I straightened. I turned my gaze up to him. He stared back with a look that was both questioning and intrigued. I gulped in a quick breath. One I needed. I was feeling unsteady, and yet the vibrancy of what had just happened had every nerve singing to a tune I'd not sung in a year.

He saw my reaction. The bastard saw it. It was clear in eyes that were brighter now than they'd been a minute ago. Pupils grown larger as they scanned me. Steve's penetrating gaze was capturing me just as his hand had a moment ago. As I gaped back at him it was clear he fucking knew *something* had happened. The cocky grin that split his face a second later was all the confirmation I needed.

"So, what do you think, Ms. Boyd? Should we go with my idea?"

His tone spoke volumes. The question might be legit, but the dash of arrogance in the tenor of it had nothing to do with floor pockets, baseplates, or an exhibit on the show floor in Chicago, Illinois. At least that's the way I was processing it. I was a hot mess. I had not felt this kind of thrill, this level of attraction towards someone in... well, since Thomas. No. No, that was a lie. I hadn't felt *this* even with Thomas. Ever. This was different. This was not testing the waters of something new. This was slipping back into something old. Familiar. Given my current disposition and state of mind, my reaction to what Steve had done was not what I'd expected. I should have calmed myself down and slapped on my best Professional Jen expression. Instead, I did the last thing I expected.

I went all in.

I dropped my eyes to the floor and clasped my hands in front of me. Letting a long second pass, I looked up at him from under lowered lashes. His eyes widened at the posture I took, then narrowed. His grin became predatory. That stare was all I needed. It broke me free. For the first time in over a year, I gave in to my true nature, the one I had worked so hard to suppress. I didn't ease into it. I stomped on the clutch and kicked it into overdrive.

Hooded eyes gazing up at him. Voice soft and demure.

Submissive.

"Yes, sir."

Yep. I did that. Put that shot right across his fucking bow. And as much as one part of me soared to feeling that thrill once again, another part hated myself for it even more.

SEVEN

"Yes, sir."

The voice I used for those two words was one I hadn't used in a year.

Sexual tension crackled between us like a bare wire electrical charge. For Steve, I had to believe he was more than a little curious about what had just taken place. He sure as hell had to be a *little* intrigued by my reaction. Especially as the Dominant I was now certain he was. For myself, what had taken place was the chance to engage with someone in a way I hadn't done in a long time. An opening I'd seized upon, almost without realizing I'd done so until I was knee-deep into it. Prepared to ignore all the this-is-just-so-wrong for a chance of another fleeting taste.

-Good job, Jen. Jesus Christ, you are beyond belief. Why don't you just get down on your knees and offer to—

Shut up. Just shut up.

The actions we'd engaged in made it clear we both knew what we were doing. At least to me they did, and that was part of what was tearing at me now. We were dancing a dance. The one that typically starts with a two-step of flirting, and proceeds from there. Problem here was that Steve and I skipped right past the two-step, diving headfirst into a tango. And that went way beyond my ogling him earlier. Way beyond. Deep into territory that my brain was now throwing up red flags left and right.

I had two issues confronting me. One was the small matter of us standing at a desk on the floor of the McCormick Convention Center, which was the giant concrete elephant in the room. The other one I didn't even want to address. It was a raw wound that this situation had ripped the scab off of and standing here continuing to engage with Steve wasn't helping.

On top of everything else, now was the moment that Keith chose to approach us.

"Hey, Steve, it's coming up on lunch. Do we want to break the guys?"

Keith was ignorant of what had just taken place, which was good. I sure as hell did not want to deal with that too right now. Steve gave no indication of being thrown off stride by the interruption. He turned to Keith and smiled.

"Yeah, now's a good time. I think Ms. Boyd and I have the electrical problem sorted out. We'll jump back on that right after lunch."

Keith nodded. "Sounds good. I'll let the guys know." He walked off, calling out to the rest of the crew to "Take thirty!" for their lunch.

Steve turned towards me, and his penetrating gray eyes made my breath hitch. He scanned me from top to bottom, looking as if he were sizing me up and deciding on his next move. "Can I get you anything for lunch, Jen? Or would you like to go out together for something?" Another shiver like the one earlier raced up my spine.

-*Something, huh? Oh, I bet you can think of something...*

- *Stop! Don't even go there.*

I went into second-guessing mode. Looking at Steve as he waited for me to answer his question, I did my best to keep myself from lowering my eyes, clasping my hands in front of me, or anything that appeared even remotely submissive. Instead, I slapped my Professional Jen face back on to erase any trace of what I'd done a few moments ago. I knew I needed to answer him. I needed to shove aside all these competing theories over what I thought I'd heard him say, what I assumed his reactions meant. The portion of my brain that told me to grab him and pull him somewhere private and ask him whether what I'd felt reciprocated by him was actually there. To confirm whether any of this was more than just a fantasy built upon my repressed, pent-up desires. The thought of doing that, though, scared the ever-loving hell out of me. Because what if he said yes? What if he confirmed that my suspicions were correct?

-*Yeah. What then, Jen? How are you going to deal with that?*-

I'd dived quick and deep down that rabbit hole, and I needed to get back to the surface fast. Say something. Do something. Standing there saying nothing could telegraph all the wrong signals. Signals that I did not want to send just yet.

-*Ah. Just* yet. *Nice. Hedging your fucking bets already, aren't you?*-

I was panicking. I'd done what I did because in the moment it had felt so good. So natural. And now suddenly it was feeling like all manner of shit. So, I did the only reasonable thing I could do in a situation like this.

I ran.

"I... I think I'm going to go grab a bite to eat by myself, Steve. I... I have some... e-mails and work stuff I need to catch up on."

His expression slipped, mouth falling open for a brief second before he snapped it shut. He never missed a beat, however. He squared his shoulders and nodded, stepping away from the table.

"Okay, sounds good. I'll see you when you get back."

I may have been wrong about every other signal I'd seen in the last fifteen minutes, but I know what I saw flit across his face just then. It was clear, it was genuine, and it was definitely disappointment.

He cast one more glance at me, and his eyes were piercing, assessing. My stomach did another flip.

What's he thinking?

-*What the fuck do you* think *he's thinking? Some crazy sub just threw herself at his feet, and now she's bolting like she got marked with a branding iron. He's wondering how quick he can get his ass off this call!*-

He asked me to lunch.

-*Sure. So he could get your skank ass out of here and tell you to knock it the fuck off.*-

He looked disappointed.

-*He was disappointed! Now he's got to deal with you sniffing around him like a bitch in heat for the rest of the set!*-

You know what, fuck off! That is not *what he's thinking!*

-*Sure. Whatever you say...*-

I didn't know. I didn't know what he was thinking, and for a second I considered doing what I'd thought about a minute ago. Just grabbing him and pulling him off somewhere where we could talk. But that fear, fear of what he might say, was too strong. That part ordered me to do what I did. I turned and walked out of the booth, moving across the show floor. I wasn't even paying attention to which direction I was going, because that didn't matter. All that mattered was that I was putting distance between us, trying to put my thoughts together and understand what had just taken place.

Why did I do that! What in God's name possessed me to call him 'sir' in that voice!

-*And let's not forget that whole looking down thing, hmm? Yeah, that was fucking classic, Jen! Seriously, why didn't you just get down on your knees? You know, in for a penny, in for a—*

Stop!

-*Don't you 'stop' me! Jesus Christ! Have you lost your mind?*-

Before I realized it, I found I was walking down the street, the humid spring Chicago air draping me like a wet towel. I looked around, saw a sign for a small café, and dived into it. I went to the counter and sat down.

"Hi! Can I get you a drink to get you started?"

I looked up into a young man's face. "A... ah... iced tea?"

"Sure." The server gave me a bland customer service smile. "I'll take your order once I'm back."

I looked without seeing at the menu in front of me. All that kept playing through my head was Steve's shoulder pressed against me, his hand on mine, and then my voice, over and over like a broken record.

Yes, sir.

Yes, sir.

Yes, sir.

I sighed and closed my eyes. So, this was it. It had all come to a head, and in true 'me' fashion, I'd waited to do it in the absolute worst of all places. On the show floor with some random I&D guy I knew fuck-all about.

-Perfect. Fucking typical. Jesus, Jen. You are a piece of work.-

What had happened in the convention center forced me to confront something I had never vocalized. What I'd done in there— every action, the inflection of my voice, all of it—was me being true to who I was. It was me being the *real* me. Not the person I had decided I would turn myself into by turning off my sexuality as if it were a light switch. Fifteen months ago I had convinced myself that I was no longer a person who would do those things. Persuaded myself to live a lie. But in a heartbeat I had destroyed all that. Made a lie of the lie.

A glass plunked down on the counter in front of me.

"Have you decided on something?"

I flinched at the sound of the server's voice as he broke my train of thought. I looked up from the countertop where I'd been staring towards him. "Umm... no. I need a little more time."

"Of course. I'll check back in a minute." His smile thinned as I put him off, and he stepped away.

I knew that I had, in fact, decided. It just had nothing to do with the menu. Even if it had been an unconscious one, I'd made a decision. I'd already come to terms with the fact that I could no longer deny those parts of me that were so integral to how I saw myself. Those elements of my sexuality that had reasserted themselves over the past month. The ones I now understood I couldn't just toss away at the drop of a hat because I'd once convinced myself that doing so would help me get over the pain of what Ben had done. Prevent the hurt he'd inflicted from ever happening again. Those feelings and desires had boomeranged around on me, coming back with a vengeance. And they made me admit that the lie was just that. A lie. They made me admit to myself who I truly was.

I am a submissive.

The crystalline clarity that came over me hearing those words in my head, the feeling of a weight being lifted off my consciousness left me feeling light-headed. The enormity of it was far greater than I'd conceived, and yet while one weight was taken away, another fell into its place. The choice I knew I needed to make. The one I'd been struggling with even before that night with Thomas.

I sipped at my drink, distracted as a thousand thoughts bounced around inside my head, each careening into the other.

-You can tell Thomas that you are a submissive, but you know he'll never understand. That's not who he thinks you are. That's not the person you led him to believe you were. You start down this path, you need to stop with all this bullshit that you can still salvage something out of this. Just fucking admit it right now. That relationship is over. You understand? Over.- I know.

-You know? You know? Jesus, that's cold, Jen. That man is in love with you.-

I... I'm...

-What? Say. It.-

I'm not in love with him. I love him, but...

-Spare me. I don't need to hear the rest of your bullshit. You said the worst of it.-

It's not fair for me to continue the lie.

-Oh, boohoo. Not fair for you. Cry me a river.- Okay, fine. For him.

-Damn right, for him. You created the lie, bitch. You created it, sold it, and lived it with him until suddenly you couldn't any longer. Now you're gonna screw him over because of your grand epiphany that you've been a submissive all this time, and—oh, sorry, my bad!—now you can't be the person he fell in love with.-

What do you want me to say?

-Nothing. There is nothing you can say.-

Fine.

-Oh, one other thing. How are you going to act when you walk across that street and back into the booth? Hmm?-

I don't know.

-Well, you better figure it the fuck out, and fast.-

"So, have we decided on anything?"

I looked up at the server, mouth open, no words coming out. The menu still lay open in front of me. "Another minute, please?"

There was no response this time. The server turned without a word, walking down the counter and away from me.

As I relived everything that had taken place across the street in the convention hall, I knew this must be what it felt like to have an out-of- body experience. I was watching myself sitting on this stool, fiddling with a menu I wasn't even reading. I was having an epiphany that threatened to change my life, and I'd decided the best place to do it was sitting at a diner counter in Chicago, Illinois.

Outstanding.

I was having a crisis and trying not to panic amidst all of this. However, no emotion at this point was as powerful as the one of relief that coming clean with myself gave. It was cathartic. It felt liberating. There was nothing unique about feeling regret over a poor, rash decision followed by relief once it had resolved itself. I might have felt that way at the moment, but maybe what made this revelation seem so powerful was that I knew what I was coming to terms with was not only a central part of my sexuality, but of my personality, too.

For the first time since Ben, I felt like myself again.

-Okay... So, this is how you're going to do this, huh? A few wet dreams, some idle afternoon fantasies, and now you're suddenly going to become a submissive again. Just like that.-

I didn't plan this. It just happened. I tried to keep up the lie. And when I realized I couldn't do that, I tried to tell Thomas what I am.

-Bullshit! You never even spoke to him about anything.-

Umm, hello? 'Are you talking about rough sex?' 'I'm going to fuck you hard, Jen.' Did you fucking forget that? Because I haven't. I. Tried.

-Well how about you try a little harder?-

No.

-No?-

Yes, no. I'm done. Because trying again wouldn't make any difference. There's no way I can turn off being a submissive. It was stupid as hell for me to think I could. And what did my one attempt at trying to talk to Thomas get me? Sex doggy style. The lie is killing me. And we both know what would happen if I tried to come clean with him and tell him who I am.

-So, that's it?-

This has always been the only real option. I just didn't want to admit it.

-Admit what?-

That I need to end it.

I caught the server moving back down the counter towards me out of the corner of my eye. Before he reached me, I put up both hands in mock supplication with a weak smile. He stopped, took a deep breath, and moved back to where he'd been.

-So some guy comes along, holds your hand, makes you feel all squirmy inside, and that's all you needed to decide your relationship is over? Six months of stringing Thomas along, tossed down the drain.-

That wasn't what caused this. This has been fifteen months in coming. And we both know how this is going to end.

-No, we don't! You haven't even tried yet! That's pure supposition on your part!-

Now who's lying?

There *was* only one option. I knew this now with undeniable clarity. Continue to perpetuate the lie? No. Dead end. Talk to Thomas, admit to him I was not the person he'd thought I was, then expect that he'd accept this and want to be with the real me?

I recognized that for the bullshit it was.

The epiphany, my decision regarding my relationship, all of it centered on the power being a submissive held for me. My desire to submit for the pleasure of my lover and for myself. I enjoyed being a submissive. No, wait. I didn't just enjoy it. I *loved* it. I craved with every fiber of my being engaging in those acts which were at the core of my personality. My kink. My dynamic. They were all part of what made being submissive powerful for me. I owned that. It was mine. Mine to give, and mine to receive.

I had tried to deny that part of myself. Tried to remake myself into something I wasn't.

And I had failed.

As those thoughts streamed through my head, I came face to face with reality. It was clear there were challenges ahead of me. What I had done after Ben was nothing more than a screwed-up attempt to escape the pain he'd created. I had to accept that there would be a great deal more pain in my future, but this time of my creation. Pain of an intensity potentially greater than anything I had experienced in the past.

Thomas was a good man. But he was not the right man.

I would have to tell him that and tell him why. There was no Ben to push the blame onto this time. I was the Ben now. But I was determined I wouldn't be like Ben. I wouldn't hide anything from Thomas. I would talk to him, come clean, no matter how difficult and painful it would be for the two of us. And I knew it would be. Probably more than I had any concept of. I sat there, idly spinning my tea glass around in circles through the condensation that pooled on the counter top. Even as I considered all the challenges that faced me, through it all there was one overriding emotion. Relief. Nothing I was doing diminished the sense of liberation that flowed like an undercurrent beneath the thoughts rattling around my head. I was freeing myself from the self-imposed prison I had built. The inmates had rioted, stolen the warden's keys, and now they were marching out the front gate, never looking back.

It felt good. Scary, but oh so good. And unlike in the past, I wasn't going to put this off. I would do it right now.

I pulled out my cell just as the waiter started to come back towards me. I scrolled to Thomas' office number and hit DIAL. Just as he drew close, I brought the phone up to my ear. He stopped, and I shot him an apologetic smile and half-hearted shrug. He didn't even bother to hide his disdain as he turned and moved away. *Asshole.*

The phone rang. And rang. And rang.

Hi! This is Thomas Kiernan. I'm on the phone or away from my desk right now, but your call is important. Please leave your name and number at the tone and I'll return your call as soon as I can. Thank you!

"Hey. It's me. Listen, can you give me a call when you have a sec? I need to talk to you about things. It's lunchtime here, but even if it's later don't worry about it. Just call me when you can and I'll take it. Thanks. Bye."

I knew I was two hours ahead of him, so he wouldn't be at lunch yet. Maybe he was in a meeting. It didn't really matter. When he called, I'd slip away and take it. What was I going to say? Was I going to break up with him over the phone? Of course not. Probably not. I didn't know. That was the thing; I had no idea what I would say or do. All I knew was I was going to do something, finally. Because I needed to. Had to. Because letting this go on was wrong. For both of us.

There was nothing but melted ice cubes in the bottom of my glass, the tea gone. I looked for some symbolism or metaphor in that, but if there was one, it eluded me. And for some reason even that made me smile.

"Could I have the check, please?" Embarrassed, I smiled at the waiter as he turned to look at me. He frowned, and I grinned sheepishly in return. I smiled as I paid, and I smiled as I left him a tip. I smiled because even though I hadn't known just how tremendous the weight I'd been carrying on my soul had been, I did now. And feeling it falling away left me happier than I had been in a long time.

-You're scared. Admit it.- Of course I am!

-When you do get in touch with him, or if you decide to wait until you get home... This is going to hurt, Jen. It's going to hurt like hell.-

I know.

-Think about it. We can still walk this back...-

No, we can't. You and I both know it.

It scared me. I feared what would take place when Thomas found out I wasn't the woman he thought I was. When I told him the mistake I'd made. When I confessed to my lie. Not just that, I was a little scared of what would happen when I walked back across the street and into the hall. Into that booth where Steve was waiting. But I could deal with all of that. I could deal with anything now. Because I was Jennifer Boyd. I was once again me. The person I was and had always been, and not the person I'd tried to force myself to become.

And that felt too good to ignore.

EIGHT

I crossed the street from the café where I'd had my epiphany and ducked back into the hall. I hadn't paid attention to how long I'd been gone, but as I walked back towards the exhibit, I could see other people still eating and talking, which meant less than thirty minutes had passed since I'd left. As I came up to our space, I caught sight of Steve sitting on a crate, using it as a make-shift table. With one hand he was eating something out of a small plastic bag sitting next to him, a book in the other.

"Oh! Hey there." He moved as he noticed me approach, arms bracing against the crate, muscles flexing as he leveraged himself forward.

"Please! Don't get up, it's fine," I said, waving him back.

With a deliberate grin, he ignored my entreaty, slipping off the crate until he stood in front of me. "Did you get something to eat?"

"No." I gave him a sheepish smile, glancing down. "Honestly, I got so caught up in stuff I completely forgot."

"Oh! Well, here." He motioned towards the small bag on the crate. "It's only trail mix, but it's good stuff, I swear."

He took up the bag and held it out towards me. I started to demur, but at that moment my stomach answered for me, giving off a growl loud enough to be heard by both of us. Heat crept across my cheeks, trailing down onto my neck as Steve pinned me in place with a mock stern gaze.

"Well, I guess something's telling me I should." He handed me the bag with a grin, and I reached in, taking a handful. He was right. It was good. The taste and texture screamed homemade. If it wasn't, it was something purchased from a specialty store, and not one of those processed bulk-bin places. I ate one handful, then took another while we both stood there, looking around.

"If you'd like, I can go grab you something. There's not a lot around here, but I know a couple of decent places—"

"No." My hand came up to forestall him, fingers wide. "No, it's okay. Thank you so much. This is fine, really." I shook the bag to show how much lighter it was than a moment ago and offered it back to him.

He pushed it back towards me. "No, please, take the rest. I'm good."

I shrugged and reached into the bag, taking out another mouthful. He smiled as I followed it with another, my hunger now getting the best of me. Steve made no comment as I ate, but watched with a look that suggested he didn't mind in the slightest that I was scarfing down all of his food. While I was embarrassed, my hunger was enough to override it, and his grin grew wider at each handful I took. He was trying not to let it show, but the twinkling of his eyes as I reached for another handful showed he was pleased I was enjoying the food.

"Can I ask you a question," I asked between bites. The food hitting my stomach was welcome and though it gave another low growl, I knew my hunger was abating.

"Sure!"

I motioned towards his face, almost reaching out to touch him before I stopped myself. "Do you, um, ski?"

His eyebrow arched upwards. "I do," he drew the answer out, head leaning to one side. "How did you know that?"

This time I moved my hand a little closer, tracing the air in front of him to the contour of the tan lines I had noticed. "It's just... I can kind of see..."

His eyebrows beetled as he followed the path of my finger before he caught on to what I was indicating and laughed. "Oh, yeah. I didn't even think about that. It's been a few weeks, but I guess it's still showing."

"It is."

"So..." He mirrored my smile, running a hand through his hair. "I'm going to admit something to you."

My stomach did a little flip, adrenaline spiking. A flash of anticipation of what he might say made me gulp as I waited for him to continue.

"I'm not from Chicago."

I cocked my head. Okay, not exactly what I'd expected, but still interesting.

"I'm not a local guy. I'm an out-of-towner from Colorado. Marty's been bouncing me around a few cities since I started working for him. He wants to get me experience before he lets me take on my own city."

"Oh!" I understood now. "Well, congratulations! How long have you been doing this?"

"Five months. When Marty's satisfied I've gotten enough experience, I'll take over an opening in Denver if it's available, or wherever else he might have."

"Oh, Denver. I've done a few shows there. And now I think I understand the whole ski face." I traced a finger in the air once again towards his tan.

"Yeah." His smile was assured, the laugh self-deprecating. "Season's actually still going back home, but I got called for this set, so off the slopes for me." He looked down, and then his eyes came up, locking onto mine. "And I'm glad I did."

Ho boy.

"Well." One corner of my mouth came up in a coy smile before

I shied away from his scrutiny to stare at my feet. There was heat in my cheeks as I said "I'm glad you did, too."

For a moment, we stood in silence. I kept my eyes on the concrete at my feet, but I could feel the heat of his penetrating gaze tracing over the contours of my body. As the silence grew awkward, Steve cleared his throat.

"Well, we should get back at it. You good with us proceeding with the plan we discussed before lunch?"

I looked up at him. That warm smile, the searching gaze, a look that showed nothing dismissive, nothing judgmental. If anything, it was poised, honest, and respectful. The impact of all those things was immediate, a calmness that lulled me into a sense of security playing right into everything I had come to terms with during my lunchtime epiphany.

"Yeah. Go with it."

"Thank you." He gave a brisk nod and an appreciative grin. I swore for a moment he was going to wink, but he turned and walked to the crew as they gathered together, ready to start back to work.

I sat at the table and did my best to get my thoughts into reasonable order. That there was a lot going on inside my head was a gross understatement. I was thinking of what had taken place at lunch. I checked my phone to see if Thomas had returned my call. Nothing. When I knew it was lunchtime there, I tried calling him on his cell.

Hi! This is Thomas. I can't take your call right now...

"Hi. Me again. Left a message on your office phone. Could you give me a call when you have a sec. I need to talk to you, okay?" I looked down at the table, lips pursed tight. "I'm working, but don't worry about it. Just... call me. Please."

I ended the call. I was nervous. The longer this went without Thomas returning my call, the more I worried that I'd lose my resolve. I didn't want that to happen. I couldn't let that happen. I needed to ride the wave of determination I'd found in the café. Even as those thoughts whirled about inside me, I found myself watching Steve. Doing so was both frustrating and affirming. Frustrating because there was still a part of me that felt guilty for gawking at him the way I was. Affirming because I was one-hundred percent convinced he was a Dom, and the thoughts that bounced around inside my head knowing that, coupled with what had happened right before lunch, sent the occasional shiver coursing through me. If there was ever a time I could relate to the 'right place, right time' cliché, this was it. I didn't know much about Mr. Friess, but I was confident in my suspicions, and those were enough to beguile me in a way I hadn't experienced since Ben.

We were scheduled for a ten-hour day, and the crew used every hour of it. I alternated between checking my phone and stealing glances at Steve. Between those, I thought of what I was going to say to Thomas when we did speak. Hint at what was coming or be direct. As the afternoon went on, I was arguing two sides of the same coin. One part of me just wanted this over, and another part contended this had to be put off until later. The former was the one saying to cut right to the chase and be done with it. That Thomas deserved to know the truth and pretending for the balance of this trip that things were 'just fine' was both cruel and unnecessary. That we were adults and that continuing to lie to him was just childish and unfair.

-And if you don't do it, it's just another excuse to put off yet again what you've been doing for how long now, Jen? Hmm? Let's be honest. You don't have any intention of following through with this, do you?-

I do!

-Then prove it.-

I was sitting at the table lost in these thoughts when the afternoon break came up. I wasn't aware that Steve had come over and was standing nearby until he cleared his throat.

"Sorry. Didn't mean to break your train of thought, but it's break time."

"No, no, it's fine. I was just... thinking." I waved away his explanation, looking up at him apologetically.

"We're looking to be in really good shape, Jen. Even with the floor pocket hiccup, we seem to be back on track now. The carpet and pad are down, and I am certain we're gonna have most of the tower set before we break tonight, if we don't finish it completely."

"I can see that. You guys are really busting it out."

"Thank you. The guys are kicking it hard. I hope you're satisfied with everything so far?"

"I have no reason not to be! That little issue this morning aside, we're right on schedule. Can't complain about that."

"Good to hear. If you see anything that doesn't look right, or anything you want to double-check on, please don't hesitate. You aren't going to hurt my feelings." His face glowed with pride from my compliment, a broad smile tugging up the corners of his mouth.

"I don't think I need to do that, Steve," I said, my voice quiet. "I trust you."

His eyes narrowed as I finished, and he stared for a second before nodding. I had a strong suspicion why he reacted that way. Trust was a loaded word in the BDSM community and carried a different meaning than it might for those not in the lifestyle. From his reaction, my confidence in my previous theory was only reinforced. I couldn't help but wonder if he was having similar thoughts as I. It appeared we were on parallel paths, and that idea produced a growing sense of anticipation in me.

-*For what?*-

Nothing.

-*Oh, right. Sure. Nothing.*-

There is nothing going on here.

-*Goddamn. You seriously cannot stop lying to yourself, can you?*-
I am not lying to myself!

-*Sure. Whatever. I am so done with you...*-

After Steve moved off, I took out my phone, checking it one more time. *Fuck.* Nothing. I decided to take another approach.

Hey, it's me. Tried calling you a couple of times. You must be

pretty busy. Could you give me a call when you can? Or if you're
slammed, just shoot me a text. Thanks! :-)

I hit SEND and then stared at my phone for a moment. This was odd. Thomas was usually very prompt about returning calls. Maybe he'd gotten pulled into an emergency or something and hadn't had time to call back. I was certain he'd at least be able to shoot me a text. I wished he'd done it by now, but maybe he hadn't gotten my voicemails yet. I pushed down anxiety that was making a concerted effort to claw its way forward. I wasn't going to fall prey to that. I shoved the phone into my bag. He'd call me. I knew he would. I just needed to be patient, and not freak out.

I took a quick walk around the booth to see where we were before the scheduled stopping point for the night. Steve's prediction about their progress proved true. My personal feelings about him aside, he'd done a better job with the crew than Mitch ever had, and that was saying something. I had never been displeased with Mitch and the way he handled things, and I knew the local guys here had loved him, but there was no denying that Steve had really pulled the guys together and gotten the booth further along than expected. At the end of the shift, Steve gathered the crew together at the table.

"Everything looking okay, Ms. Boyd?" Steve turned to me, asking the question in a quiet, serious tone. He scanned the booth space, making a final quick assessment of the exhibit before his gaze came back to mine. The chatter from the crew tapered off as all eyes focused on me, awaiting my judgment.

"You guys did fantastic. You really did. I am very happy."

There were big grins from the crew arrayed in front of me, including Steve. I caught the small nod of thanks directed my way before he turned to Keith and the rest of the crew.

"Thanks, guys. You kicked ass today. You keep making me look good, maybe Marty won't can me after all."

There was laughter and good-natured ribbing directed towards him at the comment. He shook hands with each of the men as they grabbed their toolboxes and headed off, drifting out of the booth.

"Back at 7:30, Keith." Steve clapped his assistant on the shoulder.

Keith gave a brisk nod and glanced around. "Yep. I don't see any reason why we shouldn't have this knocked out tomorrow."

"I like the sound of that. We get this booth squared away in less than eight tomorrow, might even make the client happy." Steve's easy grin, and the humor that suffused his voice made his appreciation clear.

Even Keith, who to this point had maintained a serious look throughout the day, cracked a smile. "Let's hope so." Keith shook Steve's hand and then gathered his tools and moved across the hall.

Steve watched as Keith walked away, and then it was just the two of us left in the booth. He turned towards me.

"Are you satisfied with the progress today, Ms. Boyd?"

"Please. I told you to call me Jen."

His eyes narrowed, and the smile changed ever so slightly. It was... different. It was still good, but... different in a way that sent a tiny shiver up my spine.

"Very well, Jen." Now his voice had changed. It was a subtle shift in tone, the timbre less warm, traces of a more dominant quality woven through his words. A rush of blood thrummed in my ears, pulse thumping to his inflection as he continued. "You didn't answer my question, however."

My breath hitched as he stepped towards me. Close to me. He canted his head, giving his look an almost challenging vibe. "Are you pleased with how things are right now?"

And here we go.

-Goddammit, you haven't even talked to Thomas yet. Listen, don't do this, okay? It's not too late to stop this. Nip it in the bud.-

Pretend that there's nothing going on here? I thought you were the one telling me to stop lying to myself.

-You know exactly what I am talking about!-

Yes. I do.

In response, I lowered my eyes, letting my gaze slip down the length of him until I stopped at his feet.

"Yes, sir." *Boom.*

"I want you to have dinner with me tonight."

My head snapped up. The invitation was more command than question. It was a daring, provocative tone that made my knees tremble and my legs feel rubbery. I was slipping into my old headspace, dropping back into behaviors I hadn't acted on in almost a year. As I stared into those cool gray eyes, my mind and body leapt at the chance.

Eager. Hungry.

"I know a very good restaurant here. I think you would enjoy it. And I'd really like your company."

It was his voice that sealed the deal. A good Dom can wield their voice like a weapon, and Steve had that voice. He was taking a risk, but he kept it neutral enough he could still back out with some degree of grace if needed. Not that he had much to be concerned in that regard. He'd pegged how I was responding to perfection.

And I wasn't hiding it, no matter how appalled I was with myself for what I was doing.

"I'd like that." With careful deliberation, I slipped into my demure voice, the one that came from a place inside me that felt as natural as if I was pulling on a comfortable pair of jeans I'd just rediscovered. I knew how to do this and falling into the pattern was instinctive. Pulling my eyes away from his gaze, I let them drift down. "Sir."

There was a thunder of silence between us. The sound of his steady, measured breathing louder in my ears than it should have been despite how close we stood to each other.

I should step closer to him.

-What? Oh no. No, Jen, goddammit, stop.-

Why?

-Enough is enough.-

He knows. There's no pretense now.

-You move that foot one step closer to him, and there sure as hell won't be!-

Fine. I won't. For now.

His eyes kept me pinned the entire time. The intensity of his gaze might as well have been fingers gripping my chin, holding me in place. Neither of us had any misconception of what was going on here.

"You're staying nearby?"

"Yes. The Hyatt." I kept the tenor of my voice the same as I'd switched to a moment ago. Steve wasn't the only one who could use tone to their advantage.

"Perfect. I'll pick you up at 7:30. Does that give you enough time?"

"Yes, sir." I wanted the assurance his voice promised, the gentle press of his gaze urging me to give in as he waited for my reaction.

"All right. I'll meet you in the lobby." He released a soft exhalation. "Thank you, Jen."

His aura was a physical thing. A circle of heat that grazed against me as he passed by. If my legs had felt unsteady before, they quivered as he moved past. There was a gentle brush of fingers at my shoulder that ended with a quick, sharp squeeze, and the jolt it sent through me sent already jittery nerves exploding in a hundred directions.

I stood motionless as he left the booth, my eyes glued to the carpet at my feet. As the sound of his boots faded, I absorbed what had just happened. I felt both tension and excitement, my pulse still racing at what we'd both done. A bead of sweat made its presence known as it slid down the back of my neck to come to rest under my collar, hanging there.

-Wow. So, you're seriously going to do this, aren't you?-

Yes. It's just dinner.

-Yeah, it's just dinner. With a fucking Dom, you idiot! Not only that, but a goddamn Dom you just met.-

It is just dinner!

-Oh, really? So, remind me. The way you were acting with him just now, is that typical of how you act anytime someone asks you to dinner?-

That has no bearing—

-Yeah. I thought so. Oh, and here's one other thing. I know you had this great big epiphany this afternoon, but you have still not talked to Thomas. Did you forget about that? Because it looks like you might have. And all your big insights and revelations aside, let me remind you that he's still your current fucking boyfriend, you hypocritical bitch!

There I went. Right back down the self-loathing rabbit hole. I raised my head and glanced around. I took a deep breath and gritted my teeth. Closing my eyes, I reminded myself everything I had agonized over during my lunchtime epiphany.

I would no longer be anything other than who I was.

I would no longer try to convince myself I could be something that I wasn't for Thomas.

I would be truthful about who I was, and what I desired.

I would end the bullshit charade I had created to ease my pain. Now.

It was only dinner. Nothing more. Yes, it was dinner with a man I was one-hundred percent certain was a Dominant. A man who was not Thomas. Fine. What was the big deal? Why did I feel the need to beat myself up over this?

-Seriously, Jen? You're seriously asking yourself that?-

I am. I have to. I need to.

I took a deep breath to calm nerves that demanded it, letting it escape only once I began to move. Crossing the now quiet hall, I walked out into the muggy heat of the fading evening. It didn't take me long to make my way to my hotel room, and the entire way I kept playing out all those things I had gone over at lunch and inside the booth. I cycled through them as I got ready for dinner. As I stood staring at myself in the mirror, I realized the seeds of what had happened this afternoon were planted long before I'd left home.

What was happening now had started with my initial conversation with Thomas, sown in the soil of our night of 'rough sex'. It had sprouted as I stood with him before boarding the plane, grown during the flight here, and bloomed into fruition as I lowered my eyes in front of Steve on the show floor. I looked one more time at my phone. There were no messages I had missed. I brought up the Messages window. *Read.* I stared at that tiny little word next to the text I had sent earlier, and sudden, irrational anger flowed through me.

What the fuck, Thomas!

For a moment I was livid. I typed out another text to him, fingers smashing at the keys.

Hey. I can see you got my text. I'm heading out to dinner soon. Could you please call me? We need to talk. Jen.

I slapped the SEND arrow and then tossed the phone onto the bed. What the hell was going on? What was so goddamn important that he couldn't spare me fifteen seconds for a text. Or give me a return phone call. I shook my head, and with a growl I headed into the bathroom. I shrugged out of my work clothes and turned on the water to a hair's breadth of scalding. Standing in the shower with fists clenched, I knew the games needed to end. Afterwards, dried off and getting ready, I wiggled into my dress and with gritted teeth resolved that I was done pretending. I was dressed for an evening out with a man who I damned well knew was my type, and all pretense of lying any further slipped away. However, my self-loathing wouldn't give in so easy. It fought back.

-So, that's it, huh? You're going to go through with this, aren't you?-

Yes.

-What about you and Thomas?-

Is there really a Thomas and I anymore?

-Oh. My. God. You haven't even spoken to him yet!-

We both know what's going to happen.

-We do?-

Yes.

-Wait... you're going to sleep with this guy tonight, aren't you? Aren't you?-

I don't know.

-Yes, you do!-

I. Do. Not! This is not a guaranteed!

-Fucking. Liar.-

My hands clenched in frustration as I watched the haze of fog on the mirror condense into streaking rivulets. There were all these warring parts of me, clamoring inside my head, fighting to be heard above the others. There was the Disgusted Me, the Excited Me, and the Analytical Me. Each one was trying to storm the ramparts I'd built up, sensing the weakness from my epiphany of earlier in the day, all trying to take control. I barely knew this guy. Sure, he seemed nice, but he was still just some guy I knew fuck all about. I should be careful! And those images that had been running through my mind like pictures from some submissive kink catalogue were ones I shouldn't even be contemplating. That I was an overall horrible fucking human being to even be *considering* those things was a given. I needed to think of Thomas and reflect on what a shitty thing I was doing to him. That brought me up short. Why was I thinking that? I was jumping the gun here. I'd not made up my mind yet. Right now, it was just dinner. Nothing more. With perhaps some random daydreams about the *possibility* of what I could be doing later if an opportunity arose. Not that it would. But if it did, it had all the hallmarks of being of being wonderful. Intense. Something I hadn't experienced in fifteen... I shook my head, a sharp snap of irritation. I needed to stop that train of thought. Now. I needed to remember that this was just dinner, and concentrate on the shit I needed to take care of with Thomas.

Except I couldn't.

My mind kept swinging from the thrilling thoughts of What Could Be, to the angst-filled What You Should Do, to the Don't Be A Fucking Bitch, only to be whipped back to the fantasies that refused to stopping playing themselves out. I felt like I should be crying. Feeling anger. Grieving. But I wasn't. I wanted to feel hollow, to feel pain, remorse, agony—something that would be appropriate to what was going on. But I didn't. I looked at my eyes, at the red lipstick I'd applied, and all I felt was a sense of anticipation. I was slipping back into myself, into a familiar skin which I had shed nine months ago.

And it felt good. Dammit, it felt good and *right*.

I glanced down at my watch. 7:10. I did one final pass over my make-up, grabbed my small handbag, and then headed towards the door. My conscience made one final attempt.

-*Fine. Go. I won't be here when you get back.*-

Oh, really? Who's the liar now?

-*Fuck you. Bitch.*-

I moved to the door, flicking the lights out. Hand on the knob, a resigned whisper pleaded with me.

-*If you're bound and determined to go through with this, Jen, be careful, okay? Please.*-

It's only dinner.

-*Of course it is.*-

I took a deep breath as I waited for the elevator. I felt exhilarated. It was a hundred little electrical jolts that spread through me as various thoughts flitted through my head. Considerations for all that this evening might hold, and the thrill of facing the unknown. I glimpsed myself in the mirrored wall of the elevator, and straightened slightly. How should I look at him? What tone should I take? Should I hold the handbag in front of me with both hands, wrists crossed? My imagination was kicking into high gear, reconnecting with all those submissive traits I hadn't engaged with in a long, long time.

God it felt good.

The elevator reached the lobby floor and I stepped out. There was a small crowd near the bar, and a few groups sitting in the chairs and chaises spread about. I checked my phone one more time.

There were now two *Read* messages. I gritted my teeth. *Fuck, Thomas. Seriously?* I looked at the time on the front screen. 7:20. I slipped the phone back in my bag, fingers flexing. Scanning the lobby, I looked to see if he was already here, waiting. After several searching passes of the room, it was clear he wasn't. Sitting down in an empty chair not too close to anyone, I positioned myself so I could see the front entrance. A fluttery feeling rose and fell in my stomach, and I did my best to suppress it.

It's only dinner...

Even as all those other thoughts continued to crawl over the ramparts in my head, I continued to recite those three words over and over. *It's only dinner...*

It was my mantra. One I kept repeating right until the very moment he walked through the lobby doors.

NINE

Damn.

Damn, damn, damn.

As much time as I'd spent staring at him during the day, I already knew Steve was an attractive man. However, as he stepped through the lobby doors that observation was ratcheted up by several degrees. He was wearing tailored charcoal slacks that hugged his hips, a black linen jacket stretched across his shoulders, accentuating them as his shirt had done, but with greater refinement. In fact, everything about Steve right now screamed casual sophistication, from the light blue button-down that pulled tight across his chest down to the patterned tie in blues and grays that complimented his shirt. Black belt, black shoes. As I was thinking about tonight, I had worried that I might have overdressed for wherever he might be taking me. He was here to work, not to wine and dine a client. Staring at him now, I could see my concern was unfounded. He had come prepared. And well prepared. He looked good.

No, he didn't just look good. He looked fucking incredible.

He scanned the room, his gaze sweeping across the lobby until he found me. His focus locked onto me, the intensity of those twin gray pools great enough that I was rising even before I realized it. His piercing stare was a hand at the back of my neck, a whispered command that tugged me to my feet. As he walked through the lobby, his eyes refused to track on anything other than me. I was a butterfly pinned to a board by his scrutiny, but the feeling that shot through me wasn't one of fear. It was one of possession. The single-mindedness of that look made it clear that nothing or anyone would stop him until he was next to what he wanted. Me.

Yep. I was gone. Undone.

He navigated the space between us until he was beside me. Close, but not as close as I had a sudden urge for him to be. I could see the steel gray of his eyes up close now. They were light, cool, assessing; an alluring shade that was highlighted by the color of his shirt and tie. The trace of stubble on his cheeks and chin gave his features an irresistible ruggedness that was set off against the easy grace of his clothing. Earlier his work polo shirt had showed the breadth of his shoulders, now they appeared even broader as they filled out his suit. His eyes never left mine, and I could not have broken that gaze to save my life.

"Good evening, Ms. Boyd."

Oh no. No, no, no. Not that voice. God damn you, not fair. Not fair to use that voice.

"Hello." It was all I could get out. I wanted it to sound strong, in control, but it didn't. It came out just as I felt; excited, filled with anticipation, thrilled to my core at the way he stared at me.

"You look incredible." The hint of his smile grew wider, pushing cheeks up towards his twinkling eyes.

I drew in a sharp breath, and my eyes snapped down, breaking the contact I'd maintained so far. My hands clutched my handbag in front of me, a picture-perfect replication of what I had envisioned earlier. Without being fully conscious of it, my body had taken over, falling back into mannerisms and patterns that had once been so much a part of me.

"Thank you."

"I've got a cab waiting. Shall we?"

My eyes came back up to his and I nodded. He stepped aside so I could pass, and as I did, he placed his hand in the small of my back, guiding me. It was a bold, dominant move, and there was no way he could have missed the shiver that went up my spine.

"I think you'll enjoy this restaurant," he said once we were in the cab, the hotel receding behind us. "A friend of mine recommended it, and Marty told me he's heard nothing but good things about it."

"I'm sure I will." I glanced over at him, smiling as I caught the lights from the passing city reflected in his eyes. I turned away, watching the twilight fade from reds and oranges into the purple of evening. For a while we rode in silence, and I could feel his presence next to me, a cocoon of intimacy that left me warm, at ease. When the cab turned a corner, the edge of his leg brushed against mine and the touch set my nerves alight for seconds afterwards, anticipation of further touches a feather brushing over my skin. And his eyes. I could feel the pull of his gaze drinking me in.

"I don't mean to stare. I swear I'm not trying to make you feel uncomfortable. But I'm not gonna lie. You look amazing. I'm really glad you agreed to have dinner with me."

I smiled at the way he'd said it with such ease, complete self-confidence that was both a balm and made me a bit edgy with eagerness. I stared at my hands clutched together in my lap. "It's a little... disconcerting. But... thank you."

Steve's shoulders followed the rise and fall of his chest as he released an elongated sigh. "To be honest, ever since I started working in this business, I've had to go out on business dinners way more than I ever expected. Most of the time it's with a group of people, mainly clients. I think this is probably only the second time where it's been just one-on-one. I'll tell you this much. I can't think of a single time when it's been with someone as smart and show savvy as you."

My head came up at the compliment, but my lips pursed at the same time. His tone seemed genuine. There was a part of me, though, that wondered if he was flattering me because he felt obligated to. A cynical voice that questioned if he'd truly meant what he said. I was about to respond when his hand came up, cutting me off even as my mouth started to open.

"I mean that seriously. You are the first client I've ever worked with who knew dic—" He grimaced, but before I could laugh and tell him it was okay, he continued. "Who knew anything about what the hell was going on while the booth was being set. Honestly, most clients don't even show up until the evening before the show, if not the day of. And they certainly don't understand a single thing about what setting up an exhibit entails. You have no idea how refreshing it is."

"Thank you," I said, trying to temper the eagerness in my voice. "I appreciate that." There was no way I could hide the smile his praise teased out of me. Even with my head down, a quick glance showed approval tugging up the corners of his mouth. Praise was a big trigger for me as a submissive, and between his words and the way he was looking at me my nerves were antsy, jittery in that same fluttery-in-the- stomach feeling I used to get when told I was a 'good girl.' I rode in the floaty bubble his words created, jonesing for more. Steve was good. There was no mistaking that, and yet everything he said seemed to be sincere.

"Can I ask a question?" He turned, leaning with one shoulder into the seat, brows knitted together.

"Of course."

"Why *do* you know so much about the business? Did you work in this field before?"

"No, not really. My father, however, taught me that if you are going to take on something new, at least do your homework first. Don't go into something being completely ignorant. It doesn't take much effort to do a little research, even if it is just the basics, rather than go into something blind. And the payoff can be substantial. I did that with the first trade show I ever worked on. Funny thing was, I found I actually liked it. The part that you do." I motioned towards him with my hand. "So, over time I've found that I can get things done efficiently and have better control over my budgets by knowing exactly what is going on when my booth is being set. Getting my hands dirty, so to speak. Does that make sense?"

"It does."

"To be honest, it's had other benefits too. Over the years I've been able to keep control of our show costs and save money that used to go into our vendors pockets. No offense intended."

"None taken."

"What all that boils down to is that I've become indispensable to my bosses in many respects. Because, you know, not many people will do what my dad taught me and make that extra effort."

"Smart man."

"He is."

"He's got a very smart daughter, too."

I blushed. As much as I hated that I was doing it, I did.

-Oh, this bastard is smooth. You are so fucked.-

He's just being sweet.

-Uh huh. And he is going to sweet talk his way right into your panties.-

It's. Just. Dinner.

-Oh, sure, sure. Hey, by the way, has Thomas called yet? Hmm?-

Shit. I started to reach for my bag to grab my phone and check it again, but I stopped. No. I was enjoying Steve's company too much right now to ruin it by looking at my phone. I knew what I was likely to find. Nothing. I knew there'd been no call, because if there had I would have known. And I was betting there was no text either. Those thoughts alone were enough to start irritation building in me, and I forced apart fingers that wanted to clench. No. Fuck the phone and fuck Thomas Kiernan. I didn't know what his problem was right now, but I'd be damned if I was going to let it impact this evening. I'd check the phone at the restaurant, deal with whatever bullshit reason he had for ignoring me later. Right now, I was going to live in this moment. Because—goddammit!—I hadn't felt so good, so *me* in a long, long time and I was selfish enough that I wasn't about to give it up for whatever game Thomas was playing.

I hadn't been paying attention to where we were going while I sat thinking, and when I felt the cab slowing, I looked out to see we were pulling up to a two-story building. I gave a quick examination of the brick façade of the structure. As the cab glided to the curb, I caught sight of the warm and subtly lit interior of the restaurant. People seated at tables could be seen through the floor to ceiling windows that stretched across the front of the building. Above the front door was a simple neon sign with a single word: GRACE. I had been taking all this in and hadn't noticed Steve exit the cab. He came around, opened my door, hand extended. I stood on the sidewalk as he turned back to the cab and paid the driver. Even from my cursory examination it was clear this restaurant wasn't an establishment for the budget conscious. This place was fancy. The crisp white linens on the tables, the elegant clothing of the clientele visible through the windows, the understated yet refined architecture of what seemed to be a repurposed warehouse of some sort, it all screamed sophistication. This was an upmarket joint. And by all appearances expensive.

That made me a little nervous. I'd been in plenty of places like this in my career, usually with clients, or with my bosses. It wasn't that I didn't enjoy going to a nice restaurant like this, however, I saw no reason for Steve to fork over what I was certain would not be an inconsiderable sum of money just for the pleasure of dining with me. The thought of what this would cost him left me uneasy.

-*Because he's an I&D guy, and how much money can he be making, right?*-

I didn't say that. Maybe he's not aware of what a place like this...

-*Yeah, he's pretty dumb. You should say something. Just to set him straight.*-

It was arrogant to second-guess him, but he didn't need to put himself into debt just to sit across the table from me while we ate and flirted. We could do that anywhere.

As Steve finished with the cabdriver, I glanced at the people standing just inside the door. Compared to some of them, what I was wearing bordered on being under-dressed. Steve looked fine, but that was my bias speaking. As far as I was concerned, he looked fucking hot. Still, between my thoughts and taking everything around us into consideration, I began to tense up.

Well, one thing's for certain. If he was trying to impress, he definitely nailed it!

Steve put his hand against my lower back, escorting me as the doorman ushered us in. Steve held a murmured conversation with a young woman at the reception counter as I scanned the room, lips pursed.

"Yes, of course. It will just be a moment," the woman said, smiling.

Steve turned away from the counter with a self-satisfied look. The moment his eyes caught mine, however, the smile slipped. His eyebrows etched a sharp thin crease into his face, and all that satisfaction slipped away.

"Is there something wrong?" He took a step closer to me, leaning down to whisper the question into my ear.

I should have taken the tone as a warning.

"This looks..." I paused, searching for the right way to say what I was thinking.

"Jen..." His face came away from mine, and his eyes went resolute as he stared down at me. He didn't look angry, but there was no mistaking his demeanor. Whatever I was thinking, he was determined to cut off my apprehension. "Don't. Please. It's fine."

The heat in my cheeks increased, and I turned away from his gaze, self-conscious as I looked at anything other than him. "I... it's just that..." I stammered, and instinct had my face angling downwards. "I don't want to..."

"Jen. Stop." His hand landed on my arm, squeezing gently. "I made the reservation, okay? I need you to *trust* me."

Oh, shit.

He emphasized the word. There was no mistaking it. A word I knew he understood in the same context I did. Trust. I had no doubt his use of it wasn't happenstance.

-Of course it wasn't. He knows what he's doing. Both of you do.-
I don't want to assume...

-Oh, for God's sake. I'm pretty sure you guys are beyond the whole hidden subtext thing by now. Just relax. Let it go. Trust him.-

"I'm... you're right. Sorry. Bad moment."

"It's okay." His tone was calm, gentle, and along with his smile, it worked to soothe me. "I understand."

That look was what really did it. It crumbled whatever concern I had been using as a defense to hide behind. The kindness that stared back at me sent a shiver running up my spine, and that gave me the final nudge I needed to do what I'd struggled with all evening.

I gave in.

The last remnants of the wall I had built up—the one I had created as the foundation for the notion that this was 'just dinner'—I now let fall. I let myself be swept up in what was happening. I let myself trust not only in Steve but also in myself, too.

I leaned in towards him, and he tilted his head so I could whisper into his ear.

"Okay, I have to be honest with you. This place looks amazing! And you..." I lowered my voice even further, my lips nearly brushing against his skin. "Are spoiling the fuck out of me."

His head came up, and the smile that lit up his face was boyish with delight, and yet lost none of the assertiveness he'd dressed me down with a moment ago. My own smile tugged at me, the look on his face infectious and as ego gratifying as any I could have imagined.

Before he could respond, the receptionist called to us, motioning towards the maître d' who stood waiting nearby.

We slipped through the room, past tables with groups and couples, until we arrived at our own. Steve remained standing while the maître d' pulled out my chair for me. Once we were both seated, the waiter handed us a wine and drink list and waited while we both ordered. Then we were alone.

"I'll try not to talk about work, but... were you happy with the progress we made today?"

"Yes, very. Thank you."

"Good. I'm glad. I really wanted to make a good impression."

"You did."

The way he smiled at my answer, confident, almost cocky, made it clear that was what he'd wanted to hear. Seeing his response sent another tingle shooting through me.

"I have never actually eaten here before, so I have no idea what's good." Steve was looking down at the menu, finger slipping along the edge as he reviewed the selections.

"It all looks wonderful." The choices were minimalist, but everything in the descriptions sounded incredible.

I scanned for the prices, and that's when I noticed that dinner was *prix fixe*. Doing the math in my head it was clear that between us the bill would easily run into triple digits. In any other circumstance, I would have been appalled. But Steve had asked me to trust him.

So, I did.

By now there was one thing I was certain. He didn't do things without being prepared. He'd done his research on me before I'd even stepped foot inside the booth. Knowing a simple, mundane thing such as how I liked my coffee. It was obvious that he was a planner, and not someone who half-assed things. I'd little doubt now he'd known what this place was going to set him back even before we stepped into the cab.

"Do you know what you'd like?"

"Yes."

"Tell me." The way he said it was a command. Not harsh, but firm, nonetheless. Given my current mindset I was already inclined towards obedience. His gaze never wavered as he waited patiently for my response.

"For dinner I'd like the squab with the butternut squash, please."

"Anything else?"

"No. That will be fine."

He studied me with approval, a slight uptick at one end of his mouth, corners of his eyes crinkling as the light of the room danced in them. "Perfect. Thank you."

The waiter returned with our drinks, and Steve ordered our meals. When the waiter asked if we wanted wine, Steve made no pretense he knew what would be appropriate.

"I'll have the sommelier come by to assist. He'll be happy to help you with your selections."

Steve leaned forward as the waiter moved away. "I really should know what to order, but inevitably I screw it up. Red when it should be white, white when it should be red. Besides, I think I should make them work for every red cent they're getting, considering what we're paying."

I held a hand up to my mouth to stifle a laugh that threatened to be louder than appropriate. His grin tugged across his face right into eyes filled with merriment. The ones I was suddenly falling into again.

The sommelier soon came, and the two discussed the dishes we were having and chose wines. I thought I'd misheard at first, but it was soon clear that—yes—it was wines, plural. One wine, whether red or white, was simply not going to do. We had to have a wine appropriate for each dish, and nothing less would be acceptable. Steve questioned and discussed the wine steward's suggestions, showing zero self-consciousness over his lack of knowledge. When he seemed confident he'd questioned the steward enough to ensure he wasn't being taken advantage of, he accepted the suggestions and ordered.

"Excellent choices, sir."

"Well, it's not as if I did much. You pretty much pointed out what we needed, and I just nodded my head."

"I am sure you will be pleased." The sommelier chuckled politely, then slipped away, leaving us alone once again.

I took a sip from my glass, looking at him as he took a sip of his drink. His mouth curved up, and his gaze caressed my face in a way that was pure temptation. I knew I could give in to desire and spend the rest of this evening in flirtatious, teasing banter, but I was still curious about a few things, so I went for deflection instead.

"So, you were a Marine?"

He stiffened, his eyes narrowing. His entire demeanor shifted from seductive to somber in less time than it took me to suck in a breath. My smile slid away on tension that crept up my spine at the abrupt change in mood. *Crap.* Had I brought up a subject that was taboo? His eyes fixed on mine for a long moment, and panic welled up inside me.

Dammit, Jen! What the hell have you done now?

His gaze flicked to his left and then back front and center. Eyes narrowing even further, one brow quirking up at the corner, he assessed me in silence before the smile stole back across his face.

"Hmm. I'm impressed. Figured that out, did you?"

"Well..." I blew out the breath I'd been holding, relief washing through me. "I'm smart like that." I took another sip of my wine. "How long have you been out?"

"Just over three years now."

"Ah. How long were you in?"

"Four months shy of twelve years." He matched my movement, taking a sip of his drink.

"Decided to get out while the getting was good and try something different, huh?"

He stared at me for a moment with eyes that suddenly went

cool. When he spoke his tone was curt, but polite. "I suppose you could say that."

I didn't understand the sudden change in demeanor. I'd tried to be light, amusing, but Steve's terse response definitely said he was not taking this the way I'd intended. I cocked my head, scrunching my face up into a quizzical look.

"I was surveyed out." He answered my unspoken question.

"I'm afraid I still don't understand."

"Sorry." He smiled apologetically, holding his hand out towards me. "Marine lingo. It means I was medically discharged."

"Oh... God." I grimaced, awkwardness pulling my eyes from his. "I'm sorry. You just look... I mean, you don't seem to be—"

"Jen," Steve cut in and saved me from saying anything further. "It's fine. You couldn't have known. The shrapnel busted up a couple of my vertebra pretty bad. The docs pinned everything back together, but they said there'll always be a risk of one of them failing if they get overstressed. When I was all healed up they wouldn't release me back to active duty, so they let me go on a medical."

"Shrapnel." I whispered the word, face coming up to stare at him. I knew that word. I'd heard that word before from my father, and it was never in a good way.

"Yeah." His nod was brief, his voice terse again. "Stood in the wrong place at the wrong time."

"Oh, God, Steve, I'm so sorry. I feel like an idiot..."

He reached over and clamped his hand down on mine. He squeezed tight, our eyes locking once again. "Jen. It's fine. It's okay. It's why you didn't see me out there doing a lot of the heavy lifting today. I mean I move fine, I feel great, but..." He shrugged, smiling. "Just not good enough to be a Marine."

"I feel so stupid," I whispered, biting down on my lip. I fidgeted, embarrassed for having acted so flippant even though there was no way I could have known. I tried to think of an appropriate apology but couldn't. Instead, I stared with eyes fixed on fingers that clenched the stem of my wineglass.

"Stop." He gave my hand a gentle tug, waiting until I brought my face up. His gaze met mine, and he showed no sign of being offended by anything I'd said. Instead, his smile was a balm, doing all it could to soothe my distress. "Seriously, stop. I'm fine. It's in the past. All good."

While that calming look worked its magic, brushing away my anxiety, I forced myself to relax and not let this become more than what it was. I couldn't—wouldn't—let what had happened screw up our dinner. I took another sip of my wine and then noticed something that buoyed me more than his smile, or his words.

He was still holding me. He hadn't let go of my hand.

"Where did it happen?"

He shook his head as if trying to push away a thought he did not want. His eyes clouded over, and then they weren't focused on me or anything in the room, but somewhere distant, halfway around the world. His voice was as remote as his gaze. "Some place you've never heard of."

"Try me." I pursed my lips, chin thrust forward. My embarrassment over my comment about his getting out of the service still nettled. I wanted to show him I wasn't completely ignorant of the military and the Gulf, and that just maybe we had something in common. If I could do that perhaps he wouldn't judge me as harshly as I was judging myself right now.

His gaze refocused, returning from wherever his mind had pulled him off to. He blinked once, and then his attention was back to the here and now. I couldn't tell if he took my statement as a challenge or not. If he did, he masked it well, only the slight narrowing of his eyes giving any indication of what he might be thinking. "The Al Nehardea Bridge."

"You're right," I said after pausing a second to see if the name dredged up any memory. I shook my head. "I don't recognize that name."

"I'm not surprised." He gave me a tight smile that was more sympathy than grimace. The clipped way he'd spoken the name, the hard snap he'd put to each syllable as if it was an affront to force them past his tongue made clear this bridge was a place he'd rather not have spoken of.

"It was just outside a city called Fallujah."

"Oh."

Yes. *Oh*. That was a name I recognized. My father had spoken of it. He'd almost been sent there but had retired before his unit had deployed. He knew people who had gone there, though. Fought there. Died there. I had read the news reports of the battles fought in the city.

I recognized Fallujah. It was a bad place.

"I know about Fallujah."

"Really? And why would you know anything about Fallujah?"

A part of me knew I should be offended by that remark, but at the same time I knew why he would question it. It was not as if Fallujah was a common household name. And Steve had no idea of my background, or that of my father's. I decided I should clarify.

"My father was a solider."

"A Marine?"

"No. He was Army. A Major. He's retired now."

"Oh." Steve drew the word out, contemplating my explanation. "All right. Makes sense. He served in the Sandbox?"

"Several times. First Gulf War. Then the invasion. He got out in 2003, right before Fallujah. He knew people who went there."

Steve gave a slow, thoughtful nod, taking another sip of his scotch. "First Battle. I wasn't there until the second in 2004."

He pinned me with an assessing gaze. I tried not to shift in my seat or show any sign of discomfort under his scrutiny.

He cocked his head, exhaling a short huff. "You were an Army brat, weren't you?"

"I am." I lifted my chin, staring at him boldly.

"Fuck yeah." The curse came out softly, but the satisfaction in his voice made clear what he'd said was an honorific. He contemplated me, taking another slow sip of his drink. As he lowered his glass, a smile of satisfaction tugged up the corners of his mouth.

The tone he'd used was the same I'd heard my father and his friends use when talking about their unit, or their men. It was a recognition of comradery, of a shared belonging to a fraternity of sorts. That Steve had addressed me that way puffed me up with pride. I shot him a grin that was no less cocky than the one he'd given me.

"So, what gave me away?" Curiosity imbued both his voice and the look he directed towards me.

"I saw the tattoo on your arm. I recognized the emblem."

"Should have guessed." He gave a slight shake of his head, expression amused.

"I saw another one." I took a hasty breath. "The one on your wrist."

His hand stopped as he raised the drink to his lips. Even though I knew it hadn't, it was as though all sound in the room had paused, the entire space stilled as if the soundtrack had been muted. My eyes were on his, and I waited for his reaction. We both knew what we'd been dancing around for half a day now, but this was it. Moment of truth time. All cards laid out on the table, no hiding behind innuendo, no more words loaded with assumptions. No more bullshit. Just honesty, and truth, and trust.

His hand continued and he took a sip. His eyes had been assessing before, they became weighted with confirmation now. The glass came down, and when he spoke it was with *that* voice. The Dom voice. The one he'd used on me in the booth, the one that made bursts of electricity flick over nerves gone sensitive with anticipation.

"You know what that means. Don't you, Jen." It wasn't a question. It was a statement. A firm, no-nonsense tone that said he wasn't asking for clarification. It was an inflection I knew all too well. I'd heard it often enough from my last Dom. Hearing it now coming from Steve was all it took to send me back to a place I hadn't been in fifteen months. To react as I would have back then. The tremble that shot through me was anticipation of more, my reaction an oh-so-easy tilting of my head down to gaze at the tabletop.

"Yes."

"Yes?" His voice was firm, demanding. Sensual. "

Yes, sir."

I said it softly. I did not raise my eyes until he squeezed my hand almost to the point of pain. That brought my head up, and I saw heat and desire in that stare, an open door to a world I had walked away from. A door I had not stepped through in so long that now beckoned enticingly. He was holding it open for me, watching to see if I would step through. I wanted to, I wanted to so very, very much.

So, I did.

"How long have you been involved?" he asked, voice steady.

"I've known for a long time. Actively?" I gave a slight upward hitch of my shoulder. "Only the last eight to ten years."

"Are you involved with someone right now?"

"No."

And there it was. I lied. I didn't even try to stop myself. I hadn't talked to Thomas yet. He hadn't returned my call or any of my texts in over eight hours, and that nettled me because it made no goddamn sense. I wouldn't have needed to lie if he hadn't suddenly decided to play whatever fucking game he was playing right now and avoid me. Because he *was* avoiding me. Those two READ messages proved that. So I made my decision and it came out so quick, so easy, because— goddammit—I wanted this! I needed this. I had given up any pretense I didn't, that I wasn't going to pursue this. I wasn't about to let my decision of fifteen months ago dictate otherwise now.

Maybe telling the lie made me a terrible, horrible person. However, I didn't feel that way right now. Not for a single second.

I was being selfish beyond belief. But at this point I was bound and determined to put an end to the lie I had perpetuated on myself. In ways I had not even realized until right then, I felt a sense of liberation. I had become me again. The Jen I had once been. Not the Jen who'd taken the pain Ben had inflicted and conflated it into an indictment of her sexuality. Who had bottled all of that into a vial filled with poison, and then swallowed it under the pretense I was curing my problem. The reality was I had let it fester into a gangrenous wound that had polluted me. Now I was coming clean. And that feeling was not something I could walk away from. Not now, or ever.

"I'd hoped you'd say that." Steve's eyes remained cool on the surface, a sober assessment of me that didn't falter, but there was heat behind them too. A simmer of building need I understood because I knew it rested behind my own too.

I sat there and melted under Steve's gaze. It was hunger. Hunger, lust, desire. It was pupils blown wide with yearning. A look of greed that growled to claim possession of me. It was a cocktail of swirling emotions that blew down my nerve endings like a runaway rocket. I wanted that look so much right now. Needed it. I don't know what he saw in return, but I hoped it was enough. I needed it to be enough. I saw the heat flare, and then he drew in a tight breath. Releasing it slowly, that fire banked, but was still there hidden behind a gaze that now turned imposing, assertive.

"So, your father was a Major?" His mouth pursed, tone sardonic. "Must have been nice, being an Army officer's brat."

For a moment, I started to get angry, but then I saw the gleam in his eyes.

Oh, okay. Two can play at that game, mister.

"Oh, yes, it was, it was. You have no idea. I had my own enlisted people to take care of me, do anything I commanded. It was like a fairytale..."

"I'll bet it was." His eyes went beady, grin wrinkling his nose until the look was more smirk than snark. I bit down on my lip and gave him my best brat smile.

Hell yes. I was back in the zone.

Our conversation continued, weaving from subject to subject, and the banter between us became easier, natural. Steve asked me about my dad, what bases I had lived on. I asked about the places he'd been deployed. We traded stories about crummy base housing, post exchanges that looked like looted K-Marts, places where the off-base amenities were a single strip mall filled with fast-food restaurants, a smoke shop, and five bars, two of which were of the 'titty' kind. The conversation was soon less like that of two people who'd only met a few hours ago, and more one between two old friends. The gentle teasing and repartee Steve engaged in had me laughing more than I had in a while. One thing that did not escape my attention during all of this was that Steve always steered the conversation back to me.

"Oh, God, you have to be talking about the Red Barn." Steve leaned his forehead into his hand, shaking his head.

"I guess? I was only twelve, and I wasn't allowed out of the car while my mother went in and peeled him up off the floor."

Steve laughed, using a hand to stifle most of it. "Had to be the Red Barn. Biggest bar between Fort Eustis and Norfolk. A battle-ground every weekend between Marines and anybody who got in their way. Including people like your dad."

"Well, all I know is my mom somehow got him poured into the backseat. I just remember my dad saying over and over, 'Resa, I think I left a tooth back there. You gotta go get my tooth!'"

I had mentioned my mother several times during our conversation, and it was clear he'd picked up that I referred to her in the past tense. His questioning was gentle, circumspect, and I told him of her cancer, the abruptness of her passing. It was the one point in the conversation I saw him falter. He sat in silence, and suddenly he wasn't trying to look or act like a Dom. His face was pinched, a man clearly trying to deal with something that ached inside. The smile he forced across his face was there to keep the pain from showing, but the grief etched in his features clearly showed he'd suffered through deaths of his own. He glanced down, took a breath and then with a new calm reached across the table and gripped my hand, squeezing down until it was almost too tight.

"I'm sorry, Jen."

"It's okay." I blinked back tears that wanted to form in the corners of my eyes. Swallowing, I forced my voice not to break. Our conversation had been so nice up to now, and I did not want to lose that. "Both dad and I have said there's a... sense of gratefulness we have that it happened as quickly as it did. She didn't suffer or linger in pain."

"Still..."

I pressed my lips together hard enough that the bite of pain took the edge off the memory of my mom's passing. I pushed the thoughts away, determined to turn the talk back to where we'd been earlier. Keeping my voice neutral, I said, "It happens. You know?"

Steve nodded, and he directed the conversation away from the topic to inconsequential things, all of it light and trivial and with none of the pain of the previous subject. It was a deflection. A deviation to steer the discussion away from talk of death, and on to something else. Specifically, to a topic we'd both been dancing around. One which we had only briefly touched upon earlier. It was the matter we both knew by now was ultimately where we were headed this evening.

"So, how long has it been since you were involved with someone?"

"Fifteen months." The lie flowed off my tongue without hesitation.

"Was he your Dom?"

"Yes."

He nodded, halting the conversation as the server approached with the first course of our meal. It was only then, as the warmth of his fingers slipped from the top of my hand, that I realized during our exchange he had not let go of me. It's absence now became irritating for how much I wanted it back.

The food was everything I'd expected, my earlier apprehension aside. A sublime and yet superb meal that was prepared and served with aplomb. The wines that the sommelier had paired with our dishes were perfect. Everything came together in one of those instances where it seemed unreal, as if scripted in a way that was almost dreamlike. The soft sounds of the dining room, the lighting, the quiet whisper of the wait staff as they came and went. And then there was Steve. He was both commanding and attentive, warm, yet firm. He was what I needed right now, and the sheer relief I found in being with him was like finding a life raft in an ocean storm.

"Was it okay?" He motioned to the table after they had cleared the last plates away.

"It was incredible, sir."

"I'm glad you enjoyed it. Thank you for coming with me tonight."

"No, sir, thank *you*."

Steve and the waiter talked quietly, discussing whether we wished dessert, coffee or something they kept referring to as a *pousse-café*. I was so damned comfortable right now that not knowing what the hell a 'pussy café' was only made me chuckle, drawing me deeper into this nest of contentment Steve had created. I was happy, dammit. Happier than I had any right to be.

Even happier than you were with Thomas, right?

My back snapped upright, rigid. I grit my teeth at the thought. Not because it was wrong, but because it brought back the one thing that threatened to ruin every good, wonderful, incredible feeling I'd experienced this evening so far. While Steve and the waiter continued their discussion, I snuck a peek at my phone. Nothing. Not a single goddamn word. A frisson of anger ran through me that turned my thoughts suddenly irrational. Fuck him. What right did he have to blow me off like this! An entire fucking day, and he couldn't even send me a two-word text to let me know what was going on? He'd never gone this long without responding to me, never avoided me like this, and now? He chose now to be unavailable so that I could let go of the nagging guilt at the back of my mind. It was bullshit. It was bullshit and I didn't know what his fucking game was here, but I was done with it. Things were over between us, they'd been over for a while, and I'd just been prolonging it by trying to be someone I wasn't to make it work. To make it work for *him*. And for my efforts?

Rough sex, Thomas Kiernan style. And then today, blown off and ignored.

No. No, I wasn't going to settle for that anymore. I recognized the mentality I had dropped back into during the day, this evening, and I seized upon it. Held onto it for dear life. I'd slipped back into old body language from my past, tumbled back into words and phrases I only drew on when in my submissive mindset. I'd not felt this alive in fifteen months. The last time I'd felt like this was the last time I'd allowed myself to be true to who I was. And I'd be fucked if I was going to give that up for Thomas Kiernan now. As the waiter walked away from the table I came out of my reverie.

"I ordered us something to share for dessert. Then coffee." Though his smile was as warm as before, there was a change. His gaze was a furnace of desire banked behind eyes that were a storm on the horizon bearing straight down upon me. For much of the evening I'd caught him gauging me, and I suspected he was making decisions as much as I was.

"And then we should get you back to your room."

And there it was. The next step. Back to my room. That was where this was going to lead, one way or another. Even now, the words barely out of his mouth, I wondered if it would end up being nothing more than that. A murmured thanks at the door for a wonderful evening, a gentle brush of his lips on my cheek, and then his back retreating down the hallway as he left.

He knew there was more than that going on between us. He had to know. Right?

He had to recognize the subtext behind much of what we'd spoken about tonight. To acknowledge all the subtle confirmations that littered our conversation were breadcrumbs on a path that led to something more than just a 'This was nice. See you tomorrow.' The anxiety of earlier returned. That all of this might be a construct of my imagination. It was obvious now that certain aspects of it weren't, but... what if where I saw this heading wasn't the reality? Despite every desire that screamed otherwise, it could be he was simply curious about me and nothing more. He might fear complication. Sleeping with a client wasn't considered the best form, but I knew firsthand it did occur, commonsense be damned. In a sense, that was what would be happening here. I was a client to the company Steve worked for. A very good client. A lucrative client. That could, in fact, be exactly what he was thinking. Everything I had shared with him aside, he could be weighing all the risks, trying to decide whether this was worth pursuing or not. That idea made my stomach flutter. God, I did not want that. I would be in no position to blame him if he did, however. At some level, it was the right choice, the safe choice — for both of us. What right would I have to feel rejected if he chose to do so?

And there it was again. I'd thought I was beyond self-loathing for the evening, but I was wrong.

-Yeah! What if he decides you're just too big a risk to mess with? Didn't consider that possibility, did you?-

Fuck. Off.

-You're welcome. I'll just be here waiting...-

Frustration became a coil of tension that squeezed my jaw until my teeth ached. I did not want to consider that this could be the ending to what was up to now a perfect evening. I wanted Mr. Steve Friess to come to my room, take me to bed, and give me a taste of what I had abandoned fifteen months ago. To give me the things I now craved. Everything about him said he could do that, screamed it. I knew those looks, I knew that voice, the presence he projected and all that it promised. Ben had done that for me once, and there'd been a point where I'd given up on ever feeling moments those intense ever again. Steve promised a return to that even if for only one night. Now fear that my inner voice was right made me ache at the thought that all of this was just a fanciful chimera, my imagination run wild.

"Jen, what's wrong?"

Shit. Dammit!

His voice snapped me back to the present. My anxiety was showing, the thoughts displaying themselves despite my best efforts otherwise. My shoulders hunched up defensively, and I tried to wipe from my face whatever look he had taken notice of.

"Nothing."

Steve's eyes narrowed, cooled to tempered iron, pupils flicking back and forth as he tried to gauge what was going on inside my head. Lips pinched into a tight line of skepticism, he leaned across the table. Once again there was the electric arc of his touch as his hand closed over mine, fingers pressing into me.

"Jen."

His voice was low, commanding, and I quivered with equal parts frustration and desire. Was I so obvious that he could read the turmoil I was putting myself through? I sat rigid under his silent scrutiny, my eyes turning down to stare at the table. I didn't want to look weak. I hated the idea of him thinking of me that way.

"Jen." The imposing tone he put into my name broke through my thoughts, drawing my eyes back up to his.

I took a deep breath to push down a surge of irritation, steeling myself for how he might respond to what I was about to say.

"Where is this going, Steve?"

He blinked once, grimacing as confusion clouded his face. Thoughts chased each other from brows to eyes to mouth, until something clicked into place. His expression softened, eyes crinkling at the corners as he tilted his head to one side. Any uncertainty there'd been a second ago vanished, and the gaze he contemplated me with was composed once more.

"Where do you want it to go, Jen?"

"Please don't do that." I shut my eyes, then pulled in a breath to calm a statement I knew I could make waspish. I didn't want my frustration to show, but Steve had to understand how important this was. I let out the breath slowly, opened my eyes wide, trying to emphasize this to him and still make my answer as level as the one he'd given me. "Please don't answer my question with a question."

He went neutral on me, mouth a flat line devoid of expression.

"Okay, Jen. What do you want me to say? I can't answer you any better than you could answer me if I'd asked you the same question."

There was no mistaking the tinge of frustration in his voice, no missing the tension of his jaw as he did his best to keep his response even.

"Where is this going?" He ran a hand across his face, blew a sigh through lips gone thin. "Beyond tonight, I don't know and I'm not even going to try. But where would I like it to go?" He leaned across the table, and the cool shade of his eyes shifted, need becoming a glowing ember that matched the low intensity of his voice. "Right now, what I want to do is take you back to your hotel. And then I would like to spend the night with you, Jen. There you go. There's my answer. It's the only one I can give you."

Oh, God. Oh, thank God.

His words buoyed me up and away from my insecurities once more, and I gave an internal cry of triumph. The giddy feeling of victory coursed through me, mixed with a surge of want, need, and anticipation all in response to what he'd just said. I wanted to grab him, thank him, let him know how much those words meant to me right now. But I didn't. I kept my eyes locked to his, biting into my lower lip. After letting my stare linger on him for a moment, I let my gaze fall.

"I'm ready to go when you are, sir." My self-loathing shrugged.
-Okay, you win. Knock yourself out. Just... be careful. Please.-
I will.

The flare of Steve's desire was palpable. He leaned back, and the penetration of his gaze became prickles at the back of my neck, an unspoken contract that was signed and sealed in my agreement to go with him back to my room. I watched as one finger of his hand traced a circular pattern on the tabletop, and it was as if that finger was sketching an outline on my skin rather than the white linen. I knew my words had cast the die, and his scrutiny pinning me in place was all the confirmation I needed. There was no way he could mistake my response and not know exactly what I desired. I knew it. He knew it. I was confident in my conviction, and, dear God, was I ready. I had tried to have the conversation with Thomas that I knew I needed to, but he had decided that now was the time to play some lawyer head game with me. Fine. His choice, not mine. It might be delayed, but my decision was final. It wasn't going to change, and I couldn't go back in time to have it at the apartment, or the airport. I had wanted it to be today, but Thomas had chosen otherwise. So be it. It would be tomorrow. And then it would be over and done.

"We have dessert and coffee coming. Once we've finished that, then we will leave." His voice was full Dom once more, all power and unambiguous confidence.

"Yes, sir," I said, a shiver of eagerness flitting over nerves already afire.

We sat in silence as I stared at the linked fingers of his hands. His presence was a palpable thing, an authority that allowed me to do what I had so long missed. To be submissive. To grab that feeling, hold on to it, pull myself into it and just let go. When he cleared his throat, the effect on me was immediate. My head snapped up to the sound.

He sat regarding me with a look I'd expected, but which still made my body flush. I remained still for him, waiting, obedient until his mouth curled upward at one corner.

"Good girl."

It was all he said, and I melted.

TEN

Desired.

Craved.

Most of us hunger to be longed for like that. It's a universal feeling. And though we may rail against being objectified, when we are in the company of someone who we desire, and we see that desire mirrored back, it is an incredibly powerful feeling. It empowers us, affirms us, and wipes away the demons of self-doubt we can all fall prey to. Desire is the yin to the yang of affection.

Now, as we sat waiting for the waiter to return, Steve's gaze spoke to me of both those things. The passionate look he gave sent little jolts of excitement shooting across my nerves, the buzz of anticipation making me edgy as he studied me from across the table. All pretense gone now, Steve did nothing to conceal his hunger, hand moving in a slow pattern along his chin.

It was those unknown thoughts he kept hidden behind those slow- moving fingers, his eyes ablaze, that I was eager to discover. The last act of this dinner was playing out and I dived into the deep end of my desire, thoughts of what awaited me fueling cravings I hadn't felt in a long time. And I felt no shame in it.

The dessert came, and we shared it in silence. And though the words between us were few, what we did share across the table bordered on telepathic. When I reached for another bite and my spoon touched his, the contact was electrical, as if both implements held a charge only released when the separation between us linked. As we ate I replayed our conversations in my head, and two thoughts kept coming forward. In terms of 'us', Steve wasn't thinking beyond tonight, the same as I. He wanted to take me back to the hotel, and he wanted to fuck. Crude as that may sound, it really was as simple as that. And if this was going to be nothing more than a one-night stand, it was contingent on neither of us being involved with someone.

At least on the face of it. As far as we were willing to tell each other.

As I was mulling all that over in my head, I realized there was one final piece of the puzzle I needed to fit into place. For me, there was still one thing that could bring all this crashing to a halt. I'd answered Steve's question of whether I was involved with anyone when he'd asked me. Even though I'd technically lied because in eight hours— nine now—Thomas still hadn't returned any of my texts or call, it wasn't because I hadn't tried. I'd *tried*, and I knew exactly what I would tell him when he finally did get in touch with me. To me, the finality of that was enough, even if Thomas was prolonging it by acting out the way he was. Whatever reasoning he had to justify that I didn't know, but this was squarely on him now.

Which brought me back to Steve. I'd answered his question but hadn't asked him the same one in return. That's what I needed to hear. I needed to hear Steve's answer, yes or no. If he said yes, that would finish this right now. Put an end to the perfect dream this evening had become. And if he said no...

"You asked me a question earlier that I need to ask you in return."

Steve pursed his lips, head cocked to the side.

"Are you involved with anyone right now?"

His eyes narrowed, a knife edge crease forming between them.

Where a moment ago the way he'd regarded me had made me flushed, now a chill filled the space between us. As this evening had gone on, I had slipped into submissive patterns because I loved the feelings that doing so invoked in me. The responses that engaging in the simplest of those things produced in the Dom who sat across from was a heady thrill. One I latched onto with the eagerness of a junkie. I longed for it to continue, to give into it even more, but right now the question I had just posed to him pulled me out of that mindset, turning me stone-cold sober. It had to. The answer to that question could put an end to all of this, and I needed to hear his response without being mush-minded with lust, desire, all those emotions that I was so ready to give into.

His eyes continued to bore into me. He was not frowning or smiling, but his eyes had an air of cold efficiency that for the moment seemed less to reflect the light of the room than absorb it. That his answer hadn't been immediate, unequivocal, had tendrils of fear creeping up my spine.

"I think you know the answer to that, Jen."

I closed my eyes for a second, pursing my lips. Okay, that was an answer, and his voice made me want to believe. I wanted desperately to have faith that my hopes and suspicions were true. However, a stubborn part of me wouldn't let it go at that. I needed to hear the words.

"I do. Really, I do. But..." I pressed my lips together hard, trying not to let my voice belie any fear, or emotion.

Just be cool and collected. Just ask him, Jen...

"Please don't ask me to explain. I just need to hear you say it."

Steve scrutinized me, and a small frown pulled the corners of his mouth down. His jaw set, the fingers of one hand splayed out, then slowly clenched together.

He wasn't happy about this questioning of trust, that was clear in every inch of his body language. I couldn't help that. I had run through so many scenarios in my head since this morning. So many thoughts, fears, insecurities, and anxieties, all of which had concluded that afternoon in my grand epiphany. The self-loathing monkey on my back be damned, it had reached this moment of culmination. Here. Now. And all I needed, all I swore I wanted right at this moment was one final affirmation, a final signature on the dotted line.

"Please." I did not plead. I did not beg. I kept my voice firm, poised. Strong.

Say something. Please.

Words. I needed to hear his words.

For a second Steve did something he'd rarely done this entire evening; he broke eye contact with me and glanced down at the table. That act gave me a slight jolt.

Oh, God, I was wrong. He is with someone. He's trying to find the words to tell me, to explain that he doesn't believe in limiting himself and his partners to societal constraints...

The next second his eyes came back up, locking back onto mine. His frown, the look of displeasure, all of it was gone. Whatever had gone on inside his head, he'd come to some conclusion, because the look he gave now was the same as the one he had earlier this evening. It was an assertive look, and yet one that contained a vestige of sympathy at the same time. It was a look that was little different from those which had done such a damn good job of shattering and cracking the foundation of the wall I had built up.

"No, Jen." He reached across the table and his hand took mine, clasping it. "No. I am not involved with anyone right now. That is not who I am. And I need you to trust me on that."

And I was gone.

"Thank you, sir," I whispered, letting my relief carry across on a sigh that followed the words. I needed him to hear that in my response. I was jumping into the deep end of the pool here, all of it based on those last nine words.

-*But Thomas...*-

Stop. I am done *with that. I did my best. I* tried.

And tomorrow I'd be free. Free of the last nagging shreds of guilt in my own head.

Tomorrow I'd be me again. Completely.

We finished the dessert. As we sipped our coffee, staring at each other across the table, I wanted to believe we each shared a sense of relief that something had resolved itself in a way that maybe we both had been afraid it wouldn't. It was certainly true for myself and watching some of the earlier tension drain from Steve's face, I was confident he was feeling the same way. Whatever the case, the looks he now sent me were back to the ones which earlier had shot thrills of electricity through me. Intense and full of desire. With each action I took, I saw his corresponding reaction. The precision with which his eyes focused on my every move, when I tilted my chin down to the tabletop, drew my lower lip between my teeth, biting down. The way he leaned closer at the sound of my soft voice. Each 'yes, sir' I gave him was spoken with the confidence of knowing the response it would elicit. Looking back up at him, shy and questioning from under hooded eyes. All these things I did because I wanted to wind him up as much as he had me. When we had finished our coffee, I sat with my hands folded on the table, quiet, watching as he spoke with the waiter to settle the bill. As we waited for him to return, Steve cleared his throat.

"I hope you enjoyed dinner."

"I did, sir."

"Good. Thank you again for coming tonight."

"Thank you, *sir*."

He chuckled at my emphasis, and knowing he'd caught my intention made me grin. The tension from earlier was completely gone now, and any reservations I'd had before left with it.

The waiter came back, dropping off the receipt, and then Steve was standing. He moved to my chair as I stood to leave. We walked through the restaurant, Steve's hand in the small of my back once again, and everything was so picture perfect I scanned the room purposely, doing all I could to capture this moment with crystalline clarity. I wanted to remember this, every part of this evening for the happiness it had brought me. All my issues and anxiety aside, it had been incredible. And I had this warm, fuzzy feeling of anticipation which suggested it was only going to get better.

We stood outside the front door, waiting as the valet hailed a cab. Steve's presence behind me was a cocoon of reassurance that wrapped around me. I let myself lean back into his chest, and his hand drifted from my hip up my side to my shoulder. He held me there, his fingers caressing me, my body soaking in his warmth as the slight chill of the evening stirred around us. His fingers pulled my shoulder tighter to him, and I trembled without thinking.

He leaned down, the soft intake of his breath in my hair a whisper over the sounds around us.

"Are you cold?" His voice was low, comforting. "No, sir. I'm fine."

"I felt you tremble."

Closing my eyes, I let the tingling running through my body carry me. "That wasn't because I was chilled..."

"Ah." It was all he murmured, his lips so close to my scalp, his warm breath sending another quiver arcing down my spine. The cab pulled up to the curb, and Steve guided me inside. Once I was in, he came around and slid in from the opposite side. He slipped across the seat until there was no space between us. Steve's arm came up and glided across my shoulders, pulling me in tight.

"Mmm." I nuzzled against his chest. My anxiety from earlier was gone, and I pulled the blanket of contentment that Steve offered around me. I closed my eyes, the lights from outside casting diffused patterns across my eyelids as the sound of the car whispering along the streets provided a comforting white noise. It was a lulling sound, one that let me bask in the calmness his proximity provided. I wasn't certain how far we'd traveled when he shifted, his hand brushing over my hair, his fingers moving until they cupped my cheek. Calloused fingers grazed my skin, soothing me, coaxing me deeper into this nest of wellbeing he'd created. I looked up into his eyes, watched as they caressed my face. He leaned down, and his lips pressed against mine. The kiss was sweet wine on a summer's eve, the taste of something fresh, exhilarating, exciting. He moved with assurance, and I let my hand come up to cradle his face, fingertips drifting down to trace the edge of his jaw. At my touch, the kiss went from gentle to fierce, every part of us that touched turned into a starburst of electrified nerves, and I fell into the dark pool that was my desire. I could feel him, taste him, and his every action let me know he was doing the same. These explorations were without hesitation, only hunger, each of us confident in what we were doing. When Steve pulled back, I knew only that the cab was not back at the hotel but still moving through the streets of Chicago on a trip I did not want to end and yet wanted to be over at the same time.

"You are so incredibly beautiful." His voice was soft but filled with an unmistakable rumble of desire. Desire that was for me.

I bit down on my lower lip, staring up at him. "Thank you."

His eyes traced the outline of my face, embracing me no less than if he had with his fingers. I watched as he drank me in, my body pressing tighter against him. He drew me in close until his face was touching the top of my head. I heard him murmur something, and then his hand slipped to the back of my neck, gripping me, fingers digging in to tilt me back. Those five points of pressure shot delicious tendrils of pain through me, each dimple in my skin radiating sensation outwards. It was something I had not experienced from a lover's touch in so long. Too long. I know I moaned. It was low, yearning, and I could only hope that the driver did not hear it. Even if he could, I didn't care. All I cared about in that moment was Steve. Pleasing him and in return taking the pleasure he was giving me.

I couldn't say how long he held me like that. Time was playing tricks with me. When he loosened his grip on my neck, I let out a sigh that was both contentment and dismay. Chuckling at my reaction, he pulled me close, cradling me tight to him. I nestled against his chest for the rest of the ride until the cab swung into the semicircular drive of the hotel. It was just so good to be there, held close to him, letting my mind wander with delighted anticipation, contemplating how the rest of this evening would play out. The cab pulled to the curb, and Steve pulled me up from his chest.

"We're here."

I sighed with satisfaction, looking up at him with hooded eyes. He was shifting, trying to subtly edge towards the cab door on his side at the same time he continued to hold on to me, tugging me across the seat with him. It was clear he wanted to get us out of this cab and inside, and that sense of urgency mixed with anticipation was not far from my own. He let go of me, and slipped the remainder of the way across the seat, exiting the cab. I took his hand when he opened my door, stepping out and waiting while he paid the cabbie. When he was done, he ushered me past the doorman and inside. The lobby was quiet, far fewer people than when he'd picked me up earlier in the evening. We walked across the floor to the elevators, and he pushed the UP button. I stood next to him, leaning against his shoulder, not wanting to leave his touch for even a moment. His arm came around my back, his hand resting on my hip as we waited.

"What floor," he asked as the bell chimed. "Twelve."

He ushered me inside the elevator, pressed the button for the twelfth floor. As the doors slid closed, he turned, capturing me in his gaze once more. He trapped me with a scrutinizing look that was one of pure possession, and my mouth went dry. I was buzzing with eagerness, waiting to see what his next move would be. He stalked towards me, and I backed into the corner until there was nowhere left to go. He stepped in until he was on me, close, so very close and God I wanted him. Wanted him to know how much I wanted him, and not to stop what he was doing.

Please don't stop.

His hand came up, fingers latching to the back of my neck. His grip was firm, neither gentle nor rough. He held me in place, turning my face up to his. I was his now. His mouth pressed to mine, and we both gave voice to the heat, desire, want, and need we felt. I in little cries that slipped from my throat and he in a growl of approval from his. I kept my hands to my side, giving complete control to him as he captured me, possessed me as he wished to and as I thirsted for. The elevator slowed as we reached my floor, but Steve did not release me. He kept me trapped in the corner, my back pressed against the cool stone and glass of the wall. I shivered with unease as it came to a stop, unsure if people might be standing and waiting outside when the doors opened, catching Steve as he held me cornered. Part of me didn't care, only wanted to be obedient to what Steve demanded of me. To take what he offered in return. His dominance. My submission. To give, to obey, and to take what I desired in return.

The doors slid aside on a metallic whisper and Steve pulled away slowly. I couldn't stop myself from glancing beyond him. The hallway was empty, and relief washed over me. He smiled at my reaction, and then grabbed my hand, pulling me from the elevator.

"Room number?" His voice was low, husky, and that sent another shiver coursing through me.

"1237."

He drew me down to where the hallway teed off in two directions, glancing at the wall plaque with numbers pointing left and right. I couldn't help the grin that twitched my face as I trailed in his wake.

Tugging me along, I was almost trotting to keep up with him. The way he was moving, his head snapping back and forth as he scanned the little metal plates on the doors, it all made clear he was as wound up as I was. He had me bent like a bow with anticipation, and I had him taut as the string. Alert, ready, waiting for the moment we would be released and set free.

We came to my door, and I slipped the key out of my clutch, inserting the card until the light flashed green. As he dragged me inside, the dim light from the bathroom provided the only illumination in the room. It was enough I could see the outline of his face, see cheeks flushed with anticipation. There was no mistaking the nervous buzz of excitement surrounding him. The jerkiness of his movements as he guided me into the room made that clear. Raw energy animated us both, and there was little fluid about our motions. All that mattered, though, was that we were here. In my room. Alone together.

I headed for the bedroom, but as I moved past, Steve grabbed me by the wrist. I gasped in surprise as he tugged me back into his arms, his mouth crushing to mine. Our tongues twined as he slowly marched me backwards, our bodies moving together. If his aura had been a smoldering ember before, he was fire now, a furnace turned to full, and I clung to him to blanket myself with it. He jerked me to a stop, and we stood, gripping each other. Our mouths came together again, teeth on lips, pressure and bites that were sometimes pain, always pleasure. He pulled back with my lip caught between his teeth until he drew a carnal cry from me. Letting go, he gazed down with eyes that were freshly forged steel, still glowing, his desire never more apparent.

His breathing slowed as we stood, staring.

"Tell me, Jen. Tell me what it is."

I blinked. Tell him? Tell him...what? I stumbled, confused. He was about to fuck me, and all of a sudden we were playing Twenty Questions. My heart was racing, I wanted nothing more than to rip his goddamn clothes off, and out of the blue he hits me with some stupid question.

What the hell!

And then it hit me. It came flooding back, and in a flash I knew exactly what he was asking. What he wanted from me. A wave of emotion washed over me. The sensation of relief and gratitude that only being with someone who truly understands what you are can give.

My safeword. He was asking me for my safeword.

"Bubblegum," I whispered, watching him, pressing my lips together.

"Bubblegum?" He repeated it slowly, his face equal parts incredulous and amused.

"Don't judge me..." I lowered my eyes, my voice soft, almost pleading.

He chuckled, and then his fingers were under my chin, lifting my gaze up to his. "I may do many things tonight, Jen, but judging you will definitely not be one of them."

Then, before I could think to say anything further, he was kissing me again, and I felt alive, so very alive.

He'd asked me for my safeword.

Almost the first thing out of his mouth once we were in my room. No, wait. It *was* the first thing out of his mouth. Earlier I might have been curious about Steve's experience as a Dom, but that single question drove any doubt away. I may have had trust issues with Steve earlier in the evening, but the moment he asked me for that word those issues disappeared. He was watching out for me. He wanted me to feel safe, to feel secure while I was with him, and that simple request confirmed both things. Steve had given me a sign of a true Dom. A good Dom. A caring Dom. Which made submitting to him so very easy now.

I let him control me, communicate his lust and desire with lips and tongue. His teeth captured my lip, then moved my neck, biting, teasing, testing. At first a nip, an almost negligible taste of pain. The next harder, sharper. Then a third, followed by a fourth, and by the sixth I couldn't hold back the cry that burst from me. I didn't want to. I wanted him to hear it. I wanted to feel the sharp intake of his own breath, feel his hands tighten into me. Fingers digging into my flesh, pulling me closer until—yes—I could feel his arousal pressing into my hip. With each further bite, I responded with a cry, with each nip a soft whimper. I heard his approving growl as my body formed to his, grip fierce as if to pull me inside him. To possess me whole, devour me. I didn't know what Steve's next move would be, but I was ready for it. Ready for this to begin. To take everything I'd built up in my head as this evening had progressed from a tentative possibility and turn it into reality. To carry out what was now playing out in breaths which became rapid gasps, blood which pulsed through veins that surged to his every move. Nerves that fired to teeth on flesh and then converted to noises from my throat that had me fucking wet to the point of no return.

I wanted Steve. I wanted what he offered. And—goddammit!—I wanted to get back to being the real me.

All I needed now was for Steve to be the Dom he'd proven he was and take me there.

ELEVEN

I wasn't sure how long we stood there, but eventually Steve pulled back, looking down into my eyes. Lips slightly parted, pupils wide as they danced over the surface of my face, every aspect of his gaze exuded pure hunger, and I reveled in it. His hands came up to graze across my shoulders, gripping me before taking a step back.

"Take your dress off for me, Jen." It was his Dom voice, but now it was deeper, tinged with lust and desire that made it even more exciting.

"Yes, sir." I slipped out of my shoes, flicking each away to be clear of us. Keeping my gaze lowered to the floor, I reached behind me, unclasping the top of my dress, slowly pulling the zipper down. Tiny hitches in his breathing let me know he was watching my every movement, eyes tracing my body with laser-like focus. I wriggled until the dress began to slide downwards, dropping clear of my shoulders until I caught it before it slipped past my hips. Never lifting my eyes, I let it fall until it pooled around my feet. I brought my hands together clasped in front of me, remaining still. He moved beside me, his fingers coming up underneath my chin, lifting until my eyes met his.

"The underwear, Jen." The command was soft yet forceful, a

tone that brooked no questioning.

"Yes, sir." I nodded, trembling ever so slightly.

For the moment, he continued to grip my chin, holding me in place as I completed undressing myself. I used my hands to slip my bra straps free, falling off my shoulder on one side and down my arm, the other clinging stubbornly. I shrugged until it too fell. Reaching behind, I undid the hooks, and then held it in place for a millisecond, watching for Steve's reaction as I pulled my hands away and let it fall to the floor. I let my fingers drift to my panties, and then, without my eyes leaving his, I began slipping the fabric down. Steve broke the gaze only then, watching as my hands slid them off. The hiss of his breath the moment my sex was exposed made me giddy with glee.

"God, you are beautiful." His gaze took in every inch of me in a languorous pass, his fingers tracing a path along my arm.

The feeling of triumph that surged through me at his words, the shiver that danced up my spine at his reaction was deliciously powerful. I basked in it, reveling in what I done. Steve's fingers stopped their trail down my arm, moving to return to their place under my chin, his eyes locking back onto mine.

It was that look. An intense gaze that pinned me in place, eyes hammered steel that captured me like a band around my throat. That is what I had once lived for, and was now doing so again. All of this a part of what drove me, inspired me, gave free rein to every submissive desire I'd ever had. That primal look. I created that. I owned it with my voice, my downcast eyes, the submission I offered. I saw it reflected back in eyes that hungered, the quickening of his breath, in the sexual tension that passed between us. My nose caught the faint scent of something familiar. A bright tang I knew was my arousal. If I could smell that trace of my essence, then I knew damn sure Steve could too. I didn't care. I wanted him to smell it. Wanted him to know how much I wanted him. Whatever it was he was going to do with me, that is what I wanted. I wanted more of the yearning I'd drawn out from within him.

"Present." The word came out in a soft, demanding tone.

I shivered at the command. Yes. *Oh, yes, yes, yes.* This I knew. This I could do. This was what I wanted so very, very much.

I dropped to my knees slowly. His fingers never let go of my chin as I fell until I came to rest kneeling at his feet, my head tilted back at a sharp angle. Once there, his fingers released me and I remained still, looking up into his eyes. He surveyed me, pupils gleaming with a severity that shot through me like a bolt. His mouth was a hard line, no part of it upturned to indicate approval or pleasure in my stance. I knelt obediently at his feet under that cool gaze but felt no discomfort in it. Rather, it was perfect. It was everything I could have hoped for. He may have had me as a submissive, but I had him in my own way, and I savored it.

He reached up, undoing the top button of his shirt, and then began removing his tie. He took it off slowly, his eyes never leaving mine. For a second, I contemplated looking down, letting my eyes fall to the floor, but then I thought better of it. Maybe I was being selfish, not lowering my gaze as I probably should. Maybe he'd see this as an act of defiance and punish me for it later. I didn't know, and I didn't care. I wanted to watch him because I needed to see everything he was about to do.

He slipped the tie free, holding it in his hands. His eyes narrowed as his features shifted, lips curling up at one corner into a calculating grin, cheeks dimpled, so goddamn self-assured and dominant.

"Hands above your head."

My lower lip trembled with anticipation. I obeyed, raising them up until they stretched above me. I had spent years dancing this dance, and now I was about to step back out onto the floor after a long hiatus. That feeling, the passion and desire for everything we were doing, made me shivery with joy. The fabric of the tie slithered over my skin as his fingers worked to loop it back on itself into an effective cinch. Even though ties make crappy bindings compared to rope, I didn't care. I was being bound, and that alone sent jolts of pleasure pulsing down from my fingertips right to my pussy. Steve did a wonderful job, and I loved the feeling as he wrapped and knotted the smooth fabric around my wrists, yanking it as tight as he could. As he completed the knot with a final tug, my eyes closed as my body quivered with exhilaration, nipples painfully taut as my chest jerked in shallow breaths to keep me from going lightheaded. I was bound. Hell fucking yes. God, it had been so long, but here I was, Steve using the tie to pull my arms up with the most satisfying tension. I was gone down the rabbit hole, a submissive Alice crying out with glee.

My eyes opened to find him staring down at me, eyes hooded, body exuding an aura of need. I immediately shoved my gaze back to the floor, and that earned a low murmur of approval. He held me suspended in silence before his hand moved to lower my arms down across my chest. He was moving, cloth brushing against my skin as he crouched to bring himself to my level. I kept my eyes down as his bent knees came into view. He held me in silence, still gripping the tie that bound my wrists.

"Look at me."

I brought my head up. Steve gazed back, a smile tugging at his cheeks that made those dimples I found so fucking sexy even more pronounced. It wasn't only his smile that captivated me. It was pupils that never stopped moving, little quirks at the corners of his mouth when he caught something I did that I wasn't even aware of. It was strokes of desire painted across his face, all topped with that confidence that screamed dominance. That very essence of him that had first attracted me this morning before I had even fully recognized it. The firm lines of his jaw, the angle of his lips, those beautiful eyes were all things I wanted to lose myself in. To do whatever I could to keep that look there forever, to please him, to make him happy with me.

"Jen." He gave the tie a slight tug, waiting patiently for me to respond.

"Yes, sir." I shivered, biting down on my lower lip.

His free hand stroked my cheek, then cupped my chin. He was smiling softly.

"Okay, this is new between you and I, but neither of us is new to *this*. You know how much I want you. I'm not going to insult your intelligence by assuming otherwise. However, I'm going to be up front with you. I'm going to be cautious tonight. I have a gut feeling you can probably handle more than I'm going to give, but I really, really need this, and I don't want to fuck it up. I need you, Jen. I want everything you're offering, but the last thing I want to do here is make a mistake. So I'm going to trust you, Jen, but I'm also going to go slow. I'm trusting you to tell me in all the ways that I know you know how if you aren't comfortable with something, and you need me to stop. I'm trusting you not to let me do something just because you think that's what I want. I'm trusting you not to let me fuck up and cause you pain that hurts except in the way you desire. You understand that, don't you." It wasn't a question. It was a statement borne out of the trust that Steve had already placed in me.

"Yes, sir."

He stroked my cheek again. I leaned into it, closing my eyes and letting a soft moan escape my lips.

"Good. Because there are so many things I want to do, Jen. Starting now..."

He tugged me up by the tie until we were both standing. He spun me around roughly, one hand coming to grip my shoulder at the same moment he let go of the tie. As he did, I let my hands fall in front of me. Now facing the foot of the bed, he held me in place at shoulder and hip. He moved me forward to the edge of the bed until my knees were touching it. His hand moved from my hip to the small of my back, guiding me down until my knees were digging into the mattress. Wrapping his arm around me, he bent me to fall forward, my legs dangling over the edge, my feet barely off the floor. I was ass up, exposed, arms stretched out ahead of me. Steve moved onto the end of the bed, perched next to me. There he waited, motionless, silent, until he gave a low growl and brought a calloused hand up to caress my backside. Splayed fingers brushed over my skin, dipping into the crack between my cheeks and then out again, goosebumps rising in their wake. I trembled as his hand crested the top of my ass on one side, gliding down to my inner thigh, coming ever so close to where my body craved for him to touch. Then it was moving back, tracing the same path on the other side, mimicking what he had just done. Again he stopped, denying me the touch to my sex I ached for. I spread my legs wider. If I could make him see my pussy, see how my lips glistened with want, maybe he would understand my need. His hand continued to stroke me, and I wiggled, letting out a soft whimper of frustration. Suddenly the hand left me, a half-second later coming back down with a sharp snap. I gave out a little yelp as the smack landed, a tiny blossom of pain adding to the throb of now-heated skin.

"Be still." He snapped the command at me with a stern tone, clipped syllables that did not request my compliance, but demanded it.

His hand returned to caressing and stroking me, a delicious thrum that forced me not to give into a desire to show him how I wanted his touch lest he take it away. His fingertips prickled nerves which bloomed into a field of gooseflesh, a teasing sensation which pulled me away from everything happening around us and condensed it to those five drifting spots tracking across the flesh of my ass. Every pass held my body in check to obey his command, remaining still sweet torture of anticipation for what might come next. His hand moved further up, tracing my spine. His skin was rough, calloused, not smooth as I'd grown used to. His fingers drifted to where my shoulder blades met, and then he raked them down my back, fingernails digging into my flesh as he tore a prolonged cry from me. My back arched to the fiery trails he left in my skin. Again, he swept his hand over my ass, cupping the curve of my cheeks before dipping to the insides of my thighs and then moving back to repeat what he'd just done. I held as still as I could, struggling to adhere to his command. It took effort not to twist to the blaze of stinging left in the wake of his nails, my body growing taut at the prospect of what might follow each pass.

Steve's murmurs of appreciation were a balm. Counterpoint to the subtle agony of suspense as his fingers played against my skin, confirmation of the pleasure he had in what he was doing. After the fourth pass, the bed shifted under his weight as he moved further up, leaning on an elbow to speak into my ear while his other hand continued caressing me.

"You're such a good girl, aren't you, Jen?" His voice was throaty, a low, smooth tone that came from deep within his chest. The sound had my pulse increasing, even though I suspected something hidden behind it.

"Yes, sir." My answer was stifled, barely above a whisper.

"However…"

That word brought me up. I gulped in air, eager for what was coming next, and yet with tension ratcheting up as muscles stiffened in response. Oh, there was pain incoming. Sweet, scrumptious pain that had my stomach clenching, calf muscles drawing tight as toes curled. None of this was out of fear on my part, but rather exquisite anticipation of what that word promised.

"I am reminded that earlier tonight at dinner I had to ask you to trust me. I had to say 'please.' You wouldn't accept that I am capable of deciding how I spend my money, where I spend it, and on whom I spend it. You questioned me, and my decision. Is that something a good girl does?" He leaned in closer, breath warm against my skin. "Should a good girl be rewarded for that kind of behavior?"

"No, sir."

He gave an approving chuckle, the tiniest of nods indicating his agreement. "I thought as much. Are you ready, Jen?"

"Yes, sir." My answer was thick with need, the two words melded almost into one as I rushed to get my answer out. Nerves jittery and eager to feel the first taste of what Steve offered. Yes, I was ready. I was absolutely fucking ready.

He shifted back down to the edge of the bed. The hand that

he'd been tracing a lazy pattern over my ass with hadn't stopped during our conversation, and even now it continued to glide over my skin. His other hand came to my hip, and I felt his fingers grip me, digging in and holding me in place. The hand that had been moving over me stopped.

And then they came. Four sharp, stinging swats.

They were nowhere near as hard as he could have inflicted. This wasn't my first rodeo, and I knew Steve could have gone much further. But as he'd said, he was being careful. Taking it easy. Though none were hard enough to make me cry out, each one drew an audible gasp out of me. The skin on my ass stung from the smacks, and the warmth left in their aftermath was delicious. I fully expected—wanted—cries to be drawn out of me later. If I was a good girl and deserved them.

His hand returned to my flesh, soothing over where he had just struck. The touch of his fingers over the warmed, tingling skin sent little electrical currents running up my spine. My body began to move. I willed it to be still, and then changed my mind. Maybe just a bit more fuel to the fire. I gave a small wiggle, letting my hips shift back and forth. The hand on my hip gripped me hard as the other stopped in its path.

"Did I not tell you to be still?"

"Yes, sir." I let out a small whimper of frustration as the hand on my ass pulled away.

"Then be still."

Four more smacks. Harder this time. Not excessively so, but each with increased intensity. Steve knew what he was doing, and the strength of these new strikes had intensified perfectly compared to the previous ones. My ass flared with fire, burning pain radiating outwards from the epicenter of where each blow landed. Each one overlapped the other, and this time I gritted my teeth, biting back cries rather than gasps. My hands dug into the covers, twisting the fabric within my fingers. What had been little electrical tingles flitting across my skin now became a piece of heated iron, leaving my skin seared with pain, aching, throbbing. My back arched with tension, and though I had intentionally moved after the first set of strikes, this time I had no control, my body scooting up towards the head of the bed as the last smack fell.

"You just can't be good." Mock frustration lilted Steve's voice, a pronounced fake sigh closing up the end. "Can you?"

I made a frustrated whimper in response.

"Oh, well..."

Four more. This time the fire blossomed into an inferno. The pain was sweet oblivion. Oh, fuck yes it was good. Pure, delicious, scorching pain that bent my back into an arc. I held myself shakily on my elbows, teetering because of the binding at my wrists, my hands knotting the bedcover into a ball. I squirmed at each strike, and this time I did cry out. Didn't even try to grit my teeth or hold back. It just felt so fucking good.

As the fourth strike landed Steve's hand stopped in place, melded to my ass. His breathing had risen in tempo with every blow, the noise of it overlapping the fading sound of my last cry. It was thick with excitement, a pant that belied his own arousal. He didn't move, the fingers of one hand dug sharply into my hip while the others splayed where they'd landed. After a moment of stillness, he began to caress me, same as when we'd first started. I lay there basking in the exquisiteness of what he'd done. My breathing started to slow, and he shifted again, arranging himself to where he could speak into my ear.

"Checking in," he asked softly, tenderly. "Good? Green? Yellow?" I puddled at his words. Good? Good? It was fucking perfect.

"Good. Green. Green." I knew my words were broken, hoarse, but I was still wallowing in the bliss that was cocooning my body like a blanket. I wanted to say more, give him all the words rattling around in my head, but the three I got out were the best I could do.

"Okay." He leaned into me, placing a kiss on my head.

I gave a soft moan at the feeling of the kiss. Steve slid further up the bed, pulling one of the pillows down until he had it positioned near my head. I looked at it with confusion, not entirely sure why he done it. I didn't dwell on it, letting its presence slip away as he moved back down to the foot of the bed. His hand went back to massaging my enflamed butt in slow, gentle swirls. The pass of his fingers stung, and yet at the same time heightened the sensations the strikes had created.

"You know, as much as I love the feeling of my hand smacking your ass, I can't help but notice that despite spanking you harder each time for not obeying me, it doesn't appear to be having the proper effect. If anything, it just seems to be making you move even more." His voice dropped an octave, taking on a disapproving tone. "I don't think I'm going about this the right way. I think I should try something different."

I collapsed against the covers, trying to get my breathing under some semblance of control. My body was a shuddery, limp pool, and I sank into the bed, a giddy wilted mess.

Until I heard the sound of him removing his belt.

It wasn't hard to miss. The *click* of the buckle as he undid it, and then the soft *swish* as it slid through the loops of his slacks, coming free. My head came up sharply as I twisted around to look back at him. He held the belt in his hand, slowly folding it back on itself, fingers clasping the buckle and free end. I shifted up onto my elbows, wobbly as my bound wrists did little to help with my balance. I swayed as I tried to keep eyes on him as he stepped to the edge of the bed, the belt now looped and dangling. Excitement mixed with fear made my pulse race in response to what had to be coming next. I hadn't thought he would go this far. I'd hoped but hadn't been one-hundred percent sure. He let the belt trail against my leg, and the whisper of the leather's edge against my skin shot a surge of pure adrenaline through me. My body crept forward as the leather came to the cleft of my ass.

"Tsk, tsk, tsk." He shook his head, the hard click of his tongue amplifying the faux disappointment that laced his voice. "You see?

This is exactly what I was talking about." He flicked the loop of the belt against my butt cheek. "Twice I've told you to be still, and yet for a third time you've defied me. Let's see if I can make you understand what happens to good girls who won't obey..."

I watched as the belt came up with a flash, and even as I was turning my head away, gulping in a deep breath, the first strike landed on me.

Fire. Lancing fire and a streak of pain that was so much more than his hand had produced. And my body responded, flooding my system with that chemical cocktail submissives crave. The spankings Steve had administered were a taste. This was the real deal. A mainline right to my cerebral cortex. And I wanted more.

I cried out, heard how loud it was, and quickly buried my head into the pillow. *Shit.* That's why he'd placed it there, the smart bastard. I hoped I had done it swiftly enough. The last thing I needed was a neighbor calling the front desk to say that the guest next door sounded like they were being beaten. Because they were, and they didn't want it to stop, thank you very much.

I kept my head buried in the pillow as Steve struck again. And then a third time. And then a fourth, and a fifth. I could feel him crossing the lashes, no doubt painting the canvas of my ass in Jackson Pollock stripes of bright red. I wanted the pain those strokes offered, the release, the pulse of that chemical tide washing over me. Right now, in this moment, all I wanted was that belt. Again.

He stopped at five. My chest was heaving. I could feel a sunflower of fire that had blossomed on my ass, the burn of it radiating out through me. I rose from the pillow, gasping, crying. I did everything I could to keep my voice from being too loud. I gritted teeth and choked back cries that could easily have become shrieks, denying myself the pleasure of just letting loose at the top of my lungs. During the lashing my body had crept forward with every strike, inching my way until I was up to the head of the bed. It was a natural reaction, and while I had been able to control it during the spankings earlier, with this I had not. My brain was awash with emotions and desire and being still was so far down the list of things under my control that it didn't even register.

"I swear, Jen, I don't know what to do with you." Steve made the circle of leather trace crisscross patterns over my behind as he spoke. "It's almost as if you don't want me to stop punishing you. I gave you another opportunity, another chance to be still, and look where you are now." He emphasized the comment with a sharp rap of the strap against my butt.

My knees were well away from the edge of the bed, my feet barely dangling over the lip. Facing the pillow, ragged breaths became a quivering mewl bubbling up from my throat at the implied threat in his tone.

Steve moved, one knee coming up to wedge between my legs, his weight pressing into me. Before I was even fully aware of what he was doing, he had the hand not holding the belt fisted into my hair, pulling my head back. My spine bent like a sapling in a storm, my neck bowing to the tension of his grip, quivering with both yearning and apprehension as each fought for control over the other.

"I am a patient man, however." He spoke with a low voice, darker than before, threat thrumming within. "And fair. I'm willing to give you one more chance, Jen. Would you like that? Hmm? One more opportunity to... just... be... still?" With each clipped word he gave my head a brusque tug back, eliciting a moan with every pull. When he was finished he held me there, bent tight.

"Yes! Yes, sir! Please!" The words came tumbling out, punctuated by a gasp the stinging tension of his fist knotted in my hair jerked out of me. He held me there for a second longer before suddenly releasing my head, letting it fall back to the pillow.

"Okay, then. Let's try this one more time...."

He stood up from his position straddling me. Once more there was the teasing trail of the belt down my back. A tingling line that caused me to shiver as it came across the swell of my ass before it flowed in a snaking pattern down the back of my right leg. Then it was gone, and I closed my eyes, dropping my head to the pillow.

I knew what was coming.

The first blow fell, and white dots burst behind my eyes. I rammed my hips into the bed, as if that would somehow help absorb some of the scorch of the lash. I screamed into the pillow this time. The sear of the leather against my skin a torment that casually brushed aside my pain tolerance as if it didn't exist. The edge of my vision wavered, sight going blurry as the crack pulled me straight down into a burning pit of delicious agony, especially coming so soon after the first five strikes. My fingers gripped the bedcover and I yanked at it, pulled and twisted it in my hands. My voice gone raw gave vent to my suffering as it was swallowed by the bulk of the cushion. Cries rose until they became screams, and as they grew in strength, I drew the fabric into my mouth, letting saliva drool into the cloth until an 'O' shaped blotch stained it. This newest surge of pain knocked aside what resistance I had leaned on to maintain composure during the first set of strokes, and the chemicals I had ridden with pleasure then now flooded through me with a vengeance. I held on with fingertips to ride out the second lash as it coursed across my cheeks, then the third, the fourth, and I had already tumbled over the edge by the time the fifth cracked over me. I spiraled down into that mental realm a submissive lives for. I slipped under the waves and into subspace, floating in that womb-like state that pain, endorphins, all of it, creates.

God, how I had missed this. I fucking loved it.

I was in my own fuzzy, warm cocoon of bliss, and that was all I cared about. The belt was there, I could feel the lazy trace of the edge of it moving back and forth across my ass. The sensation of that small patch of leather on my skin was heightened incredibly, and as it traced a crisscross pattern, I carried on a dreamy conversation with it. *Hey there, old friend! Welcome back! Did you miss me as much as I missed you?*

I was still floating in my bubble when Steve came up onto the bed with me again. His hand pressed to my back, the belt curling against my skin. He must have leaned down, because his voice was in my ear, soft, warm, disembodied but so comforting, nonetheless.

"Jen. You there? Can you hear me? How we doing? We're gonna take a little breather here, okay?"

I wanted to giggle. I wanted to gather him in my arms, to hold him and tell him thank you, thank you so much. But I was still drifting in my own little world, and I couldn't, so I did as much as my body and mind would allow. I rolled to him, blinked my eyes until I could bring his face into focus through tears I only now realized had been coursing down my cheeks. Wetness prickled my skin as I smiled. At least I hoped it was recognizable as a smile. I tried to say something, but there weren't words, just whimpers, soft mewls of pleasure. That was the best thanks I could give at the moment, and I hoped it was enough.

It was. Steve smiled down at me, his eyes dancing as he took me in. I reached up weakly, touched that beautiful cheek, that magnificent jaw.

"Hey gorgeous." His voice was a rumble, a soothing caress as he brushed a stray lock of hair out of my face, gently wiping the traces of tears from my cheeks.

The words made me melt when they met my ears. My hands fell, and I looked up at him, blinking slowly. I leaned into his touch, moaned as his fingers lightly stroked my skin. My mind was still swimming lazily in the warm pool he had built for me, but I managed to swallow, and whisper a single word.

"Please."

"Please? Please what, Jen."

I closed my eyes and my lip quivered. God, I felt so good. I wanted to float in this sensation for hours, maybe a day, or a month. To do nothing but feel *this*. To just be, do nothing, not even speak. What Steve needed to do right now was read my mind, because it *had* to be fucking obvious what I wanted.

"Come on. Use your words..."

I whimpered in frustration. Why did he have to say it with that amused lilt to his voice? Smug bastard. He knew where I was, what he'd done to me. He wasn't playing fair. I opened my eyes, let them refocus, biting down on my lower lip. My mind settled a little, letting me draw in a calming breath. Okay. There. I can do this. I can tell you what I want, Mr. Smartass-Smart guy.

Steve had other ideas, however. He wasn't going to wait on me. He chuckled, brushing a thumb against my chin. Then he moved, sliding down the length of my body until he came to rest at the foot of the bed. His fingers brushed up my calves until his hands were gripping my hips. Suddenly he pulled me towards him. I let out a gasp, arms twisting across my chest. I arched my back, trying to lift myself up to see what he was doing, but before I could, he yanked me one more time until my ass was inches from the end of the bed, legs dangling awkwardly.

And then he slid completely off, dropping down to fall into position between my thighs.

Fuck.

Oh fuck. I knew where this was going, what he was going to do. I'd said please. He damn well knew I wanted him inside me. But the devious fucking bastard wasn't playing fair. Teasing me, mocking me with my inability to string words together. Goddammit! He hadn't even given me a chance. He knew what kind of headspace I was in, and still he'd taunted me. Now he spread my legs apart, gripping my thighs as he opened me. I strained at my shoulders and neck to keep my eyes on him as he looked up with a devilish grin.

"Hmm. Well, if the only thing you can say is 'please,' I guess I'll just have to figure this out on my own." His face disappeared, the top of his head dropping down between my legs, and then his breath was against my...

Fuck. Fuck, fuck, fuck, fuck, fuck.

My head fell back with a cry. My fingers curled into fists before splaying outwards against my skin. My body twisted, responding to a flood of overwhelming desire that the proximity of his mouth to my overheated sex tore out of me. Steve kissed the top of my mons, then moved, trailing further touches of his lips down my thigh on one side before coming back the same way then across to the other. I lay there as pure, raw pleasure coursed through me, a frisson of frustration and anticipation for what he was going to do next creating a jumble of emotions in me. Panting breaths hissed past my clenched jaw as I tried not to give exactly what he wanted from me too soon. My hands flexed against the muscles of my abdomen gone taut, my fingers fidgety as I clenched and unclenched them while Steve continued to tease me. His breath was feather light on my skin, his lips gentle pressure when he kissed me, bright points that became sharp with pain when he took me between his teeth and bit down. He had told me to be still before, and I had tried, but any chance of that was now gone. I writhed under his touch because there was no way I could control my reaction to what he was doing.

I wanted to grab him by his calculating, insidious head, but I kept my arms plastered to my body. His tongue skated along the edge of my labia, one side to the other and back. The wet drag of that broad surface over slick folds wrenched cries from my throat, each one wavering between fierce exclamations of raw pleasure to hoarse rasps of vexation. My hands writhed against my chest, moving until they were brushing against the hard peaks of my already aching nipples. I gritted my teeth to deny the hotel my screams, sucked in air to keep myself from going lightheaded. The spankings and the belt had been delicious agony. This was just downright cruelty. I pushed into him, letting him know with my body what my voice wouldn't.

"Please!" I drug the word out, as if stretching the first vowel out long enough would make him relent. Finally, breath forced me to cut the word loose, and in the immediate silence Steve's chuckle floated up from below me. Warm breath caressed my pussy, short puffs that I swore had to be him laughing. The sensation faded, and his face swam into view as he rose up to where he could look up at me.

"What was that? Please?" He grinned at me wickedly, head

tilted slightly to one side as he pretended to struggle to hear my appeal. "Please what, Jen? I really don't know what you want if you can't tell me. I'm not a mind reader..."

"Please... sir!" My groan was near-feverish with frustration, hands jittery to do something, anything to convey to him what my voice was so obviously failing to do.

Steve shook his head, grinning with delight at my distress. Fucker. He was really enjoying this. Almost as much as I was.

"Jen, Jen, Jen. You couldn't stay still when I told you to, and now you can't use your words when I've asked so politely. You really are just a hot mess right now, aren't you?" He pursed lips, taking a deep breath that he then released in a mocking sigh. "Well, you've no one but yourself to blame for this. However, as I said, I am a patient man, and I am fair, so I'm going to do my best to see if I can guess what you want." This teasing had only one purpose. To torment me, because he goddamn knew as well as I did what he was going to do. His body glided smoothly back down between my legs, hands coming to rest on my thighs. He didn't even pause, made no attempt to pretend he was going to do anything other than go back to ravaging my pussy with that fucking tongue of his.

The first draw he made through my slick heat sent my back arching, and any frustration there had been in my voice was now obliterated by a drawn out moan of gratification, a sound that was born on the air pulled from my lungs until it died in a shivery groan. The tip of his tongue flicked over my hood, grazing my clit as it slipped past. Then he was drawing back through me again, and again. I keened with adoration as his tongue painted me with both my juices and his spit, a messy smear he coated my sex with as my breathing became more labored with each pass. His tongue pushed into me, then drug upwards, the surface laving over my throbbing nub. His lips sucked an arousal and saliva-slicked hood in, lapping at me as if trying to gulp down every drop of the juices he had drawn from my pussy to glaze my clit. The next moment he plunged back into my slit, tongue lapping at the flow of my arousal as the scent grew heavier around us. I tried not to squirm, tried to keep my ass planted to the bed, and I failed. Miserably. Steve gripped me, forcing me down with nails that dug into my thighs, tearing a wail out of me. Goddamn the man was good, and it did not take him long to have me teetering at the edge of a heavenly orgasm.

And then the fucker stopped.

His head came up from between my legs, his gaze roguish as it cut up across my belly to my face. As he pulled away, I tried to follow him, thrusting my hips forward as if that could capture and bring him back down. I cried with indignation when he ignored me and continued to rise.

"Noooo!" The cry was fervent at first, a wail of displeasure that rode on that single vowel until it trailed off into a mewl of frustration.

"What's that, Jen! No? Oh... so I must have guessed wrong, huh? God, I am so sorry."

That voice. Oh, that voice so full of self-confidence, amusement, so sardonic and taunting at the same time. I lifted my bound hands up from my chest, thrusting them at him as if somehow by that gesture alone I could make him go back to where he'd been. To bring me to the release that I so desperately craved and had been so close to.

"If only you could tell me what you wanted...." He smiled at me wickedly, slowly shaking his head.

This was cruel. Maybe Steve was a sadist after all. But that smile, and the way he'd made me feel right up to the second he'd raised his head up... all I needed was to think of that to know he wasn't. Not in the truest sense of the word, at least from my experience. While I was enveloped in all sorts of warm, fuzzy, delicious feelings, I was aware enough at this moment that if I wanted to fall over the precipice I was teetering at, what I needed to do was use my words, or this sonofabitch was going to make this go on forever.

Which wasn't a totally unpleasant thought in itself, but... nope. I needed this orgasm. Now.

"Please! Sir!"

His eyes hooded. "Please. Sir. What, Jen?"

I bit down on my lower lip. I put on my best sex-crazed whimpering voice. All the stops out. Go for broke.

"Please, sir! Please... I want to come. Please let me come." I threw in an extra little pleading cry at the end. Two could play at this game.

"Oh! So now you can use your words!" His eyes flared before slowly narrowing, head shaking in a mockery of concern. He gave me a taunting chuckle, hands spread wide on the edge of the bed as he leaned down over me. "Whatever am I going to do with you, Jen?"

I made little heaving motions with my chest. I mewled. I made grasping motions with my fingers towards his head.

"Please, sir. Please make me come. It felt so good. I swear I'll be a good girl. I promise!"

Steve smiled as the words spilled out over each other, suddenly catching my hands in his.

"Be still," he said softly.

I stopped moving, and he gently laid my hands down onto my stomach. I lifted my head up so I could look into his eyes, and the grin I saw staring back up at me was wicked with triumph at what he'd done.

"Well... I suppose..." And with that he lowered himself back down between my legs, his mouth closing down on my clit.

Fuck. Steve had brought me right to the edge before he'd pulled away to tease me, and as he drew my nub between his teeth and rolled the tip of his tongue over it, my body responded with aching need. My back arched up, and I cried out, his tongue like putting live wires to my pussy. Jolts of electricity which shot through to spread out over nerves that soaked up every amp. I ached for this so fucking bad. I wanted this orgasm. Hungered for it. A need that strained more than just my body. It was a craving to be rewarded by Steve for my submission, shown with every movement of his mouth what a good girl I'd been. And he knew just how to do that, working at me with that glorious tongue of his. A man on a mission who drew wet patterns over slick, swollen flesh. Every suck of my heated sex into his mouth yanked a shudder out of me, pulling me along towards the precipice. Every nip of his sharp teeth into blood-engorged flesh jerked sounds out of me. Cries that rose in volume, stacking one atop another until they melded into a single sound that forced me bite down to keep it from becoming a scream.

The sheets became twisted flotsam as my hands thrashed at the bedcovers above my head, fingers twisting blindly to find whatever purchase they could in the fabric. I was tossed on waves that built higher and higher the closer I got to the shore of my impending orgasm. The one that Steve fucking Friess was building like a conductor to a crescendo. I rode the crest of each one, falling down the face until drawn back up on the next, rising, rising, rising further each time until I slipped over the edge to the next. Blood thrummed through me until it roiled deep through my veins, pounding in my ears. Steve moved with me, trying to lead in this tango we were dancing. He pulled me along, timing the movement of his tongue to the reactions of my body. Dipping deep one moment, the next pushing down with hands against my thighs, pinning me in place with a strength that no amount of struggling could overcome. And I tried. I shoved against the restraint. My body demanding reaction to the carnal energy that pulsed through me.

When I realized that resistance was pointless, submission became the only option. My sweat-slick thighs struggled weakly against his still-clothed body, a shivering counterpoint to the granite that was him. The crests were coming faster, building higher each time, piling one on top of the other. And then there were no more gaps, only a final summit which kept going up, up, up towards a peak where I knew what awaited me. When I reached it, I knew my body would finally relent, and I would fall. Collapse. Slip down to a place I would not come back up from. To become placid compliance to the unstoppable force he was. I wanted that now, needed it as he pushed me further up that face.

Sensations pulsated through me, my pussy contracting to the rhythm of his tongue. He slowed, and the gentling of his movement was an ache. One I thought for a millisecond might drop me once again over a crest downwards. I was wrong. Steve's tongue plunged into me before I could draw another breath. And with that my body spun out of control. Blinding bright whiteness burst at the back of my eyes as I slammed them shut. The surge of contractions became jerky convulsions as my orgasm shattered me. My fingers splayed out against the sweat-soaked bedding above me before clenching back onto themselves. Nails dug savage divots into my palms as I dissolved into a million pieces of pleasure. I fell down that final face. Down at the same time my back arched, hips rising up to meet that tongue one final time. I dove into the pool of decadence at the base of that wave, plunged into it and came up only when a breath drew out a ragged gasp I could not contain. I lay there floating in that warm blissful sensation as the pulses of my orgasm faded, the gasp becoming a moan that slipped into a whimper.

I lazed with my eyes closed, my mind drifting and refusing to take notice of the outside world. My chest was still heaving in the aftermath of coming before it finally calmed, my breathing easing back to normal. Steve gently caressed me with his tongue, peppering my inner thighs with kisses, an occasional light nip to keep me awake and on my toes. For every touch of his lips to my skin I gave back a moan, a purr when his breath whispered across my labia, a gasp to signal approval of each nip. I sprawled there in ecstasy until I felt Steve come up from the foot of the bed, strad-dling me, bringing me back to Earth as he looked down into my contented face.

"Hey there," he said softly.

"Mmm. Hello, sir."

I gazed up at him. Tousled hair, Boy Scout grin of satisfaction plastered over his face. I couldn't help but smile back. He just looked so damn good right now. Warmth radiated off him as his hands brushed gently over my languid body. His gorgeous eyes made a slow circuit as they grazed over my face, dipping down to catch the slow evening of my breath. His gaze drifted down to my breasts, my nipples tightening as I caught him doing so. I loved everything that he had just done, the teasing, the tormenting, all of it, and as his eyes moved back upwards the contentment in them made it apparent he had too.

"So," he said, cocking his head to one side. "I didn't hear bubblegum once. I'll take that as a sign of approval."

"Yes," I drew the word out, a giddy laugh bubbling up out of me. "Oh, yes. Very much approved." As I grinned up at him, he shifted, pressing his hips and abdomen into me. If I had any lingering concern as to whether he'd enjoyed what we'd just done, one very rigid part of him made it quite clear I was mistaken. I reached up and grabbed onto his shirt and pulled him down to me.

That is to say, I tried to pull him down. He held back, his eyes narrowing, the smile turning from one of satisfaction to smoldering need.

"I beg your pardon?" His voice was soft, yet forceful. Reminding me that despite this interlude, we hadn't completely fallen out of our roles just yet.

"Please... sir," I whispered. pursed my lips together, my eyes going wide as I stared up at him, pleading. A slight tremble made its way up from my toes to my fingers at both his look and tone.

He held himself up on extended arms, hands straddling me. His mouth curled upwards, tenderness that slipped up into eyes that glowed, affectionate once more. He gave a low chuckle. "Well, I'll give you a pass this time. You have been a good girl..." Then he was lowering himself and his lips were on mine, kissing me deeply.

His tongue slipped past my open lips to move with mine. A trace of a flavor I had almost forgotten followed him inside. A bite that was sharp, electrical, unpleasant and pleasant at the same time. It had been a long time since I'd tasted the tang of my sex, the—for me at least— prickly piquant kick that I'd long associated with the essence of it. Tasting myself on him became yet another tiny homecoming, a small marker on the path of my return back to who I truly was.

Steve and I lay there entwined. It was wonderful, so comforting and while not exactly aftercare, because God knew I was hoping there would be more before we got to that, it just felt so right. Eventually he leaned down and bit my lower lip, dragging it up as he pulled away. Teeth drew on the swollen flesh and I mewled until he suddenly let go. "Well," he said, staring down at me.

"I suppose I should be going..."

I froze.

What?

What the hell did he just say?

I was paralyzed. There was no way I could have heard that right. My eyes darted left and right in consternation, as if somehow I would see the correct words if I just looked in the right spot. And yet, there he was, still fully clothed, glancing away towards something before he turned back to stare at me. I looked into his eyes, searching for some sign of what he was thinking, and saw only a sober gaze staring back.

Fuck. Oh fuck, he's serious. He's getting ready to leave. No. No, God no, he can't do this. He can't leave now.

Alarm turned to panic as he pushed himself up off the bed, standing at the foot. I scrambled up, hands flailing for purchase on the crumpled sheets. I wriggled across the bed, fighting for leverage with wrists still bound. Finally, I managed to get myself up on my knees, staring at him in disbelief.

"What are you doing?" The words spilled out of me as I shoved my hands towards him, incredulous.

"I should be going. Let you get some sleep."

"I..." For a moment I couldn't find my words again.

What the fuck was he saying?

"I... I want you! I need you! You... you can't be serious?"

165

"Oh, God. I'm sorry, Jen! I... I, umm..." Steve made a vague motion with his hand, gesturing towards either his cock or his pocket. "I don't have, you know..."

"What—" For a moment I didn't know what he meant by that signal, and then it dawned on me. "You... you have to be kidding me?"

"Sorry." He lifted his shoulder in a half shrug of apology, hands spreading to his sides in a placating gesture. He gave a self-conscious, lopsided grin. "I really wasn't sure where this might be headed tonight, and to be honest, I didn't exactly come out for this job with the thought that I might run into the most amazing sub I've ever met, so, yeah..."

I must have looked completely out of sorts. Because I was. I was panicking and tumbling away from what had been such an incredible high, a flood of so many wonderful emotions, now falling away from me like leaves from a tree. I cried out in crestfallen dismay. This couldn't be happening. It just couldn't. I wanted Steve. I wanted him naked, on top of me, inside me. I absolutely loved what he had done for me, but it couldn't end like this. I needed to give back, to reciprocate. I needed to give to him what he had given to me, and now he was standing there saying he hadn't come prepared, and that he was simply going to go.

Goddammit! No. Wait, wait, wait. He'd gone down on me, right? I could do that. I could give him the best fucking blowjob he'd ever had. Okay, no condoms, that was some bullshit, but I could still salvage this. My thoughts were racing as I stared at him, eyes blinking as I scrambled to salvage what I could of this, unwilling to believe that this was how this night was going to end.

And then he smiled.

"Gotcha." He sighted down a finger pointed directly at me as his mouth curved into a broad grin. There was a gleam in his eyes as he stood there looking pleased as fucking punch with himself for what he'd just done.

"You..." I could barely choke the word out, my throat having tightened in despair. It trickled past lips that quivered, barely a whisper.

"Ooo... look at you. All squirmy and worked up into a lather." He began unbuttoning his shirt, fingers moving down the front slowly, that damned shit-eating grin still splitting his face.

"Oh, God, you sonofa... You said, and then I thought..." The words spilled out of me, tripping over each other until the syllables became an almost unintelligible jumble. I trailed off in frustration. I wanted to tell him he was an asshole for teasing me like that, but honestly, I didn't feel it deep down. Instead I sat and watched as he undressed, stomach churning with both relief and anger as I stewed, teeth setting slowly on edge in time with the methodical movement of his fingers continuing their work. The bastard. He'd played me, and now he just stood there peeling himself out of his shirt, grinning like the Cheshire Cat.

"Uh huh." Steve undid the last of the buttons, pulled the shirt from his body, and tossed it to the floor. Then he was back on the bed, facing me, that smile suddenly less humorous, and more smoldering. "You thought. What did we talk about earlier, Jen? Trust." He caught my chin, tilting my head and capturing my eyes with his. "You really thought that tonight, of all nights, I wouldn't have come prepared?"

I bit down on my lip. I was conflicted in how I wanted to respond. To tell him he was a fucking jerk for playing me like that, teasing me over something he obviously knew was important to me. Or to thank him. Thank him for both being prepared *and* for teasing me, because there was a part of me that recognized that I enjoyed the frustration of the near frenzy he'd put my nerves into. A part of me that wanted to praise him for the rollercoaster thrill of the rise and fall of those feelings. Emotions that rode to the top and then dived over the edge, plummeting downwards with stomach fluttering, only to be carried up on that sadistic grin of his, buoyant on the promise of what lay ahead. He was playing not only with my body but with my mind, and I loved every part of it. My eyes grazed over the hard planes of his now naked chest, taking in the symmetry of his form. Just seeing him revealed to me, any anger and frustration I'd had moments ago began to melt away.

"Sorry, sir," I mumbled. I followed my natural inclination to look down, but Steve stopped me, trapping my chin between thumb and forefinger as his eyes focused on mine. He may have halted my face from tipping downwards, but my eyes slipped away nonetheless, all contrition now. He gave a low growl, and then his hand tightened on me.

"Look at me."

I snapped my eyes up to his, obedient.

"What do you want, Jen?"

"You, sir."

"What do you want me to do?"

"Fuck me. I want you to fuck me, sir." I pleaded with my eyes first and then my words, "Please."

He smiled, fingers letting go of my chin with a small shake. He slipped off the bed, his abs flexing as he shifted upright. His belt was already off from earlier, and though he moved enticingly slow, it was not long before his pants were pooled onto the floor, followed soon after by his briefs.

Oh yes. Yes. This was where I wanted to be. This is what I wanted.

Steve's cock was beautiful. It was full, thick, gorgeous, and as it stood pushing up and away from his abdomen I let out a murmur of appreciation. My response clearly pleased him, a cocky, satisfied grin splitting his face. He had every right to be proud. His shaft twitched as my eyes scanned it, veined length bobbing from plumped scrotum to the head that glistened with a slight sheen of precum. His grin grew wider as the tip of my tongue wet my lips. He fetched his pants up off the floor and took out his wallet. He fished several foil packets out, and the fact that there was more than one left me giddy with what that implied. He climbed up onto the bed then, sliding past me, placing the wallet and the condoms onto the nightstand. Then he was wrapping an arm around my waist, and with a squeak of surprise, I found myself being flipped onto my back.

"Hello, there." Steve straddled me, grinning mischievously down at me.

"Hey." I stared back up at him, and though a part of me wanted to put on a sultry, submissive gaze in return, all I could do was smile, just a glow of warmth and contentment flowing through me. I reached to caress his gorgeous face, but before my fingers could make it he caught up my bound wrists, bringing my hands up to kiss them. At the brush of his smooth lips against my sensitive skin, the slight scratch of his stubble brushing my knuckles, there was no stopping the soft moan that escaped me.

He broke the kiss, twisting my wrists until he was able to give a sharp nip to the pad of one palm. Then he was staring down at me, pinned beneath him, his cock pressing firmly into my thigh.

That hot, engorged length of flesh pressing into me was an inescapable presence I yearned to take in hand. To circle it with my fingers, draw up the extent of him until I could run my thumb across the tip, and then tease back down the length until I could cradle the balls I could feel lightly rubbing against me as I squirmed. Even if I had wanted to be still, everything about what he'd done in the last five minutes would have made it damn near impossible. He had wound me up, played me like a concert pianist, and I was in tune with all of it, eager only for what was coming next. There was no part of what he'd done that I didn't find fantastic, including the teasing, having me riding the edge of uncertainty, and the fact that all of it was driving me completely out of control.

"So, Jen. I think it's pretty clear what I'd like to do right now. And you've been a good girl, and asked so nicely for me to fuck you, so..." He grinned down at me, lowering his head until his mouth was level with my ear. "Is that what you'd like right now? Would you like to fuck?" His voice was silk, soft, smooth. Velvet wrapped steel.

"Yes. Please." I tried to match his tone, but the words tumbled out on top of each other, shivery whimpers thick with desire.

"You are so fucking perfect." He moved up, reaching for one of those foil packets, followed by the crisp sound of the cover tearing. There was the crinkle of the wrapper as it fell away, followed by a whisper of latex over flesh as he slipped the condom over his shaft. He smiled as he caught my eyes drifting from his cock to his face, and then they narrowed as he dug his fingers into my hips, leveraging my body across the jumble of sheets to position himself once again between my legs.

I whimpered as those nails bit into my skin. I squirmed, bringing my legs up and hooking them around him. He moved to nest in tighter between my thighs, the remaining wetness from my climax sticky against his skin. He shifted, pushed forward, the tip of his erection coming to rest against me.

Steve slid inside me. Entered me with no hesitancy, none of that first-time awkwardness. It was as if he was flowing into me, filling me as if he had been there before. Belonged there. I lay back, my hips pushing up to meet him, gasping. It felt so good, so very good. He had called me perfect moments before, and now I was determined to return that sentiment to him. I did not use words, however. I let him know in the cry I released as he bottomed out inside me, pinning me with his weight to the bed. I made him feel it in my legs wrapping around him, drawing him in tightly. My wrists were still bound, but I shifted my arms above my head, clutching at the twisted covers. Steve's shaft began a steady glide in and out of me, hard flesh sliding against slippery warmth. The head of his cock pushed deep into me, my body welcoming it as he picked up a steady rhythm that I matched. His gaze as he stared down at me was one of pure, raw lust. His eyes danced to every twitch my body made. When they focused on my face at the torrent of whimpers and cries I let out, he showed me he recognized how much I wanted this. Needed it. His thrusts picked up speed, driving into me deeper. The tension of his straining muscles signaled his coming release. One I so desperately wanted to see as I pulled it from him. My hands ached to grip him, to rake long red lines down his back. Wrists still bound, they simply thrashed against the bed. His jaw flexed with effort, a grunt for every deep thrust he made. His cock spread me open. Filled me until my pussy was swollen and slick, walls gripping at his length. I was too focused on Steve for another orgasm. Too centered on giving to him what he had given to me. His strokes increased in speed, building towards the inevitable.

He pistoned into me hard, thighs slamming into mine. The sound of our bodies coming together was sharp, a noise similar to his hand on my ass earlier. He drove me into the bed as his thrusts became forceful but erratic. His cock swelled inside me to the point where I knew he would soon explode. His back arched as his hips hammered down against me. My hips pushed up to meet him, forcing our bodies tight to one another. He gave a deep grunt between clenched teeth as I felt him kick inside me. There was a second pulse, then a third. His hips plunged forward to each one. His grunt gave way to a groan that drew out to the final pulses of his climax. Excitement flushed my skin, and I cried out with pleasure at the feel of him coming. My voice mixed with the rumbles that came from deep in his chest. He felt so good, so wonderful, so amazing in this moment. Steve's body came to rest above me, hips still pressing down, both of us sheened in sweat. The pulsing of his cock inside me subsided, each throb expanding against my walls less and less until it stilled altogether. He did not pull out but remained joined with me, cooling skin against mine, his chest falling back into a steady rhythm as he regained control of his breathing. He stared down at me, and his expression shifted from one of fierce concentration to gentle adoration, the corners of his eyes crinkling to accent the contented smile that spread across his face. His fingers moved to my cheek, gently stroking me.

"Good," he asked softly, tracing the line of my jaw.

"Mmm. Yes, sir. Good. Very, very good."

"I'm losing my touch."

"Hmm?" I looked up, brow furrowing into creased folds between eyes that narrowed with confusion.

"If I was on top of my game, you'd have come a second time. I've spent too much time skiing and working lately. Not enough time watching porn or in the bathroom, practicing..."

At first I couldn't speak, and then looking up into his twinkling eyes, I was suddenly laughing.

"Oh my God, Steve—" I bit down on my lower lip, cutting myself off.

"Well, it's true!" He chuckled as he stared at me, eyes bright, and then his shoulders hitched up in a shrug. "Well, that, and you are so fucking beautiful, and gorgeous, and sexy that there was no way I could have held out any longer."

"Thank you, si—Steve." I bit down on my lip hard and felt tears at the back of my eyes. The cocktail of all the emotions swirling around inside me from what we had just done, this beautiful, simple joyous act bubbled up to the surface at his praise. It was such a simple thing, so easily given between two people who were like-minded, and yet, in my current state, it meant so much more than I could articulate with words.

I reached my hands up to him, but still bound, I realized that I couldn't do what I wanted to at that moment—to wrap my arms around him, pull him to me, and kiss him hard. To tell him with words and actions how extraordinary all this was to me. Instead, I lay there with them pushed to his chest, silent, smiling, my lip quivering. He stared down at me, still firmly planted between my legs. He leaned back, took my wrists in his hands and slowly undid the tie which had held them bound. When he finished, he let it fall, gathering up my hands in his, looking down at me.

"You are incredible."

It had been a long time since I had felt that way as a submissive. The shiver that raced up my spine was because Steve had made it easy to feel incredible.

And in that moment, I did.

TWELVE

"Stop. But... don't."

We both lay draped across the tangled sheets of the bed, our bodies nestled into each other as skin cooled in the wake of passion. My fingers intertwined with his, each of us moving to play in counterpart to the other, basking in the afterglow of what had just happened.

Our movements were gentle, languorous. A shift to adjust a hip that pressed to a thigh, my toes running lightly from his ankle up his calf, his leg pressing down against mine, capturing it beneath muscles strong enough to make movement impossible. Drying sweat both chilled and revived, and soon both of us settled into the other as we lay still, simply soaking in the serenity that passed between us. My arms wrapped around him, draping across his broad back. Steve leaned down, drew close until his lips were brushing against my ear.

"Are you sore?"

"A little." I tried to muster enough energy into my smile to make it bright. "It feels so good, though."

He gave a satisfied chuckle, mouth curving. "Did I mention how incredible you are?"

"You may have..."

He nipped at my ear, trailing kisses along my cheek until his mouth closed over mine, tongues slipping past warm lips, tips engaged in an intricate dance of sensuality. I lost track of time until he pulled away, tracing a pattern of soft bites against my throat and neck. I moaned in frustration as he lifted himself up, wanting his comforting presence back the moment it was gone. The mattress shifted as he pushed against it to stand, the bed moving with a slight undulation as his weight came away. He reached for me with one hand, insistent. "Come on."

I let him pull me up until my feet found purchase on the carpet. He held me in his arms, and I leaned into his chest. It felt good, and I hung there, body limp, still working to come back completely from the puddle I had been a few minutes ago. I rolled my shoulders, working out muscles tense from everything that had taken place. There was a part of me that resisted, wanted nothing more than to fall back onto the bed, pulling Steve with me. I didn't, though, and after a moment he shifted, gently turning me around as I groaned in annoyance.

With mild pressure he nudged me forward, and we padded away from the bed, moving towards the bathroom. Steve steered me in front of him and I could feel his eyes on me, confirmed by a soft growl as he followed behind. There was no doubt he was quite pleased with his handiwork, enjoying the display on my backside. We came to the bathroom door and his fingers dug into my skin, pulling me to a halt.

"You first. Just let me know when you're finished." Before he let go, he drew me tight to his chest, lacing the fingers of one hand with mine while the other traced a slow path up from my thigh. The fingertips brushed along my skin, leaving goosebumps in their wake. When his hand reached my shoulder he stopped, holding me as he placed a kiss to the back of my head.

"Thank you, sir." I waited until his hand released me, and then I stepped inside the bathroom, closing the door. I walked towards the toilet, but before I reached it, I caught myself in the mirror. I stopped, turning to look back over my shoulder at my image. I could see what had made Steve growl. His belt had left a series of red bands across my ass and thighs, some of which were already fading to a muted pink glow. A pattern of crosshatched lines still imprinted on my flesh that hadn't disappeared completely, marks probably not as red as they'd originally been, but which still indicated every inch of where he'd punished me. I smiled at my reflection. Damn. Looking at them I could still feel the tingling remains of the act which had left them there. I hugged myself, shoulders tight as a shiver ran down the length of my back. It was an incredible feeling. To stand and bask in the memory of what Steve had done. I stared a moment longer, wondering if they would still remain in five days when I headed home. Doubtful, and I didn't dwell on it any further, shoving the thought away. It didn't matter. Nothing mattered right now except for how wonderful this felt, and I'd be damned if I was going to let anything break this spell.

When I was finished using the bathroom, I took one last glance at myself and then crossed to the door. Opening it up to step out, I jumped as I found Steve there on the other side, waiting with arms crossed. A tremble of *uh oh* fluttered up from my stomach.

"And where do you think you're going," he asked in a rumbling growl, the smile pulling at his lips the only thing betraying I hadn't done something wrong. He took a step towards me as I stood frozen, his eyes narrowing as his hands came up to grip me by the shoulders. He gently pushed me back into the room, gazing down at me as I stumbled, my feet tangling up with each other as he moved me in reverse. Steve kept me upright but did not stop his march forwards.

"I thought you might need to..." I stammered, my feet trying to sort themselves out as he continued to frog-march me backwards.

"I'm good." His grin was cocky, dimpled cheeks accentuating the twinkle in those gorgeous eyes.

My gaze slipped down surreptitiously, and I saw the condom was gone. Taken off and disposed of somewhere while I had been admiring myself in the bathroom. That beautiful cock that had earlier jutted upwards, bobbing proudly to get inside me now hung relaxed against his thigh. I wanted to reach for it, to take it in my hand and run my fingers along its silky length, to see if it still radiated the heat I'd felt when it was sheathed inside me. My fingers flicked at the thought but did nothing more. As he continued to advance towards me, I retreated, backing into the room. I twisted my head, glancing to make sure I wasn't going to run into anything, and then Steve was right up against me. Before I could react, he had arms wrapped around my waist, hands cupping the cheeks of my ass to lift me. I slid along his chest as I rose, my slick skin running over the ridges of his abs, his chest hair tickling my nipples, making them grow taut at the sensation. I squealed as he held me tight, wriggling in his grasp as he advanced a few steps until my butt hit the hard edge of the bathroom counter. The cool lip of granite creased across my buttocks as his fingers kneaded soft flesh in a way that had absolutely nothing to do with keeping me in check or held in place. I hissed when those fingertips clenched tighter and he gave a final extra boost, lifting me over the edge and depositing me on the countertop.

"Steve!" I yelped, mouth opening into an 'O' as my ass met the chilly granite. I tried to wiggle off the counter, but he wouldn't allow it, pressing his hands down to pin me in place.

"Do I have to order you to be still again?" His voice was a commanding growl, a teasing, warning rumble.

"But the counter... its...cold!" A part of me wanted to do the exact opposite of what he warned. Slip off to the floor and back onto my feet. The implication in his tone was enough to override the thought of not complying, though I did scooch ever so slightly towards the edge as Steve stood there.

He gave me a stern look. "Jen, I'd think twice before disobeying me. If you think you're sore now..."

I whimpered with frustration, but immediately stopped. It was cold up here, and now my butt had not only the lingering sting from my belting, but the bite of cold from the granite. However, I obeyed, remaining perched there while he started the shower. He adjusted the head, fiddled with the temperature until he was satisfied. Steam was starting to fill the room when he turned back to me. He stalked the few paces between us, eyes narrowing in a look that was hungry, predatory, fierce with concentration on his prey. Me. A shudder pushed through me under that gaze, recognizing it as the same one he'd used to track me last night. Comprehension for what lay behind those smoldering eyes pulsed through me. That right here, in this moment, I belonged to him. Steve didn't just want to be with me, he wanted to possess me. A powerful, almost animalistic desire made clear by his actions. He would have me, because my body was his. His possession, and his alone. Not that any part of that bothered me in the least. It felt so good, so natural, to feel this way again.

As he drew close, he grasped my legs and spread them apart. I responded, wrapping them around him, pulling in tight. He cupped my breasts, fingers tensing into my flesh, thumbs moving up to brush over my nipples. I closed my eyes, drawing in a deep, calming breath. Steve leaned down, and his mouth closed over mine. As we kissed, our tongues crashed together as they had before, and the room slipped away. Steam had made the air thick by the time he pulled back.

"Hold tight." He said it softly, waiting as my arms came up and around him. Lifting me again, he turned and marched us towards the shower. As he came up to the door, he nudged it open with his foot until it was wide enough he could carry me inside. There he let me down gently until I stood wrapped in his arms, the water cascading in a sensuous staccato across my back. I leaned against the expanse of his chest, luxuriating in the warmth of it and the bliss of the water that flowed over me.

We moved with each other as we showered, and the sheer intimacy of the act was incredible. Hands slick with soap caressed a body, mine to his and his to mine. Light touches became less gentle in his hands, teasing wet skin with fingers that gripped, pinched, and held me on the cusp until I gave him what he desired. The sound of my voice filled with gratification. One moment his hands were at my hips, gently maneuvering me about the stall until the pressure of his hip against mine shifted me to face him. Then in the next it was fingers digging into me, slamming my back against the tile, his teeth raking the flesh at my neck. He made sure I knew by his every action what he wanted, with half-formed words that were more growls than coherent speech. To each I submitted, bending to his will, my fingers spread open against cool tile that warmed to the touch as he took what was his.

I loved every fucking second of it.

We didn't make love again because that's not what this was. It wasn't what either of us wanted. This was affection and tenderness, care in a way that was unique and yet oh-so-familiar. There wasn't a single moment while we bathed where Steve wasn't touching me, where we lost contact with each other, and that made what we were doing even more eloquent. This was aftercare, and the things Steve did—every touch, every pass of his hands over my skin, no matter whether tender or wild—I soaked up with greed. I gave into it, let myself go and offered myself up without reservation because it was just so damn good. When I gave back, I gave with everything, but in my mind it didn't seem enough. It could never match the way Steve made me feel. He'd melted me into a puddle, and without regret I took more than I gave, selfish, and feeling no shame.

Once we were done, he pulled me from the shower and wrapped me in one of the hotel towels. I stood facing the mirror, watching as he pulled the shower door closed behind him, grabbing his own towel. As he stood there, drying himself, I took my first long look at the scars he wore. There were at least four that I could count. One a narrow pale stroke that began just below the center of his chest, rising and falling over his abs until it wrapped around to his back where it faded, trailing off to disappear into his skin. It was on his back where most of them lay. As he turned, I could see them clearly. Three long, thin lines slashing at an angle like lash marks.

They cut rows into his muscles, faint puckering at the edges that only smoothed when they disappeared completely. Two of them crossed over his spine, jogging slightly where they wove through the line of vertebra. At the end of one there was a thicker knot of scar tissue that pushed out from the muscle, a lump of flesh that stood away from the otherwise smooth planes of his body. These were the remains of being in the wrong place at the wrong time I was staring at, and I bit down on my lower lip as everything he'd spoke of at dinner came flooding back. My eyes traced the paths they created across his body a second time, caught up in a swirl of emotions for what they represented. Seconds had passed before I realized he'd stopped moving, gone still. My gaze turned slowly up towards his. The face that stared back at me was sober, emotionless.

"Sorry," I said softly, swallowing embarrassment as I looked away, face burning.

"Why?" He stepped in close to me, one hand landing on my hip while the other brushed against my cheek, turning my face back towards his. "Do they bother you?"

"No!" The word tumbled out, a defensive reaction to having been caught. My hand came halfway up towards his, and then stopped, hovering. My throat tightened in frustration, voice turning querulous. "No! It's just... I shouldn't have stared."

"You don't need to apologize." He moved up close to me and took my hand in his. He used his other to lift my chin up until I was looking into his eyes. "I told you what happened in Iraq. These," he dipped his chin downwards, "are the remains of that day. Scars and memories, Jen. Those are what I have to remind me why I am no longer a Marine." He took the hand he held in his and placed it on the scar on his chest, pressing my fingers to it.

"I'm not ashamed of them. I hate them, make no mistake. They're a reminder every day of what was taken from me. But I earned these the hard way, so there's a part of me that's proud of them too." He stared down into my eyes, face somber. "Does that make sense?"

My lip quivered as I stood there in silence. It was such an intimate thing for him to do, to say, to share. I ran a fingertip along a portion of the scar, feeling the unnatural smoothness of it, slick and shiny compared to the nearby skin. When I came to the end, my hand stopped, and I spread my fingers, pressing into him tenderly.

"A little."

He smiled at me, and it held a trace of sadness in it, though it was clear from the tightness of his jaw, the forced set of his mouth that he was trying not to let it show. My fingers slipped from the scar, and as my arm fell to my side those strong, solid arms of his came up around me, pulling me in a tight, protective embrace. I leaned against his chest, eyes closed as my cheek pressed to his skin. His fine hairs tickled me lightly as I flattened myself to him. I soaked up the comforting strength that being contained within the cage of his arms enveloped me in, willing myself not to cry. I pressed my eyes tight to keep tears trapped, mouth and nose scrunched. I couldn't let him see me break down, not after everything he'd given me. This night had been too wonderful, too incredible for me to suddenly let sadness overtake it. If I needed to cry over what Steve had sacrificed, I would do it later. Quietly and in private where my grief wouldn't taint what we had shared. I sucked in a breath, calming myself as his hand ran up and down the length of my back, soothing both skin and nerves. We stood there holding each other, unmoving, connected in a way that didn't require words. He relaxed in my arms, pulling away a moment later to take my hand in his once again.

"Come on. Bed."

I followed him out of the bathroom. As he moved ahead of me towards the bed, I indulged myself. I admired the firmness of his ass as it shifted with every step, the way his back muscles rippled in counterpart to those two cheeks I had a sudden desire to dig my fingers into. I knew if I did that what it would earn me, and that thought did less to stop me than urge me to follow through with my desire. Before I could, however, we were at the bed. He guided me with his hand, and I crawled up onto it, knees sinking once again into the tangled sheets strewn across the mattress. I watched as he let the towel slip from his body. It slid off hips that ended where the 'V' of his upper body tapered in, sculpted lines at either side that had my teeth biting into my lower lip as it fell. I soaked in his gorgeousness, watched as that tight ass became two smooth surfaces that I could have spent an hour running my fingers over if I thought he'd let me. The muscles of his legs made sinuous outlines as he bent and rose, twisting as he tidied up our clothes from the floor. He gathered them, then draped them over the nearby chairs. Finally finished, he stretched, fingers linked as he brought bulging arms up and behind his head. His abdomen became a plane of ridges, skin pulled taut over the rippled muscles beneath it. Climbing up onto the bed, he gathered me up into his arms, pulling me into his chest. I snuggled into the warmth of him, drew the scent of soap and freshly washed male into my nose. I fitted my head to his shoulder, tucked in under his chin. Pressing myself tight to him, I let my eyes close, reveling in the sensations as I melded to his body, drawing in the heat that radiated off him. The fingers of one hand began to stroke my hair while the other lightly caressed my arm and shoulder.

We lay in silence for a while. Two people cocooned in pleasure, quiet breathing and the faint whisper of fingertips brushing against skin the only sound in the room. My head rose and fell to the movement of his chest, and his tender touches soothed me, lulling me from the state of excitement that had run through me throughout this evening. My breathing slowed, body relaxing and drifting into a half-conscious state of drowsiness that made my eyelids too heavy to keep open. I was right on the edge, hovering at the very precipice of sleep when he shifted slightly beneath me, clearing his throat.

"Jen."

"Hmm?" I didn't move, enveloped in the nest made of him and the bedcovers.

"I don't do this. I want you to know that. I need you to know that."

I froze, confusion at first quick to morph into an insidious worm of anxiety that wound through me, dragging me out of the serenity I'd wrapped myself in. Steve's body stiffened to my response, both of us now fully awake, bodies tensing to each other. Three simple sentences and all thoughts of slumber were chased away. I pulled back, my face a mask to hide the trepidation that was growing inside me. Steve eased up onto an elbow to stare down, his mouth a thin line, gaze impenetrable to whatever he was about to spring on me.

"You don't do... what?" I asked softly.

"This." His hand pulled away from my hair, hovering to make a vague wave as if he could weave the answer to my question from the air around us. "I don't go after, you know, seduce, or sleep with..." His voice trailed off with a frustrated growl. He ran a hand brusquely across his scalp, fingers clenching at the back of his head. "God, I am doing a shitty job of this. I don't do one-night stands. I... I'm just not like that."

I started to interrupt him, but before I could get a word out, his hand came down, gripping my shoulder.

"Sorry, wait. I need to finish. I'm not saying that's you, or you're anything like that. God, please don't think that. And I'm not trying to play some sort of fucked up head game here. But... this has been really fucking incredible tonight, and I need you to know that. To know how special this has been. I need you to know that this is not something that just happens all the time with me. To be honest, it's *never* happened before." He sighed, and the pressure of his hand on my shoulder relaxed, the fingers spreading against my skin. "I just needed you to hear that. I hope to fuck it makes sense."

I'd tensed up the minute he'd started, and now as it began to sink in, my body went rigid. So many conflicting emotions came bubbling up as I played his words back in my head. A part of me wanted to feel resentment at the arrogance of him thinking he had seduced me. As if I'd had no part in it, hadn't understood was happening between us from the moment he took my hand in his on the show floor. Steve was a Dom, pure and simple. He probably *did* feel that way, at least at some level. Thinking he'd been the one in total control of the situation all this time, and I had simply fallen into it. It was part of the Dom mentality, little different from my own submissive nature. That attitude was something I wanted, and I'd sure as hell got it in spades. And though some of the words stung, there were more that didn't. The ones that made up the part of his statement which thrilled me. That this evening was special for him. That sentiment was one I felt. I felt it to my core. Because this night had been the same for me. Special. Absolutely, completely, incredibly special. I chose to focus on that. That this night was something more than two random people falling into bed for a quick fuck.

"I'm a big girl, Steve. I knew exactly what this was." I turned my head towards him. I could see in his look he was gauging me, watching to see how I was going to react. "I wanted this from the moment you took my hand at that table. I don't sleep around, if that's what you're worried about."

He started to protest, but I pressed on.

"And I'm not saying that's what you were suggesting, but I need *you* to understand something. I wanted tonight. I wanted what we did as much, if not more, than you. I *needed* this, Steve. For my own reasons." I paused, pursing my lips together to let emotions cool. "So, yes, I understand what you're saying. I'm no different. I don't do this either." I stopped, mustering every bit of sincerity I could draw on. I pushed all of it into my smile, tried with everything I could to make that emotion show. "But I can tell you this. I'm so fucking glad I did."

His face slowly changed. The concern faded, his mouth turning from a thin line to curl into a smile of simple pleasure. His fingers curved to cup my cheek. At his touch, my eyes closed, and I leaned into his hand, my breath slipping away on the drawn-out breath of a sigh.

He caressed a path to touch the lobe of my ear before he bent to kiss me. It wasn't a passionate kiss. It didn't need to be. It was a simple, tender gesture, our lips meeting in a soft embrace. And yet it was the most intimate one we'd shared all evening.

"Okay," he said quietly after pulling away to look into my eyes. Again, his hand came up to stroke my cheek, thumb brushing across my chin. "Thank you."

I pressed my hand to his, palm laid over his in a silent appeal for him to hold me for a moment longer. "No, Steve. Thank you."

He smiled, doing as I wished until he tenderly pulled away. He shifted then, body slipping alongside me as he rolled to his side, the silky feeling of his skin against mine a soothing reassurance. He gathered up the bedcovers and tugged them around until he had them pulled over us. He slipped his hand under the covers, gliding up my thigh and over my hipbone until he positioned me where he wanted.

My butt wriggled into place, spooning against him. The feel of his cock nestling against my ass was more comforting than arousing, a good indication to me just how satiated I was.

"I've got about five hours before I have to get up so I can head back to my hotel and get ready for work. Until then I'd like to stay here and sleep with you. You good with that?"

"I'd like to see you try and get away." I chuckled, pressing back against him and snuggling in tight. I clamped my hand over the one he had at my hip, defying him to try and move. I knew what I was doing, and my butt went taut in expectation of how he might respond.

He tensed, and then the hand underneath mine yanked out, pulling away from me. I squirmed in delicious anticipation of what might come next. We remained motionless until Steve relented, his hand moving back to rest on top of mine.

"Hmph. You, Ms. Boyd, are treading on very dangerous ground. I've half a mind to give you another taste of what I did earlier." He leaned in closer, lips skimming against the skin of my ear. "But there's always tomorrow night for that, isn't there?"

A shiver ran down the length of my spine. There was no way

Steve could have missed it. His chuckle confirmed he hadn't, followed with a kiss to the back of my head.

We lay together in peaceful silence, the only sound that of our slowing breathing. Sleep pulled at my eyelids, and even when Steve made a slight adjustment of his hand, letting it drift down over my stomach until he had me wrapped in an embrace, I barely noticed it, drifting closer and closer towards slumber. His hand around me was a calming presence, and it wasn't long before my body finally gave in. This day had been one for the books. A plethora of emotions that pushed and pulled me in all directions. First an epiphany of epic proportions, followed up with incredible sex of the kind that I hadn't experienced in a long time. All ending on a wonderful high note that my body left me little choice but to respond to. It called for me to sleep. Demanded it. Burrowing into Steve, his arm cocooning me, I gave over to that call and drifted away.

THIRTEEN

Sleep did not give me up easily, or without a fight.

Despite the effort, I awoke to the bed shifting, mattress dipping and then settling back into place from movement somewhere. Cool air flooded underneath the covers for a moment before they fell back into place, warmth returning to blanket me. I blinked away slumber, opening my eyes to a room still dark except for the city lights coming through the window casting a faint glow across the walls.

"Hey gorgeous." Steve's voice was soft as he leaned over, lips gently grazing my forehead.

"What time is it?" I murmured, still groggy. Shifting under the covers, I looked up at him. His shirt was on, unbuttoned, and I watched as he did it up.

"5 am. I need to get back to my room and get into work clothes. I have to be on the floor at seven."

Stretching, I extended my legs until muscles ached at the strain. Shifting back, I slid one foot out until my toes found purchase on his leg and pressed against it. I wriggled them against the smooth fabric of his pants, feeling the muscle underneath. Pushing at the bedding to get out from under them, I tried to suppress the yawn that emerged from me despite my effort. "I should get up, too..."

Steve frowned, drawing the sheets back up over me. "You don't have to. Sleep. We'll get things rolling and you can show up when you're ready."

I blinked, tilting my head to give him a sidelong look. "I'll be there on time. I just need to get moving. Go exercise, take a shower and then get myself dressed."

Steve stared back at me, wry amusement fighting the serious look he was trying to maintain. "I'm both offended and delighted by that statement."

"Umm, why?" I squinted in confusion as his grin grew wider.

"I'd have thought," he said, leaning down until his forehead nearly touched mine. "That I gave you more than enough exercise last night." His grin became wicked, matched by the low growl of his voice. "Obviously I was wrong. You're a hell of a lot stronger than I gave you credit for. Something I think I'll need to put to the test next time."

I choked out a gasp as his arm wrapped around my back, pulling me to him. The kiss he crushed to my lips was fierce, promising nothing gentle. Once he let me go I caught my breath, gulping in air to slow my heart racing in response to what that comment implied. Once I had myself back in control, I plastered a devil-may-care grin across my face.

"Army brat, remember? Best you don't forget it."

"Yes, ma'am!" He snapped off a half-assed parody of a salute, laughing as he did. Bending, he kissed me one more time before pulling off the bed, the mattress flexing as he moved away.

For my part I indulged myself, just lying there as he finished dressing. Jesus, he was gorgeous. Arousal made my pussy tighten at nothing more than watching him pulling his pants on, hand roughly cramming the hem of his dress shirt into the waistband, shoving the tie into a pocket. I was half-tempted to pull him back onto the bed and help me exercise in a different way than going to the hotel gym.

I didn't, however. Work before pleasure. I was certain Steve and I shared that in common, he a Marine, and myself from an Army family where that phrase had been an inescapable mantra. I suspected if I tried to lure him back to bed it would have ended in failure. Polite kindness to my attempt, gentle rebuff to my seduction, all ending right back at square one. For now, I consoled myself with not getting a more-than-decent morning fuck by watching him with contentment as he dressed.

"Okay, I've got to go." He sat on the edge of the bed and leaned over me. His fingers brushed my cheek. "I'll see you in a couple of hours, okay?"

"I'll be there," I said, smiling back. My hand came up to touch him, holding his fingers in place.

He nodded, leaving his hand clasped in mine as he looked down at me. Then his mouth was crushed against mine, a kiss that was twisting turbulent passion as we tried to consume each other. My hand moved in blind, jerky movements that bumped against his cheek, and then his neck until it found the back of his head, holding him in an unyielding embrace. I ached to keep his mouth captured to mine, the solid planes of his body pressed tight to me. There was an almost violence to the way we clung to each other, savage, erratic movements punctuated by low growls and keening moans. Finally, they eased, and as we slowed, the hunger seemed appeased for the time being. Regaining our breath, he held his forehead against mine and I pressed back to him, my hand still splayed at the back of his head. I released him when he pulled against my grip to move away. He gathered up his jacket, throwing it on carelessly as he moved to the door. I set my jaw to stop myself from begging selfishly for him to come back to bed and fuck me senseless.

"See you soon." His voice was soft as he paused, hand on the handle. For a second it seemed he might turn, come back to the bed on thoughts as greedy as mine. He didn't, though. He pulled the door open, stepped through, closing it quietly behind him.

I remained in bed for a while after Steve left, going over the past twenty-four hours in my head. So much had happened in that time, from my epiphany, to dinner, to waking up snuggled next to him.

And a conversation with Thomas that was *still* unresolved.

Yes. That. I found my clutch where I'd dropped it last night and pulled my phone out. Nothing. Not a message or a single text. *Goddammit, Thomas. What the fuck.* Sitting here, covers pulled up around my knees, my thoughts flitted from one thing to another with abandon. Behind them all my inner demon rattled its cage, clamoring for attention that I refused to give. Gnashing teeth, it tried to throw up a *'Thomas'* or a *'hypocrite'* wherever it could, but I refused to listen. I hugged my knees tight, and though I knew there was a lot of unfinished business I would need to address soon, I couldn't dwell on it now. Not with memories still as fresh in my mind as the ache of the stripes on my backside, or the still lingering scent of Steve in my head that pushed everything else aside.

Huddling in the bed, a half an hour passed in reflection before I forced myself to get up. Digging through the closet I pulled out the gym clothes I'd thrown in there yesterday. I tugged them on, slipped into socks, shoes, and grabbed my key card. Slipping out of the room, I was almost reluctant to leave, as if the moment I did what had taken place last night would disappear forever. It was a peculiar feeling, and it lingered with me as I walked through the silent, empty hallways, making my way to the hotel gym. It was empty at this hour, and I went about my routine in quiet solitude. My mind wouldn't focus on my workout, but was back in the room, on the bed, reliving everything Steve had done, my every reaction. It was both distracting and titillating at the same time. With every stretch of my muscles the remains of the marks on my ass and thighs tingled, reminding me of what had gone on. Successive memories that built on each other until a self-satisfied grin was plastered across my face. I was just fucking happy, and I did not attempt to hide it. I finished my workout alone, the space as silent as it had been when I first arrived. As I walked back to my room, the elevator and halls were empty, quiet in the early morning calm. I threw my gym clothes back in the closet, grabbed some underwear, and then headed into the bathroom. Steve had straightened up at some point, picked our towels up and put them away. I held his to my face. Breathing deep, eyes closed, I caught the faintest trace of his scent in the damp cloth.

-*Jesus Christ, Jen. What the hell is wrong with you? Knock it off. Okay, sure, it was great. Incredible. But let's be real here. You've got a few more nights with him at best, and then you're back home and that's the end of that. And let's not forget that you still have a shitload of things to deal with when you do get back there. Did you forget about that? So, put the fucking towel down, stop acting like some lovelorn teenager, enjoy what time you've got left, and get your head back in the game, m'kay?-*

Lowering the towel, I looked at myself in the mirror. Everything I was saying was true. It *had* been wonderful, and as I'd told Steve, something I'd needed very much. However, there was no denying that this was a transitory thing, and after this show was over, it would become a footnote to a brief period in my life. A time of correction. A small though wonderful part of a greater whole. It was a bittersweet thought as I carefully folded the towel, setting it back onto the counter.

I started the shower, then stepped inside. The water washed over me, but the feeling was light-years from what I'd felt with Steve. I closed my eyes, head tilted back, swallowing a lump in my throat that threatened to turn into tears. Hands clenched, I gritted my teeth until my jaw ached. I would not second-guess what had happened or taint what might lay ahead of me. I would just fucking enjoy this for what it was and then move on with my life. Letting the water become a salve, as the heat soaked in I gathered up my emotions and did my best to compartmentalize them so I could center my thoughts. What had happened between Steve and I was the beginning of a process. The first steps towards reclaiming who I truly was and putting an end to the lies I had perpetuated. All the yummy, sexy feelings, the stripes decorating my ass aside, everything that had happened boiled down to that concept.

Reclaiming who I was.

I'd had a come-to-Jesus meeting with myself and decided that I was moving forward with my life, not clinging to a flawed past. I wouldn't let my past change me into something I wasn't. Hand-wringing over what I'd done, focusing solely on those past decisions and mistakes I'd made wasn't pushing me in the right direction. I still had things I needed to take care of. However, from here on, I needed to focus on driving ahead. Not looking back and dragging the chain of my lies along with me.

Coming out of the shower, I dried myself off and slipped into my underwear. As I put my work clothes for the day on, I glanced over and caught sight of my phone where I'd tossed it earlier. Snatching it up from the table, I flicked the screen alive.

Still nothing. *Fuck.*

I glanced at the time. 6:45 a.m. Okay, be reasonable, Jen. That meant it was four in the morning back home. Which meant Thomas was still dead to the world.

Dead to the world.

Shit. That phrase sent a tremor of panic through me. What if the reason Thomas hadn't returned my calls or texts was because something had happened to him?

-Hadn't thought of that, had you...-

But... they said READ. That meant he'd read them.

-Well, someone had. Right?-

I clenched my jaw. Okay, okay, so it was too early to call Loren to ask her if she'd seen Thomas. To send her searching to see if something was wrong. As soon as was reasonable, that would be job number one. Guilt tugged at me again, an inescapable force dragging down my happiness. I hadn't officially ended it yet. Hadn't said the words aloud or dealt with the fallout. And if the reason for that turned out to be because Thomas had been...

Don't even think that. Just. Don't.

I fired off another text: *Are you okay? I need you to call me back. Please.*

I pushed all those thoughts away for the moment. Despite everything going on, I still had my job to do. It was still early enough that I could grab breakfast in the hotel restaurant, check on my e-mails while I ate, and be back at the hall with time to spare before the 8 a.m. start. Looking over to the bed, I couldn't help but let a smile creep back to my face. Sheets still twisted, rumpled, the images were suddenly of Steve kneeling over me, belt in hand, arm rising. Playing out like my own personal porno, the fantasy had me squirming, and I stood there indulging myself in it. My fingers were drifting across my thigh towards my sex when I shuddered, bringing myself out of my reverie.

-Oh, yeah, Jen, you are in rare form. Whatever. Better get it out of your system now, because once you hit that show floor you need to be all business. What happened in this room last night—might happen again tonight—has no place being dragged down into that booth. Time to get your game-face on.-

Okay, fine. Fine. I get it. But—damn!—it's nice to think about right now.

— ❀ —

At breakfast I sat and caught up on e-mails. One was a list of salespeople who would be checking in to the booth later this evening, including those from the new company. That worried me a bit. What if they wanted me to go out to dinner with them tonight? To get to know me. That was the last thing I wanted. If they tried to press me to join them, I was going to beg off. I had other plans, and they included a dinner-for-two of the room service kind. Assuming we even got around to eating.

It was 7:30 a.m. when I finished and stepped out of the lobby doors. In the morning sunlight the colors were bright, in sharp contrast to the deep shadows the light cast. As I moved along the sidewalk a river of business attire slipped by me, all flowing towards the office towers that surrounded us. Weaving through them, thoughts of last night continued to loop through my head, and a smile creased my face as I made my way to the convention center.

My cheerfulness had not abated as I came up to the service desk to check in. Tony was there, and as I approached he came up with a smile, giving me a quick hug.

"Hey there, Ms. Jen! You're looking happy this morning. Did you have a good night last night? Go out someplace fun?"

"I had a nice night, Tony." I gave him a nonchalant smile, confident Steve hadn't spoken to anyone about taking me out last night. My suspicions at dinner of how that would be perceived, especially by his boss, convinced me he wouldn't. Tony stood by, nodding as I continued. "Nothing fancy; just a nice dinner, then back to the room and bed."

"Well, there ain't nothing wrong with that. Sometimes those are the best nights, right?"

"Absolutely."

"So... listen, I gotta ask. Is Stevie taking good care of you? Mitch wanted me to make sure you were getting everything you needed, and that Stevie's got it under control."

I made sure the smile on my face didn't falter or change in the slightest. "Mr. Friess has been taking good care of me, I assure you."

"Well, good. He's kind of a new guy with the company and all, but I think he's good people, and the boys seem to get along well with him. We just want to make sure you're happy."

"I have absolutely no complaints so far, Tony. Feel free to pass that along to Mitch too."

"Alright! That's what I wanted to hear!" Tony nodded enthusiastically, moving back behind the service desk, taking a quick look at some paperwork. "I think most of the boys are already over in the booth, and I know Stevie's there, 'cause he and I already talked things over this morning. Your booth's looking in real good shape there, Ms. Jen. I don't see any reason why you guys are gonna be running late tonight."

"That's what I wanted to hear, Tony." I gave him a big grin, moving off from the desk towards the hall entrance.

"All right!" Tony gave me a quick salute as I started across the lobby, calling out as I walked away. "I'll come over a bit later and check to see how you guys are doing. You have a good morning, Ms. Jen!"

My shoes squeaked on the smooth marble tile flooring of the lobby as I crossed it and moved into the hall. Inside, there was already quite a bit of activity going on. Last minute exhibit arrivals filled the empty aisle spaces from yesterday, crates stacked and crowded together. As I wove my way towards the booth I was careful to avoid hitting or tripping over anything. They had cleared away some of our empty crates, and the crew was already moving about the exhibit when I got there. I scanned the immediate area, looking for Steve. He was nowhere in sight, and I moved to the set-up table, plopping my bag down. I took out my paperwork and set myself up for the day, glancing up occasionally to try catching a glimpse of him. Several minutes went by, and then Keith approached, his face wrapped in the same serious look he always wore.

"Morning Ms. Boyd."

"Good morning, Keith." I gave him a bright smile, my voice chipper. "You guys are already at it, huh?"

"Yes ma'am." He gave me a short nod, his head swiveling to glance at the crew moving about the booth. "Steve asked us to make sure we got to work ASAP. I think he and Tony might want to shift a couple of guys later today to another booth that's running behind."

"Ah." I nodded at the information, glancing around the space once again. "Where is Mr. Friess?"

"He took off for a bit. He should be back shortly." The information came out in the same deadpan tone Keith seemed to use for everything.

I pushed the corners of my mouth up into a perky smile, one I hoped would lighten things and let him know how pleased I was with the progress made. For my efforts he simply stared back blankly before nodding, turning to head back to work. I tracked on him as he went, then scanned the booth space one more time. They had made good progress yesterday, despite the slight hiccup with the electrical. Unless something went very wrong, I couldn't see how they wouldn't be done with time to spare. If my mood had been good coming into the booth this morning, it now ratcheted up another notch. A giddy bubble of anticipation for what being ahead of schedule might mean for this evening. A part of me wondered if Steve had pressed the crew to do this. If the reason for his pushing had less to do with moving part of the crew somewhere else and maybe more with Steve wanting to make sure we didn't get stuck working here late tonight rather than up in my room fucking. That sent a little shiver through me. I was pretty confident that was why he had the crew shifted into high gear. He wanted me for round two as much as I wanted him.

Oh, you egotistical shit. You really are full of yourself to think he wants you that badly, aren't you?

I was still chortling over that when I felt a touch at my elbow.

"Jesus!" I spun, the word a startled yelp as the giddy feeling bolted. My knee hit the edge of the table as I whipped around, but I swallowed down a second yelp, trying to maintain a little of my composure. Steve was standing at my back, a familiar coffee cup in hand. I had been so lost in reverie I hadn't heard him approach over the din of the hall.

"Boo." A mischievous grin split his face as he silently pushed the cup towards me.

"Dammit! Don't do that!" I snatched the drink from his hand, casting a heated glare into those twinkling gray eyes. Fucker. He looked so damned pleased with himself, probably suspected what I'd been daydreaming about, the arrogant jerk. I wanted to punch his shoulder, or pull him into a hug, maybe both, but I did neither.

We stared at each other, and even though he'd startled me, that earlier feeling of exhilaration was quickly returning. A floating sensation that just being in his presence imbued in me. Jesus, it'd only been a few hours since he'd left my room, but now all I could concentrate on was having his arms around me, to feel his touch again. Memories of what we'd done the night before rattled around inside my head. Flashbacks I knew would plague me the rest of the day, fighting to override where my focus should be. Which was supposed to be my job, not figuring out how fast we could get out of here, run back to my room, tear the clothes off each other in a lust-fueled frenzy, and create a slew of new fantasies to throw me off my stride. For the rest of the day, however, there would be no outward showing of affection, no discernable indications of what I wanted to do to Steve and visa-versa. I knew I would keep things professional, and I had little doubt he would, too.

"How are you doing this morning, Ms. Boyd?" The pleased tone of his voice was unmistakable, a cadence that bordered dangerously close to lascivious, as if he was reading the script of my thoughts.

"I was fine up to the point that you knocked five years off my life." My best disapproving gaze only made him grin wider. Those damn eyes practically undressed me as I stood there, and I squirmed as my body responded in a way I really couldn't afford right now.

"Well, we'll just have to see what I can do to get those back for you later."

Dammit. My eyes widened even as my mouth clamped shut tight. The not-so-subtle insinuation made little sense, and yet it hinted at things that made my blood pressure spike.

Steve tracked my reaction, mouth curling up with impish glee. He held me in his gaze until I couldn't hold his any longer, and I looked away to the side. He released a huff of satisfaction, and then his tone became all business. "We look to be in really good shape. Are you satisfied with the progress?"

Taking a deep breath, I gathered my composure, pushing away exasperating thoughts that had little to do with getting on with the job. Steve might think he had me flustered—and he did—but I'd show him. I could do this. I took a sip of my coffee, glancing around the booth one more time. "Yes. I have to say, you guys really kicked it yesterday. I can't imagine why we shouldn't be finished and doing the wipe-down by 4 pm."

"By 3 pm." Steve's voice was firm, cutting in on top of me. "That's what I told the guys."

"Keith mentioned that you might need to shift guys off the booth onto another job?"

"Yeah." Steve sighed, bringing a hand up to rub his chin, his face turning serious. "We got another booth that's behind schedule. Not sure what happened, other than they got into the hall late yesterday. Tony and I need some of the guys off your set to help out over there. That wouldn't be an issue, would it?"

"Hmm. Cut my labor call and save me some money?" I snorted, giving him a half-smile. "I couldn't possibly agree to that."

"Fair enough." Steve arched an eyebrow, nodding as if giving my comment serious consideration. "I can increase the call instead, if that's what you'd like?"

"Ass," I said it under my breath, but I saw the corner of his mouth twitch, and knew he'd heard it. I fully expected to pay for that later. I took another sip of my coffee. My brain suddenly tripped over a random thought. A comment Steve had just made, and one Keith had earlier. A chill crept up my back, my smile disappearing. "Are you going to have to go to that other booth?"

"Would there be a problem if I did?" Steve eyes narrowed as his tone became sober.

"No, sir," I whispered, the words painted with defeat. I glanced around us. We were alone, no one else nearby. I turned back to Steve, bit down on my lower lip, my voice soft. "If that's what you have to do, I understand. I'm not going to lie and tell you I'll be happy about it, but..." My voice trailed off as I sucked in a deep breath, dreading what he might be about to say.

"Well..." He drew the word out, as if he was giving deep

thought to what would follow. "Marty's order to me was to make sure I did whatever I needed to do to make sure you're happy. I'm taking it by your response that if I want to follow that order..." He stepped close to me, a sudden compelling presence at my side. "I probably shouldn't go to that other booth, should I?" He gave my shoulder a quick squeeze as he moved past and out into the exhibit where the rest of the crew was working.

Releasing the breath I'd been holding, I felt lightheaded. He'd teased me, made me panic at the thought there wouldn't be a repeat of last night, and then yanked me back from the edge. For the second time this morning I slapped pieces of myself back in order to maintain the professional demeanor I wanted to show. Jerk. It was almost as if he enjoyed doing this to me.

I gave a short shake of my head. Of course he did, the bastard. Standing here and bemoaning how terrible it was being tormented by Steve was bullshit on my part. Because the truth was, I craved it. Thrilled to the sensation of being with someone capable of getting me that worked up.

For most of the morning work kept Steve and I apart as the crew finished setting the exhibit. We weren't deliberately avoiding each other, but for what was left to do there was little interaction necessary between us. I spent a good deal of it engaged in what I'd done yesterday, which was to stare at him. But this time I had more context, a far better picture of the man than I'd had the day before. Yes, a *far* better picture. Including an ass that would not leave me alone every time I caught him bending over to do something, nor the image of a cock that I would gladly have shoved him inside the tower unit to get another glimpse of, even if only for a moment.

-Jesus, Jen. You are something else. Oh, and by the way, have you forgotten something?-

Shit.

I *had* forgotten. So happy to be back in his company, the tickled feeling of being teased by him, the delight in fantasizing about what had been and would be again, I'd completely forgotten about checking my phone. I reached over to my bag and pulled it out. I wasn't a bit surprised to see there was no message, no text. That worry from earlier this morning raised its ugly head, though, and I brought up Loren's office number from my Contacts.

"Hello, Loren speaking."

"Loren. It's Jen."

"Jen! Oh my God, how are you doing!" Loren's voice was bright with happiness, and then it pulled up short. "Wait, is everything okay? Is something wrong there?"

"No!" I gave her a polite chuckle, grinning. "Everything's fine. Jeez, Loren. I call and the first thing out of your mouth is 'Oh God! What have you done? What's the problem!' Thanks!"

"Well..." she drew the word out. "You are pretty new at this, so I've been worried. I've been waiting for your call to tell me how bad you've screw things up."

"Thanks. Dick."

Loren laughed, and my mouth curved up into a full-blown smile. A second later it slipped away as I remembered why I had called.

"Things here are fine. I've got a great crew, and we're ahead of schedule."

"Pfft. 'Ahead of schedule.' You're *always* ahead of schedule, Jen."

"Well, this time I'm ahead of schedule of my normal ahead of schedule."

"Awesome!"

"Hey, I have a question for you..." I tried to keep my voice casual, conceal any inflection of worry or irritation out of it. "Have you seen Thomas today by any chance?"

There was a brief pause, and the butterflies in my stomach took flight.

"Oh, yeah. I saw him and Thom Paul in the atrium this morning, actually. I didn't say hi 'cause they looked like they were busy with something, but far as I know he's here." Loren gave another brief pause. "Why?"

"Oh, it's nothing." I waved my hand as if she could see it, a nervous attempt to brush further questioning aside. "I haven't heard from him... today, so I was just curious."

"You want me to give him a buzz?"

"No!" *Dammit.* I caught the strident sound of my voice, grimaced at the almost angry tone of it. "No, no, it's fine. He's probably busy with something. I'll call his office later."

"Okay. If I see him, I'll let him know to pull his head out of his ass and give the woman he loves the attention she deserves."

Laugh, Jen. Laugh and let her know that nothing is wrong, and that everything is hunky-dory and that things are just fine and that there is no reason to tell Thomas Kiernan to go fuck himself.

"Ha! Yeah, do that for me, okay?" I tried to fake as convincing a laugh as I could as my fingers gripped the phone so tight I thought I might break it in two. "Okay, listen, I have to get back to work. You know, to try and clean up the mess I've made here."

Loren giggled. "Yeah, sure, you do that."

"Thanks, Loren. I'll talk to you later."

"Okay, Jen. Take care! Have a good show!"

"I'll try. Bye!"

I ended the call, and stood there, gripping the phone with fingers that ached.

You son of a bitch. You goddamn sonofabitch. You got my call. You got my texts. What the fuck is your problem!

I lowered the phone where I could see the screen. I started to tab to the Messages screen. To type another text to Thomas.

I stopped myself. *No. No, fuck you. I'm calling. And you better fucking answer.*

I dialed his cell phone. Not his office, because that would probably go right to voicemail. On his cell I knew he'd know exactly who was calling.

Five rings, and straight to voicemail.

Hi! This is Thomas. I can't take your call right now...

"Thomas, I know you're getting my messages. I don't know what's going on, but I need you to call me. Now." I held the phone to my ear, my neck burning. "Call me, Thomas. I'm serious. Please. Bye." I slammed my thumb into the END button and then tossed the phone to the table.

God fucking dammit. What the hell was going on?

I stood for a moment, shaky. I drew in a deep breath, then let it out slowly. Moving away from the table and my phone, I made my rounds, trying to cool myself off. Irrational anger continued to pulse through me, and I needed to get rid of that before I talked to Thomas. I made two circuits of the booth, talking myself down. It helped, but only a little. I moved back to the table and sat down. Keeping a cursory eye on how things were proceeding, I flipped the phone up to where I could see the screen, watching for Thomas' call or text. Fifteen minutes passed, then twenty, then thirty, and by an hour I was done. *Fuck. You.* I pushed the phone away from me, and with an almost savage glee I turned my attention to surreptitiously watching Steve. Where earlier I might have thought that dangerous—observing him quickly became thoughts that turned into fantasies—I now embraced it with gloating fury. *Fuck. You.* That sustained me. Carried me through the rest of the morning as my phone sat silent. Steve came by at one point, and we talked, and the smile I gave him was a sunburst of latent sexual energy. When I asked him to arrange lunch for the crew—a last-day-of-the-set tradition that I had started years ago—I fucking purred.

"Do you think you could make that happen for me, Mr. Friess? Please?" I batted my eyes at him, bit down on my lower lip as I poured a carton of sex over the words.

-*Wow. Lay it on fucking thick, why don't you?*-

"I will absolutely make it happen, Ms. Boyd." If my request, and the manner in which I asked it, took Steve aback, he hid it well. He grinned as he stood looking down at me, his eyes narrowing. "I think this may be only the second time I've had a client buy lunch for the crew on a job."

"Well..." I responded in a husky voice that bordered on erotic. "I like to take care of my people."

"So I'm aware." His eyes thinned to slits, one corner of his mouth turning up almost imperceptibly.

Just before lunch, he and Keith came by to discuss the layout of the graphics in the exhibit. I had gotten myself a little more under control by that point, but I was still flinging mental *Fuck You's* at Thomas. As we walked the booth, laying out the visuals out in the proper locations, there were a few moments when my eyes met Steve's. I had no idea what he was thinking, especially given my little display earlier, but when our glances did catch, I had my suspicions. I knew what I was thinking. That this day could not end quickly enough.

The crew had chosen pizza for lunch and Tony brought the food to the booth when it arrived, spreading the boxes out on one of the empty crates. I asked him to join us, and after some half-hearted protesting, he finally agreed.

"Ms. Jen, did Stevie have a chance to talk with you about maybe cutting your crew back a bit?"

"He did." I took another scan around the exhibit before I turned back to him. "We're in really good shape. I certainly don't have a problem with it."

"Aw, Ms. Jen, you're the best!" Tony gave me a broad smile. "Thank you!"

"Don't thank me." I glanced over at Steve, shooting him a meaningful smile. "If it wasn't for the fantastic job Steve and the crew did, we wouldn't be this far ahead."

That earned me a few chuckles and a chorus of thanks from the crew. I acknowledged each of them with a brief nod until my gaze landed on Steve. My eyes locked on him, and as the voices died down, he spoke in a low, polite tone.

"Thank you, Ms. Boyd."

"No, thank you, Mr. Friess." We stood contemplating each other, and the smile he gave was thanks for far more than my praise or the pizza that lay before us. My gaze dipped, and I drew teeth across my lower lip before looking back up at him. If anyone took notice of us, it didn't show. Spirits were high, lunch seemed to have everyone occupied, and the two of us shared this private moment before we turned to other things. Throughout the remainder of lunch I forgot about unreturned calls, texts unanswered. I let the warmth of a crew well pleased wrap around me. And Steve. Gathering what I had from the look he'd given, a blanket of serenity stayed with me long after the moment had passed.

After we finished eating, the call was scaled down to three men, including Steve. That was more than sufficient for the work we had left. For the most part, the exhibit was set, the empty crates tagged, and some were already being cleared away. There were only last-minute things to take care of. I puttered about, handling minor tasks while the small crew continued working, making sure that nothing was amiss. I knew from the e-mail this morning that the salespeople planned to be here around 4:30 p.m. for the review, and it was clear everything would be in place when they arrived. As we worked, I bumped into Steve near one of the workstations.

"What time will I be able to see you tonight." he asked, voice low.

We were alone in this area of the booth, so I dropped my voice into a tone I wouldn't have risked otherwise. One I knew he'd react to. "Do you want to see me tonight, sir?"

"Yes." His response was an emphatic, quiet rumble. "I most definitely want to see you tonight, Ms. Boyd."

"Okay." His voice shot a charged thrill straight from my brain to my now slickening core. "I can't tell you exactly what time it will be, but I'll make it as soon as I can, sir."

"Good."

"The salespeople are due here at 4:30 p.m. for the pre-show review. I'm not expecting it to take long. If they ask me to have dinner with them, which I'm hoping they won't, I'll beg off. It's been a long set, I'm not feeling up to it, whatever. That will leave me all yours tonight." I glanced around once more to see if anyone was looking towards us, and then I lowered my head.

"Sir."

"Good girl."

Those two words along with his stare sent a sliver of electricity running up my spine. His presence this close, along with the knowledge of what lay ahead this evening, swirled into a heady cocktail of anticipation, balanced on an edge of giddy arousal. I stepped away from him before he could say anything further, moving off. I did not need to see him to know he was watching me. And I added fuel to that fire. Put an extra sway into my hips, ass swishing left and right as I walked away.

Yeah, Steve enjoyed teasing me. Well, I could play that game too. And I had a reason. One that I hoped would earn me something special tonight.

Something very, *very* special.

FOURTEEN

I was indulging myself in schadenfreude.

It wasn't pretty, but I did it nonetheless. The balance of the afternoon passed slow and uneventful for us, but that was not the case for other booths nearby. There was barely contained chaos all around us. Our exhibit stood like an isolated oasis of calm in a sea of disarray, work going on at a frenetic pace. A self-satisfied smirk of pride pulled up the corners of my mouth as I sat at my table, feet propped up on a literature box, watching the other exhibitor's struggles. I had been one of those exhibitors at previous shows and remembering that should have guilted me into stopping. It didn't. I was happy, feeling a little cocky, and far too smug than I had a right to.

Our booth was in good shape, and I was pleased, and not solely for a job well done. I knew the salespeople would be here in an hour or so, and when they saw the booth was complete, I had little doubt word would get back to Loren. That would equal a happy boss, so what was not to be proud of? I laced fingers behind my head and grinned. Besides, I had my own special reward awaiting me as soon as I could get off the show floor, and thoughts of that were never far from my mind.

Thomas still hadn't called. As the afternoon wore on, I went from fuming and flinging more of those mental *Fuck You's* at him to just plain indifferent. I had no idea what he was trying to prove, but right now I could shit-care-less. This was a lawyer tactic. I knew it in my bones. He was upset about my not communicating with him before. He'd been hounding me about it for weeks, and this was his childish, passive aggressive way of letting me know that he didn't like my attitude or the way I was handling whatever it was that was bugging me. I was confident he didn't know *why* I wanted to talk, but I couldn't believe he'd chosen now to pull this bullshit on me as a way of making his point. *You don't want to talk to me, Jen? Well, fine. I can play that game too.* No response to my voicemails or my texts. And now that Loren had confirmed he was okay and had been at work, I knew he'd gotten them and wasn't lying dead in the apartment or in some ditch somewhere. Nope. This was deliberate on his part, and while at first I'd been mad as hell, now I was just over it. A voice in the back of my head reminded me that what I wanted to talk to him about really wasn't the kind of thing you left on a voicemail. And I hadn't done that. I had held firm that if I wasn't going to do this face-to-face, I was at least going to do it when we could actually speak to each other. But now? After this... crap he was pulling? I was sorely tempted to go against my sense of what was right— and my better judgement—and just leave him a voicemail.

Hey, Thomas. I've been trying to reach you, but you seem really intent on teaching me a lesson right now, and I've run out of time and patience, so here's the thing. I'm not who you think I am. And I'm not the person you deserve. And we're over.

Yeah, I wanted to say some really shitty things on top of that, but that would have been emotion talking. Instead, the best thing to do would be to just leave it at that. Explain that we were over, that I'd tried to speak to him but—

No. No, that wouldn't be right. He deserved to hear it directly from me, not my disembodied voice left in a message. If for no other reason than it would allow him the chance to speak his peace. As much as it grated on nerves that were scraped raw at this point, I wouldn't sink to just leaving him a Dear John voicemail. Even as angry as I was at Thomas at the moment, he was a good person who deserved better, and despite everything I'd done—and this little incident of his aside—I owed him the courtesy of speaking directly to him at a minimum.

I pushed it aside and out of my mind. As much as I could. Until the blood pressure wasn't a throbbing drumbeat in my ears, and when I did think of it I wasn't immediately reaching for my phone to leave him a piece of my mind.

It was just after 4:30 when I caught sight of the gaggle of salespeople trickling inside the booth. Getting up from the table, I brushed my hands over my clothing, straightening myself out. I scanned the faces of the people coming in, watching heads swivel as if on gimbals as they took in the exhibit. Several of them I recognized from previous shows, while others I did not. The latter were, I suspected, salespeople that had come over from the other company. As they clumped together in the center of the booth, I stepped across to them, putting my game face on.

"Hi! I'm Jennifer." Hand extended as I approached, a few of the salespeople I knew smiled, recognizing me. One I knew by name—Andrew, a brand manager I'd worked with on several occasions—reached for my hand, shaking it in greeting.

"Jennifer. How are you? Last time I saw you was the ASTA Show in Dallas, right?"

"Andrew. Good to see you again! Yes, that's right! I'm well, thank you."

As further introductions continued, I did a quick headcount. 7 people total. My memory told me the number should be more. At least eight, maybe nine. I shrugged. Perhaps I was incorrect. That or someone was missing.

"Jennifer Boyd?" The person who spoke was another of the salespeople, one who I did not recognize. She was young, artificially bright, with that cheerfulness that seemed almost borderline manic. I gave her a polite smile as she introduced herself.

"I'm Tracy. You work with Loren, right? She's your boss?"

"That's right."

"I love Loren! She's been so much help during the transition!"

"Loren is the best." I bobbed my head in confirmation, giving her a courteous nod.

"Oh, I wish Sam was here! She really wanted to meet you."

"I'm sorry... Sam?" I crinkled my eyes, giving her a perplexed look. I didn't recognize the name.

"Oh, right!" Tracy dipped her head in an energetic nod. "Sam. Samantha Davis. She's my boss. She works out of your office now. You probably didn't hear, but her flight was delayed. She won't be here until later tonight. We were talking the other day and she mentioned your name. She was saying how much she was looking forward to finally meeting you."

That confirmed my earlier suspicion that there was a person missing. I didn't know this 'Sam', although I gathered from Tracy's comment that she too was one of the new people who had come over after the merger.

"Aww, I'm so sorry to hear that!" I gave Tracy a slightly forced smile. "Well, hopefully she gets in safe tonight, and I can meet her in the morning."

"Oh, I'm sure she'll be fine." Tracy dismissed the issue with a wave of her hand. "You guys can meet first thing in the morning and chat."

Some additional polite conversation followed, and afterwards I took the group around the booth, showing everyone to their different stations. I focused on the newer folks as the other more experienced people I had confidence in. Walking through the exhibit, I explained the layout, how various things worked, and what to typically expect during a show.

"This booth is so much bigger than the one we had at our old company!"

"Well, we want to make sure you and your products are getting the highest visibility possible on the floor. That way traffic stays brisk, and the new lead draws stay solid."

"Well, I gotta say, this is all pretty incredible."

It was gratifying to hear their responses. Everything that had happened between Steve and I aside, this was what I was here for. It felt good to see and hear their positive reactions.

Once I had everyone situated, I moved to the front reception desk, waiting to answer any questions that might arise. The crew continued to work, completing the final adjustments and wipe-down of the properties. A quarter hour slipped by before Steve approached, coming up beside me.

"Is there anything we can help with, Ms. Boyd?" His voice was quiet, relaxed.

"Hmm." I didn't turn to look at him, but my head swiveled, eyes scanning the booth and the salespeople spread about. "It doesn't look like it right now, Mr. Freiss."

"Things going well?"

"So far."

"Okay. Let me know if there is anything you need from us. We're going to keep wiping down."

"Thank you."

I remained at the desk, waiting patiently, but aside from a few minor questions there was very little that needed taking care of. The more seasoned salespeople had their act down, and spent most of their time talking amongst themselves, or looking around at our competitors. The newer folks seemed excited at the prospects our exhibit held for them. In some cases, they seemed a little overwhelmed, and I did my best to put them at ease. By 6pm I saw nothing but satisfied looks as they began to gravitate together at the center of the exhibit, chatting. I waited until they were all together before I walked from the desk to confer with them.

"So... everyone happy? Things looking good?"

"Outstanding job as always, Jennifer." Andrew gave me a broad smile, glancing around the exhibit one more time.

"Thank you." I dipped my head in quiet recognition, returning his smile.

"Yes, thank you!" Tracy's chipper voice chimed in. She was practically bouncing on her toes. "This is going to be such a great show!"

"Well, that's what we're here for. I think it is going to be a really good show too."

"Listen, Jennifer..." Andrew made a casual wave to the group behind him. "We're going to head out and get some dinner. Would you like to join us?"

"Oh, thank you so much." I gave him a weary smile, spreading my hands in regret. "But—honestly—I've had a couple of long days, so if you guys won't be offended, I think once I've gotten everything buttoned up here, I'm just going to go back to my room and crash."

A couple of the people made sympathizing noises as I finished. "Oh! Is there anything we can do to help?" Tracy jumped in with the rest, looking about as if she could fix whatever needed doing by sheer willpower. She seemed nice, and appeared sincere, but I was beginning to feel like telling her not to try so hard.

"No, no, it's fine." I smiled, waving them off with a dismissive gesture. "It's just last-minute stuff I need to take care of before I cut the crew. Please. Go have dinner. Enjoy yourselves. I'll be alright."

There were understanding smiles and nods from the gathered salespeople. I could tell from the general reactions they weren't going to press me too hard to join them. The realization that I'd done it, gotten away from the dinner obligation I'd feared, sent a balloon of elation floating up inside me. I kept up the façade of weariness as they stared at me with sympathy, even as a part of me wanted to sway in a little dance of joy. Andrew made one last half-hearted attempt, asking again if I was sure I didn't want to join them. After assuring him I appreciated the offer, the group gave me another round of thanks for all I'd done before they moved out of the booth. I stood and watched with an ever-increasing sense of euphoria as they drifted off into the hall, chatting amongst themselves. I finally gave into some of that delight, bouncing on my toes as the last of them disappeared from sight. Once they were completely gone, I whirled in delight to take in the relative silence of the now empty booth.

I'd done it. I was free.

Not long after they'd left, Steve, Keith and the other worker approached me, glancing around to see if it was only us remaining in the space.

"Everything good, Ms. Boyd?" Steve scanned my face, head tilted to one side.

"Yep." I nodded, glancing around me. "I think we're good. Let's lock everything up and call it a night."

They moved off, going around the exhibit and securing all the cabinet doors, shutting off the lights and monitors. I did my own last pass through the space, making sure that there wasn't anything I'd missed earlier. Once we'd all circled the booth insuring everything was locked up for the night, we gathered together by the desk.

"OK, gentlemen. I think we're done. Thank you for everything. I really appreciate it."

They nodded in gratitude, grinning at each other and then at me. "No problem, Ms. Boyd. Glad things went well." Steve's voice was cool and professional, no hint of anything like the suppressed excitement I was feeling.

"Well, I'm going to go grab my stuff and head out. I'll see everyone at 7am?" I glanced at the three of them in turn.

"Yes ma'am," they said in unison.

"Alright, then." I bent to gather up my things, shoving them in my bag. I tried not to let it show, but my hands were jittery with excitement as I moved. "You guys have a great evening."

As I finished, Keith and the other worker headed out of the booth, toolboxes in tow. Steve was standing nearby, his own tool caddy in hand, and I saw him steal a look towards Keith's back. He turned to face me, and I froze, watching as he walked in my direction. During the day we had both kept things professional towards each other. That ended the moment Steve stopped in front of me. As he stood there looking down, heat and desire radiated outwards from him. It enveloped me. A physical presence that gripped me, made my back taut with tension. His aura was pure male, and I breathed it in. Lowering my eyes, I looked down to the carpet at my feet.

"I will be in your room in one hour. Understood?"

"Yes, sir." My voice was a whisper that floated under the noises of work still going on in the hall.

His hand came up, gripping my chin as he raised my face up to his. I gave a soft gasp. It was a bold move. The booth was empty, but the hall was not, and someone could easily have walked back into the space unexpectedly. Caught him holding me there like that. That would definitely raise eyebrows, no matter whether a co-worker of his or mine. Gossip would fly. Despite that, the thrill that ran through me as I stared wide-eyed at him was undeniable.

"Good girl." His voice was thick, low, husky. His thumb dug into my chin, a sharp flash of pain that made my body strain even further. He held me ensnared, the entirety of me trapped between thumb and forefinger before he finally relented, releasing me with an ever-so- slight shake.

"Now go."

I swallowed hard, heart thumping in deep fight-or-flight. I stepped around him, doing as he commanded. I pulled myself out of his presence, breaking through the bubble of hunger he'd held me rapt in. A part of me wanted to go back, to feel that envelope of need for just a moment longer. The risk he'd taken touching me the way he had made me heady with anticipation. Instead, I walked out of the booth without looking back, my head swimming. As I strode through the hall, I trembled as thoughts tumbled one over the other. I was going to be spending another night with Steve. I was going to submit to him again. Let him take me as his own, and do as he wished. I had an hour before Steve arrived at my hotel room door, and suddenly I was convinced of a million things I needed to do.

I crossed out into the lobby, not even looking around me, completely caught up in my fantasies. As I stepped into the hotel atrium, a panicked thought pushed me out of my reverie for a moment. What if a co-worker was here and stopped me now? The last thing I wanted was to be drug to the bar for drinks or another attempt to coerce me into going out to dinner with them. The lobby was crowded with both exhibitors and attendees, and though I couldn't see anyone I recognized, I took no chance. Keeping to the edge of the room, I skirted the crowd to stay out of sight. As I stood waiting for an elevator to come, I chided myself. I was acting like a kid trying to sneak home late at night. It was ridiculous. I was a grown woman; I wasn't obligated to have drinks or go to dinner with coworkers if I didn't want to. Yet for some reason I was skulking through the hotel as if I was trying to slink past the guards in some sort of prison break movie. *You've got yourself worked up, Jen. Let's just ratchet it back a little, okay.*

Getting off the elevator on my floor, I made my way down the hall to my room. I let myself in and took stock. The housekeepers had come by and tidied everything up. That was good. Bed made, fresh towels, every bit of visible evidence of what had taken place the night before gone. I glanced at my watch; I had about three-quarters of hour before Steve arrived. I'd been mulling over a plethora of things on my way here. How should I greet him? What should I be wearing? *Should* I be wearing anything? Now that I was here in the room, I needed a game plan. I walked to my suitcase. I already knew what was inside and none of it was sexy, much less kinky, or approaching fetish-wear. Appearing at the door naked would definitely set the tone, but there was risk involved in doing that. What if someone other than Steve showed up? Scrambling to find something to cover myself in would be awkward. I blew out my cheeks, dismissing it out of hand. No, I had to be wearing something. Question was, what?

I pushed through my things. Decent underwear. Not super sexy, but not granny-wear by any stretch. I had a set of pajamas, but they were rather plain looking. I pulled out the top. I could wear this, and maybe just underwear below that. I yanked the top and a pair of the undies out, holding them up to me as I looked in the mirror. Hmm. It was kinda flirty sexy, but not quite the look I wanted for tonight. It was an option, but not ideal. Standing there, mouth a grim line, I realized Steve probably wouldn't give a damn what I was wearing because he likely wouldn't leave me in clothing for very long anyways. I wanted to make an impression, though. Set the stage, even if it was for no other reason than to add fuel to the fire, so to speak. I stared at the panties and PJ top, chewing on my bottom lip. Yeah, those weren't exactly the gasoline I was hoping for. I tossed them back onto my suitcase with a groan of resignation. If I couldn't find anything better, those would have to do, but I wasn't ready to give up just yet.

I looked around in the closet. My gym clothes lay on the shelf where I'd thrown them this morning. Hmm. They were sporty looking. And tight fitting. That was a plus. I pursed my lips, forehead furrowed. There was one big drawback, though. They smelled. Two mornings of use without washing had left nothing Downey fresh about them. I caught a slight whiff of funk from them. Nope. I wasn't about to pile on enough deodorant and perfume to mask sweaty gym room body odor.

Fuck. I closed the door to the closet, blowing out a frustrated sigh. I wandered into the bathroom, still thinking. Peeling out of my blouse, I slipped my pants off, unhooked my bra and folded everything into a neat pile on the counter. Still racking my brain to come up with something as time ticked away, I brushed my teeth, refreshed my deodorant, applied some perfume, and mussed my hair. When I was done I stared at myself in the mirror, and while I looked fine, I was still no closer to knowing what I was going to wear when I greeted Steve than I had when I'd walked in. Growling in exasperation, I snatched up my clothing, turning to walk out to the bedroom.

That's when I saw them. Bathrobes.

Hanging on the back of the bathroom door were two hotel bathrobes. Fluffy white freshly laundered cotton. A wicked grin tugged my cheeks high and wide. I plopped the clothing back down on the counter, and then slipped out of my underwear. Naked now, I padded to the door, pulling down one of the bathrobes. I shrugged it on, pulled the sash closed but not tight. I twisted to the left and right as I looked at myself in the mirror.

Well, son of a bitch. Perfect!

The robe came down to just above my knees. I adjusted the sash, and let the front slip open slightly. My mouth curled, eyes bright with mischief. Oh, yes. This would work. This would work perfect. Turning back to the counter, I rummaged through my bag. There it was. I had thrown in a few lipsticks for show days, and I thumbed through them until I found what I was looking for. The red one. I applied it carefully, lips pulled into an 'O' as I drew the rich red color over them. When I was done I leaned back, satisfied. This would do quite nicely. The robe left little to the imagination as to whether I was wearing anything underneath, especially with the sash as loose as I had it. There was enough cleavage showing to remind Steve for the thirty seconds before he tore it off me just what lay beneath. I loved the way the color of the red lipstick stood out in vivid contrast to the dazzling white of the robe. I stood looking at myself, smug. The robe felt warm and comfortable against my skin. I pushed the gap open a little further, letting one side catch on my nipple so the tiniest trace of areola showed. Snatching up my phone, I glanced at the time. Not bad. Twenty minutes to spare.

Gathering up my clothes, I moved back into the room and dumped them in the closet. I did a quick pass through the bathroom to tidy up. I checked my phone again. 7:35. Steve could be here at any moment. I moved to the mirror on the closet door and gave myself one more look- over. Being a person not above a certain amount of vanity, I preened at what I saw. The robe was simple, but sexy, and the lipstick was the ideal accent. I'd wanted to add fuel to Steve's fire. This, I felt confident, was going to be gasoline I'd been hoping for.

The next fifteen minutes were excruciating. It was kid-at-Christmas kind of painful, the waiting murder on nerves already strained. I fidgeted, walking from one end of the room to the other, calf muscles tight. The clock on the end table was death by slow ticks from little blue glowing numbers that never seemed to change. Twice I heard footsteps in the hallway, and I leapt up, my heart hammering in my chest. Each time they walked by, fading as they passed. I tried to force myself not to look at the clock, but three minutes would go by that felt like twenty, and I would glance over. The clock became a silent guardian, taunting me.

A third set of footsteps approached. As they grew closer, I squirmed in my chair until I couldn't stand it. I came up to my feet, standing and staring at the door.

The footsteps stopped. Then there was a single, forceful knock. I shivered.

Show time.

FIFTEEN

I swallowed, nervous.

My throat gone tight, I walked to the door, peering out through the peephole. In the narrow fisheye view I saw Steve standing there, waiting patiently. I released a *whoosh* of breath I'd been holding in.

Undoing the latch, I opened the door, easing myself behind it, head peeking around the edge.

"May I come in?"

"Please, sir."

Steve brushed past the edge of the door and into the room. As he walked by, I noticed something I hadn't seen through the peephole. In one hand he was carrying his toolbox. My eyes went wide.

His toolbox? Okay, what the hell was that for?

Closing the door behind him I spotted something else. In his other hand he was carrying what looked for all the world like a length of pipe. Leaning with my back against the door, I caught sight of something else. He had a backpack slung across his shoulder.

Okay. This was interesting. Unexpected, but interesting. I'd wanted to create a certain impression, but Steve had me beat at this game. I might look sexy, but Steve had me all manner of thrown off kilter with his get-up. *Point to you, sir. Point to you.*

He came to a stop, and then turned to face me. Pushing off, I walked as seductive as I could towards him. He watched me as I did, eyes taking me in from head to toe. As I came up close it was obvious from both his look, and the heat of desire that projected off him, he approved of my clothing choice.

He dropped his toolbox to the floor and reached up with his hand to finger the edge of the robe where it opened. His eyes rove up and down the length of me again, and then he was staring into mine, grinning.

"Very nice."

I smiled softly, lowering my eyes. "Thank you, sir." Again, my eyes were drawn to the pipe he held in his hand, and the toolbox that now sat at his feet. I suddenly recognized the pipe for what it was; the bar portion of a pipe clamp. I'd noticed one in the booth during the setup but thought nothing of it. Now I frowned, looking up at Steve.

"Sir? Not that I'm questioning, but.... are you planning on doing some work in my room tonight, rather than...?" I let the question hang in the air as I squinted at him quizzically. His grin grew wider, and he stepped closer to me.

"Oh, I plan on 'doing some work' with you tonight. Don't worry about that." He moved the hand that held the pipe, bringing the metal up to catch the edge of my robe, lifting the fabric until my thigh and the top of my buttock were exposed.

I gave a little gasp, blinking my eyes as I felt the cool metal touching my skin. After a second I swallowed, and then said, "I'm just a bit... confused."

Steve chuckled. "Last night I had to make do with what I had at hand. Tonight, I came prepared."

I pursed my lips, thinking for a moment before I responded. "OK, but... your toolbox? And a piece of pipe? I... I'm not quite sure I see where this is going?"

He leaned into me until his lips brushed my ear. His voice was whisper soft, but also full of thinly veiled portent, an omen of things that set the skin where that metal had stilled afire.

"Oh, you will soon enough, Jen. I believe I mentioned at dinner last night I was an engineer in the Marines. I was trained to improvise. To make do in the field, when necessary, with found objects. You are soon going to discover that I have all sorts of tricks up my sleeve."

He nipped at my ear, eliciting another gasp. Then in an instant his free hand was at the back of my neck, holding me as he was kissed me hard, fierce. I leaned into him, moaning against his mouth, suddenly all heat and melting to his touch. Dissolving to the promises behind those words.

"First things first." Steve dropped the pipe on the bed, and then turned, facing me.

"On your knees."

I dropped. God, it came so naturally. I fell to my knees, bending my neck so I faced the floor. The sound of Steve's chuckle floated above me.

"Nice. Good girl."

"Thank you, si—" I hadn't even finished before he'd closed the two steps between us and his fingers dug into my hair, wrenching my head back. The fire that lanced across my scalp as he bent my head up to meet his eyes yanked a cry from my throat. He was smiling, but I recognized the way his mouth curled, recognized the set of it and the gleam in his eyes. I cut the sound off as quickly as I could.

"I mentioned last night I felt you were stronger than I had given you credit for, Jen. That opinion has not changed. So, tonight I am going to put my theory to the test. And I think I am going to enjoy doing so very, very much."

I nodded ever so slight as I felt my pussy flood. *Goddamn, he brought his A-game, didn't he?*

"Yes, sir." I whispered.

"Excellent." My eyes never wavered from his as I heard the

sound of him undoing his belt followed the *zzzzick* of his zipper coming down. I smelled the musk of him even before I felt the first brush of his cock against my cheek, then the head quivering in front of my lips.

"Suck."

And I obeyed. God, did I obey.

I had thought our first night together incredible, liberating. This night... this night was soul affirming. I was back where I wanted to be, where I needed to be, and it was Steve who helped bring me there.

Who showed me just how right all this was.

"Stand up."

I'd been kneeling for minutes while I lavished his cock with everything I could. I swallowed him deep, gagged when he held my head down until the first traces of blackness rimmed my eyes. Gasped when he let me up to take in air, and then I worked his length as if oxygen itself were produced by that slick, veined member. When he gave me the command, I scrambled up as fast as I could, stood with hands at my side, eyes down.

Steve never said a word as he circled me once, a cat playing with a mouse that quivered to be taken. He disappeared behind me, and I stayed as stock-still as I could. I heard the sound of his movements, caught enough indication from the noises to know he was undressing. A part of me was desperate to turn, to accept any punishment he might mete out just to see him naked once again. But I knew how this scenario needed to play out. I knew my role. And I knew I would see all of him soon enough. If I was a good girl and obeyed.

The sounds slowed, I heard the bed creak, and then it was silent. I gasped, jerking forward as cold metal brushed against my inner thigh. The pipe came away quickly and then it smacked against my ass.

"Be. Still."

"Yes, sir." I blurted out as I resumed my original position.

"Better." Steve's voice floated from behind me a moment later. "Spread your legs."

I did as he commanded. Once I was planted, I felt the pipe come up against my inner thigh once again. It crept upwards, a slow path in which I could feel the sawtooth edges of threads scraping against my skin as they moved higher and higher towards my...

Fuck! How could I be this wet and he hadn't done anything more than let me suck his cock and run the tip of that goddamn pipe over my skin?

Steve used that piece of metal to stimulate me as if it were some sort of iron dildo, letting the edge of it play against my labia, somehow teasing me open enough so the edge was able to push up against slickness that he then drew down and painted across my skin like an artist with a brush. As he moved back and forth, he made my jaw clench as I fought to keep from moving to the sensations he was creating. When he pushed forward and the grooved metal pushed up against my clit there was nothing that could stop the moan that came out of me.

And then he stopped.

The pipe left my body and I groaned. For a moment I stood on legs gone to jelly, and then I heard him chuckle once again from behind me.

"Oh, Jen, Jen, Jen." I heard him get up off the bed, and for the first time since he'd disappeared he came into view. Yes, he was naked. And gorgeous as ever. He was holding the pipe cinched up tight towards one end, and as he brought it close to my face, I could see it glistened.

"Hmm. Would you look at this. I pride myself on keeping my tools tidy, and here you've gone and gotten this one all dirty." He stepped until he was against me, and I could feel his cock touching my thigh.

Even closer still was the tip of that pipe, hovering a hairsbreadth from my lips.

"Clean it."

I did.

I drew my tongue across the tip of the metal, licking clean my arousal. I knew what he wanted, and I gave it to him. Sucked it as if it was his own cock and showed my appreciation in turn. When he was ready he pulled it away, gripping the back of my head to stop me. He pretended to inspect the tip, as if judging from the sheen of my salvia coating it whether it met his approval.

"I suppose that will have to do." He released my hair, the tone bordering on disapproving.

For a millisecond I wanted to reach for it, to ask him for another chance to show I could finish it properly. Instead, I did nothing but stand shivering as he slipped behind me. The sound of the mattress settling drifted forward, and then his calm voice.

"Turn around."

I did as ordered and found him sitting at the end of the bed, holding the pipe like a staff, one end planted to the floor. I stopped, facing him, and then lowered my gaze until it rested on his feet. I heard him move, and shortly after felt the tip of the metal catch against the sash of my robe, pulling against it. The end caught the belt, tugged it open until the robe loosened around my waist. I kept my eyes down, watching as it moved into the cloth. Steve worked it along the robe, snaring the tie until it fell clear. The pipe continued to pull the robe open until he'd exposed my breast. He let it fall, and then did the same with the other side. I felt heat burn up my neck, flush into my cheeks. He held me exposed like that, and between what he was doing with the metal and the cooler air from the room, my nipples harden in response. A moment later, the tool slipped from view.

"Mmm. Very nice." I heard him shift on the bed. "Take it off, Jen. Now."

His tone suggested I should move quickly, and so I did. I let the cloth slip off my shoulders, shrugging it away until it pooled at my feet. Silence filled the room, and then there was the soft rustle of feet on the carpet as Steve moved up to me.

A sharp jolt of pain stabbed my ass as the pipe smacked against it once more. I came up on my toes, a yelp jerked out of me as I did so.

"Move to the end of the bed."

I scrambled to the edge, knees pressing against the mattress. I quivered as the stinging red spot on my backside continued to throb, pulsing outwards across my cheek. I pressed my lips tight, teeth clamped together. Steve had showed a bit of a sadistic streak in him last night. Tonight, he was putting it on full display.

And I was ready.

"Legs apart," he ordered. A second later he smacked his palm sharply against my thigh. "Wider."

I spread them, hands splayed to balance myself as I did so.

He moved behind me, and then his hand pushed against the center of my lower back.

"Bend over."

I did as he commanded. I leaned over the edge of the bed, resting on my elbows, and spread my legs apart a little further. I could hear him back there, the sound of latches on his toolbox coming undone. I took a chance and peeked back, looking to see what he was doing. He was bent to the box, pulling two lengths of rope out. Watching as he knelt behind me, I felt the cold metal of the pipe as he placed it across my ankles.

"Polypro would be better here. Or some nice jute. But... beggars can't be choosers, can they?" His voice was so relaxed, so amused at what he was doing. As he continued lashing me to the bar, he began to hum a tune.

You... fucker!

I couldn't help the feeling of giddy excitement that came over me even as the pinpricking sensation of the nylon fibers bit into my skin. He was not being gentle, and as I felt every delicious bite as he cinched tight each wrap of the rope. With every jerk, I could no more withhold the whimpers of pleasure that escaped me than I could have stopped my own breathing. A minute later, he was done.

Now spread and fully exposed to him as I bent over the end of the bed, I felt a level of arousal that I hadn't in forever. He stepped away, and I could hear the sound of him fiddling once again inside his toolbox, the chipper sound of the tune a counterpoint to the occasional groan I made. Eventually he went quiet, and the noise from the toolbox stopped.

A moment later his hand came up, knotting into my hair. He yanked my head back, moving his other hand under me. I felt it brush across my breast, and then as he pressed something hard against my nipple.

"Do. Not. Move." His voice was harsh, strict. I could feel his fingers moving, and then fire burst outwards from the hardened peak of my breast. It hadn't been clear at first what it was that he'd been holding in his hand, but now I knew. It was a clamp. He'd fashioned a nipple clamp. While I had thought he'd been busy during the day taking care of finishing the setting of the booth, he'd somehow found time to take the alligator clips off something and had create a set of nipple clamps.

Looking down between my breasts I could see he'd wrapped the teeth of the clamp with tape. The spring was still strong, though.

Stronger than the nipple specific ones I had experienced before. It bit into my sensitive flesh, and I keened with bliss-filled pain.

"Ehhhhnnnn!"

He chuckled. "Like that, do you?"

I answered him softly, panting. "Yes, sir!"

"Well, then you are going to love this...." And then he applied the second clamp.

He had not been lying when he said he had all sorts of tricks up his sleeve. And I loved it. I loved it all.

He bit the back of my neck hard, then released my head. I could feel him moving behind me, down once again to where I knew he'd set the toolbox. After a moment, I felt him come back up onto the bed. I felt something drag against the back of my neck, and then whatever it was he had, he pulled it over the top of my head. I couldn't immediately tell what was going on, but then I smelled the unique scent of rubber. I felt something stretchy being drawn over my nose, and then suddenly Steve was pressing it against my lips, forcing it into my mouth.

Holy fuck. He'd made a gag. He was gagging me.

I could taste the rubber of it as he forced it between my teeth. The material was thick, stiffer than what I expected, and the surface was pebbled with small dots. As Steve was cinching it tight against the back of my head, I realized what it was. He'd removed the rubber safety cover off a power tool handle and with some cording had fashioned a gag.

"Mmnnnnffggh!" I grunted against the rubber that was now drawn tight through my mouth, spreading my lips apart and forcing my teeth to bite down. Steve gave one last hard tug against the tie, and then he was leaning against me, lips close to my ear.

"Last night, when I whipped you, you cried out so beautifully, but you had to bury your head in the pillow. So we wouldn't scare the other guests. Pity, wasn't it? I would so love to hear you scream, Jen. But we both know we can't have that. Not here. However, at least with this..."—he gave a sharp tug on the gag, and wrenched my head back—"I'll be able to hear your cries a little better, even if you do still have to use a pillow."

I heard him chuckle darkly.

"And I do intend on making you scream, Jen."

Yeah. I was undone. Game over. Steve won. I was his.

Completely.

The first ten smacks he gave me were flat palmed. Last night he'd been reasonably gentle. Like any good Dom, he'd tested the waters, judged just how far he could go with his new submissive. I wasn't unaware of what he'd done, and the knowledge made me both respect him and desire him all the more. Tonight... tonight Steve ramped things up. The first couple of smacks seemed about on par with those from the previous night. But then they began to grow. Grow in intensity, and in the speed with which they fell. By number ten, my ass was aflame, and the pain washed through me like a tide.

As he spanked me, I was soon glad for the gag Steve had fashioned. The cries I would have released without it and the nearby pillow would have brought the entire Chicago PD charging into the room.

And it was only the beginning.

Ten smacks of his palm to my backside led to a brief pause, followed by another ten. After that set there was another pause, and then the gentle soothing of his hand over my ass as I lay there panting. Steven caressed me for a minute longer before he moved up to speak into my ear.

"OK, 'bubblegum' isn't going to work tonight, obviously. I'm not going to bind your wrists for now. If things hit yellow or red, I want you to smack on the bed with your hand. If you go beyond three, I'll stop. That work for you?"

I nodded vigorously.

"Good girl." He kissed the top of my head. "So if we're done with the warm-up, let's get down to business."

I jerked my head around to look at him and caught the predatory smile that creased his face. His hand suddenly darted forward, fisting itself once again into my hair.

"Eyes forward!"

He twisted, and I complied eagerly, looking ahead and down at the sheets in front of me. Once positioned as he wished, he let me go, moving back behind me.

I could hear further shifting from back there, and then the room went silent. When the first lash of the belt came, I bit down hard on the gag, and my cry came out as a high pitched "Ngheeee!" By the sixth fall, I was straining to maintain my position, and my mind was a perfect mess. At the end of the tenth I could feel drool slipping from the corners of my mouth, and my ass felt as if it was creating its own aurora. All perception was focused on it and the sensations emanating outwards from the fire that burnt there. Steve paused after the tenth strike, letting the leather of the belt trace lazy patterns over my enflamed skin.

"God damn you are beautiful, Jen." His voice was low, hoarse with lust and desire. Even through the roaring in my own ears, I could hear his labored breathing.

"I think you can handle more."

I felt so good. So incredible. So powerful in this moment. I swallowed hard as he finished the statement, closing my eyes. A sense of euphoria washed over me. I knew I could. I would. For me. For him.

I could sense his presence behind me, silent and still. I suspected he was waiting to see how I would respond before he'd proceed. I gave him what I hoped he wanted. Laying as still as I could, I thrust my backside up, flexing calve muscles to bring me up onto my toes. I presented myself to him. A moment passed, and then I heard him give a low growl.

"Good fucking girl."

And then the next blow fell.

Ten more lashes. With these, Steve held nothing in reserve. They were quite possibly the most perfect strokes that had ever touched my skin, and I cried with elation at each one. On the tenth I felt my hand moving, and I willed it to stop. I could do this. I wanted to do this.

More. I want more.

But Steve had caught the movement, and he stopped. The belt hit the bed, and then he was alongside me, whispering gently in my ear.

"OK, OK, that's enough."

I keened my disagreement, a whimpering cry that I wanted to sound like the begging I would have spoken if I could.

"Shhhhh..." he crooned softly in my ear, his lips brushing against the lobe, and then trailing across my neck. "Stop, Jen. Stop."

"Damn. You are so fucking perfect." He reached with fingers and gently stroked my cheek. "You'd go longer for me, wouldn't you?"

"ESsss!" I nodded as forcefully as I could.

Steve's chuckle was a warm breath that tickled against my ear. "No. No more. I call 'bubblegum.'" For a moment, he just knelt there, caressing me. Then his lips came close to my ear again.

"I'd rather fuck you now, Jen. Would you like that? Hmm?" he asked the question softly, but he didn't need to hear my answer. He knew my response already.

"Tell me, Jen."

It was a teasing demand, and I whimpered my approval with joy.

Steve slid off the bed. He moved behind me, leaning into me. I felt fingers dig into my ass, and I shrieked into the covers as agony radiated outwards from the ten sunspots he pressed into my flesh. I pushed forward but Steve would have none of that, pulling me back into position. I heard the familiar sound of the condom wrapper being opened, and then a pause as he slid it on. A moment later I felt the tip of his cock brushing between my lips.

"This is going to feel so fucking good." And then he drove into me.

Fire and fury. Pain and pleasure. That is exactly what I felt as he thrust deep inside until his hips landed against my ass. He held himself there as my back arched. I came up on elbows and fought against a throat that wanted to let a scream rip loose from deep in my chest. I bit down on the gag and let tears scatter from my eyes as my head twisted left and right. I watched in fascination as a thin string of drool moved from my bottom lip down towards the bedcover. It traveled in a way that seemed to defy gravity, as if it was in slow motion and completely out of sync with the movement of Steve as he slammed into me. He was not gentle. He was not kind. He was not making love to me. This was not doggie-style sex masquerading as rough. He was fucking me in the purest, rawest sense of the word.

And I loved it.

His cock spread me open to accept him without any regard to

what I was feeling. And I was feeling. God was I feeling. Pain from where his nails dug into my hips. Marks I knew that would be divots dug into flesh in moon-shaped arcs that I was going to be carrying all day tomorrow, if not into the next night. I had been riding the edge of subspace while Steve had whipped me, but this time, unlike last night, I hadn't fallen immediately into it. No, he'd brought toys, and my mind had been all too caught up in everything he was doing to let me give in and fall over the edge. 'I have all sorts of tricks up my sleeve,' he'd said. And he had. I'd been too caught up in the experience of everything Steve had done, and my brain refused to shut itself down. But, now, this... this was simple. Easy. Just raw, primal, powerful, and suddenly there was nothing my mind needed to latch onto. Just the cock sluicing in and out of me without rhythm, through wetness that smeared both of us in a physical confirmation of my need for this. For him.

The voices began to fade. To disappear into the background. From insistent to sporadic to the barest whispers until I began to fall over the edge.

I reached my peak before Steve. It wasn't much of a challenge at this point. Everything he had done had put me at such a fever pitch that I'd known it wasn't going to be long before I fell into that vortex. I slipped over the edge and went down, pulled along by the same things that had pulled me into subspace the night before. I dove, followed them, chased after them until the world became only the totality of the sensations my body sent back to me. I knew Steve was fucking me, but not in the same fashion as I normally did. Everything now was narrowed down to the sensation of swollen flesh stretching more swollen flesh, nerves responding to friction and sending back bright pulses of energy in the most primeval of terms. When the world went white, I screamed. Buried my head into the sheets and screamed in a voice that was the purest note of pleasure I could summon. I held it there, an uninterrupted tone that went on until I felt faint from lack of air. And yet I didn't care. I wanted him to know. I wanted Steve to understand the perfect bliss of this moment. I must have succeeded. When I finally stopped, laying there quaking as my body attempted to put itself back together from the pieces it had shattered into, his strokes slowed. Finally, he came to a stop deep inside me, leaning over.

"Did that feel good? Because it sure seemed like it did from here..." With a voice laced with mirth, his breathing slowed, evening out from where it had been a moment ago.

I could not answer him. I simply nodded my head slowly.

"OK, well we're not done yet, are we?"

I giggled around the gag and shook my head.

Steve chuckled, and then he lifted himself up, sweat-slick skin leaving my own as he rose back up to continue where he'd left off. He began slow, long deep strokes that stretched me back open to take his engorged cock. My pussy sucked him in, clamping down in spasms that were the lingering remains of my orgasm. His fingers gripped me as fiercely as they had before, and now I knew there'd be two sets of marks he'd leave in my flesh. His thrusting became erratic once again, hips slamming into my still burning ass one second, the next the plunges slow and going as deep as he could inside me. I knew he was close. I could feel it in every inch of him that pushed against my walls, in the grunts of exertion as he drove himself to reach his own peak. And when he did, when eventually the final lunge came and he sank as far into me as he could, the exclamation he let loose nearly matched mine, a groan that rose in pitch until it was almost a shout.

"FUCK!"

I felt his orgasm pulse inside me. A rhythm that matched the throbbing of his cock as he came. As if I could feel his heartbeat in each one. That one shout was followed by sounds that became rumbles that tapered off to the noise of his labored breathing as he came down from his orgasm.

"Jesus Christ..." He leaned down against my back, sweat mixing with mine, his breath warm against my neck. "I am seriously out of shape to be fucking a sub as incredible as you. You damn near killed me!"

My laughter was a choking wheeze around the gag, but I knew Steve could feel it in the way my back quaked beneath him. A long moment went by where we simply lay there together, and then Steve rose up. Without warning his hand came down and smacked my ass. Hard.

"Think that's funny, do you?"

"Oo srr!"

"Uh huh." I could hear the grin in his voice, even though I couldn't see him. For another moment he stayed there, still hilted inside me, and then he was pulling out. "Let me get rid of this, and then I think I'll just leave you here spread open for me while I take a little nap."

My back arched, and I twisted my head to look back over my shoulder towards him.

"AAaat!"

"Tsk, tsk, tsk. Such a disobedient sub." He shook his head, but the smile I saw was nothing short of complete satisfaction. "If you hadn't worn me out so much, I'd have to seriously consider whipping that ass of yours again."

Which sounded absolutely fine by me.

Later, spreader bar and the gag gone, he nestled me in his arms on the bed, my head buried into his chest. The words of praise he lavished on me were a low rumble that I caught in bits and pieces while I drifted lazily in a pool of decadence. My ears had burned red as he went on, and finally I slid up and kissed him hard to make him stop.

"I'm not *that* good."

"The fuck you say."

Steve cuddled me. He fucking cuddled me, nuzzling into my hair, brushing fingers lightly over my skin, peppering my neck, cheeks, forehead, and eyebrows with kisses. And while I might have wanted a bit more of what he'd done earlier, I had to admit this was nice too. I had almost drifted off when he picked me up in his arms, carrying me into the bathroom. He never put me down, but held me tight even as he awkwardly got the shower going, waiting until the water was warm and steam filling the room before he stepped us both in.

I gave a little groan as he set me on my feet, holding and caressing me until I could barely stand.

"Mmm... someone had a good time, didn't they?" Steve's voice was a pleased growl in my ear as the warm water beat against my skin. He held me close, holding me up as I burrowed into him, returning my own pleased murmurs.

"Yes, sir. I did. This is so wonderful."

He kissed the top of my head, drawing in my scent. "You are fucking incredible, Jen. You really, truly are." He enveloped me in those arms, and I pulled him tight in mine.

I wanted this. Him, all of it, everything. I didn't want it to end.

Later, when we lay in bed together, I had time to think. Snuggled tight to his chest, his fingers idly stroking my hair, I reflected on my past. I'd once had an entire playroom full of toys, devices, and kinky accoutrements to play with. And yet right now, here in bed with the still lingering taste of rubber in my mouth, the sting of rope marks on my ankles, nothing from the old playroom seemed as distinct in my memory as these new things did now. What Steve had cobbled together from found items put it all to shame. At least that was my perspective as I pushed into his chest, eyes closed in contentment. Everything about what he'd done felt perfect. Was perfect.

And I regretted nothing.

Even as a tiny part of me realized that this was all going to end soon, coupled with the heaviness of what awaited me when I returned home, I couldn't find the slightest feeling of regret within me. All I could do was revel in this moment. I was me again. The me that I liked, that liked and loved what I'd done over the last two days and nights. And I knew right now if I had the opportunity, I'd do it all over again. Without a moment's hesitation.

I liked Steve. I cared about him. He was a good man, and a fun, sexy, and wonderfully skilled Dom. I knew that once everything in my life was sorted out the way I knew it would need to be, I would always remember him. And even though there were a few moments a part of me tried cobbling together a way that I could be with him, in the end I knew it was nothing more than a fantasy. There was little chance beyond the next four days for us to be together. Like this. When this was over, what I would have were memories, fond ones I would cherish even long after we'd both moved on and, hopefully, found someone else.

We slept together that night, and it was the wake-up call I'd set when I'd first arrived which roused us. I rolled into Steve after I'd set the phone back into its cradle, watching him as his eyes opened. The smile he gave me grew from one of muzzy warmth to pleasure, and then to a devilish grin as his arms pulled me in, wrapping me close.

"That was your exercise alarm, wasn't it?"

I chuckled. "Nice guess."

He leaned in, and I felt his breath on my ear, his teeth taking the lobe between them. "I have a different exercise option in mind than the gym...."

And he did. And it was good. So much better than the gym.

We showered, and then dressed. Steve gathered all the things he'd brought with him. I kept stealing glances at him, watching him as he moved about. I caught him looking at me, and twice he looked hesitant, as if he wanted to say something. Whatever it was he let it pass, going on with what he was doing. I considered saying something to him, asking what was going on in that head of his, but I didn't. It was easier this way. Don't overthink it. We still had a few days—well, evenings at the very least, if I could arrange it left to spend with each other, so why bring anything heavy into this like the thoughts that were suddenly rattling around in my head.

Which is what we both did, in the end. Neither of us broached whatever subject had us both preoccupied. We made polite conversation as we got ready for the day, gentle touches and brushes against each other as we moved about the room. We both neatly dodged the five-hundred pound gorilla that was the 'what is happening here between us.' I was in the bathroom, finishing putting on my jewelry when Steve came up behind me. I felt his arms on my shoulders, and I looked up into the mirror as his eyes stared back into mine.

"I'm going to go, Jen," he said softly.

I swallowed. For some reason I couldn't speak for a moment. I felt tears at the back of my eyes, which I blinked away quickly. This was silly. I was going to be with him again in just a little bit. Down there in the booth when both of us would be preparing for the first day of the show. Sure, after that I probably wouldn't see much of him during the actual show hours, but there was always tonight, once the show broke for the day. Worst-case scenario would be I'd have to go out with my co-workers, pretend to enjoy dinner with them, and then get my ass back here as quick as I could. I'd give him my room key. He could be here, waiting, planning. For me. So why was it I felt like there was something passing between us, an event horizon we were crossing over, and with it tears that threatened to spill down my face.

Come on, Jen. What are you doing? Dropping? Little late for that, don't you think? You can't afford this right now. Get your shit together. Game face on. Save the subdrop for later. You've got a job to do.

"Sure. I'll see you in the booth in a bit."

He smiled at me, and it was kind, gentle, but I swear I saw a trace of the same sadness I felt mirrored in it. Maybe it was because since that first night we'd had ourselves to each other. And now we wouldn't. He knew as well as I did that my job starting today would be to support the salespeople, and that meant potentially socializing with them if they wanted. On top of that, he wouldn't be in the booth all day. He'd be back at the Service desk, maybe even off at another exhibit working. During the set we'd been together all day. And then all night. Now...

That had to be it. And it made sense. He leaned in, kissed the back of my head, trailed kisses along my neck until his breathing became a comforting sound in my ear. For a moment my focus tightened solely to him, his touch, the essence of him there right behind me. I closed my eyes, drifted back into his chest, and just stood silent as he held me. I wasn't sure how long we both remained like that, but it felt all too quick. He kissed me one more time, and then let me go.

"See you soon."

I opened my eyes as he left. I stood staring at myself in the mirror as I heard him out in the room, gathering his things. There was a second of quiet before the sound of the door opening drifted back to me.

And then it closed.

SIXTEEN

I forced myself not to cry.

But a part of me wanted to. I realized at some level I was overreacting to a set of circumstances that didn't exist, but that didn't stop me. I stood there, looking at my reflection in the mirror and groaned.

Okay, Jen. Enough. You'll be back here tonight and get another good whipping and then the fucking you want. For God's sake, dial the emotional shit back. All you have to do is just get through the day...

Fortunately, this little emotional hiccup I was having didn't last long, and I got myself gathered together. A little pep talk to get my head back in the game, and I was under control. I touched up my make-up and hair, got what I needed, and then headed out of the room to face the day ahead of me.

Steve and I had spent enough time together this morning that breakfast was pretty much out of the question. I went by the small hotel store and bought a banana, eating it as I walked to the convention center. As I wove through the people heading the same direction, I realized something. I hadn't checked my phone. It hadn't even crossed my mind once to do so. It was an afterthought now, and I debated whether I really wanted to deal with this right now.

Sighing, I reached into my bag, pulling it out. I thumbed the screen alive.

Nothing.

I checked my messages, looked for a text from him even though I knew there wouldn't be one. And I was right. I had to bite back the surge of raw anger that shot through me. Thomas was still ignoring me. *You bastard.* I'd called Loren yesterday, confirmed he was alive and well, and I'd be damned if I was going to bother her again today. *You goddamn bastard.* He'd spent the last month pestering me, asking me what was wrong, pushing me to talk with him before I even knew what I wanted to say. And now that I knew? Nothing. Nada. This was a game. This was some of Thomas' lawyer throw-the-client-off-balance bullshit, but I wasn't playing. *Don't want to talk to me? Fine. Have it your way, asshole.* I tossed the banana peel in the trash with more anger than was appropriate, and then worked to pull myself back into a professional expression. Because, while there was no text from Thomas, there was one from the salesperson who had missed her flight the previous day.

'Sorry I couldn't make it yesterday! I'm here now! Looking forward to meeting you in the morning!'

So. Many. Exclamation. Points. I sighed. An exclaimer. Great. While it didn't surprise me—that seemed to be the type that gravitated towards sales—I wasn't sure why she was making such an effort to make sure I knew she was here. I was just the Marcomm person for the show, nothing more. Maybe she wanted to make sure if I reported back to Loren that I'd met her I'd say she was a real go-getter, enthusiastic about being here, or some bullshit like that. Impressions were definitely important to salespeople, and since she was new to the corporation, she was probably covering all her bases. That was fine. I was the last person she needed to worry about, so if she wanted to make sure she was on my radar it was no skin off my nose.

I crossed the street into the McCormick lobby, and even though it was just past 7am, people were already starting to fill the hall. It was a whole different vibe than in the previous two days. No men in jeans and tool belts, forklifts buzzing about, and the humid air was now pleasantly air conditioned. I walked through the lobby, and then through the doors into the hall. Compared to yesterday the convention center was oddly silent. There was the murmur of people talking quietly as I walked past the other booths, the sound of the occasional vacuum cleaner as someone did some last minute sweeping, and the gentle hum of the huge overhead A/C ducts pumping chilled air into the hall. All the other loud noises that had made up the background ambience during the set were gone, replaced by the calm that prevailed as I walked to the booth.

Once there I found both Keith and Steve already working, doing a final wipe-down of everything. No one else had arrived yet, which is what I had expected. Those who had come yesterday evening were already set and didn't need to be here this early. Anyone else who might show up this morning probably had little they'd need taken care of. All of the monitors had been turned on, all the lights brought up, and everything looked perfectly in place. I walked to the reception counter and set my stuff down. This is where I'd be spending the bulk of my time during show hours over the next two days, and I intended to stake my claim for space while I could. I opened a door and threw my bag inside. As I rose up, I found Steve standing in front of the desk, a by now familiar coffee cup in hand.

"Morning, Ms. Boyd."

"I could kiss you right now." I said softly as I reached for the cup. "I like the sound of that," he said in return, smiling.

There was a tingle of electricity that passed between us as our fingers touched as the cup went from his hand to mine. Although part of me would have loved nothing more than to kiss him, I didn't, obviously. Instead I let my eyes linger on his as I took a sip. He returned my stare, and the look he gave me sent a small shiver down my spine.

"How are we looking?" I asked, glancing about to break the

spell. "Things look good. Honestly, there's not much left for us to do except finish the wipe down, and then see if anyone needs anything when they show up."

I nodded. I could see Keith across the booth, wiping down a cabinet at one of the workstations.

"Thank you, Steve," I said quietly. "For everything."

"Thank you, Ms. Boyd." he smiled back at me sincerely. "For everything."

We both stood there looking at each other. There were so many unspoken yet still spoken-without-words things passing between us. Just as I started to take advantage of this quiet moment we had together, I caught movement out of the corner of my eye. I turned to look in that direction, and watched as the first contingent of my co-workers began to trickle into the booth.

"Well, here we go", I said ruefully, turning back to look at Steve.

"So it begins." He had caught what I'd seen, and now he grinned at me. "Let me know if you need anything." He reached over and gave my hand a gentle pat before he moved off to continue wiping down the exhibit.

As I watched him go, I felt a wave of warmth and gratitude wash through me. I could do with more of that. At least a few days and nights more of it. I was still basking in that thought as the group of salespeople approached me. We made polite chit-chat for a minute as I took a headcount. A quick once-over told me that at least one person was missing. The bright, bubbly trying-too-hard young woman I'd met last night. Terry? Tina... no, no Tracy. That was her name. Tracy. She wasn't here. And I did not see another unfamiliar face which I'd expected. The woman who would be her boss, the flight delayed exclaimer named Sam.

"We seem to be missing a couple of people," I said casually.

"Oh, yeah... Trace and Sam are still over in the restaurant, finishing breakfast. Trace was bringing Sam up to speed on a few things since she didn't get in until late last night."

"Ah," I said, nodding. It didn't surprise me that they were both running late. Unfair as it may be, I'd already pegged them as the type.

"They'll be here shortly, I'm sure."

I smiled politely. Of course. Sure. Shortly.

"Well, we should start getting everyone set up for the show. If you have any questions, please let me know and I'll be happy to help." I moved away from the counter with the group in tow, and we began setting up for the opening of the show.

Fifteen minutes later I was back at the reception desk, explaining to Andrew and one of the new salespeople how to use the presentation stage monitor controller when I saw the two missing women come into the booth. I watched from the corner of my eye as they approached Steve, speaking with him briefly. He nodded, pointed towards me, and then led them over. They came up and stood politely as I finished my explanation.

When Andrew and the other person had left, Tracy approached, smiling. She motioned to the woman who came up with her. "Sam, this is Jennifer Boyd, the Marcomm manager for the show. Jennifer, this is Samantha Davis, our Senior Brand Manager for the Sinaxsys product line."

The woman reached forward for my hand, smiling brightly. "So, you're Jennifer! Thomas' girlfriend!"

I froze.

"I've really been looking forward to meeting you!" She leaned forward and gave me one of those little hugs that people do when they want you to think you're already old friends. "Thomas has told me so much about you. He just goes on and on about how wonderful you are!" She pulled back, letting go of my hand. "I'd wanted to meet you back in Irvine, but you know, with how hectic things have been the opportunity just never seemed to come up!"

An accident you can see coming you can prepare for. Even if it's only for a moment or two. The worst are the ones that come from out of nowhere. The ones that blind-side you completely. In the moment those happen, in the split-second before impact, time slows. You can sense what is about to take place, feel the flood of absolute terror in anticipation of the pain you are about to suffer, and yet there is nothing you can do to stop it. You are simply left in free-fall, distanced only by the sheer knowledge that nothing you do, even if you could do something, will stop what is about to take place. It is all completely and utterly out of your control.

And then it's over.

Suddenly time begins to move again, and there is such unbelievable chaos internally as you react to what has just taken place. The world seems to explode, and it feels almost as if you might come apart at the seams. I experienced that once when I was young. On a trip with my mother and father we were driving through an intersection when another car T-boned us. I turned my head at the exact moment the car ran the red light. I stared in horrified fascination as the front hood of the car filled the window next to where I was sitting. What had made me turn my head at that exact second, whether it was from some sound or a flash of movement, I'll never know. I had never experienced an adrenalin induced thrill of fear in my life as I did in that millisecond. Had never felt so completely out of control of a situation until the very moment before the car slammed into us.

Until now.

There was a smile plastered onto my face. I could feel it. It felt unnatural, though, as if my skin was stretched across bones in some sort of horror movie death rictus fashion. The woman continued to speak, and at some level I was processing the words, but only on the surface. Inside... inside I wasn't hearing anything. I could see Steve standing behind her, to one side. He had gone stiff, rigid. It was as if I could feel his body through the space that separated us. Feel the tension that coursed through him, his eyes boring into mine for a brief second before they flicked away. He no longer acknowledged me, staring off into space as if I no longer existed. I wanted to go back in time, back to a moment before this woman had opened her mouth. No, back further, back to last night, or the night before that, or over a year ago when all this had truly started. Back to the exact moment when in some sort of fucked up moment of pain I had decided that the best way to deal with what had happened to me was to start down a path of cascading lies that led to this. This right here. This moment of car crash intensity.

I couldn't do that, of course. That's not how life works. Life makes you own up to shit, and sometimes in the most painful way it possibly can. Life makes you see your mistakes in all their glory, and it gives fuck-all about the timing of when that happens. Nor how terrible the ramifications might be.

I stood and watched as my life slowly unraveled in excruciating detail. This woman Samantha continued to go on about Thomas, how they'd worked together at the other company, how much she *loved* him, what a great guy he was, it had been so good to hear when he found someone, and even better someone who worked at the same place. At one level, I was processing all of this, standing there with a smile glued to my face. Nodding when I knew I should, smiling, best professional face I could muster glued on like a cheap Halloween mask. And yet, inside, in my head, where everything that truly mattered was going on, I was completely numb.

The shock had set in.

My eyes flicked back and forth between the woman and Steve. What I saw when I glanced at him filled me with despair. He looked like he was standing at attention, on parade. His eyes were not aimed in my direction, and nothing I did appeared to catch his attention. As Samantha continued to babble on gaily, I realized he had no intention of looking at me. A moment before I'd had a brief second of fantasy that 'Maybe he hadn't heard her'. But now I knew that wasn't true. Steve's stance, the mannequin-like stiffness of his posture, the anger and betrayal that exuded from him put the lie to any notion he hadn't heard Samantha refer to me as 'Thomas' girlfriend,' and everything else she said afterwards. If I was desperately trying to maintain a professional demeanor in front of these people, Steve was matching mine no less.

It was terrible. Horrible.

Finally, Samantha stopped speaking. I responded somehow; words that must have made some degree of sense, because she smiled back at me, nodded at whatever I managed to mutter out, and then I was leading her away from the desk, away from Steve. I took her across the booth to where her other salespeople were gathered. I got them together, asked questions that meant something rational I assume, and then when they seemed to be in a good place on their own, I stepped away. Spinning, I looked back across the booth to where he'd been standing when I'd walked away.

The space was empty. There was no one there now. I whirled, taking in the entire booth in a frenzied glance.

Nothing.

Steve was gone.

SEVENTEEN

I panicked.

I panicked, but I kept my exterior under control, maintained my professional demeanor as best I could. I walked back to the reception desk, head swiveling left and right to catch any sight of him. I got to the desk, and braced my hands on the counter, doing everything I could to calm myself. I kept looking around the booth, through all the salespeople that were now moving about, hoping against hope to catch sight of him. Had he walked out? Off the job? Not that I would have blamed him, but it seemed inconsistent with the way he'd conducted himself up to now, the fucked-up nature of current circumstances notwithstanding. I was close to convincing myself that he had when I caught movement coming around the corner of the tower structure. It was Steve and Keith walking together, talking. I stared at Steve, willing him with every ounce of my being to look my way. I just wanted him to take notice and come to the desk. Alone.

After a moment, the two of them stopped, and then Steve looked my way. Our eyes locked for a second, and then he turned away, saying something to Keith. I did not take my eyes off him, could not. I needed him to come here. So I could ask him to give me one minute. Not to explain myself, but to beg for the time to do so later. There was too much I needed to say, too much I needed to pour out to him than I could in a minute, and there would be no time for it right now. It was impossible. I watched as he finished with Keith, and then he looked my way again. As he began moving towards me, I felt relief wash through me. *Oh, God. Oh, thank God. He's coming over to talk. He'll listen. Of course he will. He has to.*

He has to.

Steve walked up to where I stood at the counter. His face was a mask of cold stoicism, eyes boring into mine. That look cut me worse than any knife could. He stopped and stared at me, wordless. I tried to say something, opened my mouth to speak, but nothing would come.

"Is there anything I can do for you, Ms. Boyd?"

It was his Dom voice, and yet it wasn't. It was deep, command-ing, and yet so brutally dispassionate, so clinically professional, that I sucked in my breath to his words. He might as well have reached out and slapped me when he finished. As badly as it hurt, I could not fault him. What else did I expect him to do? We stood staring at each other, and then I lowered my eyes, desperate not to cry.

"I..." It was as far as I got. The best I could do. The only thing that would come out, and the silence that hung seemed forever before he gave a contemptuous sigh.

"If you have nothing you need, I am going to go back to work, Ms. Boyd. Do you understand me?" He snapped the words out harshly, and if anyone had been close by to hear them I'm sure eyebrows would have been raised. However, it was just the two of us, and though no word he'd spoke was itself untoward, the barely concealed anger and disdain in his tone pierced me.

"I..." I tried to speak up, but the words caught like burrs in my throat. "I just wanted... need to..." I trailed off as someone approached. It was Tracy, the salesperson from last night. I stopped, turning to look at her.

"Umm... sorry, don't mean to interrupt, but Sam has a question regarding the presentation scheduling..." The young woman smiled at us both, unaware of what was going on. I started to tell her I'd be with her in a moment, but it was too late. Before I could open my mouth, Steve turned and walked away without a word.

In my mind, I ran after him. I ignored Tracy, Samantha, all of them and pursued Steve. I caught up to him, grabbed his arm, moved in front of him until I could look up into his face.

"I need to talk to you, Steve! I can't do it right now, please understand. But... please... please, give me ten minutes of your time. Just tell me when, and where, and I'll be there. Sir."

That's what I wish I'd done. But I didn't. Instead, I stood motionless as he strode away.

I followed Tracy over to where Samantha and Andrew stood in front of the presentation stage. I spent the next twenty minutes reviewing the scheduling with them. I know I was saying the right words, but my mind was in a different place. By the time we'd finished, and I had walked back to the reception counter, there was no trace of Steve. I stood there, trying to gather my thoughts into something cohesive, less panicked. On the surface, I hoped I was behaving professionally, because inside I was not. I was body bag material. Emotionally blown apart, pieces everywhere, and no idea if I could put them back together into anything remotely whole. Leaning back against the counter, I scanned the booth, hoping to catch sight of him. I just needed to corner him, give me a minute that even with all his suppressed anger and rage I'd have a chance to finish what I wanted to say. An impassioned plea that he had every right to ignore. Aside from a few co-workers coming up to ask questions, I stewed alone with thoughts that grew increasingly desperate. There was still no sign of him by the time the announcement came over the convention center loudspeakers that the show would open in ten minutes.

I moved from the counter, heading through the booth. I finally caught sight of Keith loading a cabinet with literature. I took a breath, did everything I could to make it so my voice would not sound as desperate as I felt as I walked up to him.

"Keith, have you seen Steve?"

He looked up at me. "Oh, he's gone, Ms. Boyd. He said that he needed to take care of some paperwork and that if I needed him to just give a call over the radio. Did you want me to get him back here?"

I went numb with despair. I shook my head no. "Thank you, Keith. It's fine."

"If you need anything, just let me know. I'm going to head out too once the show opens."

I nodded, and then turned and walked slowly across the booth, back to the reception counter.

I felt so hollow inside. Both numb and helpless in this situation at the same time. I wish I'd exhibited the strength of character that I so prided myself in. Marched myself out of the booth, tracked Steve down, and at a bare minimum apologized for what I had done. But I didn't. I stood there, rooted in the same spot at the reception counter I'd been at all morning. As the show opened I put my game face on, smiled, and made all the right noises while everything else inside me went over the edge and into an endless black hole. I did my fucking job, and by every metric I could take stock of, I did it with my usual thoroughness and acumen.

Yay fucking me.

Throughout the morning, I kept seeing Steve's face in my head. That cold look he'd cast at me just before he turned and walked away. I analyzed it from every angle in my mind, and I came up with a hundred different thoughts on what he'd been thinking about me. None of them good. How could I think anything other than that? Steve had caught me out in my lie. And it was the worst possible lie he could have discovered. Not *'Oh, yeah, I'm actually 42 not 32...'* or *'Yeah, not really a fan of being spanked; I faked that just to make you happy.'*

No, I went for the mother of all lies.

'I'm still technically in a relationship, and I just cheated on my soon-to-be ex-boyfriend. With you.'

I knew by Steve's look and demeanor just how much that had affected him. Hurt him. Angered him. The worst thing, though, was what I didn't know. Just how horrible of a person he thought I was. Whether he truly hated me now. If he would ever give me a chance to apologize and try to explain. He owed me answers to none of those. He owed me nothing. But the desperate part of me wanted the chance.

Wanted those few minutes I should have run after him earlier and asked for. It was selfish, but I clung to the idea that if I could just explain things to him, tell him the terrible choices I had made, that somehow I might soften that look from the icy disgust I was convinced I'd seen to maybe just mild repugnance. I would take that as a victory, right now.

At lunch I made my way to the service desk for the I&D company. I looked for Steve, but there was no sign of him when I got there. I forced myself to go up to the desk and speak to the two women behind it.

"Is Steve around by any chance?"

The one woman frowned and then shook her head. "No, I haven't seen Steve since this morning. Did you need some help over at your booth? I can get one of the guys to come over right away."

"No, no," I waved my hand. "It's nothing urgent. I just had a question about the call in the morning."

"You're booth 2235, right?" The woman gave me a helpful smile. "I'll make sure Tony knows you came by. I'm sure he'll get back to you right after lunch."

I smiled weakly. "Oh, no, it's fine. It's nothing, honestly. I was just checking..." Before I could dig that hole any deeper, I gave a slight wave, and then turned, walking away.

I sat at a table in the convention center's atrium, but didn't eat lunch. I couldn't. The thought of food made me nauseous, and the tension that racked me only made it worse. I had no way of contacting Steve. I'd never asked for his cell number, and I had no idea where he was staying. I wasn't about to press anyone at the I&D company for a way to get in touch with him. The last thing I needed to do now, on top of everything else, was get him in trouble with his employer. If I pressed Tony or someone else to get his phone number, or asked about where he was staying, it would raise eyebrows for certain. There'd be questions followed by assumptions, and none of them good. He deserved my continued discretion, considering everything else I'd put him through this morning.

Sitting there, I had a momentary surge of anger directed at Steve. He'd walked away from me, leaving me there, not given me my moment to explain things to him. To offer my apology. He could at least have had the courtesy of doing that, but instead he'd abandoned me. As I was building myself up into a good head of steam, my self-loathing—who'd mostly gone into hiding since the other day—came back full force.

-Oh, yeah.... that's rich. You think this is his fault? That he owes you anything? That you have any right to be mad at him? What a bitch...-

He could have at least given me an opportunity!

-To what!? To lie to him some more!? Hmmm? He owed you a chance to do that, eh? God, you are a fucking piece of work.-

I wasn't going to lie to him!

-Sure you weren't. He'd have no reason to believe otherwise, right? RIGHT!?-

Fuck off.

-Make me. Oh, wait, you can't. Because you fucked things up bad, Jen. And you know I'm right.-

My internal dialogue was everything I didn't need right now. There was no having a clear, rational discussion with it. I was my own worst enemy, and what really hurt was coming to realize that all of this wasn't just a function of what had taken place this morning. This was just the last move in the end game of something I had started fifteen months ago. The denouement now playing out was one I'd set the stage for a long time ago, and it was following the script life gave it. To punish me for my lies and hubris. And I deserved that. Every damn step of the way.

In the end, the anger towards Steve dissipated. I had no rational way of maintaining it. He hadn't done anything wrong except to be in the wrong place at the wrong time. I was an emotional IED that had had remained hidden until I could blow up in his face. And the pain I suspected he was feeling was all me. I owned that, and goddamn if it didn't slice into me like a knife.

After an hour trying to think through and process all the things I'd done, I accomplished nothing of any real value other than I felt like crawling into a hole and disappearing from the world. That didn't happen. Instead, I dragged myself back to the booth and plastered on a plastic altogether unconvincing smile I'm sure made me look like some sort of blow-up doll. No one seemed to notice. It was the first day of the show and people were amped up, especially those who'd come over from the other company. I wasn't even registering on anyone's radar right now. When I returned from lunch, the girl who had taken over for me held up a business card. I recognized the logo. It was from the I&D company.

"Ms. Boyd, some guy came around looking for you while you were at lunch."

My heart leaped to my throat, and with an effort I stopped myself from snatching the card from her hand. As she held it I reached over smoothly and took it. I looked at the front eagerly.

It was from Tony.

"Oh." I said, feeling my heart sink back into my chest. I flipped it over, but there was nothing written on the back. It took a moment, but I realized that one of the women at the service desk had obviously passed along to Tony that I had stopped by. He'd come around at lunch to find out what I needed. That was all. No Steve.

"Thank you," I said politely, putting the card into one of the desk drawers. This day was going to be a long one. As I sat at the counter I became more and more preoccupied with my internal misery, and despite my efforts, it began to show.

"You OK? You seem a little out of it." Tracy had snuck up on me, and her hand on my shoulder broke me out of my trance.

"Oh," I gave a little start, turning on the stool. I saw who it was and took a deep breath, forcing a too-bright smile onto my face. "Oh, thank you. I'll be fine. Just a little post set-up exhaustion. It happens sometimes."

Her head bobbed energetically in sympathy. "Oh! Yeah, I can imagine. This booth is so big! It must be a ton of work!"

"Yeah, it is." I nodded, putting on my best world-weary look. "Sometimes it catches up with you, you know?"

She gave me a reassuring pat on the shoulder as she moved off. I closed my eyes and hoped that exchange would buy me some understanding later when I announced this evening that I wouldn't be up to joining them for dinner. Because I was going to do just that, even if it got back to Loren. I could hold it together during the show, but no more than that right now. I needed to corner Steve tonight during the check-in. And if I had the tiniest sliver of karma left to my name, maybe he'd give me a few minutes. To grovel and apologize for having lied to him. And if I was lucky, maybe he'd give me enough time to explain how I'd tried to end things with Thomas, how he'd blown me off, refusing to return my calls and texts. At this point, I'd just be happy if he'd listen to *anything* I had to say. Before he told me what a piece of shit I was and walked off.

The rest of the day passed in fits and starts. There were times I kept busy handling something going on within the exhibit. At others, I sat at the reception counter wallowing in misery. No matter what I kept that smile taut across my face. I appreciated the times when I was busy because it stopped me from brooding. Still the day seemed to drag on interminably. Thoughts of Steve, the look on his face, the tone of his voice continued to plague me. Added to everything else, now that my self-loathing had kicked back into high gear, it began flashing mental images of a different Steve to me. The one who had looked at me with such affection. Lust. Desire.

-*Hey, do you remember when he looked at you like this last night? Good times, huh? Ooo, but then you fucked that up, didn't you? When you shit all over him this morning. Wow! Good job, Jen! Fucking impressive!*-

The announcement at 6:15pm that the show would soon close for the day was like a reprieve from the warden. For the first time in hours I actually smiled a real smile. One of relief. I watched as people began to move out across the hall towards the exit doors. I looked around at my co-workers. They'd congregated in small groups, talking amongst themselves, and I guessed that maybe two or three clients at most remained. I wanted things to be over as quickly as possible, so I would have as much time as I could to speak with Steve alone. In spite of all of my self-pity and self-loathing over the course of the day, I'd spent some time coming up with a plan of how I wanted the conversation to go. I would bare my soul to him, and though I didn't expect it to garner me much sympathy, at least I would walk away knowing I'd tried. One thing was for certain, I would not lie about anything, no matter what he asked. If he chose to humiliate me and make me bare every mistake I'd made, I'd do it. No reservations. Dignity didn't play much part in my plan. But honesty sure as fuck did.

I was mulling this over when Samantha and Tracy approached.

"Oh, Jen, I cannot tell you how great things went today! Thank you so much for all of your help!" Samantha was gushing, standing shoulder to shoulder with me. Arm around my waist, she gave me a tight hug. Under different circumstances I would have eaten it up. Right now, it was like nails on a chalkboard, and it took everything I had not to stiffen and pull away from her.

"Oh, I am so glad to hear that! That's what all the hard work I put into the last few days is all about."

"I hope you'll come have dinner with us tonight. I'd really love to hear all about you and Thomas and catch up on other things. I have so many questions!"

She giggled as if we were going to be best friends, and it was no fault of hers that I had the sudden urge to grab her by the throat and tell her she was the one who had destroyed what I had had planned for this evening, and—no, no thank you—I would not be having dinner with her tonight. I had my own plans, and they most definitely did not include her or talking about Thomas.

"Oh, can I be honest, Sam?" I played the same card I done with Tracy, angling for sympathy. "I mentioned to Tracy earlier that I am really feeling kinda out of it today. I think some of the stress of the set-up is catching up to me. Could I take a raincheck on dinner tonight? I just need a night to recoup, and I promise I'll be ready to go out tomorrow evening."

Samantha smiled at me sympathetically, giving me a gentle squeeze. "Of course, Jen! Of course! I totally understand! You've worked so hard, and today was just fantastic! You take the night off and rest. I'm sure we can catch up tomorrow evening."

"Thank you so much." I smiled wearily, nodding my head. "I really appreciate it."

After more pleasantries and thanks for all I had done, Sam and Tracy moved off to the large group that had formed at the center of the booth. I sighed, glad to have at least that one thing out of the way. Now it was just the small matter of waiting for Steve to show for the check-in. Yeah, small matter. No big deal. Just going to spill my guts out on the floor in front of him and hope that he didn't ask to rip my heart out too.

The show now closed, the salespeople began to drift out of the exhibit. As they did, I caught movement out of the corner of my eye. It was someone in a gray shirt and jeans, walking into the booth. Pulse tripling, I turned to face him.

It was Tony. With Keith trailing not far behind.

I frowned, watching in nervous silence as they approached.

Where's Steve?

"Evening Ms. Jen," Tony said genially, smiling. "Sorry I missed you earlier today. Everything OK? Anything you need done tonight?"

I need to know why you're here and not Steve.

I swallowed, then shook my head, keeping the smile plastered to my face, my voice calm and level. "No, no, everything's fine, Tony." I took a deep breath and then tried to make my voice as casual as possible. "I think we're good with everything for tonight. The guys can handle anything that comes up in the morning during the wipe down."

Okay, he was too angry to come for the check-in tonight. I get it. That's fine. Slight change in plan, but I'll see him tomorrow morning and I can talk to him then.

Tony nodded. "OK, sounds good, Ms. Jen. Just wanted to make sure you were taken care of." Tony inclined his head towards Keith. "Keith and Toby will be by first thing in the morning to take care of the wipe down and handle anything you need."

No. No, that's not right.

"Keith... and Toby." I stammered, pulse racing like a humming-bird's heart. Forcing myself to regain my calm, I shoved composure back into my voice. "Steve won't be here?"

"Oh, yeah, sorry, Ms. Jen. Stevie went home. He said something came up, family emergency I think, and he needed to head back early. But don't you worry, Keith and the guys will make sure you're taken care of. We gotcha covered."

No.

For a second, I felt an eerie sense of disassociation. I was looking down, seeing myself standing there at the desk, Tony and Keith on the other side facing me. I froze as everything crumbled and fell to rubble at my feet. An observer watching as the final bits of my hubris piled up around me.

No. Please.

"Ah. I see." I tried. I tried so hard not to let any emotion show in those words. I had no idea if I succeeded or not, other than Tony's look did not change as he stood watching me. I absorbed the shock of Tony's announcement in agonizing silence before my instincts kicked in once more.

"Well then, I'll see the guys in the morning. Thanks, Tony." I smiled as firmly as I could, and this time I heard something approaching poise in my voice. All phony and blandly professional as I could make it to overcome the absolute hollowness that was my soul. Tony gave me a smile as Keith stood by as impassively as ever.

"Alright then, Ms. Jen. We'll see you in the morning!" The two men walked off, leaving me in the exhibit. Everyone else had left while we were talking, and now I was alone, unable to move.

Steve had gone home. 'Something had come up...' Yes something had. I had. I had come to Steve professing honesty, truth, and trust. What I had given him instead was lies and betrayal. Betrayed the trust he had put in me, deceived him about the very thing we'd spoken about that first night. He had been truthful and honest with me. I knew it in my heart. Steve had been first to tell me how this wasn't something he did, wasn't who he was. And then later how much being with me had meant to him. And I had rewarded that honesty and sincerity by lying, right up to the moment that life slapped him in the face with the truth of who I really was.

So, sure, something had come up. Falsehoods and treachery had come to Steve in the form of me. So, what did I expect him to do? Stay here and give me additional chances to lie to him? To create more stories and false narratives to justify what I had done? Why should he—why would he—give me that opportunity?

My dad had once taught me a lesson on fighting. He'd said 'Sometimes, Jen, you have to know when to make a strategic retreat. There's no sense in letting your enemy beat on you when there is nothing to be gained by standing your ground.' I realized as I stood there what Steve had done. He'd retreated. There was nothing for him to gain by staying here. By giving me a chance to make up some sob story about how this was all just a big misunderstanding. A case of mistaken identity, or some bullshit lie like that. What would give him any cause to think that over the course of the afternoon I'd had a sudden epiphany to turn over a new leaf and stop lying now? Not a fucking thing. In his place, no reasonable person would have done anything different. Cut your losses and move on. So, he did. He got himself as far away from me and my toxic presence as he could. Back home to where he could lick his wounds in private. To forget about the cruelty of a person who had promised honesty and truth, but who had proved to be nothing more than a compulsive liar.

The one thing that had held at bay the full weight of my despair and self-loathing during the afternoon was the thought that maybe, just maybe, if I could speak to Steve, I might be able to convince him I could be truthful, at least once. I would lay all my cards on the table, tell him with every bit of honesty and candor what had happened with me, and why I had done what I had.

And now that was gone. Not a chance in hell of that happening.

I don't remember how long I stood there. I know I didn't cry. One hand on the reception counter, I leaned against it as every part of me drifted away into darkness. A simple sound broke me from my reverie. A cleaning person somewhere nearby was already at work, and the *vmmmm* of a vacuum being run across the floor finally caused me to move. I looked slowly around myself, and then I was walking. I walked, and the next time I was aware of where I was, I was stepping into the lobby of the Hyatt.

That was when the tears started.

Why they started then I couldn't explain. Maybe it was because I remembered when Steve had picked me up in this very lobby two nights ago. The night that had been so incredible that even now thinking about it tore like claws ripping through flesh. I felt my eyes brimming, and then tears were spilling down my cheeks as I hurried across the floor. There were so many people there from the show, gathered together and talking, laughing. I ignored them, moving across the lobby until I was in front of the elevators. I kept my face down, watching in fascination as my tears fell and landed like tiny beads of glass onto the polished marble of the floor. I felt completely disjointed from my surroundings. All I could see was those drops falling, moving as if in slow motion. My vision wavered, blurring the sight of the splash and spread of each one as they impacted with the tile. When the bell sounded for an elevator God took pity on me, and I slipped into one alone. I punched my floor number. The door slid closed before anyone else got in, and I choked out a sigh of relief. I could see myself in a mirrored section of the wall. I wanted to see some monster, some hideous being that reflected the way I felt inside. It wasn't there. It was just me. Red eyes, wet streaks across my cheeks. An empty shell that had once been a human being.

That was the moment I hit rock bottom.

I got to my door, fumbled for my keycard, got it in on the second try. Reeling into my room, I let the door close behind me with a click. I did not reach for any lights, but simply threw my bag to the floor, and collapsed on the bed.

And then I really cried.

I lay there and cried. Despair hollowed me out for what I had done to Steve. For what I had done to Thomas. And then I cried for what I knew I still had to do. Eventually, I cried for myself. For what I had done to me. I curled up on the bed, and into myself. I grieved over the memories of what had taken place over the past two days. Accepting the misery that came from acknowledging the consequences of my past decisions had culminated in what had taken place on the booth floor this morning. Tearful recognition that I had to take ownership of them. There was no lessening of the pain in any of this. No sense of catharsis. I knew what I had done. I knew what I still had to do. And fuck me if it didn't hurt so goddamn much.

At some point I got up and took a shower. Afterwards, I wrapped myself in a towel, and climbed back into bed. I didn't feel as if I was in control of my body, but that someone else was inside me, running the show.

*Just get under the covers. Fuck PJs, just burrow deep. Eyes closed.
I'm shutting you down for your own good.*

And I did. I collapsed into sleep. My dreams were all anxiety,
fear, and an almost crushing tension. I slept, not awaking until my
alarm went off at 5:30. To begin another day.

It would be nice to say as I got up and went about getting myself
ready for the coming day that I pulled myself together. That I put
my 'big girl' pants on and did everything I needed to do to move on.
But that would be another lie. I struggled. I skipped my morning
workout—a mistake. I drank coffee I picked up from the hotel
restaurant but skipped breakfast—another mistake. I did, however,
manage to drag myself over to the booth and get there on time somehow. I slapped on my professional work face, got Keith and Toby
started on wiping down the exhibit, and I tried not to see Steve in
every glance of gray shirts. When the rest of the staff showed up, I
made every day idle chit-chat, let Samantha know how much I
appreciated the alone time of the previous night, and got the show
up and running for the second day. It wasn't my finest work, but I
made it through the day. I had only one breakdown where I fled to
the bathroom, sitting on the toilet and crying for a few minutes. I
pulled myself through it. Bore down and got my head back in the
game. And though the day was long and my thoughts as unfocused
and disjointed as they had been the day before, I made it to the end
in one reasonably cohesive piece.

After the show was tough. It didn't go as easy as I had hoped it
might. As much as I wanted to beg off going to dinner with my co-
workers once again, I knew I couldn't. Corporate politics being
corporate politics, I knew I'd be treading a fine line if I tried to skip
going out with Samantha and the staff a second night. This would
be the last chance for us to have dinner together, as the show was
closing the next day. Once the tear-down began I would be busy, so
it was tonight or never. And while I would have much preferred the
'never,' that wasn't a realistic option.

"So, Jen... Thomas has told me so much about you!"

I winced internally. I was trapped at dinner with Samantha, and this was going to happen whether I liked it or not. And there was no viable exit strategy here.

"Well, I hope it's all been good!" I gave her a bright, fake smile, masking my chagrin.

Samantha reached over and patted my hand. "Oh, it's been nothing but wonderful! It is so good to see he finally found someone as incredible as you!"

Yeah. Great. She had a scalpel, and was carving me into pieces, and she didn't even know it.

Somehow, I made it through the meal. Smiled when I was supposed to smile, laughed when it was appropriate, and I didn't break down into tears or scream when a part of me so desperately wanted to. I even managed to be gracious when Samantha pulled me into a hug and told me how wonderful it was to finally get to talk with me. How she was so "looking forward to working with me", and "how lucky Thomas was." She had carved me up emotionally, but outwardly I held it all together. I clutched at the bloody pieces of me until I made it back to my room.

And then I fell apart.

I collapsed on the bed and sobbed. I curled up and cried until exhausted. I drifted in and out of sleep for some time after that, switching back and forth from crying to tension filled torpor, and then back to weeping again. Eventually I forced myself up and undressed, heading to the shower. I leaned against the wall of the enclosure, and then let myself slip down until I was curled up at the bottom, squeezed into a far corner. The water pounded down on me like a million tiny fists, and I cried. I cried until there was finally nothing left. I was empty, and in its own way that was liberating. Finally, I stepped out of the shower, grabbed a towel, and as I dried myself, I gazed into the mirror, staring at the person who stared back.

It was just me. Nothing more. Just the person I was, looking back, exhausted.

I wiped the last of the water from my hair, dropping the towel unceremoniously to the floor before walking back to the bed. I crawled in, pulled the covers over my head, and fell almost immediately into a dreamless sleep.

The next day passed in a blur. I'd thought I'd spend most of it in self-reflection, contemplating my past and future—except I didn't. I just moved from one thing to the next, and in between my mind was a blank slate. At some deep, core level I knew what challenges faced me in the coming days and weeks, but for the moment I was a spent force. I had no energy for any of it, and the best I could do right now was pull my work face on and make it through the day. Everything else would come eventually, and I would face what I needed to face, but for now I needed a vacuum, and that's what I created for myself.

The end of the show was a celebration of sorts for my co-workers, but for me it was just another checkbox ticked off on my list of things that I could put behind me. I made big smiles when I needed to, accepted the praise and accolades from everyone on what a great show this had been, and before I really had a chance to process it, they were gone. In the past, the close of a show often left me feeling melancholy. This time it was different. There were no wistful feelings. Only a finality that was neither oppressive nor liberating. It was just done. Over. Keith and the crew arrived to begin the dismantle, and I went about my job efficiently if perfunctorily. We would only work a four- hour minimum tonight, so I knew what to expect we'd get done. A part of me began thinking of Steve, fixating on the fact he wasn't here, but I pushed the thoughts away. I wanted nothingness. Just clear mental space where I could operate on autopilot. The past was over, and the future would handle itself in due time. For now, I simply wanted to be.

We finished up for the night, and after the crew was gone I took stock of where we were. They'd done a good job. We were exactly at the point I'd expected us to be, if not slightly further along. Tony had stopped by just before the end of the shift to check up and see how things were going. I started to ask if he'd heard from Steve, but stopped myself. Why would I? To Tony and anyone else Steve was just another worker. An installation and dismantle supervisor on an exhibit for a show that was over and done. He was gone, replaced by another who had performed just as efficiently. Why would I ask about Steve? Why should I care?

So, I didn't ask. I thanked Tony for everyone's hard work and then let it go. Tomorrow they would be back and we would finish the dismantle. After that the exhibit would be packed on the trucks to return to the warehouse. And I would head home.

To Thomas. To fix the final thing that needed fixing.

I ate dinner by myself in the hotel restaurant. After finishing my meal, I went to my room, showered, and then packed most of my things. I still had one more night here after this, and then the following morning I would be on my way to the airport, heading home. It felt right to be preparing, making the motions to move away from this room, this place. When I completed packing, I sat in a chair looking out the window at the lights of Chicago, to the edge of the waterfront, the water of Lake Michigan beyond. Even though the final day of the show was behind me, I didn't allow myself to obsess over everything that had taken place beforehand. I kept my mind as blank as I could. The demon that was my self-destruction was there lying in wait, and it clamored to be let loose. To tear at me and drag me down to its level. It smelled blood in the water, the raw meat that was my psyche. But it was patient. It knew—I knew—that there would be opportunity aplenty for it to rip me apart later. For now, it only needed to bide its time, knowing I would eventually unlock the chains so it could run loose.

I slept without waking that night. It was not a restful sleep, but I did not wake up crying multiple times as I had the night before. The next morning I drug myself down to the gym, forcing myself through my workout routine. When I finished I felt a sense of having accomplished something. Something for myself. Something that was good, not destructive. I went back to my room, cleaned up, grabbed a quick breakfast. I was back at the booth before the crew even arrived.

The convention center had changed already. The atmosphere was back to what it had been during the install, and not that during the show. The air conditioning had been shut off, and the humid air coming in from the dock doors settled back into the hall. The aisles were full of client crates and skids, and the sound and smell of forklifts moving about filled the space. As I stood inside the booth it stabbed at me; memories of everything that had started four days ago came flooding back. I clenched my hands, forcing thoughts and images down. No. No, not yet. Too soon. I still needed time, and space, and distance. I needed to be away from here, away from Chicago, back home. Then I could allow myself the luxury, if I could call it that, of giving in to all the emotions that wanted to overwhelm me. There would be time for that later. But not now.

"Ms. Jen!" Tony's voice carried through the booth as he showed up with the crew a short time later. "You're here early! I didn't even see you come by the desk."

I smiled at him. "I didn't, Tony. I'm sorry. I just wanted to take a look and see where we're at and go over a few things in my head."

"Well, Keith and I were just talking about that, and we think you're gonna be in good shape, Ms. Jen. I don't see any reason you ain't gonna be down and packed by this evening, if not sooner."

Keith was nodding solemnly as Tony spoke, and I grinned.

"That's good, Tony, because I have a 9am flight tomorrow morning, and I'd love to be on it. Much as I love Chicago and all..."

That got a chuckle out of the assembled crew, including Tony.

"Well, we love having you here, Ms. Jen, but we understand. We're gonna make sure you ain't gonna miss your plane."

The crew lived up to Tony's word. The day went by in a blur as the exhibit came down, and then packed away. I spent most of my time double-checking every crate before they sealed it up and then filling out and applying shipping labels to each once they were ready. At lunch we were more than halfway completed, and there seemed little to stop us from being done before the normal 5pm quitting time. I'd already heard discussions amongst some of the crew that they were eager to get the job completed; another exhibit that promised overtime was waiting, and they were eager to jump on that. By 4pm they had all the main exhibit properties disassembled and packed away. Keith approached me quietly.

"Ms. Boyd, I was wondering if you'd be okay if I cut a few of the guys to go on another call? All we have left is to pull up the carpet and pad, and I think me and a couple of the guys can handle that ourselves."

I gave him an understanding smile. "I heard the guys talking earlier, Keith. It's fine. Let them go get some OT. As long as you can finish off what's left, we're good."

"Thank you." He nodded, a slight grin coming over his normally serious face. "The guys'll really appreciate that." He motioned with his thumb towards them. "I'll go let them know, and then we'll start pulling up the carpet."

I nodded as he headed off. We were in a good spot, and I'd little concerned with what we had left to do. Unless something fell apart, even with a reduced crew I knew we'd be done in plenty of time.

By 5:30 Keith and the three guys that had remained behind had finished everything. They'd rolled all the carpet, strapped the padding to the pallets, and all that remained was loading the pieces to onto the truck. Keith and the crew came up to me, toolboxes in hand.

"Ms. Boyd, unless you need us for anything else, we're gonna bounce onto that other booth."

"No, go, go." I waved them off. "Everything here is done. Go make some real money."

That earned another chuckle, and Keith stuck out his hand.

"Thanks, Ms. Boyd. See you next show."

"Thanks Keith." I smiled, taking his hand. "See you next show."

They moved off, leaving me standing in the space where the exhibit had once been. Now it was just a congregation of packed crates and pallets. There was nothing for me to do but wait, so I moved and sat on the stacked carpet rolls, my feet dangling over the edge.

I looked around silently.

It was over.

Feet kicking back and forth, I gave into reflection. It was funny sometimes how something that ends up being the catalyst for a huge shift in your life can begin from such an innocuous event. I had come to Chicago for just another trade show, one of hundreds I had done in my career. It was supposed to be easy. Simple.

Life had other plans.

I would be leaving in the morning, heading home to yet another tectonic shift in my current life. One that was needed. Required. Long overdue. I could sit here now and realize that the underpinnings of what had taken place the four days I'd been here had started back home. Begun the night Thomas announced *he* understood what I wanted. That he was going to take care of me. 'Fuck me hard.' Back then I'd been frustrated with myself. With why I wasn't happy. Why I couldn't just be overjoyed and *in love* with a man like Thomas Kiernan— but I knew why now. The thing was, knowing that didn't make it any better. I looked down at my feet, watching them as they swung back and forth in a slow arc. Pursing my lips, I bore down to stop tears that suddenly wanted to flow.

No.

No, that was wrong. It hadn't started the day of Thomas' discovery. It had started the day I'd said to myself I was over being sexually submissive. The day I had created that lie. The most painful lie of all, and I'd told it to no one other than myself. After that, the lies —the *other* lies—started piling on top of each other until we'd reached this moment. Lie after lie after lie, and a trail of bodies in their wake. I took a deep breath and then let it out slowly.

And one more yet to go.

"These your crates?"

The voice startled me out of my thoughts. A gruff looking Teamster was standing to one side, paperwork in hand, his forklift idling nearby.

"Yes, they are."

"Well, I'm here to take them. Anything special I should know?" I looked around at them. Gazed at the now-empty exhibit space, the hall, everything I could see. I turned back, staring at him for a moment.

I shook my head.

"No. Not now. Nothing special at all."

EIGHTEEN

I flew home the next morning.

I had a direct flight from Chicago O'Hare. A little over four hours' time in the air. I made it out of the hotel, to the airport, and all checked in with plenty of time to spare. I was still in damage-control mode, though. Still in a sort of mental free-fall where I kept waiting for the parachute to deploy, wondering if it would.

I was sitting in the departure lounge when I felt my phone vibrate. I pulled it out idly.

A text message. From Thomas.

Your flight gets in at 11. I'll pick you up in baggage claim.

A surge of rage shot through me. *Seriously? Now you can text? You fucker!* When I arrived home, I'd every intention of taking an Uber to my apartment. I had no desire to talk to Thomas right now. I was still raw. Clenching my phone as I read the message, my teeth set on edge.

Having second thoughts about your little snit fit, aren't you? Fucking asshole. Well, fuck you. You started this, not me.

I began typing out a reply. *Sorry, Thomas, but I don't want a fucking ride from the airport. I don't want a fucking anything from you.* I paused, my thumb over the SEND button. Wait. No. No, that was exactly what he wanted. Sending that made things easy on Thomas. Gave him the perfect out. Turned everything he'd done from *his* problem into *my* problem. Screw that shit. Change in plans. I deleted the message. I sent him nothing. He'd wanted to have his teachable moment. *That's what it feels like not being communicated with, Jen. Not fun, is it?* And now he was having second thoughts. Too fucking bad. If that was his strategy, it failed. I had my own lesson plan. And when I got home, this was going to be finished. A surgical strike that ended it once and for all. Over.

Thomas met me in baggage claim. He approached, coming up to give me a hug. I flinched as his arms came around me, and the glee I felt when he hesitated, almost jerking back, was the most joy I'd had in days. To Thomas' credit he followed through, but the awkwardness of it was undeniable. I brought my arms up, hugged him—if you could call it that—in return. The stiffness between us was palpable. A tension that pushed us part like magnets in polar opposition.

"Hey." he murmured, pulling away. He stared at me, and the assessing look in his eyes spoke volumes. *Did you learn your lesson?*

"Hi Thomas." I gave him a tight smile, and then turned to the carousel, ignoring him as I watched for my bag. *I did, but not the one you're thinking of.*

During the car ride back to the apartment we rode mostly in silence. There were brief moments of strained conversation, followed by longer periods where the only sound was the road noise.

"Good trip?"

"Yes."

"Show go well?"

"Mmhmm."

I kept thinking I should say it now. Tell him. At the very least start the conversation. I glanced at him once, twice, each time intending to begin. But I didn't. The words wouldn't come. My inner demon chortled.

-I knew it. I knew it! You're going to give in, aren't you? You fucked things over with Steve, and now you're going to lie to Thomas and try to salvage something out of this mess. Aren't you?-

I am not.

-Then do it, Jen. Say. It. SAY IT!-

My anger from earlier was still there, but now there was another layer added to it. The growing irritation I had with myself, my sudden inability to '*just say it*', became an acid burn. It aggravated me that I was hesitating. I should just tell him he was an asshole. That his little game had achieved nothing because we were over. Had been for some time, as he would have known if he hadn't begun behaving like a dick. Not only that, I rationalized to myself, I wasn't the only one who could start a goddamn conversation. He was just as capable as I was. And he sure as fuck had something to say. I didn't need to be a rocket scientist to sense that.

In the end, nothing happened. Beyond the trivial two to three-word questions and answers that went back and forth between the long silences, neither of us said anything substantial. We were with each other, but we couldn't have been further apart.

He took me to my apartment. It was a surreal situation. We were like two gunfighters staring each other down. Waiting for one to make the first move so the pistols could come out and the shooting begin. I went to my bedroom, unpacked my clothes. Thomas stayed out in the living room, doing something on his laptop. Half an hour went by, then an hour. I grew more and more angry, more and more frustrated, and more and more determined that he would be the one to fucking blink. Not me. No. He started this fucking game, but I'd sure as fuck show him how to finish it. I could do this. I'd pretend like nothing was going on. Just another day in the life. I put the last of my things away, grabbed the basket of dirty laundry, and walked out into the living room. Thomas looked up as I came in.

"I'm going to start a load of laundry. Did you want lunch?"

"Sure."

Goddammit.

I marched to the alcove where the washer was and dumped in the dirty clothes. *Okay, he's going to match you tit-for-tat, isn't he?* I slammed the door closed.

-Well then, do something about it, Jen. Go in there and finish this. Tell him the truth. Tell him it's over.-

No! He needs to break! He needs to go first! He started this! Not me!

-Oh my fucking God. Are you kidding me?-

I tossed the empty basket on the floor, went and looked in the fridge. I cobbled something together from what I had, making as decent a lunch as I could.

"Here." I handed the bowl of salad to Thomas.

"Oh. Thanks." He took it absently, began eating.

'Oh, thanks?' That's it? That's it! You motherfucking DICK!

I sat in the chair across from the couch, doing my best not to show my fuming. He was pretending to focus on his laptop, doing the lawyer bit to the hilt. Calm, cool, collected and not giving a hint that there was anything he wanted to discuss. I had to give him credit. He was good. But I was better. He wanted to play games? Oh, I could fucking play games too.

-Oh, Jesus. Are you serious, Jen? That's what this all about now? All this bullshit just so you can one-up the man you're supposed to be breaking up with? What the hell is it with you?-

I didn't start this. He did.

-I swear to God. Are you twelve or something?-

The rest of the afternoon we barely spoke five words to each other. Thomas moved only to get up and put his empty bowl in the sink and get another bottle of water.

"You want one?"

"No, I'm fine, thanks."

I sat across from him with my own laptop balanced in my lap, pretending to look at e-mails and catch up on work stuff. What I spent most of my time doing was arguing with myself.

-Let me help you. 'Thomas, we need to talk. Our relationship was

based on a foundation of lies I created, and now it's over. I wish you the best. Get the fuck out.'-

Go to hell. I am not saying that.

-Okay, fine. I don't give a fuck what you say, but say something, goddammit! Or... wait a minute. Hold on here. Or just admit you are going to flake out and give in and just let this ride because you're too weak to do what's right.-

Fuck. Off. Go. To. Hell.

The afternoon became the evening, and finally Thomas got up, stretching.

"Chinese for dinner?"

"Umm... sure. Sounds good."

He went to the kitchen, pulled the menu of our favorite place off the fridge. I listened as he called, placed the order, and then hung up. He sat back down and looked over at me.

Holy fuck. Finally. Here it comes.

"Did you want to watch a movie tonight?" My eye twitched.

What? Are you fucking kidding me?

"Umm, honestly, I think I might go to bed early. I'm kinda tired after the show and the trip."

"Oh. Okay. I understand."

You understand? You understand? Oh, I bet you fucking understand. Well guess what, fucker! I'm not giving in first!

I was as irrational as I could be. Even I recognized that what I was doing was childish, and wrong, but I couldn't stop myself. The part of me that exerted the most control right now was the part that told me in no uncertain terms that I would not cave. I would not be the first to broach the subject that hung between us. Thomas had started this by refusing to take my calls or answer my texts. Now it would be him that had to finish it. To speak up first.

And then I would tell him we were done.

He picked up dinner, and we ate it in near silence. By nine I gave up. My rejection of the movie had sent him straight back to his laptop, and the more I sat there, the angrier and more frustrated I became. The worst part was I couldn't let it show. If I did, then he gained the high ground. I couldn't stand the idea that he'd perceive my being the first to talk as tacit admission that I'd done something wrong, and not he.

-*But that's the truth, isn't it?*-

That's not... I tried... I tried! He started this! Not me!

Tired, irrational, and frustrated at my wits end, I feinted with my own move.

"Thomas, I'm really starting to fade. I think I'm going to head to bed."

"Oh, okay."

And he immediately buried his face back to the screen of his computer.

Oh. Okay.

I nearly exploded. But I didn't. I clenched my jaw until I thought my teeth would crack and didn't say another word. Getting up, I closed the screen of my laptop down with a *snap*, and then padded silently to the bedroom.

I don't know what time Thomas came to bed. Simmering in a stew of anger and exasperation exhausted me, and I hadn't been curled up in bed for half an hour before I drifted off into a broken sleep. I woke up sometime late at night, and Thomas was there, back to me. I rolled towards him, instinctively reached with my arm...

And stopped.

I couldn't finish the move. What had once been as natural as breathing now felt foreign. As if to touch him would be to take a step backwards. To admit and give in to what my conscious had accused me of earlier.

No.

I rolled out of bed, slipped silently to the bathroom. Once I was finished, I stole back in. Thomas never stirred, the gentle rise and fall of his chest the only movement visible. I scooched under the covers, staring at his back. I grit my teeth, then rolled to my side, back to him.

Goddamn you, Thomas Kiernan. Tomorrow. You better fucking do it tomorrow. Or I swear, I will.

-*Yeah, right. Sure. This is* exactly *how it begins...*-

I woke the next morning to an empty bed. Thomas was gone. For a moment I thought he might have gotten up sometime during the night and left. I sat up, my gut tightening. *Shit.* If he'd taken off, I would have to find him. Track him down. Do this on his turf. Maybe he'd realized that, gotten up deliberately just so he could set the stage for...

I heard movement in the kitchen. A cupboard door opening, then closing. The sound of the Keurig humming as he made a cup of coffee. A second later the smell of it drifted into the bedroom. *Thank God.* He was still here.

I rolled out of bed and walked down the hallway and into the dining area. Thomas was in the kitchen, making a second cup. As he worked, he silently handed over the first to me. I took it without a word, taking a sip.

Just the way you like it.

I pinched my lips together painfully. That first morning with Steve was a bright memory that exploded over nerves already tense since I'd awoken. I stared down at the cup, doing everything I could to savagely shove that memory into a box where I could lock it away forever. I did not need this. Especially right now. In the background I heard the Keurig stop, and the room went quiet.

"Okay, Jen. You know what, fuck this. Who wants to go first? Me? Or you?"

The room, my mind, everything suddenly cleared away. Pure, crystalline clarity replaced every thought, every emotion that had been rattling around in my head this morning. I looked up slowly from cup to Thomas. He stared back at me, and for the first time since I'd arrived home, I saw a glimpse of the man I'd known six months ago. The kind, gentle, caring man who I'd fallen in love with. Who'd fallen in love with me. Then his face clouded over, his anger as deep and abiding as mine.

"Thomas, I'm not who you think I am." I took a deep breath, letting it out slowly. "And I'm afraid we're over."

Neither of us moved. There was no sound. Not even our own breathing. And then each of us were moving. Out into the living room to the couch.

Where we both sat down.

Together.

— · ✹ · —

"That's it, huh? 'We're over.'"

"Yes."

"Jesus fucking Christ, Jen. You are something else. That's all you have to say? That's all I'm going to get?"

"Does it really matter?"

"Of course it fucking matters!" Thomas' fist slammed into the couch, and I flinched. "What the fuck kind of comment is that! 'Does it really fucking matter?' You are way too fucking intelligent for me to buy that bullshit, Jen. You have fucking lied to me and lied to me and kept whatever the fuck has been going on away from me, and now you just want to sit there and wipe it all away with this 'does it really fucking matter' shit!"

He rose, stepping towards the window.

I curled my legs under me tighter, hands clenching around my cup. When he whirled towards me, I did not flinch, but faced him head on.

"No." His finger stabbed at me. "No, fuck you. I don't know what the fuck has been going on for the last month, but you do not get off with that crap. Maybe you fell out of love with me a month ago, or even before that. I don't know. But I sure as fuck know you did love me at one time. And I loved you too. And you do not get to just fucking walk away with from this with four fucking words,

Jennifer Boyd." He'd stepped towards me as he spoke until he stood over me, looking down. I could have been afraid. Should have been. But I wasn't.

"You. Owe. Me." His finger jabbed downwards with each word. He stood staring, anger rolling off him in waves.

I stared back, defiant.

He turned slowly, moving back to his end of the couch before sitting down. The next words that came out of his mouth were controlled, unyielding.

"You owe me, Jen. I don't care what the fuck you think of me right now, but you owe me the goddamn courtesy of telling me exactly what the fuck happened here. And what the fuck is going on." He turned, and stared at me with eyes that were cold, dark.

"And you are going to do it. Right now."

"Wait. Are you fucking trying to tell me you think this is *my* fault!"

"You were the one who ignored my calls. And my texts."

"Because I was tired of being ignored myself, Jen! Of being lied to!"

"I didn't lie..." I started to protest and then stopped.

-Yes you did.-

"Yeah." Thomas gave me a knowing look, his lips pulled into a tight slash across his face. "That's right. I'm not fucking stupid, Jen. I knew something was going on. And I got tired of you never being truthful with me. Every time I asked, I got some lame bullshit excuse that it was nothing. That it was work. To just leave it alone. I put up with that for, what? A month? Yeah. After that, I decided that I was going to force the issue, one way or another. I thought you were going to say something that morning before you left, but—nope. Same bullshit. I was done with it. So, I'll be the first to admit it was petty, but if you wanted to treat me that way, I figured I could fucking treat you the same way in return."

"Well, that's really fucking great, Thomas. Bravo to you. You sure showed me. Put me in my place, didn't you?"

"Don't even try to twist this to—"

"Fuck. You. I'm not trying to twist anything. You did this! You! Not me. I was trying to talk to you! I was trying to tell you the fucking truth!" I slammed the coffee cup down onto the table. "Fine, sure, maybe I waited until the worst possible moment. But that excuses you for nothing. Because your fucking timing was for shit, Thomas. Not just mine. And I want you to know something else. If you fucking think for one second that you're the only one who suffered here, that this was something that wasn't tearing me to fucking pieces..." My throat was raw. The words had built almost to a scream, and I could hear it. Feel it in the way my body shook. I stopped myself, my chest heaving. I sucked in one breath, two, doing everything I could to bring myself back under control. "If you really think that, then you can go fuck yourself. I was scared, Thomas. I was frustrated. I didn't know what the fuck to do. All I knew is that I was tearing myself apart. And that the longer I lied, lied to myself *and* to you, the more it was going to hurt."

"Well it seems like you did a pretty fucking bang-up job of that."

"I know." I laughed desolately, a rictus-like grin stretching skin. "I did. Oh, and by the way—fuck you."

— ❀ —

"I remade myself. Into a person that wasn't who I truly am."

"That's the second time you've said that."

"Said what?"

"'I'm not who you think I am.'"

"Oh."

"Oh?"

"What?" I stared at him, shrugging my shoulders.

"Oh my fucking God, Jen!" He shook his head in derision. "Are you seriously going to fucking play that game right now?"

"What game?"

"You are!" He threw up his hands. "Holy shit, you're going to try and act like you have no idea what I am talking about, aren't you?"

"I'm not playing a fucking game, Thomas—"

"Bullshit! Bull fucking shit!" Thomas jabbed a finger towards me. "You know exactly what I am talking about right now but you're going to play this fucking passive aggressive ignorance card like I'm a fucking idiot or something."

"What do you want, Thomas? What's your fucking point here?"

"Okay, I guess we're fucking doing this…" He muttered under his breath. Sighing, he enunciated his next words slowly, as if speaking to a child. "What does that mean? What did you mean by that statement?"

I paused. I looked down at the coffee table. To the empty cup sitting there. I was acting like a child. But I wouldn't admit it. Because he'd acted like a child too. I chuckled bleakly.

"You know, it's funny. Now that I think about it, that does pretty much encapsulate everything." I grinned ruefully, shaking my head. "In all honesty, it's what this all boils down to."

"Honesty." Thomas snorted. "That's pretty ironic coming out of you right now."

I turned my face slowly towards his.

Low blow, dickhead. Low fucking blow.

"You know what, asshole? Fuck off."

"Okay, okay! Fine, I shouldn't have said it. There. Satisfied?"

I sat, taking in deep breaths. Ten minutes of arguing with Thomas to make him concede he'd acted like a dick had me dancing back from the edge of fight / flight.

"Yes. Thank you." I blew out an elongated sigh.

There was a moment's pause and then he rounded on me. "You still haven't answered the original question, though."

"What question?"

He rolled his eyes. "What. Does. That. Mean. The statement you made. Statements." He held up his hand as if to ward off what he assumed I was about to say. "What did you mean with the whole 'I'm not who you think I am' and 'I remade myself' thing?"

I blinked my eyes.

"Where do I begin?"

— ❧ —

"Dominance. And... submission?"

"Yes." I nodded, my voice gentle for the first time since we'd began. "You understand that term, right?"

He shot me an annoyed glance. "Don't fucking patronize me, Jen."

"I'm just asking." I threw up my hands.

He looked down to his lap and then huffed out a long sigh. "Okay, I do. In a sense. I'll admit I'm not well-versed, per se, beyond what little I've picked up from things. Bits and pieces of *Fifty Shades of Grey*, that kind of stuff." He turned his gaze back to me. "I'm guessing it's a lot more complicated than that, isn't it?"

I smiled.

"Yeah. You could say that."

— ❧ —

"Wait, wait, wait." Thomas cut me off, holding up his hand. "I want to make sure I've got this straight. This guy Ben was your... Dom?"

"Yes."

"And you guys were in this relationship for three years. And you were his submissive?"

"Yes."

"And all that time, he was fucking these other... submissives... behind your back?"

Even after all this time it still hurt.

"Yes." I sat my empty cup down and stared across to my living room window. "It's somewhat common in the lifestyle for some couples to engage in—"

"Jen, stop." Thomas cut me off again abruptly. "You said you told him you were strictly monogamous. I did hear you correctly, right?"

"Yes."

"Then why the hell do you sound as if you're trying to defend what he did? It's bullshit, Jen! It's complete and utter bullshit. I don't care what happens in the 'lifestyle'," he rose his fingers into air quotes, "what he did to you was wrong. Wrong. It was cheating, Jen. He cheated on you. No two ways about it."

How easily that blade slipped between my ribs and straight into my heart.

"I... I suppose."

"There's no 'suppose'. There's no two-fucking-ways about it."

— ❀ —

"That's what you meant by 'remaking yourself.'"

"Yes."

"And that was your plan?"

"Umhmm."

Thomas chuckled hollowly, shaking his head.

"Not gonna lie to you, Jen. That was a pretty fucking stupid plan."

For the first time since we'd started, I felt tears slip down my cheeks.

"I know."

— ❀ —

"Can I ask you something?"

"Of course." I glanced over at him. His face was serious as he stared back at me.

"Was there someone else?"

It felt as if he'd punched me. For a moment I couldn't breathe. *Don't tell him. Don't tell him. Think up a lie! Quick!*

"Yes. But it didn't work out."

I turned to him, waiting for his reaction. I watched as his hands clenched in his lap. His jaw went tight, achingly taut. I remained still as he sat in silence, rigid.

When he spoke, his voice cracked at first, then became firm.

"I'm sorry to hear that."

"Why?" I whispered.

"Because you deserve someone. Someone who is right for you. Who can be for you what you need. And someone out there deserves you, Jennifer." He turned, and his gaze latched onto me. He held me with his eyes, and I waited for the blow.

"But that person is not me."

The room was silent. Neither of us moved. Finally, Thomas shook his head.

"I could never be that person for you. Never. It's just not who I am, Jen. That... those... things are just not a part of me. And unlike you I'm not willing to lie and claim it's someone I could become."

"Ouch. Touché." I sniffled, wiping the tissue across my nose.

"Well, it's not like you don't deserve it. And it's a lesson that bears driving home." He gave me a sardonic grin. "Right?"

"Again, touché." I smiled weakly and looked away.

"Here's the shitty thing, Jen," Thomas' voice was harsh again. For a while we'd been speaking to each other calmly. Evenly. Civilly. Without the underlying river of anger from each of us that had been there at the start. But now Thomas' demeanor had shifted back. His voice was resentful. Incensed. Not the angriest that I'd heard all morning, but close. He stabbed a finger at me. "It's not that you lied to me..."

"But—"

"Stop!" He cut me off, his tone a single step from a shout. My eyes went wide, a tiny shiver shooting up my spine. "Be quiet while I finish."

"Yes, sir," I whispered.

"It's not that you lied to me. As a lawyer, I get lied to all the time. Believe it or not, I'm pretty good at recognizing it." He paused for a moment, staring at me pointedly. "The shitty thing is that you lied to yourself. Whatever fucking made you think doing what you did was a good idea, whatever made you think you could reinvent yourself into something you aren't, and that somehow *that* person would be a better person than who you truly are... It was bullshit, Jen. It was fucking bullshit. Because the person you *are* is good. I may have been smitten by the fake you that you created, but I know as God is my witness the person I fell in love with was the *real* you. The one you lied to yourself thinking you needed to hide to be whole again."

I sobbed.

"I'll probably never fully understand why you did something so incredibly fucking stupid. But I'll get over it in time. I just hope to God you never do it again. To anyone. But most importantly, to yourself."

I couldn't respond. I couldn't choke out words. Chest heaving, I did nothing but sit and stare at him through a veil of tears. Thomas didn't move. He didn't attempt to come over and comfort me. To console me. He simply sat and watched in silence as my heart shattered into a million pieces.

— ⚜ —

"God, you must hate me." I crumpled the tissues between my fingers, feeling them ball into a sodden knot.

"Not in the slightest." He sighed. "I am angry as hell with you, but I couldn't hate you even if I wanted to."

"You should." The words came out a soft, ragged whisper. "You should despise me. I'm a terrible, horrible person."

"You know what, Jen?" I could feel his teeth gritted in the bite of his tone. "That is not for you to say. You have no right to deny me my feelings, okay? You don't get to dictate to me how I should react, or feel, just so it will make things easier on you."

-Oh, this guy is good. He can see right into you. He's cutting right through your self-serving bullshit. I like him.-

"And I'm going to tell you something else. Don't come at me again with that 'I'm a terrible, horrible person' bullshit. You're not. You made a mistake. We all make fucking mistakes in our lives. I've made plenty of them. I did not fall in love with a 'terrible, horrible person.' And if you want to spout that crap about yourself, you keep it inside around me, okay? Because I like the person you are. The *real* you. And as mad as I am right now, you keep that shit up and you'll really see me get angry."

-Oh, yes. I like this guy a lot!-

— ⚙ —

"Oh, I remember that." Thomas smiled, looking down the couch at me. "I stood there and watched you and thought 'Whoa. This woman is hot as hell. I hope her husband doesn't work here or I'm going to be in deep shit.'"

I laughed. "My... husband?"

"Hey! I couldn't tell if you had a ring on it. It wasn't until we were at lunch that I saw you weren't wearing a wedding band. Even then, I figured you had a boyfriend."

"You figured." I shook my head.

"Jennifer," his voice went serious, "there was no way I would have believed someone as intelligent and beautiful as you wasn't taken."

I blushed, looking away from him.

Please. Please don't be this way. Be a bastard. Uncaring. Self-absorbed. Anything but the good man you are.

"Those are the sorts of things I find pleasurable." I kept my head down. I'd slept with Thomas for six months, and yet with this I couldn't look him in the eye. Couldn't stop the heat that climbed into my cheeks.

"That's what you meant that night. Wasn't it?"

I nodded, continuing to stare into my lap. "Yes."

He blew out a deep breath, his head shaking slowly. "Wow. Do I feel like an idiot."

"No! Don't say, that. Please. You couldn't have known. I didn't exactly tell you..."

He stared at me as my voice trailed off.

"No. You didn't." He shook his head and then looked away across the room. "And I sure as hell would never have guessed."

I felt the world fall away. For a minute we sat in silence. I listened to the sounds of birds in the tree outside my apartment. They called to each other, a tête-à-tête of chirps that ended in a burst of chattering as they flew away.

"I suppose that's it, then?" I whispered.

"I suppose it is."

My eyes filled. "Why does this hurt so much?"

"Because it's supposed to."

He stood.

"I'm going to go now, Jen," he said it quietly, yet his voice was firm.

I stared up at him, and the tears began to flow once more. As he gazed down at me, I saw tears slipping down his cheeks. Silent tracks that made me choke.

I rose and wrapped my arms around him. I crushed myself to his chest, as if somehow I could pull a piece of him inside me to hold onto forever. At first he didn't move, but then he carefully enfolded me in his arms, and we held onto each other. I was still sobbing when he gently gripped my shoulders, prying himself away from me.

"I'm so sorry, Thomas." My voice was a cracking, gasping thing.

"I know you are, Jen. So am I."

With that, he turned, strode across the room, and walked out the door.

— ❀ —

I spent the rest of the day in bed. I cried until my body became a mass of knotted muscle that wouldn't allow my chest to heave another sob. In the end I just lay there and drifted in and out of consciousness. Restless sleep where I dreamed nightmares that had no definition. Amorphous falling sensations, brain coral like objects I tried to flee but stuck to me no matter how hard I ran, scraping my flesh raw. I didn't get up to eat, to shower, to do anything. When I awoke the next morning, I stumbled to the bathroom, urinated, and then shambled right back to the bed. Right back into the dreams. When I awoke out of one, I glanced at my phone. 3:25pm. *Jesus Christ.*

-Why get up? I'm enjoying this. I love watching you wallow in misery of your own creation. Because I told you this was going to happen. I knew it would!-

You know what? Fuck you. I'm so fucking tired of letting you think you're going to win.

-Oh, yeah? Ha! Then do something about it.-

I dragged myself up. I showered. Heading to the kitchen, I ate the remnants of the Chinese. I sat on the couch and did what I shouldn't have done, but that I knew I needed to. I went over it all. Again. In excruciating detail.

"You made a mistake. We all make fucking mistakes in our lives."

Thomas' words rang in my head like a preacher from a pulpit, but even though I could accept the truth in those words, the reality of everything I'd done, all the fallout and the consequences of my actions laid heavy on me. Coupled with the now growing strength of my self- loathing and its companion guilt, for every time I clung to those words, they threw a dozen examples back at me of just how badly I had fucked up.

-Hey, remember the look on Steve's face when Samantha said 'Thomas' girlfriend'? Aww... that was incredible wasn't it? Destroying someone's faith in you with two simple words? Exquisite.-

-You are the worst, Jen. You destroyed Steve, ruined what you had with Thomas. Pity you couldn't be as good a person as him. You certainly didn't deserve to be treated as well as he treated you.-

I dug fingers into my palms until it felt as if the divots would run red, teeth grinding on teeth as I let my demons run wild while I clung to those words.

"You made a mistake. We all make fucking mistakes..."

Tomorrow I had to be back to work. I had to return to my job. Start back at a square one I hadn't been at since Ben. I let guilt and self-loathing have this day. I knew there would be others. But I took solace in one thing. I hadn't lied to Thomas. I'd told him the truth. And if there was anything that I was determined I would do from here on out, it was that.

I'd barely made into my office the next morning when I got an e-mail from Loren.

Come see me as soon as you can.

I didn't know what to expect. Doubted that word of my break-up with Thomas could have spread so fast, but who knew? Stranger things had happened. The look on Loren's face as I stepped into her office didn't make it seem that was the case. She was practically beaming.

"Jennifer. I want to you to look at this." She motioned me to come around to her side of her desk. I glanced at her computer screen, saw it was an e-mail from Samantha.

"Read it."

I cannot begin to tell you how much of an absolute pleasure it was to work with Jennifer on this show. Having been limited by our own internal budget constraints for past shows, I was a bit nervous on how we'd adjust to the much more elaborate exhibit you have. Jennifer took away all of those worries right from the start. She was beyond the consummate professional and made sure that we had anything and everything that we needed. I'd be lying if I didn't say I'm jealous; I would kill to have someone on my team with the skills and acumen she showed. I hope you will pass along my thanks to her for everything she did. I am looking forward to many, many successful shows in the future!

Loren smiled up at me. I lowered my head, grinning.

"That'll do, Jen. That'll do."

I laughed, punching her in the shoulder. "I am not Babe, thank you!"

"Well, you're *my* Babe, so don't let this go to your head." Her eyes twinkled at me, bright with appreciation. "Or get any ideas about going off and joining some other team. Okay?"

I smiled. "Yes, ma'am."

"Good job, Jen." She reached and gripped my shoulder. "Seriously. Good job."

That morning was the beginning. I went back to my office. Back to my job. Back to square one. I began rebuilding my life. Rebuilding who I was. Rebuilding me. The days went by, became a week. Thomas and I shared a few e-mails, but he never sought me out to talk face-to- face. I gave him his space. Respected that he might need some distance before he'd be willing to go beyond the *Hope you are doing okay*.

My self-loathing and guilt had a field day. We had some great times, the three of us. Tearing myself down. Destroying some self-worth. Making sure I knew just what an absolute worthless piece of shit I was. It became very intimate. The loving way I ripped pieces of my soul out, examined them, found every flaw I could and then exploited them to their fullest. And yet each time it always ended the same way. With a voice in my head. One that drove my demons crazy. A voice that even they could not drive out.

"You made a mistake. We all make fucking mistakes in our lives."

I hadn't been sure how long it would take, but it ended up being my second week back when word got around that Thomas and I were no longer a couple. It became a topic of gossip around work, more so than when my relationship with Ben had fallen apart. It was perfectly natural. We both worked at the same company, and word of things like this spread quickly. Loren was kind as ever, accepting with simple grace my explanation that things just hadn't worked out between us. Thomas—damn him—was ever the gentle-man. I heard from no one that he spoke ill of me. Even when Samantha came by to say how sorry she was, she said only that Thomas had told her he felt that he'd never find someone quite like me.

"But in the end, he said it was the only realistic outcome. That when you knew something wasn't going to work, when two people just weren't the *right* two people for each other, it was better to part ways. So that each could heal and move on with their lives."

I cried when she told me that. Samantha hugged me, and I saw tears in her eyes too. I had spent a lot of time being angry with her. For what had happened that morning in Chicago. She had been the catalyst for a moment of incredible pain. But that had not been her fault. That had been on me. I had no right to blame her for anything, and now, as she smiled crookedly at me and said how sorry she was for both Thomas and I, I felt no hatred towards her. She was a good person who had not known the terrible person that I was. In an odd twist, much like Steve, she'd just been someone in the wrong place at the wrong time.

Two weeks became three, and things settled into the new norm. Thomas and I met twice; he at my place to gather his things, and then I at his to do the same. It was awkward, at least from my perspective, but there was no animosity, no overt signs of anger. There was just sadness. Plenty of sadness, and I spent no small amount of time alone dissecting the state my life was in. My demon helped with that, but eventually even that slowed. All those self-destructive thoughts it wanted me to buy into, the ones I held constantly at bay with Thomas' words, began to fade into a dull ache, a numbness that became my personal state of mind when I wasn't buried in my work. As I had done after Ben, I turtled. I pulled into my shell and blocked out the things in the world I was just not prepared to deal with right now. Still shadowboxing at times, biting my own tail, I continued to tear myself up over all that I had done. But even that became pro forma, rote over time. I knew I had fucked up and fucked up bad. However, I also knew that eventually the day would come when I would accept that while I had made some pretty stupid decisions, those were behind me. I had learned from them. And that my life could and would go on.

It was almost six weeks to the day after I'd left Chicago that I got the letter. They'd dropped it in my work mailbox, and I picked it up that morning as I was going past, headed to my office. The envelope was marked with the logo of trade show I&D company I used. I gave it a cursory glance. It was probably an invoice for show services. No big deal. I knew payment was due net thirty on receipt, so there was no rush. I'd get to it in due time.

After lunch I picked up the envelope again, opening it casually. There was a single page inside. It wasn't the invoice I'd expected. It was not a printed letter, but a handwritten one. The writing was in neat, careful block lettering. As I started to read, my heart rose into my throat.

Dear Jen,

I wasn't sure if I would ever write this, and then once I did if I would finish it. Or send it to you. You're reading it now, so I guess it's apparent I did. There is a lot I want to say, a lot I want to tell you, but I've had a long time to think about this, and I think that there's too much that I want to make sure is said exactly the right way. I'm not the best writer, so I guess I'm afraid my words won't be the right ones. I don't want that. I need them to sound the way they do in my head. The way they would if I could say them to you face to face.

What I will say is this. You hurt me, Jen. You hurt me bad. I have no idea what made you do what you did. But there has not been a single day since I left Chicago that I have not thought of you. And not a single day I haven't told myself there must be a reason. And if there is no reason, then I suppose that's an answer in and of itself.

I told you I was a Marine. I am used to operating in environments with half-assed information. I served twelve years, and half the time I was working completely in the dark. When command deemed we were not on a need-to-know basis. But I'm also an engineer, and I hate leaving a problem unresolved. Maybe you don't have an issue with what happened in Chicago. But I do. And I'd like to suss it out so that maybe I can stop worrying about it any more.

A city manager position is coming open in Anaheim in two months. I'm pretty sure that's near you. Marty's asked me if I'd be interested in considering the position. He's going to fly me out to take a look at things for a few days. I would like one hour of your time. That's all. One hour, just to ask you a few questions, and maybe get some answers if I can. I know you don't owe me anything, but if you'll at least give it some consideration, I'd appreciate it. I'll be in town on the dates below, and you can reach me at that cell phone number. If you choose not to respond to this, I'll take that as an answer of its

own, and draw my own conclusions. I hope that won't be the case.
Thank you.
Sincerely,
Steve Friess

Below that, he'd written the dates he'd be in town, and his cell phone number.

Life teaches us hard lessons. Necessary lessons. People get hurt learning them, even people who may not deserve it. At times, however, life offers up a reward for a lesson learned. Compensation for the pain you've gone through in gaining a bit of life's hard knocks. I knew exactly what Steve wanted to ask me. What he wanted to know. And as I sat there at my desk, my heart beating in my chest, blood rushing in my ears, all I could think of was this; I wouldn't lie this time. He wanted to talk. To me. And I would tell him the truth. Tell him everything about me, who I really was, the decisions I'd made and the consequences thereof. I didn't know how he'd respond. Maybe he'd tell me what a complete piece of shit I was for doing what I'd done. I hoped that wouldn't be the case. What I really wanted to believe was that he wanted to hear from me if I felt the same way as he did. I wanted to believe he wanted to know whether I, like him, had not had '*a single day since I left Chicago that I have not thought of you.*' That's what I hoped he would ask. Because I knew how to answer that question. It was simple.

"Of course not. There hasn't been a single day."

That's what I wanted. What I needed to tell him. Because it wasn't a lie. It was the truth. And I needed him to hear it from me. I needed for him to see that I was capable of speaking without it being a story. A lie.

I knew if I could just talk to him, I could do it. I would do it. Was I sure he would believe me?

No.

But I was damned sure going to try.

EPILOGUE

His hand closed around my throat.

"You like that, don't you? You like how that fucking feels."

I keened out my approval. Did I like this? Fuck yes, I liked this. It had been so long since someone had held me this way. Had treated me this way in bed. It felt good in a way that made the entirety of me quiver. A way that at one time I was certain I would never feel again.

I could feel his cock brushing against my thigh. So close to an entrance that was already coated thick with arousal. I looked up into hooded eyes, brows that closed until they were dark slits. The fingers tightened, the smile cruel.

"You want that cock inside you." The hand gripped my neck ruthlessly. "You want me to fuck you with this cock, don't you?" He leaned closer, voice hissing in my ear. "Don't you!"

I wanted to speak. To tell him *yes, sir, yes, please!* But I couldn't find my voice. I couldn't form the words. All I could do was nod, my eyes pleading.

Yes! Please. Please!

His lips brushed against my ear.

"Well that's too fucking bad. Only good girls get fucked. Lying, cheating sluts..." The fingers squeezed. "Get." I felt my vision go black. "Nothing!"

I screamed. I shot up in bed, gasping in sharp staccato breaths as I fought to choke back another cry. There was no man. I was alone. I sucked in a lungful of air, my heart pounding as if to escape my chest. My sheets tangled around me in a sweaty mass.

God dammit! Not this again!

It was the third time this week. The third time. Nearly always the same dream. The same nightmare. I could never see the man clearly. But I knew who it was. Who it was supposed to be.

Steve.

He was the man haunting me in those dreams. The ones which had started the night after I'd received his letter.

And today was the day I was going to meet him.

I was still in a tee shirt and underwear when I glanced over at the alarm clock on the nightstand. 12:45pm. I groaned. The arrangement I'd made was to have a late lunch with Steve at 2:30. I planned for a minimum of thirty minutes travel time to get the restaurant, just to be safe. I needed to get my ass in gear. Time to put my game face on, get dressed in the clothes I'd picked out, make-up applied, and then out the door. I caught a flash of something from my nightstand. The message light on my cell phone blinking.

I froze.

It hadn't been doing that before I'd gotten in the shower. I was positive of that. It was blinking now, and for a moment I couldn't move. Thoughts scattered through my head like windblown leaves. He's changed his mind. He's texting me to cancel. A note to tell me he'll e-mail me later to outline just how much he despises me.

Yep. Right down that rabbit hole.

I walked over to the phone. Picking it up as if it would strike me the moment I touched it, I thumbed open the screen. Two text messages. I tapped the button.

Afternoon, Jen. Just checking in to make sure we're still on for 2:30. Also, could you check this map link and let me know if I have the correct place? Greatly appreciated. Steve.

The next message was a Google Maps link that showed the location of the restaurant I'd chosen to meet at.

The breath I'd been holding came out in a *whoosh* of relief. I couldn't help the smile that crossed my face. This was the Steve I remembered. Ever the Marine, ever the Dom, ever the engineer he'd once been. I tapped out my response.

Sorry for the delay. Yes, we're still on. I'll be there at 2:30. The map is perfect. There should be parking in a lot up the hill right behind the restaurant. I'll see you there. Jen.

I hit SEND, and then set the phone down.

Okay, okay, calm down, Jen. Everything's fine. Nothing's changed. He was just checking in. Steve being the Steve you knew.

I blew out my breath, stood with my hip leaning against the edge of the bed.

Okay, no time for standing around. You have stuff to do. Now. So. Get. Moving.

I was glad I left the apartment when I did. I hadn't considered how bad traffic would be heading into Dana Point on a Saturday. When I finally made it to the parking lot I glanced quickly at my watch. 2:17. Okay, good. Still ahead of schedule. I was fine.

"Hi! I have a reservation. Jennifer Boyd. Party of two."

The hostess smiled, glancing down at the log. "Oh, yes. Right here. 2:30, party of two, reserved table outside on the deck." She looked up at me. "If you'll follow me, please." I walked behind her, moving past tables crowded with guests. She led me out onto the deck, and then down and around the corner. She strode the short distance to the last table, but I'd stopped.

Steve rose from where he'd been sitting, waiting.

He'd beaten me here.

Sonofabitch.

— ❀ —

"Hello, Jen."

"Hello, Steve."

He stood while I seated myself. Once I settled into my chair, he returned to his own, motioning towards my side of the table.

"I ordered you a glass of wine."

I spotted a glass I hadn't noticed. A rosé, slightly chilled, beads of condensation sweating on the surface in the warm sun.

"Thank you. That was very kind."

"You probably don't remember, but that night at dinner in Chicago... I had to have the sommelier make all our wine choices for us." He leaned in slightly, motioning towards the front of the restaurant. "I kinda let the waitress choose for me this time. I hope it's okay."

Biting down on my lower lip, I grinned. I picked up the glass, nodding.

"I remember." I took a sip of the wine. "It's very good. Thank you."

"Good." His voice sounded relieved, but there was something else about it too. The tone was reserved. Not cold, nor distant, but it wasn't the voice of the Steve I remembered. Not even from that first morning on the show floor. It was... different.

-Well, what did you expect? That he was just going to show up here and be all warm and friendly with you? After what you did to him?-

No.

I pressed my lips together for a second, and then took another sip of my wine. We sat across from each other, together and yet alone, in silence.

I heard him take a deep breath.

"So, I'm not going to waste time here. I asked for an hour, and I don't expect anything more than that, Jen. So, I'll just cut right to the chase."

God his voice sounded so... clinical. It wasn't the harsh voice he'd used that morning after Samantha had outed me, but neither was it the voice he'd used the day we'd first met. The one traced with mirth. The one filled with pride when I'd pulled that Starbucks cup back in surprise for his getting it just the way I liked it. This was a completely new voice. Detached. Collected. Military precise.

I almost wished he'd be angry. I deserved that. That I could deal with. This... this I wasn't sure what to make of.

"I won't lie, Jen. I'm really not good at this sort of thing." His eyes locked onto mine. "I've spent a great deal of time going over what I wanted to say, but right now..." He gave me a tight smile. "Right now I'm having a hard time remembering a fucking word of it." The expletive was harsh, but his voice was low enough that I doubted anyone around us would hear.

"So, I'm going to go with my gut here." He paused, and his eyes flicked from me to the tabletop and then back again.

"You lied to me, Jen. You lied to me, and that's what hurts. It hurt back then, and it hurts sitting here right now. You told me all sorts of things, and I believed you. Trusted you. But when that woman started going on about your boyfriend back here, and how she'd heard so much from him about how wonderful you were, I knew that everything you'd said to me was bullshit. A lie. It hurt, and it made me really fucking angry. And so I did something I *never* do. I bounced. I walked off a job. I made up that shitty excuse about suddenly needing to get back home. And I'll tell you why. Because right then I couldn't deal with the idea that a woman as incredible as you had lied to me so casually. So fucking *easily*." He'd maintained a neutral voice to this point, but now I heard anger. As slight as it was, there was no mistaking it. A tightness to the jaw. The ember that flared in his eyes.

And suddenly, even though I'd said different a moment ago, I didn't want him to be that way. I wanted the other Steve back. Because this hurt far more than I expected.

He paused, and I could see in the way he stiffened that he was collecting himself. Pushing the anger down, reverting to the composed demeanor he'd had when I'd first sat down. His face went smooth, the jaw unclenched, the eyes cooled. He reached for his glass, took a sip, and then continued.

"I was honest with you. I answered your questions. I did not hide anything from you or lie to you when you discovered who I was, and what I was about. I could have made up some bullshit story about this..." He turned his wrist up at me. The wrist with the triskelion tattoo upon it. "That this was just some crappy little ying and yang symbol I'd gotten tatted up with when I was a Marine. But I didn't. I told you the truth. And you responded. God damn did you respond so perfectly. And I swear to God I could not believe what was happening. I told you back then. Shit like that does not happen to me. It was incredible, Jen. It was incredible, unbelievable, and too good to be true. And that's just it. It *was* too good to be true. I don't know what your fucking deal was, or how much of what you said to me was really *you*, or if it was all just some weird, fucked up act you were putting on. Doesn't matter. You had me. You had me right up until the moment when it all came tumbling down. I walked off that convention floor, and I'll be goddamned if even then, as angry as I was, I couldn't stop thinking. Why? Why? I asked myself that fucking question about a million times on the way back to Denver. I've probably asked it about a million times more since. Why? Why did you do it? What was in it for you? Why did you *need* to lie to me?"

Steve looked down for a moment, and then back up at me. His eyes were hard, that intense grey that had made me shiver the night he'd picked me up at the hotel in Chicago. My knuckles went white as my fingers gripped the wine glass in my hand, and yet I didn't move a muscle as he continued.

"I was not lying to you when I wrote that letter, Jen. There has not been a single day since I walked out of that booth that I have not thought about you. And not just to ask why. But about you. As a person. The person I wanted to believe you were. So, here's the thing. I asked you for an hour of your time. I know I've burnt up a little bit of that, but I'd like an answer to that question. I'd like to know why. Why did you do what you did? Why did you lie to me?"

Steve's eyes scanned back and forth across my face, his mouth tight. "And, I'm not an idiot, Jen. Trust me, I know you can just tell me another fucking boatload of lies right now if you want to. Same as you did in Chicago. I'll have no way of knowing whether you're telling me the truth now any more than I did back then. But I'm giving you a chance. Convince me. Convince me there's a *reason* behind why you did what you did. Convince me that you're not lying to me all over again. I just want an explanation. Something. So at the very least, if nothing else, I can just put all this behind me and get on with my life."

He stopped, and we both sat in silence. Even though I felt tears pressing against the back of my eyes, I didn't cry. I owed Steve a calm, lucid explanation of all that I had done. Not a response that might make him think I was using emotions in a play for sympathy. I didn't want his pity. What I wanted was his trust. I wanted to repair the damage I had done. And if I couldn't do that, I at least wanted to give him the best explanation I could for what had motivated me. Why I had done what I'd done.

The waitress approached our table. We both looked up at her simultaneously.

"Have you had a chance to look at the menu? Is there anything I can explain?"

I shook my head. I hadn't even spared a moment for it or to think about food. Steve had been my sole focus. I picked up the menu, flipping the cover open, searching quickly for something to choose. Even as I did, Steve spoke.

"The lady will have the chicken Florentine with the side vegetables. I'll have the skirt steak with mushrooms, please. No side."

I looked up at him. He turned his gaze from the server to me, eyebrow cocked. I felt a tremor run through me. *This* was the man I remembered from Chicago. In charge, confident, commanding, self-assured. The Dominant I'd suspected he was, and which circumstances had proven true. I gave him an imperceptible nod, lowering my eyes back down.

"Sounds good! Another glass of wine?" The server motioned towards my glass, and I shook my head no. "I'm fine for the moment, thanks."

"And you, sir?"

"Water's fine, thank you."

The woman nodded, smiling. "Okay. I'll get your order in and check back in a bit to see if there's anything else you need. Thanks!"

She turned and walked away. I looked up from the tabletop to Steve.

"Thank you."

He looked at me, his face assured. "I remembered what you chose for dinner that night in Chicago. I thought this would be OK."

"It is. I appreciate it. I was so focused on what you were saying I hadn't even looked at the menu...." My voice trailed off, and I found myself glancing down at the tabletop again.

We didn't pick up the conversation where we'd left off. Instead, Steve made small talk while we waited for our meals to arrive. It was all bland pleasantries. The weather, what he'd been doing, what I'd been doing, Marty sending his regards. I was only half-listening to most of it. My fixation was on what Steve had said at the end.

'Convince me. Convince me there's a reason behind why you did what you did.'

I wanted to do that. Convince him. Convince him I wasn't the horrible person I was sure he must think of me. That the person sitting across from him right now was the real me. Not the half-me he'd left on the show floor. How I would do that I had no idea. There was only one thing I was certain of. No matter what, I wasn't going to lie to him.

About anything.

Our conversation continued, a chain of banal trivialities inter-spersed with silences that were tense only because I wanted desper-ately to tell Steve what I thinking. I was chewing my lip raw trying to think of things to say when the server finally arrived with our food. She placed the dishes in front of us, and then asked if we needed anything else.

Steve smiled politely at her. "No, I think we're good. Thank you."

"Okay! I'll be back by later to check up with you and see if there's anything you need."

She walked off, and I looked down at the plate in front of me. It might as well have been ash for all the appeal it held. I pushed a bit of it around, taking one small bite.

"So..." Steve cleared his throat. I looked up to find his gaze fixed on me, eyes serious. Waiting.

I took a deep breath.

"Yes, I lied to you. I know that's stating the obvious, but I think the first step here is for me to admit to you that I did. I also want you to know that it wasn't just you. I lied to a lot of people, Steve. I lied to myself. And that's the thing. That lie, the one I told myself... That's what really set everything in motion. It caused me to make some really bad decisions. To tell some really bad lies to some really good people. Honestly, I can't justify any of what I did. There is no justification. I can only explain what happened."

And so I told him. Of Ben. Of my decision. Of Thomas. Of everything.

"And then I met you."

I explained everything to Steve as the summer afternoon drifted past us. The breeze from the ocean came across the deck occasion-ally, the low murmur of nearby conversations a background white noise to my own voice. The sun was warm, but as I poured out my soul to Steve, I felt cold. Reliving all of this again absorbed whatever heat I should have felt. Not that that stopped me. I drove on. No excruciating detail left unsaid. I explained to him every decision I'd made, every lie I'd told, all of it. I tried to make him understand *why* I had done what I'd done without giving the impression I was trying to defend it. When I came to the part where I told him of my break-up with Thomas, how we had fought, and then argued, and then realized that it was truly over, that it had been over for a while... my voice stopped. We sat in silence, staring at each other. I could hear laughter from somewhere in the distance, and the breeze carried the scent of salt and sea by.

Steve looked at me with eyes that bore straight through me. Searching for a way to discern whether this was yet another pack of lies. Or the truth.

I had done everything I could. I'd told my story. I had hidden nothing from him. There were no lies this time. Nothing to lessen the impact of my confession, and now I sat looking at him like a criminal before a jury, waiting for the final verdict.

Steve gave a slight shake of his head, lips pressed together. "Jesus Christ, Jen." It was all he said. The silence stretched on, and his eyes never left me.

"I can really be stupid sometimes." I said it in a soft voice, to break the quiet.

"No." He grimaced, and this time when he shook his head it was stern. "No. That's a cop-out. You made some bad decisions. That's all. I mean, they were really, really, *really* bad decisions, true, but... people do that all the time. You know that as well as I do."

I pursed my lips, and then nodded. "Fair enough."

"Making a bad decision doesn't make you stupid. It just makes you human."

I couldn't think of a word to say. And I was afraid if I did, I'd cry.

Steve took a drink from his glass, and then ran his hand across his jaw.

"Well, I asked for an explanation, and you sure as hell provided one."

I swallowed the lump in my throat down.

"There's nothing I can say that justifies what I did, Steve. All I can do is say I'm sorry. And hope that you'll be able to forgive me someday" I said it softly, trying to keep my voice as neutral as I could, the tears at bay.

The space around us went still.

"I want to."

I let my eyes close. Opening them only when he began speaking again.

"I didn't bullshit you, Jen. When I said how much I've been thinking about you. Because I have. And maybe part of the reason for that is I had a...feeling. A sense that there had to be more behind what you did than I understood." Steve paused, looking away.

"I don't know. It just bothered me. What you did to me was shitty. Really fucking shitty. And yet when it all went down, it just didn't make sense. I knew you for two days, Jen. Two fucking days. And even after what happened, I still couldn't stop thinking about you. It didn't add up. It wasn't the you I'd formed in my head." Steve took a deep breath, and then let it out slowly. "None of it made sense to me, and I've come at this thing from every angle I could since I left Chicago. And every time I just end up with the same questions, the same frustration." He pointed his finger at me. "I couldn't tell you why I thought the way I did, or what made me so goddamn sure I was right, but I did. Whatever was going on back then, it just wasn't you."

"But it was." I whispered the words, my voice cracking with a sadness that wanted to spill out of me.

"I know. But the difference is now I know *why*, Jen. I know the why behind what made you do what you did. Something that even then I knew, deep down, really wasn't *you*." He stared at me, and for the first time this afternoon I saw something more than the neutral look he had been maintaining all this time.

I saw compassion.

I turned away, looking out over the deck railing. "It was me, though. It was stupid and dumb and selfish and yet I did it anyways. I became the very thing I hated most. A liar who kept building lie upon lie to try to get myself out of a situation that I'd created from the worst lie of all. The one I told myself. That I could change who I am by simply willing it to be." I stopped, biting my lip to regain control I felt slipping.

"You think you're the first person in the world to do that?" Steve's voice was gentle but firm.

"No. But is knowing that supposed to help?"

"Probably not. About all it's going to do is help you understand that it has happened to people before you, it will happen to people after you, and to help try and recognize that it doesn't define you forever. People have recovered from it. People have survived and gone on to lead happy lives. Even with the very people that they once lied to."

I pushed my lips together tightly as he said that. I did not waver as his eyes locked onto mine.

"Okay." I took in a steadying breath, then let it out slowly. "So here we are. You wanted an hour, and my explanation." I spread my hands open. "There it is. In all the gory details." I slowly let them fall into my lap.

"What now?"

A lifetime seemed to pass. Steve glanced down at my plate. "You haven't eaten."

"I'm really not hungry. Sorry." I looked down at his own plate. He followed my gaze, saw where I was staring.

"Yeah, my appetite isn't any better. I've been stressing over this meeting for weeks now, and the thought of trying to eat" His voice trailed off, his mouth a crooked, rueful grin.

"Oh, thank God." I grinned back at him. "I thought I was the only one."

His smile. God, it was so warm now. So much what I remembered about him. Those gorgeous eyes, that beautiful face, the sexy smile. The timber of his voice the one I remembered from the show floor. I couldn't stop the grin from spreading until it was a beaming smile I'm sure made me glow.

"Nope." He shook his head, laughing. "Despite all my planning, when I got here, I swear I had no idea exactly what I was going to say. Hell, Jen, I had no clue if you were even gonna show. And if you did, what you'd say to me. I knew I needed to do this, and I'm glad I did. But—Jesus Christ—the build-up was like being back in Iraq."

"Oh, come on." I rolled my eyes, giggling. "It couldn't have been *that* bad."

He gave me a dour look, and I thought back to how much today had preyed on my own nerves.

"Okay, maybe a little..." I conceded.

Steve reached across the table and placed his hand on top of mine. As his fingers closed, I felt lightheaded. A sudden buoyant, giddy feeling enveloped me. Silence seemed to descend over us once again, the ambient noise fading almost to nothing. For a moment all I could feel was his fingers pressing down, holding me. I stared at him, my eyes widening. He stared back with that look that I remembered all too well. The one that sent a jolt of electricity shooting up my spine.

"Thank you, Jen. Seriously." His voice was soft, but every syllable was a balm to me. I felt a weight lifted that had been crushing me for weeks. Months. Sure, I had no idea if anything more would come from this. But right now, it was enough. It was good, and it was more than I'd dared hope for.

Steve pulled his hand away gently. The absence of his fingers on mine made me want to reach out, to grab him and pull him back greedily. I wanted to do that, but I didn't. It wasn't right. There was no point in assuming anything. We'd talked. And listened. I couldn't — wouldn't—push for more than that right now. Maybe this was a beginning. Or maybe this was all it would ever be. A fresh start, perhaps. One where I could show Steve that I was not the person I'd been in Chicago. The person who had lied to him the way I had. I was back to being me. The real me. And if that was a person who he might want to know, then I was more than happy to oblige.

"So." I looked across the table at him, watching as the light played off his eyes. "What are your plans now?"

Steve sighed. "Well, I took a tour of the shop this morning. Tomorrow, Bryon, the city manager here, is going to take me down to the convention center to meet with the union steward." Steve glanced around, looking out towards the ocean nearby. "As for the rest of today... I dunno. Maybe do some sightseeing, I guess?"

"Ah." I smiled, playing with my wine glass. "Well, if you want a tour guide, I'd be more than happy to play the role."

Steve's gaze snapped back to me. For a moment I thought I might have gone too far. Pressed forward when I should have held back. I'd admitted a lot to him today. He probably need time to process everything. And now here I was making a comment that might be construed in a way entirely different than I had meant.

Liar.

"What are you doing for dinner?"

My heart skipped a beat. For a millisecond I wasn't there. I wasn't at this table, under this sun, sitting across from a man who I had once thought I'd never see again. Suddenly I was standing on the floor of a convention center in Chicago, Illinois, staring down at my feet.

"I have no dinner plans." I said quietly.

The sound of my heartbeat thudded in my ears. I could hear my own breathing, and the faintest trace of his across from me. I stared at the base of my wine glass. Waiting. Hoping.

Please.

"Well then, I have an idea. I'd like for you to fix dinner for us. Tonight."

"At your place."

My head came up slowly. I gazed into his face. Watched a thumb and forefinger tracing a slow pattern back and forth across his chin. Saw the slight uptick at the corner of his mouth. The heat that glowed in the burnished gray of those eyes.

My pulse raced.

"I can do that."

For a moment there was silence. The hand stopped. The eyes narrowed.

"Sir."

Steve smiled.

"Good girl."

And I was gone.

ACKNOWLEDGMENTS

"Easy way, or hard way. Your choice."

A good, dear friend of mine once said that to me. And at the time I didn't realize what an apt metaphor it was for not only my path as an author, but, in many respects, for my life itself.

But I do now.

The book you hold—one I'm hopeful you've read—is a testament to how consistent I seem to be about choosing the "hard way." I wrote the very, *very* rough draft of *Submissive Lies* over 4 years ago. Back then, it was simply called *Jen's Story*. It was a fourth wall breaking, stream-of-consciousness in places tale in many respects little different from the story you have here, but in a much rougher, less polished form. I gave it to my lifelong beta reader, and for the thousandth time regarding my writing she said:

"This is really good, Shane. You should try to get it published."

As I had done for the 25 years prior, I rolled my eyes.

"No one wants to read my junk."

And I filed the story away.

Fast forward two-and-a-half years, and a friend of mine has her second novel published. Both are romances, and suddenly I am reading in a genre that I would never have thought I would. I mention to her how much I loved her books, that I've written things but done nothing with them, and also how jealous I am that she's made the leap to become an author. She asks me if I would let her see some of what I've written. So I do.

"You have a real voice, Shane. These are rough, sure, but every shitty first draft is. If you love doing this, you really should pursue it."

Oh.

That wasn't the response I'd expected. But it got me thinking...

I was reading romance novels as quick as I could. I found this one author, and I really connected with her work. Her words and stories struck a chord with me, and I was reading everything of hers I could get my hands on. After one particular set of stories, I started writing a fanfic centered around one of her minor characters. I was three quarters of the way through my story when she made mention on her Facebook page she would be writing a novel based around the same character I had built my fanfic around. I was both disappointed and excited at the same time. In one of my moments of sheer *chutzpah*, I messaged her what I'd done, finishing by saying "No point in continuing with it now."

"Can I read it?"

"Why!?"

"Because I'd like to."

"Okay..."

I sent it to her. A few hours went by and I heard nothing back and I thought 'Well, she probably only got through the first page before she threw it away.'

Which was wrong. "This is good."

"Really?"

"Yes, really. This is very good. I love what you've done with these characters!"

"Well, it's yours, because there's not going to be any more of it."

"Oh yes there will be. You are going to finish this."

"I am? I don't think so..."

"Yes you will. Easy way or hard way. Your choice."

And thus did Jennifer Bene out me on her Facebook page the next morning. And I finished my little 80+k word fanfic taken from the books in her *The Thalia Series*.

I called it *The Wedding Gift*.

Oh, and that beta reader from before? The one who said *'You *should try to get this published.'* Yeah, that's my wife. Ms. Starrett. The one you now hear saying *'I told you so.'*

There's a great number of people I would like to thank for helping me to achieve the goal that *Submissive Lies* is. However, to mention every single one would take a book of its own. Therefore, I will start by offering thanks to every person out there who encouraged me. Whether it was reading the serialized version of *The Wedding Gift*, or responding to my posts on Facebook, you have no idea how much every comment helped carry me through the points in this process where I was quite ready to say, 'I've made a huge mistake.' Thank you all!

There are a few people I wish to give personal thanks to.

To Sheri Cordell and Karen Jackson. You two took the second draft version of *Jen's Story* and gave me the push to keep going when I needed it. And you've been standing there watching and encouraging me ever since. Through *The Wedding Gift* to what morphed from *Jen's Story* into *Submissive Lies*, this Dude owes you both a debt of gratitude I'll never be able to repay in full. But as Jen says, I'll damn sure try.

To KB. You know what you did. Through it all, you were a harsh taskmaster, but my writing is all the better for it. Thank you for sticking through it all with me, as irritating as I was.

To Nerine Dorman. You gave me the first edits I've ever had, and guidance far more than I'd expected. And you also gave me thirteen words that helped me carry on when I needed it most: 'I reckon you've got a hot story here, that has a satisfying tie-up.' Thank you. I needed that.

To Addison Cain. Who bolstered my spirit in a way you probably do not recognize. A simple dedication that made me feel as if I truly belonged in a community where I'd felt I was an outsider before. And who put up with quite possibly the most awkward first meeting ever in LV. If I stepped in all the filthy, filthy mud, you stood by with grace and aplomb and never batted an eye as I tracked through it. Thank you.

To Niki Roge. "You, sir, are a goddamn idiot." Never have those words been said to someone in such a way as to fill them with the immense pride and joy as they did me the day you sent them. And for every push, tug, and threat of the whip since then, you've been a kind, yet stern, friend. And I will win that bet still. Oh, yes... I will. (Editor's Note: He did not, in fact win the bet)

To Measha Stone. Fine. You were right. Don't let it go to your head.

To Eris Adderly. You, ma'am, have the soul of a goddess and the patience of a saint. Taking a video call from some weird dude you hardly knew after a black widow had bitten you, then accepting a dinner invitation so I could fanboi all over you, and then after *that* accepting us into your home shows you're either a closet masochist, or you have compassion and empathy in far greater measure than you recognize. I'm hedging my bets on the latter (although perhaps I should discuss the former in greater detail with Mr. Adderly, eh?). You guided me through the process of creating the cover for my book and put up with every inane question I've asked since. I never came into this community thinking I would find someone like you, and if I never write another word, I will consider this entire endeavor a success. Much love, Eris. Much love!

To the first of the two Jens.

Jennifer Sable. You of the first two romance novels I read when I started down this path. You of the "You have a real voice, Shane." You of the "Now go forth and write!" Thank you for being there to give me that first gentle nudge. I know your muse has left you for the moment, but it'll be back, and when it is, it'll be stronger than ever. Thank you for being there at the beginning.

And to the second Jen. Jennifer Bene.

Hey, braintwin...

I did it.

No, scratch that.

We did it.

Because the truth is, none of this would have happened without you. You inspired me, encouraged me, pushed me when it was necessary, listened to me when I needed an objective ear, made me frustrated, made me laugh, and helped to me fall in love with my book all over again when I needed it most. You have given when you've had no need to give, even when your own life has been absolutely crazy out of control. You let me take your characters and create my own world for them in *The Wedding Gift*, and you provided guidance on *Submissive Lies* to help me put it back onto the right track. You've listened to every crazy, kinky, disturbing idea I've ever had, and said "That's so cool." or "Whoa, that's HOT!" Both of which, to be honest, are rather disconcerting, because you're *supposed* to find those things troubling, not interesting. However, you were the first to recognize braintwins so I suppose I just need to lean into it, right? You know how much I love you, and how much I will forever be in your debt for everything you've done. And who knows, maybe someday we'll work on something together!

Stranger things have happened, right? And finally...

To Cynthia.

Twenty-five years.

Twenty-five years you waited. Ever patient. Ever supportive. Ever my perfect submissive. This story is our story in so many ways, and while I may have written the words, everything in it belongs to you too. I won't even try to describe how much I owe you. How much I care for you. How much I love you. It'd take an entire library of books to do that. You are what drives me every day. You are what completes me. You make me strive to be a better human being in all things, if only to see that shy smile that slips over your face when you look up at me. The one I saw that day in the scene shop in college, the same one I saw the day I first told you I was in love with you, and the same one I have spent thirty years craving since. And as much as I frustrate the hell out of you, you are ever the very thing I've called you from the day we married.

Mein Amboss.

My Anvil.

Shane Starrett July 22, 2019

ABOUT THE AUTHOR

Shane Starrett has spent twenty-five years writing steamy, erotic technical documents (okay, the erotic part is probably a bit of a stretch) for major companies in the live events industry. When he isn't writing, which isn't often, he can be found hiking, working in his shop, or just staring off into the distance, probably thinking of something very, *very* naughty.

To the delight of his very patient support team, Shane has new and exciting stories in the works! If you're interested in following him you can find him online at...

Website: http://shanestarrett.com/

Printed in Great Britain
by Amazon

48486739R00179